3
2
6
1

THE DARK ANGEL

Also by Mika Waltari

THE EGYPTIAN

THE ADVENTURER

THE WANDERER

A STRANGER CAME TO THE FARM

MIKA WALTARI

THE DARK

ANGEL

TRANSLATED BY NAOMI WALFORD

G. P. PUTNAM'S SONS · NEW YORK

Library of Congress Catalogue Card Number: 52–13647

MANUFACTURED IN THE UNITED STATES OF AMERICA
CORNWALL PRESS, INC., NEW YORK

THE DARK ANGEL

The Diary of John Angelos, During the Siege of Constantinople, 1453, at the End of the Christian Era.

12 December 1452

Today I saw you and spoke to you for the first time.

It was like an earthquake; everything in me was overturned, the graves of my heart were opened and my own nature was strange to me.

I am forty, and I believed I had reached the autumn of life.

I had wandered far, known much and lived many lives. The Lord had spoken to me, manifesting Himself to me in many ways; to me angels had revealed themselves and I had not believed them. But when I saw you I was compelled to believe, because of the miracle that had happened to me.

I saw you in front of the Church of St. Sophia, by the bronze doors. It was when everyone was coming out, after Cardinal Isidor amid icy silence had proclaimed in Latin and Greek the Union of the Churches. In celebrating the splendid Mass that followed he recited the creed, and when he reached the interpolation "and from the Son" many covered their faces, while from the women in the galleries could be heard bitter sobbing. I was standing in the press of people in a side aisle beside a gray column; when I touched this I felt that it was moist, as if even the chill stones of the temple were sweating out their anguish.

Then they all left the church, in the order prescribed many centuries ago, and in the midst of them walked the Basileus, our Emperor Constantine, erect and solemn, his head already gray beneath the golden hoops of the crown. Each one walked in the appropriate clothes and colors: the officials from the Palace of Blachernae, ministers and logothetes, the senate in its entirety, and then the archons of Constantinople in order of lineage. No one had dared stay away and so let his views be known. On the Emperor's right I recognized all too well Phrantzes, the Chancellor, as with cold blue eyes he surveyed the people around him. Among the Latins I noticed the Venetian bailo and many others whom I knew by sight.

But the Megadux, Lukas Notaras, Grand Duke and Commander of the Imperial Fleet, I had never seen before. He was a head taller than the rest, and a swarthy, haughty man. His glance was keen and scornful, but in his features I read the melancholy common to all members of the ancient Greek families. When he came out he was agitated and wrathful, as if unable to endure the deadly shame that had fallen upon his Church and his people.

When the chargers were led foward there was some disturbance among the people, who began to cry out upon the Latins. There were shouts of "Down with unlawful interpolations!" "Down with Papal rule!" I would not listen, for I had heard more than enough of it in my youth. But the hatred and despair of the crowd broke out like the roaring of the tempest—like an earthquake—until the practiced voices of the monks led them into a rhythmic chant of "Not the Son, not the Son!" It was the feast of the holy Spiridon.

By the time the procession of the noble ladies started, some of the Emperor's suite had already mingled with the crowds that were surging and waving their arms in time to the howling chant. Only round the sacred person of the Emperor was there space, and as he sat his charger his face darkened with sorrow. He was dressed in a purple, gold-embroidered mantle and his purple boots were adorned with the two-headed eagle.

So it was that I witnessed the fulfillment of a dream cherished throughout many centuries: the Union of the Eastern and Western Churches, the submission of the Orthodox Church to the Pope, and the abandonment of its original, unadulterated creed. Having dragged on for more than ten years, the Union had at last gained legal force through the reading of the proclamation by Cardinal Isidor in the Church of St. Sophia. Fourteen years before, it had been read in Greek in the cathedral of Florence, by the great, round-headed, scholarly Metropolitan Bessarion. Like Isidor he had been made cardinal by Pope Eugenius IV as a reward for his services in the great work of reconciliation.

That was fourteen years ago. That evening I had sold my books and cloth, distributed my money among the poor and fled from Florence. Five years later I took the Cross. Now as the people shouted I remembered the mountain road to Assisi and the field of corpses at Varna.

But as the shouting suddenly died away I raised my eyes and saw that Megadux Lukas Notaras had leaped onto the ledge in front of the yellowed marble colonnade. With a wave of his hand he claimed silence, and the biting December wind carried his cry: "Better the Turkish turban than the Papal miter!"

At this defiant watchword people and monks burst into thunderous applause. Exultantly the Greeks of Constantinople roared and yelled "Better the Turkish turban than the Papal miter!" just as once the Jews had shouted "Release unto us Barabbas!"

A group of distinguished gentlemen and archons gathered challengingly about Lukas Notaras to show that they supported him and were not afraid to defy the Emperor publicly. Then at last the mob gave way and allowed Constantine to pass on with his diminished following. The women's procession was still moving out through the great bronze doors, but scattered immediately and vanished among the turbulent crowd.

I was curious to see how the people would receive Cardinal Isidor, but he is a man who has endured much for the sake of the Union, and is himself a Greek. Therefore he never appeared. He has not grown fat in his office of cardinal: he is still the same lean little peppery-eyed man and looks even thinner since shaving off his beard in the Latin fashion.

"Better the Turkish turban than the Papal miter!" No doubt the Grand Duke Notaras shouted this with all his heart, for love of his city and his faith, and hatred of the Latins. Yet however sincere the feelings which gave fire to his words, I could not regard them as anything but a calculated political move. He had flung his cards on the table before a rebellious mob, to win the support of the great majority of the people; for in his heart no Greek approves this Union, not even the Emperor himself. He is merely forced to submit and to set his seal upon it, in order to conclude the treaty of alliance which in this hour of need will ensure for Constantinople the support of the Papal fleet.

This fleet is already being fitted out in Venice. Cardinal Isidor affirms that it will sail to the rescue of Constantinople as soon as certain news of the proclamation of the Union reaches Rome. But today the people shouted after Emperor Constantine *"Apostata, apostata!"* The emptiest, most terrible and most destructive word that can be shouted at a man. That is the price he has had to pay for ten warships—if they come.

Cardinal Isidor has already brought a handful of archers with him, recruited in Crete and other islands. The gateways of the city are walled up. The Turks have ravaged all the country round, and closed the Bosporus. Their base is the fortress which the Sultan caused to be built last summer, in the course of only a few months, at the narrowest part of the Straits. The fortress lies on the Pera side, the Christian side. Only last spring the Church of the Archangel Michael stood on that spot, but now its marble columns serve to strengthen the thirty-foot-thick walls of the Turkish bastions, and the cannon of the Sultan stand sentinel over the Straits.

I thought of all this as I lingered by the massive bronze doors of St. Sophia's. Then I saw her. She had contrived to break free from the mob and was on her way back into the church. She was breathing hard and her veil had been torn to shreds. It is the custom for Greek ladies in Constantinople to hide their faces from strangers and to live in retirement, guarded by eunuchs. When they mount their horses or step into their litters, servants hurry forward with spread cloths to protect them from the eyes of passers-by. Their complexions are white and transparent.

She looked at me and time paused in its flow, the sun ceased to move round the earth, the past mingled with what was to come and nothing existed but the instant—that single instant of life that not envious time itself can snatch away.

I had seen many women in my day. I had loved, selfishly and coldly. I had enjoyed and given others enjoyment. But for me love was no more than a contemptible lust of the flesh which, when gratified, left the soul disconsolate. Only from pity did I feign love, until I could feign no longer.

Yes, I had seen many women, and in the end I renounced them, as I have renounced much else. For me, women were merely a physical experience, and I loathe all that binds me to my body.

She was nearly as tall as I am. Her hair was fair under the embroidered cap, her mantle was blue sewn with silver, she had brown eyes and her complexion was ivory and gold.

But it was not her beauty I looked at—then. It was her eyes and their expression that held me captive, for those eyes were as familiar to me as if I had already beheld them in a dream. Their candor burned away all commonness and vanity. They widened in surprise, and then suddenly they smiled at me.

My rapture was too clear a flame to hold any earthly desire. I felt as if my body had begun to shine, as I had once seen the hermit huts of the holy monks of Mount Athos shine with transcendent radiance, like bright lanterns on those mighty cliffs. And this comparison is no sacrilege, for my rebirth in that instant was a holy miracle.

How long it lasted I cannot say. Perhaps no longer than the breath that in our last hour frees the soul from the body. We were standing a couple of paces apart, but for the space of a breath we stood also on the threshold between the temporal and the eternal, and it was like the edge of a sword.

I turned back into time. I had to speak. I said, "Don't be afraid. If you like, I will take you home to your father's house." I saw from her cap that she was unmarried. Not that this signified; whether she were married or single, her eyes were in my confidence.

She drew a deep breath as if for some time she had taken none, and said inquiringly, "You are Latin?"

"If you like," I said.

We regarded one another, and amid that noisy mob we were as much alone as if we had awakened together in Paradise at the beginning of time. Shyness glowed in her cheeks, but she did not lower her gaze, for each of us recognized the other's eyes. At last she could master her emotion no longer and asked in a trembling voice, "Who are you?"

Her question was no question. It showed merely that she knew me in her heart as I knew her. But to give her time to recover I said, "I grew up in France in the town of Avignon until I was thirteen. Since then I have traveled in many countries. My name is Jean Ange. Here I am called John Angelos."

"Angelos," she repeated. "An angel. Is that why you are so pale and grave? Is that why I was frightened when I saw you?" She came nearer and touched my arm. "No, you're no angel—you're flesh and blood. Why do you wear a Turkish saber?"

"I'm used to it," I answered. "And the steel is tougher than any of Christian forging. In September I escaped from Sultan Mohammed's camp, when he had finished building his fortress on the Bosporus and was to return to Adrianople. Now that war has broken out your Emperor won't surrender any Turkish slaves that have taken refuge in Constantinople."

She glanced at my clothes and said, "You do not dress like a slave."

"No, I do not dress like a slave," I said. "For nearly seven years I was a member of the Sultan's suite. Sultan Murad promoted me to the charge of his dogs and later gave me to his son. Sultan Mohammed tested my understanding, and read Greek and Roman books with me."

"How did you become a slave of the Turks?" she asked.

"For four years I lived in Florence. At that time I was a rich man, but I tired of the cloth trade and took the Cross. The Turks captured me at Varna." Her eyes led me to continue:

"I had been secretary to the Cardinal Giulio Cesarini. After the defeat his horse was drowned in a bog and the Hungarians stabbed him to death with their knives as they retreated. Their young king fell in that battle. My cardinal had induced him to break the peace which he had sworn to keep with the Turks. So the Hungarians blamed him for bringing disaster upon them, and Sultan Murad treated us all like perjurors. He did me no harm, though he executed all the other prisoners who would not acknowledge his God and Prophet. But I've been talking too much—forgive me! I had so long been silent."

She said, "I'm not tired of listening; I would like to hear more about you. But why don't you ask who I am?"

"I shan't do that," I said. "It's enough for me that you exist. I didn't believe anything like this could ever happen to me now."

She did not ask what I meant. She looked about her and saw that the crowd had begun to disperse.

"Come with me," she whispered, and taking me by the hand she drew me hurriedly into the shadow of the bronze doors. "Do you acknowledge the Union?" she asked.

I shrugged my shoulders. "I'm a Latin."

"Step over the threshold," she urged. In the porch we paused at the spot where for a thousand years the iron-soled boots of the guards had worn a hollow in the marble floor. People who had lingered in the church for fear of the mob were eying us; yet she flung her arms about my neck and kissed me.

"Today is the feast of the holy Spiridon," she said, crossing herself in the Greek fashion. "From the Father only, not the Son. May my Christian kiss seal a pact of friendship between us, so that we may not forget one another. Soon my father's servant will be here to fetch me."

Her cheeks were hot and her kiss was not Christian. Her skin smelled of hyacinths, her high, arched eyebrows were thin lines of dark blue and she had painted her mouth red as is usual among distinguished ladies of Constantinople.

"I cannot be parted from you like this," I said. "Though you dwelt behind seven locked doors I should not rest until

I found you again. Though time and space should separate us I will seek you out. You cannot prevent me."

"Why should I?" she retorted, raising her eyebrows in mockery. "How do you know that I'm not burning with impatience to hear more of you and your strange adventures, Master Angelos?"

Her playfulness was enchanting and her tone said more than her words.

"Then tell me the place and the time," I persisted.

She frowned. "You don't realize how rude that is. But perhaps it's a Frankish custom."

"The time and the place," I repeated, and seized her arm.

"How dare you?" she stared at me, paling with astonishment. "No man has ever dared to touch me before. You do not know who I am." But she did not attempt to free herself from my grasp, and it seemed as if after all my touch were not displeasing to her.

"You are you," I said. "That is enough for me."

"I might send you a message," she said. "What does decorum matter, after all, in these troubled times? You're a Frank, not a Greek. But it may be dangerous for you to meet me."

"I took the Cross once, because I lacked faith," I said. "I had achieved everything else—everything but faith. And so it seemed to me that I could at least die for the glory of God. I ran away from the Turks to die on the walls of Constantinople. You can't make my life more dangerous for me than it has been, and still is."

"Be quiet," she said. "And at least promise not to follow me. We have attracted enough attention already."

Drawing her torn veil over her face she turned her back upon me.

Servants in blue and white livery came to fetch her. She

went away with them without a glance toward me, and I stayed where I was. But when she had gone I felt as weak as if I had bled from many wounds.

14 December 1452

This day, in the Church of the Holy Virgin near the harbor, delegates from different nations headed by the Emperor Constantine voted, by a majority of twenty-one over the Venetians, to commandeer the Venetian vessels now lying in the harbor for the defense of the city. Trevisano registered a protest on behalf of the owners. The vessels were allowed to retain their cargoes after their captains had sworn by kissing the cross not to try to escape with their ships. The rate of hire for the vessels was fixed at four hundred bezants a month. An exorbitant price, but Venice knows how to profit by any situation—and why should a drowning man count his gold?

The Emperor has conferred with Gregorios Mammas, whom people call the Puppet Patriarch, and with the bishops and heads of monasteries, about melting down and minting church plate. This plundering of church and cloister is regarded by the monks as the first true sign of the Union and of its recognition.

Land and house property have reached rock-bottom prices. Interest even on short-term loans has risen to forty per cent in a few days, and long-term loans are not to be had. For one small diamond I have bought carpets and furniture worth sixty thousand ducats. I am now furnishing and decorating the house I have rented; the owner is willing to sell it cheaply, but what would be the sense in buying? The future of this city can now be reckoned in months.

I have slept little these last two nights. My former sleeplessness has returned; restlessness impels me to walk the streets, but I stay at home in case someone should inquire for me. Reading is impossible. I have read enough already to perceive how vain all knowledge is. My Greek servant watches my every step, but this is natural and hitherto it has never bothered me. How can they trust a man who has been in the Turkish service? My servant is a poor old man, deserving of pity. I don't grudge him his extra earnings.

15 December 1452

Just a folded piece of paper. A hawker of greenstuff brought it this morning. *In the Church of the Holy Apostles this afternoon.* Nothing more. At noon I announced that I was going to the harbor and I sent my servant to clean out the cellar. As I left I locked the door upon him; I wanted no spying eyes on me today.

The Church of the Apostles stands on the highest hill in the very middle of the city. It was well suited to a tender meeting, for there were only a few black-clad women there, plunged in their devotions at the rail before the holy icons. My clothes attracted no attention, for the church is often visited by Latin seamen who come to see the tombs of the Emperors, and the relics. Immediately on the right of the door, surrounded by a plain wooden railing, stands a fragment of that pillar to which our Savior was bound when He was flogged by the Roman soldiers.

I had to wait a couple of hours in this church, and they dragged heavily. But no one noticed me lingering there. In Constantinople time has lost its meaning. The praying women had loosened their hold on the world and sunk into ecstasy. When they roused themselves they stared about as if they had been asleep, and their look regained the ineffable melancholy of all this dying city. They veiled themselves once more and went out with lowered eyes.

After the chill outside, the church felt warm. Beneath its marble floor run hot air channels in the ancient Roman manner. Even the frost in my soul thawed out. A glow of expectation brought me to my knees to pray, which I had not done for a very long time. I knelt at the altar rail and prayed in my heart:

"Almighty God, Who in Thy Son took flesh upon Thee in a manner beyond our understanding, to save us from our sins, have mercy upon me! Have mercy on my doubting and unbelief, which neither Thine own Word, nor the writings of the Fathers nor any worldly philosophy has been able to cure. Thou hast led me about the world as it seemed good to Thee, permitting me to know all Thy gifts: wisdom and simplicity, wealth and poverty, power and slavery, passions and tranquillity, desire and renunciation, pen and sword; but of these things not one has been able to cure me. Thou hast driven me from despair to despair as the pitiless hunter drives his wearying prey, until in my guilt I had no choice but to venture my life in Thy Name. Yet not even that sacrifice hast Thou been willing to accept. What is it that Thou dost require of me, most holy, most hidden God?"

But when I had thus prayed I knew that it was only my ineradicable pride that had colored my thoughts, and I was ashamed, and prayed again in my heart:

"Thou Who art, have mercy upon me! Forgive me my

sins, not through my merits but of Thy grace, and free me from my dread guilt before it crushes me."

When I had prayed thus I felt cold again—burning cold, like a piece of ice. I felt strength in my limbs and firmness in my backbone, and for the first time for many years I experienced the joy of being alive. I loved, I waited, and all the past fell away in ashes behind me as if I had never loved and waited before. Only as a pale phantom did I remember the girl in Ferrara who wore pearls in her hair and wandered in the garden of philosophy, with a bird cage of gold wire held high in her hand, like a lantern for her own illumination.

And later. I had buried an unknown woman whose face the foxes of the forest had devoured. *She* came to me, seeking the buckle of her belt. I was tending plague victims in a tarred shed, because the endless disputes over the letter of the faith had driven me to despair. She too despaired, that lovely, elusive girl. I had drawn off her plague-infected clothes and burned them in the salt merchant's stove. Then we lay together and gave one another warmth, though I had believed such a thing could not happen to me. She was the daughter of a duke and I was only a translator in the Papal secretariat. It is nearly fifteen years ago now, and nothing stirred within me when I thought of her; I had to search in my memory for her name. Beatrice. The duke admired Dante and read French romances of chivalry. He had beheaded his son for adultery and seduced his own daughter. In Ferrara. That was why I found the girl from the garden in the plague hut.

A woman with a pearl-embroidered veil over her face came up and took her place beside me. She was almost as tall as myself, and wore a fur cloak because of the cold. I smelled the scent of hyacinths. She had come, my beloved.

"Your face," I begged. "Show me your face so that I may know you are true."

"I'm doing wrong," she said. She was very pale and her eyes feared me.

"What is right and what is wrong?" I asked. "We live in the latter days; what can it matter now what we do?"

"You're a Latin," she said reproachfully. "An eater of unleavened bread. Only a Frank could talk like that. A man feels in his heart what is right and wrong—Socrates knew that. But you're a mocker like Pilate, who asked what truth was."

"By the wounds of Christ!" I swore. "Woman, have you come to teach me philosophy? Verily, thou art a Greek!"

She broke into sobs of fear and excitement, and I let her weep herself into calmness, for she was so frightened that she shivered, despite the warmth of the church and her rich fur mantle. She had come; she was weeping for my sake and her own. What better proof did I need that I had stirred her soul, even as she had rolled the stones from the tombs in my heart?

At last I laid my hand on her shoulder, saying "Everything is of little value. Life, learning, philosophy—even faith. Everything is but kindled, to burn fiercely for a time and then die. Let us be two grown people who through a miracle have recognized one another's eyes and can speak together frankly. I have not come to quarrel with you."

"Why have you come?"

"I love you," I said.

"Although you don't know who I am and have seen me only once?" she objected. I spread out my hands; what was there to say? She lowered her eyes and once more began to tremble as she whispered, "I was not at all sure that you would come."

"O my beloved!" I said, for a sweeter confession of love I had never heard from any woman's lips. And again I was aware of how very little can be said in words. Yet men, even the wise and learned, believe that with words they can explain the nature of God.

I stretched forth both my hands, and fully trusting she let me take her cold ones in mine. She had slender, firm fingers, but they had known no toil. For a long time we stood facing one another, hand in hand. We needed no words. Her sad brown eyes surveyed my hair, forehead, cheeks, chin and neck as if, in insatiable curiosity, she wanted to imprint every feature on her memory. My face is weather-beaten, fasts have hollowed my cheeks, the corners of my mouth are deeply lined by disillusionment and my brow furrowed with thought. But I was not ashamed of my face. It is like a wax tablet closely written over with a hard stylus, by life. I willingly let her read the writing on it.

"I want to know all about you," she said, pressing my hard fingers. "You shave. That makes you look as strange and frightening as a Latin priest. Are you a scholar or a soldier?"

"I've drifted from land to land and from one estate and condition to another, like a spark in the wind," I answered her. "In my heart I have walked in the depths and on the heights. I have studied philosophy with its nominalism and realism, and the writings of the ancients. Then weary of words I took to expressing concepts by means of letters and numbers, like Raymondus. And still I could not attain clarity. And so I chose the sword and the Cross."

Presently I went on. "At one time I was a merchant. I learned bookkeeping by the kind of double entry that makes wealth an illusion. In our day wealth has become no more than writing on paper, like philosophy and the sacred mysteries."

After some hesitation I lowered my voice and said, "My father was Greek, though I grew up in the Avignon of the Popes."

She started and dropped my hands.

"I thought as much," she said. "If you let your beard grow your face would be the face of a Greek. Was that the only reason that you seemed so familiar to me from the first moment, as if I had known you before and were seeking your former face behind this one?"

"No," I said. "No. That was not the reason."

She looked about her fearfully and hid her mouth and chin in her veil.

"Tell me everything about yourself," she begged me, "but let us walk about meanwhile and pretend to look at things, so that people will not notice us. Someone might recognize me."

She laid her hand trustfully on my arm and we began walking around, looking at the sarcophagi of the Emperors, at the icons and the silver reliquaries. Our steps fitted one another's. It was as if a feather of fire had brushed my body when her hand touched my arm; but the pain was sweet. Half aloud I began to tell my story.

"I have forgotten my childhood. It's like a dream and I'm no longer sure which is dream and which fact. But when I played with other boys by the city wall or river bank in Avignon I used to preach long sermons to them in Greek and Latin. I knew by heart a great deal that I didn't understand, because after my father became blind I had to read aloud to him all day from his books."

"Blind?" she asked.

"He went on a long journey when I was eight or nine," I said, searching in my memory. I had banished all these things from my mind as completely as if I had never known them, but now the horrors of my childhood returned like an evil dream. "He stayed away a whole year, and on the way home he was set upon by thieves; they blinded him so that he wouldn't be able to recognize them afterwards and bear witness against them."

"Blinded," she said in wonder. "Here in Constantinople only deposed emperors are blinded, or sons who rebel against their fathers. The Turkish rulers learned that custom from us."

"My father was Greek," I said again. "In Avignon he was called Andronikos the Greek and in his last years simply the Blind Greek."

"How did your father come to the country of the Franks?" she asked in surprise.

"I don't know," I answered. I did know, but I kept it to myself. "He lived in Avignon all the rest of his life. I was thirteen when he fell over the cliff behind the Papal Palace and broke his neck. You asked about my childhood. I used to have visions of angels when I was a child, and thought they were real; my name after all is John Angelos. I don't remember much about this myself, but everything was brought up against me at the trial."

"The trial?" She frowned.

"When I was thirteen I was condemned for the murder of my father," I said abruptly. "People gave evidence that I had led my blind father to the brink of the precipice and pushed him over so as to inherit his fortune. There were no eyewitnesses, and so they scourged me to make me confess. At last I was sentenced to be broken on the wheel and quartered. I was thirteen. Such was my childhood."

She took my hand quickly, looked into my eyes and said, "Those are not the eyes of a murderer. Tell me more—it's a relief to you."

"I haven't thought about these things for many years," I replied. "I've never wanted to speak of them to anyone. I had wiped them from my memory. But it's easy to talk to you. It was long ago: I'm forty now and I have lived many lives since then. But I did not kill my father. He may have been stern and irritable—he may have struck me sometimes; but in his best moods he was good to me. I loved him. He was my father. Of my mother I know nothing—she died when I was born, vainly clutching a miracle-working stone. . . .

"Perhaps father tired of life because he was blind. That's what I thought afterwards, when I grew up. In the morning of that day he had told me not to worry whatever happened. He said he had a great sum of money, no less than three thousand ducats, which the goldsmith Gerolamo had in safekeeping. He had bequeathed everything to me and appointed Gerolamo as my guardian until I should attain the age of sixteen. This was in the spring. Then he asked me to lead him up onto the cliff behind the palace: he wanted to hear the wind and the sound of birds coming in their flocks from the south. He said he had made an appointment with the angels, and asked me to leave him there alone until the hour of evensong."

"Had your father forsaken his Greek faith?" she asked sharply. She was a true daughter of Constantinople.

"He heard Mass, went to Confession, ate the Latin bread and bought indulgences to shorten his time in purgatory," I said. "I never even imagined that he might have a religion different from everyone else's. He said he had an appointment with the angels, and I found him dead at the bottom of the cliff. He was tired of life—he was blind and unhappy."

"But how could they blame you for that?"

"It was all laid at my door," I said. "All, all. I was after his money, they said—and Master Gerolamo was the one who witnessed most vehemently against me. With his own eyes he had seen me bite my father's hand when he thrashed me. As for the money, there was none; it was an old man's delusion. Gerolamo had indeed received a small sum when my father was blinded, but that had long ago been spent on his keep. Out of compassion Gerolamo had continued to send us provisions from his estate, he said. The Blind Greek was easily contented and fasted often. This maintenance was not to be regarded as interest on any sort of deposit, as the blind man imagined. It was purely and simply a work of charity. To lend out money at usury would have been a great sin for both parties. Yet to show his good will Master Gerolamo promised to give a silver candlestick to the Church in memory of my father, though his ledgers plainly showed that in the course of years my father had got into his debt. Of his generosity he proposed that I should settle the debt with my father's books, though no one could read them. But I am wearying you."

"No, you're not wearying me," she said. "Tell me how your life was saved."

"I was the Blind Greek's son, a foreigner. Therefore no one spoke in my defense. But the bishop came to hear of the three thousand ducats and demanded that I should be brought before the ecclesiastical court. The formal charge related to the visions I had had when I was flogged, for I had been delirious with pain and raved about angels, as I had done when a child. In the temporal court they had quickly skimmed over the theological aspects of the case, and merely noted in the record of proceedings that my mind was unhinged. By chaining me to a wall in the tower and flogging me every day the judges believed that they could easily drive the tempter from my soul before the execution. But the money question complicated the case, and the charge of parricide soon resolved itself into a dispute between the temporal and spiritual authorities as to the right of trial—as to which of them was entitled to pronounce sentence upon me and confiscate my father's fortune."

"But how were you saved?" she asked impatiently.

"I don't know," I admitted, with truth. "I can't claim that my angels saved me, but one day my fetters were struck off without any reason being given, and early next morning I noticed that the door of the tower had been left unlocked. So I went. After so long in the dark I was dazzled by the daylight. At the western gate of the city I met a peddler who asked if I would go with him; he seemed to know me, for he at once began asking inquisitive questions about my visions. Once well into the woods he brought out a book which he had hidden under his wares: it was the four Gospels translated into French. He asked me to read it aloud to him, and so I came to belong to the Brotherhood of the Free Spirit. Perhaps it was they who had released me, for many belong to it whom one would never suspect of such a thing."

"The Brotherhood of the Free Spirit," she said in wonder. "What is that?"

"I don't want to be tedious," I said evasively. "I'll tell you about it some other time."

"How do you know there will be another time?" she asked. "It was very difficult for me to arrange this meeting—more difficult than you might guess, used as you are to the freer customs of the west. It's easier even for a Turkish woman to make an assignation than for a Greek, if one may believe the stories."

"In the stories the woman always outwits the guard," I said. "You should read them carefully. Perhaps they could teach you something."

"But you," she said, "of course you have learned it all?"

"You needn't be jealous," I said. "I was busy with very different things in the Sultan's seraglio."

"I, jealous? You flatter yourself!" she retorted, flushing with indignation. "And how am I to know that you're not a common seducer, like other Franks? Perhaps like them you'll profit by having made the acquaintance of an inquisitive woman, to boast of your splendid conquest, in ships and taverns."

"So! Is that how it is?" I said, squeezing her wrist. "Is that the sort of acquaintance you have among the Franks! You're that kind of woman. Don't be afraid—I can hold my tongue. I simply made a mistake about you, and it will be better if we don't meet again. No doubt you'll easily find some captain or Latin officer to keep you company in my place."

She snatched away her hand and rubbed her wrist.

"Yes, indeed," she said. "It would certainly be better if we didn't meet again." She breathed quickly and looked at me with darkening eyes and back-tilted head. "Get back to the harbor—you'll find plenty of women there, more easily won, who will suit you better. Get drunk and start a brawl, as all Franks do! You'll find someone to console you. And so God be with you."

"And with you," I answered, in equal fury.

She walked rapidly away over the glassy marble floor. Her movements were graceful. When I swallowed I tasted blood, so hard had I bitten my lip not to call her back. Her pace slackened, and when she reached the door she could not resist looking round. Seeing that I hadn't moved from the spot or made any attempt to hurry after her she became so enraged that she turned, ran back to me and slapped my face hard. One ear was deafened and one cheek smarted, but my heart rejoiced. For she had not struck me so impulsively but that she first looked to see that no one was watching us.

I stood still and said nothing. After a pause she turned again and left me, while I remained where I was and watched her go. When she reached the middle of the floor my will caused her to relent, slacken her pace, stop and turn. She was already smiling, and her brown eyes shone with amusement.

"Forgive me, my dear sir," she said. "I have been badly brought up, but now I am cowed and meek. Unfortunately I have no books of Turkish tales; perhaps you could lend me one so that I may learn how woman's cunning may outwit man's intelligence." She took my hand, kissed it and pressed it to her face. "Feel how hot my cheeks are."

"Don't do that," I said warningly. "Anyway, one of my cheeks is hotter. And you needn't learn cunning: I fancy the Turks have nothing more to teach you."

"How could you let me go without hurrying after me?" she asked. "You hurt me deeply."

"It's still only a game," I said with burning eyes. "You can still draw back—I won't pester you. I won't follow you. You must choose."

"I have no longer any choice," she answered. "I chose when I wrote a few words on a scrap of paper. I chose when I didn't send you away at St. Sophia's. I chose when you looked into my eyes. I couldn't draw back now even if I wanted to. But don't make it too hard for me."

Hand in hand we left the church, and she was startled to find that dusk was already falling.

"We must separate," she said, "at once."

"May I not go with you just a little way?" I pleaded, unable to help myself.

And she could not refuse me, incautious though it was. We walked side by side as twilight sank over the green domes of the churches, and lanterns were lit before the fine houses in the main streets. Behind us slunk a thin yellow dog which for some reason or other had attached itself to me; it had followed me from my house to the Apostles' church and waited shivering until I came out.

She didn't turn off toward the Palace of Blachernae as I had expected, but in the opposite direction. We passed the ruins of the Hippodrome. On this ancient race course the young Greeks practice archery, or play ball on horseback with sticks in their hands. The dilapidated buildings looked even larger in the twilight. The tremendous dome of St. Sophia's soared into the sky, while the palace of the Emperors loomed darkly ahead. Not one light was burning there; its deserted halls were now used only for rare ceremonials. Dusk was merciful and concealed a dying city. Its marble pillars were yellowed, its walls cracked, its fountains played no longer and withered plane leaves filled the moss-grown basins in the neglected gardens. By tacit agreement we slackened our pace. The evening star was already lit on the horizon when we paused in the shadow of the pillars of the old palace.

"I must go now," she said. "You mustn't come any further."

"But your fur mantle may attract robbers or beggars," I objected.

She raised her head proudly. "In Constantinople there are neither robbers nor beggars. Near the harbor, perhaps, or on the Pera side. But not in the city itself."

This is true. In Constantinople even beggars are thin and proud. There are few of them, and they squat here and there near churches, staring before them with a veiled look as if they were gazing a thousand years into the past. When they receive alms of some Latin they murmur a blessing, but no

yet greater efforts. Even his aged viziers had to roll stones and mix mortar. Never before, I believe, has so strong a fortress been built in so short a time. When I escaped from the Sultan's camp nothing was lacking but the leaden roofs for the towers.

Orban the gun-founder's great bronze bombards have withstood their powerful charges and shown their strength. Since one huge stone sank a Venetian galley no vessel from the Black Sea has put in here. Her captain refused to strike his colors, and his corpse still hangs on a stake near the Sultan's fortress, while the limbs of his crew lie scattered and rotting on the ground about him. The Sultan spared only four men, whom he sent into the city to tell of what had happened. This was a month ago.

Yet it looks as if the Emperor Constantine means to defend himself in earnest. Reinforcement work is going on all along the city wall; even flagstones from the burial grounds outside are being used. This is prudent, for otherwise the Turks might turn them to account when they begin the siege. But a rumor is rife among the people that the builders are scamping their work and pocketing large sums. No one condemns this; on the contrary, they rejoice. The Emperor is an apostate and has turned Latin, and therefore may legitimately be swindled. Truly this city loves the Turks better than the Latins.

And in the Palace of Blachernae they have Panaghia, the miracle-working Virgin, on whom to pin their faith. The baker's wife told me today in all seriousness that when Murad laid siege to the city thirty years ago, the Holy Virgin appeared on the battlements in her blue mantle and so terrified the Turks that they set fire to their siege-engines and their camp and withdrew during the night—as if Murad had not had more pressing reasons for his retreat!

How long a week can be! How strange it is to be waiting, when I fancied I had nothing further in life to wait for. Even waiting is delight, now that the mad fever and impatience of youth have departed. But I cannot believe in this any longer. Perhaps she is not at all what I imagine. Perhaps I am only deceiving myself. Yet I do not miss the warmth of a charcoal brazier, despite the icy wind off the Marmora and the snowflakes whirling in the air. My body is a furnace, radiating heat.

22 December 1452

The Feast of our Savior's Nativity is at hand. The Venetians and Genoese in Pera are preparing to celebrate it. But Greeks pay little attention to Christmas; their chief festival is Easter. Not in commemoration of Christ's Passion, but of the joyful Resurrection. Their faith is devout, ecstatic, mystical and forgiving. They do not even burn their heretics, but permit them to enter a convent and repent. They have not stoned Cardinal Isidor, but only shouted "Take your unleavened bread back to Rome!"

Such glowing faith and devotion as one sees here on the faces of churchgoers is no longer to be found in the west. There people buy forgiveness with money.

But this city has grown ever more desolate. Its gigantic walls once encircled a million people, but now the place has shrunk and survives only on the hills around the central squares and on the slopes near the harbor. Ruins and wasteland stretch between the inhabited parts and provide bleak grazing land for goats, donkeys and horses. Coarse grass, thorn bushes, abandoned, roofless houses—and ever the wind off the Marmora. Dreariness unspeakable.

Venice has sent two warships. Pope Nicholas of Rome sent fifty mercenaries with Cardinal Isidor. Apart from these we have only vessels forcibly commandeered, and Latins pressed by hook and crook into the service. But I was forgetting the Emperor's five warships of Byzantine pattern; they lie in the harbor, bilges awash, sails gone and the rotten smell of them spreading far and wide. The cannon in their bows are green and blocked with corrosion. But today there were men on board, so it seems that Megadux Notaras means to put them into commission, even though the Emperor cannot afford it. Warships are costly things.

From the islands in the Aegean a few cargoes of grain, oil and wine have arrived. It is rumored that the Turks have devastated the Morea, so no help can be hoped for from there, even supposing Constantine can place any reliance on his brothers. Demetrios at any rate opposed the Union even in Florence, and after Emperor John's death it was entirely owing to their mother that no war broke out between them.

I don't know them. I cannot reach their hearts. They will always be foreigners to me; even their measurement of time is different. For them, this is the year 6960, counting from the Creation; for the Turks it is the year 856 after the flight of their Prophet. What a mad world it is! Or am I too much of a Latin at heart?

I have paid a visit to Genoese Pera on the other side of the bay. No one questioned me. Boats laden to the gunwales ply back and forth. Genoese trade is prospering; if I chose I could make a quick fortune by dealing in arms. Perhaps I should be better received by the Greeks if I could offer them old-fashioned weapons at extortionate prices; they might trust me then and regard me as an honest man.

In every wineshop in Pera one may sell or exchange information, for the Genoese are not at war with the Sultan. That too is madness. Through Pera, Mohammed can learn all that goes on in Constantinople, just as we may hear how the Sultan's preparations progress day by day.

She didn't come. No doubt she only wanted to gain time to drop me in a becoming manner, and cover her tracks. I do not even know her name.

And she's Greek, as Greek as I am by virtue of my father's blood—that enfeebled, sly, treacherous, cruel Byzantine blood! If it be true that women, whether Christians or Turks, are the slyest creatures in the world, then a Greek woman must be the slyest of all women. She has two thousand years of experience behind her.

My heart is lead, and leaden is the blood in my veins. I hate this dying city which stares only at its past and refuses to believe in the approaching cataclysm.

I hate because I love.

26 December 1452

My servant surprised me this morning by coming to warn me.

"Master, you should not visit Pera too often."

I looked closely at him for the first time. Up to now he had been simply a necessary evil that went with the house when I rented it. He saw to my clothes and bought my food, looked after the house in the interests of the landlord, swept the court and no doubt supplied the Dark Chamber at the

Palace of Blachernae with information as to what I did and whom I met.

I have never had anything against him. He's a pitiable old man, but I have never wanted to look at him. Now I did look. He's a little old fellow with a thin beard, he has pains in his knees, and Greek eyes full of a fathomless sorrow. His clothes are threadbare and spotted with grease. I asked him. "Who told you to say this?"

He was offended. "I'm thinking only of your own good. You are my master so long as you live in this house."

I said, "I'm a Latin."

But he protested eagerly, "No, no—you're not! I know your face!"

To my speechless amazement he threw himself on his knees before me, groped for my hand to kiss it, and pleaded, "Don't despise me, master! It's true that I drink the wine left over in the jar and even take care of the small change you scatter about. And I gave some of the oil to my sick aunt, for our family is very poor. But if this displeases you I won't do it again, for now I have recognized you."

"I haven't been stingy with the housekeeping money," I said in surprise. "It's the poor man's right to live on the crumbs that fall from the rich man's table. You're welcome to maintain your entire family at my expense for as long as I'm your master. I set little value on money. The hour approaches when both money and property will lose their meaning. In the face of death we're all equal, and in God's scales the virtue of a mosquito weighs as heavily as that of an elephant."

I kept on talking to him so that I might observe his face meanwhile. I thought he looked honest, but faces lie—and can a Greek trust a Greek?

He said, "Another time you need not lock me up in the

cellar if you don't want me to know what you're doing or where you're going. It was so cold in the cellar that my joints froze. Ever since then I've suffered from a cold and from earache, and my knees are even worse than they were before."

"Get up, you dolt, and cure your aches with wine," I said, and took a gold bezant from my purse. To him this was a fortune, for in Constantinople the poor are very poor and the few rich extremely rich.

He looked at the coin in my hand and his face cleared, but he shook his head saying, "Master, I was not complaining in order to beg. You needn't bribe me. I will neither see nor hear anything you don't wish me to see or hear. Only command me."

"I don't understand you," I said.

He pointed to the yellow dog which had already begun to put on flesh, and which lay on its rag mat by the door with its nose on the ground, watching my every movement.

"Does not even that dog obey and follow you?" he said.

"I don't understand you," I repeated, and threw the gold coin onto the mat in front of him. He bent to pick it up and then looked me in the eye.

"You needn't disclose yourself to me, master," he said. "How could I suppose it? Your secret is sacred to me. I take your money only because you order me to do so. It will bring me and my family great happiness—but it is even greater happiness for me to serve you."

His hints stung me, for of course like other Greeks he suspected that I was still secretly in the Sultan's service and had only pretended to escape. Perhaps he hopes to profit by me to avoid slavery when the Sultan captures the city; such a belief would be an advantage to me if I had anything to hide. Yet how could I rely upon a man of such low birth?

"You're mistaken if you think you can gain anything

through me," I told him. "I'm no longer in the Sultan's service. Ten times over and to the limit of my patience I have repeated this to those who pay you to watch me. But I repeat it once more to you: I no longer serve the Sultan."

He said, "No, no—I know that. How could you be in his service? I have recognized you, and it's as if the lightning had struck the ground beside me."

"Are you drunk?" I asked. "Delirious? Feverish? I don't know what you mean." Yet in my innermost self I was strangely stirred.

He bowed his head and said, "Master, I am drunk. Forgive me. It shall not happen again."

But his wild words sent me to a mirror. For some reason I had decided not to visit the barber any more, but to shave myself, and more carefully than before. From apathy and dejection I had neglected this for the last few days. Now I have even altered the fashion of my dress to show that I'm a Latin.

2 January 1453

She came. In spite of everything she came to me.

She was dressed in a light brown mantle and soft brown shoes. Perhaps she thought herself well disguised, but not the most simple-minded could have taken her for a woman of low birth. The cut of her mantle, her headdress, even the fashion in which she had wound a gauzy veil about her head to hide her face revealed her rank and breeding.

"You're welcome, in God's name," I said, unable to restrain the tears that came to my eyes. The yellow dog wagged its tail at her.

"It's madness," she said, "madness and witchcraft. I shall be found out, but I couldn't help coming. I had to come, although I didn't want to."

"How did you get in?" I asked quickly. She was still holding the veil before her mouth.

"A little old fellow with a cough opened the door at my knock," she said. "You should give your servant better clothes and tell him to comb his hair and beard. As it was, he was so much ashamed of his appearance that he turned his back without looking at me." She glanced about her. "Your room would be the better for some cleaning, too." She averted her eyes quickly from one of the corners.

I threw a rug over my sleepingplace and hurried out. My servant was standing in the yard staring at the clouds.

"A beautiful day," he remarked with a sly grin.

"A glorious day," I agreed, and crossed myself in the Greek fashion. "The best day in my whole life. Run and get wine, cakes, sweetmeats, fried meat and preserves. Bring plenty. Buy the best you can find—buy a whole basketful so that there'll be enough for you too, and your cousins and aunts—your whole family! If you meet beggars on your way, give them alms and a blessing."

"Is it your birthday, master?" he inquired innocently.

"No, I have a visitor," I told him. "A common, low-class woman has come to solace me in my loneliness."

"A visitor?" he repeated in feigned astonishment. "I saw no visitor. It's true that a gust of wind shook the door so that it sounded as if someone were knocking, but when I went to open it I saw no one. Can you be joking?"

"Do as I tell you," I urged him. "But if you say one word about a visitor to anyone I'll take you by the beard and cut your throat with my own hand." As he started to fetch the basket I seized him by the arm and said, "I've never asked your name. Tell me what it is."

"This is a great honor for me," he said. "I'm called Manuel after the old Emperor. My father served him as wood carrier in the Palace of Blachernae."

"Manuel!" I exclaimed. "What a beautiful name. Manuel, this is the happiest day of my life." I caught him by the ears and kissed both his bearded cheeks, then thrust him on his way.

When I went back into my room my visitor had thrown off the brown mantle and uncovered her face. I could not gaze my fill of her; the words stuck in my throat, and my knees failed me so that I sank to the floor before her and pressed my cheek to her knees. I was weeping for ecstasy and joy. Shyly she stroked my hair.

When at last I looked up she was smiling. Her smile was like the sun. Her eyes were golden-brown flowers; her blue eyebrows curved high and even, in exquisite arches; her cheeks were tulips, her soft lips were rose petals and her teeth were pearls. I was dazzled as I beheld her. I told her all these things.

"My heart is seventeen," I said. "I must borrow words from the bards, for my own fall short. I am drunk with you. It's as if I had never experienced anything—as if I'd never so much as touched a woman—and yet I know you as if I'd known you all my life.

"You are all Byzantium to me," I said. "You are the city of the Emperors, Constantinople. It is because of you that I've yearned all my life to come here. It's you I dream of when I dream of your city; and just as your city was a thousand times more beautiful than I could have guessed, so you are a thousand times more lovely than I remembered. Two weeks is an endless time—a dead, dead time. Why didn't you come when you promised? Why did you forsake me? I thought I should die."

She looked at me, closed her eyes lightly and with her fingertips touched the corners of my eyes, my cheeks and lips. Then she opened the radiant, smiling brown eyes again and said, "Go on—you talk well. You're pleasing to listen to, though no doubt you don't mean a word of what you say. You had forgotten me—you were surprised to see me. But you did recognize me."

I embraced her.

"No, no," she said, and thrust both hands against my chest. But her resistance was like an invitation. I kissed her. Her body melted and weakened in my arms—until at last she pushed me away, turned her back and held her head in both hands.

"What are you doing to me?" she complained, and burst into tears. "It wasn't for this I came. Oh, my head—my head is aching."

I had not been mistaken. She was indeed inexperienced, a maiden. Her mouth told me so—her body told mine. Proud, maybe; passionate, easily kindled, capricious, and jealously guarded, but of sin she had made no trial. In her thoughts, perhaps, but not with her body.

From her face I could see that she was in pain. Gently I took her lovely head in my hands and began to stroke her brow.

"Forgive me," she said, sobbing. "I expect that I am too sensitive. I feel as if someone were pricking me with red-hot needles. Perhaps I was frightened when you took me in your arms so suddenly."

Strength passed from me to her—strength from my hands. In a little while she sighed deeply, her limbs relaxed and she opened her eyes. "Your hands are gentle," she said; she turned her head and kissed my hand lightly. "They're a healer's hands."

I looked at them.

"A healer's and a destroyer's," I said harshly. "But believe me, I mean you no harm. Even just now I meant you none—you should have known that."

She looked at me, and her glance was once more open and familiar to me. I could drown in it again, until everything about me grew dim and unreal.

"I was mistaken, then," she said. "Perhaps *I* meant harm, but not in my innermost self. But all is well again now. It is good to be with you. My own home has grown strange and tedious. Your strength has drawn me constantly—through walls and right across the city. Can you have bewitched me?"

"Love is witchcraft," I said. "Love is the most terrible witchcraft. It was you who bewitched me when you looked into my eyes outside the Church of the Holy Wisdom."

"It's madness," she lamented. "My father would never consent to give me to a Latin. You don't even know your own lineage—you're a wanderer and an adventurer. Father would have you slain if he knew."

My heart stopped. To gain time I boasted.

"My lineage is written in my face. My father's name is Sword, my mother's Quill. The thinking stars are my brothers, angels and demons my kinsmen."

She looked me straight in the eye and said, "I did not mean to hurt you. I spoke only the truth."

Haughty words stuck in my throat. The truth was simpler.

"I am already married," I confessed. "It's true that I have not seen my wife for nearly ten years, but so far as I know she is very much alive. Our son is twelve. The truth is that I took the Cross because I could live with them no longer. They believe I fell at Varna. It's better so."

She had started violently at my first words. We did not look at each other. She drew a finger along the collar of her gown and straightened the brooch at her bosom. The skin of her neck was very transparent.

"What does that signify?" she said at last in an icy voice. "This—our meetings could not have gone on." She still fingered her brooch, looked at her hand and added, "I must go now. Will you help me with my mantle?"

But I would not let her go, and she hardly wished it herself. She had spoken those words merely to wound me.

"We're both grown people," I said, and I could not keep the roughness from my voice. "Don't be so childish. You know very well what you're doing. You came here with your eyes open. What do I care for marriage—what do I care for the holy sacrament of the Church? I care neither for heaven nor hell since you exist and I've found you. They are not what we think, they are not what we are told. You're mine and you cannot deny it. But again I tell you, I mean you no harm."

She stood silent, staring obstinately at the floor. I continued:

"Perhaps you don't yet realize what is in store for us all. Under the Turks there can be only death or slavery for us. One of those two things you must choose. We have only a few months left—half a year at most. Then the Turks will be here. And what will custom or decorum matter then?" I shouted, bringing my fist down so hard on the back of a chair that the bones of my hand cracked and the pain of it blinded me for a moment. "Marriage, home, children, are things a man may think of when he has all life before him. You and I have not. From the outset our love is doomed. Our time is short. But you—you would take your mantle and go your way because many years ago divine judgment forced me to marry a woman older than myself—a woman I gave my body to, from pity. My heart she never reached."

"What do I care about your heart?" she cried, with flaming cheeks. "Your heart is Latin, as your words show. Constantinople can never fall; once in every generation the Turks have besieged it in vain. The Holy Mother of God herself guards our walls, and how shall a youth pull them down—that Mohammed whom the Turks themselves despise?"

But it was as if she were saying this for the sake of talking, so evident was her fond faith in the walls of Constantinople.

More softly and with averted eyes she asked, "What was that you said of divine judgment? And is your wife really older than you?"

Her questions made my heart rejoice again, for it showed that curiosity had awakened in her woman's mind. At that moment my servant returned, slamming the door and treading heavily on the stairs. I went and took the basket from him.

"I shan't need you again, Manuel," I said.

"Master," he replied, "I will watch the house from the tavern opposite. Believe me, it is best." In his eagerness he touched my arm, drew my head down and whispered in my ear, "For God's sake, master, teach her to dress differently! As she is now, she attracts all eyes and arouses more curiosity than if she went with her face uncovered and her cheeks painted like the trollops in the harbor."

"Manuel," I warned him, "my dagger sits loose in its sheath."

But he only sniggered as if I had said something witty, and rubbed his hands in benediction.

"You have the soul of a pimp, like the barber," I said, and kicked him away. "Think shame of your notions." But my kick was a gentle one, that he might accept it as a mark of favor.

I carried in the basket. I blew on the embers and put on more charcoal, poured wine into a silver cup, broke a wheaten loaf, put sweetmeats in my Chinese bowl. She raised her hands in deprecation. But then she crossed herself in the Greek manner, took a sip of the dark wine, bit off a piece of the bread and ate a honey caramel on a stick. In the same way I tasted everything too. I was no hungrier than she.

"Now we've drunk wine and broken bread together," I said. "Now you know I cannot do you any harm. You are my guest, and all that I have is yours."

She smiled and said, "Weren't you going to tell me about the judgment?"

"I've already talked too much," I objected. "Why should I talk so long as you're here? Besides, people use the same words for different things; words sow misunderstanding and mistrust. It's enough that you're here. When you're here I need no words."

I warmed her hands over the dish of charcoal; her fingers felt cold but her cheeks glowed.

"My beloved," I said softly. "My only beloved. I thought that life's autumn had come, but it wasn't true. My thanks to you for existing."

Later she told me that her mother had been ill and so it had been impossible for her to come before. I saw that she would have been glad to tell me who she was, but I forbade her. I did not want to know. Such knowledge only increases care. There is a time for everything, and it was enough for me that she should be with me then.

When we parted she asked, "Do you still seriously believe the Turks will attack this spring?"

I could not help flaring up afresh. "Are you all mad, you Greeks? Listen: dervishes and teachers of Islam are wandering from village to village all over Asia. The European troops under the Sultan's command have already received their marching orders. In Adrianople they're casting bombards. The

Sultan means to assemble a greater army for this siege of your city than any of his ancestors—and you ask me, 'Does he really mean to come?'

"Of course he does!" I shouted. "And he's in a hurry. Now that the Union has come into force the Pope may after all be able to induce the princes of Europe to sink their quarrels and embark on a new crusade. If the Turks are a deadly menace to you, Constantinople in the heart of the Turkish Empire is a mortal threat to the Sultan. You don't know the extent of his ambition: he thinks himself another Alexander."

"Hush, hush," she said soothingly, and added with a dubious smile, "If what you say is true we shall not meet many more times."

"What do you mean?" I demanded, seizing her hands.

"If the Sultan really intends to march from Adrianople, Emperor Constantine will be sending the ladies of the Imperial Court to the Morea in a fast-sailing vessel, for their better safety. There will be other ladies of rank on board; I have my place there too." She rested her brown eyes upon me, bit her lips and said, "I ought not to have told you that, I suppose."

"No," I said hoarsely. My lips were dry. "I might be the Sultan's secret agent—that's what you mean, isn't it? You all suspect that."

"I trust you," she said. "You won't misuse this information. Tell me if I should go."

"Of course," I said. "You must go. Why shouldn't you preserve your virtue and your life, if opportunity offers? You don't know Sultan Mohammed—I do. Your city will fall. All the beauty of it, all its fading glory, all the power and wealth of its great families—all these things are already shadows without substance."

"And you?" she asked.

"I came here to die on the walls of Constantinople," I answered. "To die for all that is past—for all that which no power on earth can restore. Other times are coming; I have no wish to see them."

She had put on her brown mantle and was fingering her veil.

"Aren't you going to kiss me in farewell?" she asked.

"It only gives you a headache," I replied.

She stretched up and kissed my cheeks with her soft lips, stroked my jaw lightly with the palm of her hand and for a moment pressed her head against my chest as if to possess me.

"You make me vain," she said. "I'm beginning to think too well of myself. Don't you really care to know who I am? Is it simply as a woman that you want me for your friend? That is sweet to hear, but hard to believe."

"Will you come again before you sail?" I asked.

She glanced around the room and patted the yellow dog abstractedly.

"It is good to be here," she said. "I will come again if I can."

6 January 1453

The Greeks are becoming uneasy after all. Evil prophecies spread from mouth to mouth; women tell their dreams, men see omens. In the streets frenzied monks with eyes aflame preach death and destruction to the city that has forsaken the faith of its fathers.

All this agitation originates in the Pantokrator monastery, whence the monk Gennadios sends out letters to be read aloud to the townspeople. Women weep to hear them. By the Emperor's command he may not show himself in public, but I have read a proclamation that he caused to be nailed up on the monastery gate.

Wretches! Whither have ye strayed? How came ye to forsake your faith in God and set your hopes on Frankish aid? Ye hurl your city to destruction and with it your religion! Lord, be Thou gracious unto me! Before Thy countenance I testify that I have no part in this sin. Bethink ye, O most miserable! As slaves ye shall pine and languish, having cast off the faith of your fathers to embrace false doctrines. Woe, woe unto you upon the Day of Judgment!

The most important question at the moment is whether the Pope's fleet will arrive in time and whether its aid will be sufficient. I can scarcely believe there will be a general crusade. Christendom had been making ready for five years before its defeat at Varna. The Hungarians won't dare to break the peace as they did then. If help does not arrive in time the only result of the Union will have been to arouse bitterness and despair. Why indeed should the people of Constantinople renounce the consolation that their faith can bring them?

Gennadios has the people with him. The Church of St. Sophia is always empty now; only the Emperor with his ceremonial suite hears Mass there. What the politicians believe is of no importance; they would pay lip service to any faith. But I think the deserted church frightens them. Some of the priesthood have fallen away too, and those who remain to serve in St. Sophia's have been threatened by the rest with excommunication and the interdict.

8 January 1453

A fresh rumor sent me to the monastery of the All-Ruler to meet this Gennadios. I had to wait a long time. He prays and scourges himself all day long to expiate the city's sins. But he received me when he heard that I had belonged to the Sultan's suite. Truly they love the Turks better than the Latins.

When he observed my shaven chin and my Latin clothes he drew back, crying "*anathema*" and "*apostata.*" It was not surprising that he did not recognize me, for I hardly knew him at first glance, bearded as he was, with matted hair, and eyes sunken with fasting and watching. Nevertheless he was the former Georgios Scholarios, secretary and keeper of the seal to the late Emperor John—the man who in Florence had signed the Union with the rest—the fiery, learned, ambitious, vital young Georgios.

"I am Jean Ange," I said. "Giovanni Angelo, the Frank to whom you showed kindness in Florence many years ago."

He stared at me as if he beheld Satan before him.

"Perhaps Georgios knew you," he cried, "but there is no longer any Georgios. Because of my sins I have renounced my position in the world—my rank as scholar and my political honors. Only Gennadios the monk remains and he does not know you. What do you want of me?"

His fever and spiritual agony were not feigned; truly he suffered and the death sweat of his people and his city stood on his forehead. Briefly I told him my story, so that he might trust me.

Then I said, "If you sinned in signing at that time, and if you're now expiating that sin, why do you not do it privately to God? Why do you drag all your people into your pain, and sow dissension just when all forces should be united?"

He answered, "Through my tongue and my pen God will scourge them for their grievous betrayal. If they had trusted in the Lord and rejected help from the west, the Lord Himself would have fought for them. Now Constantinople is lost. The building of walls and amassing of weapons is vanity: God has turned His face from us and delivered us into the hands of the Turks."

"And even if God is speaking through your mouth," I said, "the battle is still before us. Do you suppose Emperor Constantine would give away his city of his own free will?"

He looked at me searchingly, and into his rapt eyes there came the keen glint of an experienced statesman.

"Who speaks through *your* mouth?" he demanded. "The Sultan will protect the lives, livelihood, property and above all the religion of those who submit. Our Church will live on and flourish even in the Turkish Empire, under the protection of the Sultan. He makes war not on our faith but on our Emperor." As I made no answer to this he added, "By his faithlessness Constantine has shown that he is not the true Basileus. He is not even lawfully crowned. He is a worse enemy to our religion than Sultan Mohammed."

"Demented monk!" I burst out. "Do you know what you're saying?"

Somewhat more calmly he rejoined, "I have made no secret of my views. I have said the same thing to Constantine himself. I have nothing to lose. But I'm not alone: behind me stand the people and many of the nobles who fear the wrath of God. Pass that on to those who sent you."

"You are mistaken," I said. "I no longer serve the Sultan, but I have no doubt that it will be easy for you to deliver your message to the Sultan's ears through other channels."

10 January 1453

I was summoned again to the Palace of Blachernae. Phrantzes showed me remarkable courtesy and attention, and gave me wine; but he never once looked me in the eye. He just twisted his signet ring, which is as big as a baby's hand, and surveyed his well-tended nails. He's a clever, learned man who doubtless has no longer any religion; he is faithful only to his Emperor. Constantine and he grew up together from childhood.

Among other things he said, "This winter will be decisive. Grand Vizier Khalil in Adrianople is doing all he can to preserve peace. He is our friend. Quite recently we have had encouraging messages from him through the Genoese in Pera. There's no reason why I should keep it from you. He urges us to have confidence in the future and to equip ourselves as best we may; the more strongly we arm, the more certain will be the Sultan's defeat if he really dares to embark upon a siege."

"This winter will be decisive," I agreed. "The sooner the Sultan gets his bombards cast and his army mobilized, the sooner Constantinople will fall."

"Our walls have withstood many sieges," Phrantzes said with a smile. "Only the Latins succeeded in reducing the city, and only once, and they came from the sea. Since then we have had no love for crusades; we would rather live at peace with the Turks."

"I'm taking up your time," I said. "I'll detain you no longer."

"Why, no!" he said. "I had something to say to you. I'm told you visit Pera too often, and you've also been to see the monk Gennadios, though by the Emperor's command he must remain within the monastery walls. What are you after?"

"I am lonely," I said. "No one seems to trust me. I only wished to renew an old acquaintance. But Georgios Scholarios is evidently dead. I had no pleasure from my interview with Gennadios the monk."

Phrantzes threw out his hands in a gesture of indifference.

"Why should I argue with you? We shall never understand each other."

"In God's name, great Chancellor!" I exclaimed. "I ran away from the Sultan. I left a position that many envied me, expressly to fight for Constantinople. Not for you, nor for your Emperor, but for this city which was once the heart of the world. The heart alone remains of a mighty Empire, and beats its last, slow beats. That heart is mine too. With that heart I shall die. If I am caught, the Sultan will spit me on a stake."

"Childishness!" said Phrantzes roughly. "If you were twenty years old I might believe you. You, a Frank and a Latin—what have you in common with us?"

"The will to fight," I answered, "vainly, in the face of downfall and the deluge. I don't believe in victory—I fight without hope. But what does that matter, so long as I am willing to fight?"

For a moment I felt that I had convinced him, that he was ready to dismiss me from his political calculations and regard me as a harmless eccentric. Then he shook his head, and his pale blue eyes were filled with melancholy.

"If you had been like the rest—if you had come from Europe with a cross on your shoulder, begging money like all the Franks—if you had demanded trade concessions in return—

then I might have believed you; I might even have trusted you. But you're too learned a man—too experienced and cool—for your attitude to indicate anything but hidden motives."

I remained standing before him. My feet itched to be gone; but still he twisted the signet ring and looked at me askance without daring to meet my eye, as if he felt the deepest repugnance for me.

"When you reached Basel where had you come from?" he demanded. "How did you win the confidence of Doctor Nicholas Cusanus? Why did you sail with him to Constantinople? You could speak Turkish even then. Why did you stay behind so stubbornly with the synod in Ferrara and Florence? And where did you go from there? Why did Cardinal Julius Cesarini choose you as his secretary? Was it you who took his life at Varna, so that you might more readily go back to the Turks? And don't stand there staring at me!" he roared at last, waving his hands before his face. "The Turks say you have some spiritual power that makes brute beasts obey you and enables you to win the confidence of anyone you choose. But you won't get the better of me! I have my signet and my talisman—but that's all nonsense. I rely most on my own good sense."

I was silent. There was nothing to say. He rose and smote me on the chest with the back of his hand as if annoyed, but it was only to disconcert me.

"Man, man!" he said. "Do you think we don't know? You were the only one who could keep up with Sultan Mohammed for a day and night, when he rode from Magnesia to Gallipoli after his father's death. 'Who loves me, follows me'—remember that. You followed him, and they say he couldn't believe his eyes when you caught him up at Gallipoli."

"I had a good horse," I said. "And I was taught by the

dervishes. I have hardened my body to endure all privations. If you like, I will take a glowing coal from the dish without its burning me."

I took a step toward him and at last managed to catch his eye; I put him to the test and he failed. Irritably he waved me aside, not daring to bid me try. If I had succeeded he would not have known what to think of me, so superstitious was he—superstitious because he no longer believed in anything.

"Yes, indeed I loved Mohammed," I said, "as one may love a splendid wild beast, while aware of its treachery. His youth was like a seething cauldron in need of a heavy lid to keep the contents from boiling over. At times, by Murad's command, I was this lid. But Murad hated him because his favorite son Aladdin had been drowned. As father and son they never agreed, yet secretly Murad was proud of him. Murad wished him to learn moderation, justice, self-control. Murad wished him to humble himself before the One, and perceive the vanity of power and the life of this world. And Mohammed has learned moderation only in order to be immoderate, justice in order to abuse it, self-control in order to indulge his desires—and to guide all with his will. He performs his devotions, but in his heart he believes in nothing. To him all religions are equally worthless. He reads Greek and Latin, Arabic and Persian. He is familiar with mathematics, the map of the world, history and philosophy. Constantinople is his touchstone, and ever since boyhood it has been his dream to capture it. By subduing this city he can prove to himself that he is greater than his ancestors. Do you understand the meaning of these signs? He is the One who shall come. In his era I have no desire to live."

Phrantzes blinked and roused himself as if from sleep.

"Mohammed is a passionate, impatient young man," he said. "We on our side have statesmanship that has been tested and tried through many centuries. Older and wiser men, both here at the Blachernae and in his own seraglio, expect him to break his own neck, and they're rejoicing in advance. Time is on our side."

"Time is up. The sands have run out," I said. "Peace be with you."

He went with me to the door of the Palace, walking beside me down the chill stone corridor, each step echoing dismally against the walls. The doorpost was embellished by the double eagle with its hissing heads.

"Don't leave your house too often," Phrantzes warned me, "and don't row over to Pera. Don't seek the company of conspicuous men, or it may be you will have to exchange your cozy timber house for the marble tower. This is friendly counsel, John Angelos, offered in your own interests."

Suddenly he seized me by the front of my clothes and hurled his last question: "And the Megadux, Lukas Notaras! He has offered you his friendship!"

It was an attempt to catch me off my guard. When I made no answer he said, "Beware lest it come to our ears that you have sought to link yourself with him. If this can be proved you are lost!"

The doorkeeper led up my hired hack and I rode off along the main street at full gallop without heeding the crowds or the travelers coming the other way. Those who didn't step aside in time would have only themselves to blame. But people, hearing even at a distance the thunder of my horse's hoofs on the worn and hollowed paving, yelled, shouted, swore, and whipped their donkeys to one side. From the Palace to the Hippodrome I tore with a loose rein until the foam flew about the bridle of my steed. I was aghast and in a fever of agitation.

"Better the Turkish turban than the Papal miter!" rang in

my ears. The Grand Duke, Commander of the Fleet, the most powerful man in Constantinople after the Emperor—Lukas Notaras. He too!

16 January 1453

I stay indoors now, but rumor runs riot; no one can stop it. It pierces all walls.

The Sultan is building ships in all the ports of Asia.

The Serbs have been compelled by their treaty of alliance to send cavalry to the Sultan's army. Christians are coming to besiege Christians.

I am alone. I am suspect, and therefore useless.

Time passes. Pitilessly day follows irrevocable day. She does not want to come back, then, or she would have done so.

Even the very poorest. . . . On sunny days they lie on the withered slopes of the Acropolis, on the cold ground beneath the trees, to embrace. Men and women in rags, heedless of observers. If only you were poor, my beloved, ragged and ugly! No one would hinder us then. But I should know you by your eyes—your brown eyes would have told me who you were—even if you were old—even if you were dirty and your hands as hard as wood from toil.

If you really wanted to, you would have come.

21 January 1453

For three days I've been among the workmen who are strengthening the wall by the Gate of St. Romanos. I have rolled stones and carried mortar; I am covered with dust and cuts. My hair is stiff with lime.

Shut in my room again I relax. I must keep my body strong and my arms hard, to be fit to draw a bow and wield a sword when the time comes. Did I not help to build the Sultan's fortress on the Bosporus for a whole summer?

I won't accept the daily wage, but I share the laborers' bread, oil and dried meat. They think I'm mad.

23 January 1453

Today Emperor Constantine rode around the walls with his suite. He talked kindly to his master builders and foremen. My face was dirty and I kept my head bent; but when he had spoken to the others he turned and faced me, saying, "Go home. This work does not become your rank."

It was no accident. I saw by his expression that he gave me this order reluctantly. In him is no deceit, and therefore deceit is not the first thing he looks for in others; but Phrantzes and the rest keep him on leading-strings.

To console me he said, "There are worthier tasks for you." But it was not true. He never meant it. He meant only to make my humiliation easier to endure.

Fifteen years ago he was as obstinate and haughty as the rest of the Palaeologos brothers, but time has rubbed off the corners. He is forty-nine now, and his beard is gray. He is also childless. He lost two wives while still young, and ever since the death of Emperor John he has cherished plans of a third marriage. It is said that he asked the hand of Murad's widow, Mara, whom Mohammed allowed to return to Serbia. But she preferred the convent. Murad had allowed her to retain her Christian faith, and she had even taught young Mohammed the Greek prayers.

Years have worn down Constantine. He is a very lonely man, and everything in his life happens too late. The Doge of Venice was willing to give him his daughter, whereby he would have gained strong support from the west—but he dared not wed a Latin woman. The Emperor of Trebizond was far too poor and already the Sultan's ally. At last they found a barbarian princess on the further shores of the Black Sea. The Prince of Georgia confesses the true faith, and he promised a sufficient dowry; he was even willing to send his renowned warriors to the support of Constantinople. But it was too late. Phrantzes returned from his mission of courtship only just before the Sultan's fortress was completed. Now the Bosporus is closed. No princess can come here across the Black Sea, no dowry, no fierce warriors from Georgia.

Constantine was born under an unlucky star. He is hated by his own people because of the Union. But there is no deceit in him, nor is he cruel. After war broke out he had all Turks in the city imprisoned, but on the third day he let them go their way.

They could imprison me; they could torture me by all the traditional methods, to force me to utter the confession they require. But Constantine will not have it, and Phrantzes dare not. I might indeed be a secret agent of the Sultan, and one does not drag such a man to the torture chamber when the enemy is at the gate.

But he is torpid, sluggish. . . . Constantine is slow to act, tender of his dignity as Basileus. How could the divine Emperor dismount from his horse to lever stones or handle a trowel side by side with common workmen, to encourage them as the young Sultan did on the Bosporus? Yet what a spur it would be! Now the work is nothing but soulless day labor, slow and apathetic.

So I am not even allowed to lay stones and carry mortar to strengthen these eternal walls. I do not hate Constantine, but I find it hard to forgive him this.

I returned to my house, bathed and let Manuel wash my hair, and then I put on my own clothes. When I told him I had met the Emperor Constantine and stood face to face with the divine Basileus, my servant Manuel began laughing his sly, piping laugh. I drank wine and gave him some, and he told me about the room whose walls are faced with the first slabs of porphyry ever fetched from Rome. Only a few have seen it. In this purple chamber the Emperors of Byzantium are born, and from a little balcony high up on its façade wall their birth is proclaimed to the people.

"To your imperial name, Manuel!" I said, pouring wine into his earthenware mug.

"To yours, Master John," he answered, and drank so eagerly that he spilt it on himself.

24 January 1453

If she had gone away I should be sure to know about it. Even if the vessel had sailed secretly, rumor would have babbled of it afterwards; from the low hills in the city anyone can see what is going on in the harbor, and here nothing ever remains a secret.

The coast of Asia lies blue beyond the water. Longing stabs at my heart.

Were I nameless, without honor, without a past, I would sink myself in the mob-ocean. I would live from day to day, content, biding my time. But I have tasted the bitter bread of knowledge; my will lies inert within me, like a stone.

26 January 1453

Something unexpected has happened. Two big warships slipped into port under full spread of canvas today, and while the hands were furling the sails our people surged up onto the slopes and the harbor wall to shout and wave. The bigger of the two is a mighty vessel, comparable to a Venetian.

Her military commander is Giovanni Giustiniani, a Genoese, former podesta in Kaffa and a well-tried professional soldier. He has brought with him seven hundred seasoned men-at-arms. The townspeople are in an ecstasy of joy, although these troops are Latins. Their equipment is impeccable: many carry two-handed swords, and in their plate armor each one of them is equal to ten lightly armed men in buff coats. They are accustomed to stern discipline and they respect their commander, as could be seen when they disembarked in good order and with clattering accouterments marched through the city to the Palace of Blachernae.

The Emperor inspected this force. If he knew beforehand of their coming he kept his secret well; as a rule there are leakages—to the highest bidder—from even the most private councils.

Perhaps after all the western nations have not forgotten Constantinople. Giustiniani must have come with the good will of the Genoese; how else could he have found means to fit out his ships and pay his men?

But already the Sultan's janissaries number twelve thousand, and at Varna not even the iron-clad cavalry could halt them.

27 January 1453

She came. She came again after all. She had not forgotten me.

She was thinner and very pale, and there was anxiety in her brown eyes. She had suffered. Words and questions died on my lips; what had I to ask her? She had come.

"My beloved," I said only. "My beloved."

"Why did you come here?" she cried. "Why didn't you stay with your Sultan? Why do you torment me—why do you not release me from your will? It's shameful. I used to be happy and self-assured, and now I have no will left. My feet carry me whither I would not. And you—a Latin, a married man and an adventurer! You make me loathe myself."

I could say nothing.

"How little even the best and noblest upbringing can avail one," she complained. "Of how little use is learning, judgment, birth, pride and fortune! I am as much at your mercy as a slave, and I blush for every step that brought me here. . . . And you've not even touched me! Yet there are dark eddies in my blood—the darkness in my body cries aloud. Once I was clear-sighted—once I was pure. Now I don't know what I am or what I want.

"A dagger in your breast, poison in your cup!" she cried. "Better you were dead. That's what I came to tell you."

I took her in my arms and kissed her mouth. Now she no longer felt the pains in her head; in these days of separation she had grown into a woman. She trembled in my arms.

How I hated that trembling! How I hated the flush of desire that sullied her cheek. I had known it all so often before. But there is no love without the body—no, no love without lust.

"I am not going to lie with you," I said. "There's a time for everything. That was not why I missed you."

"If you tried to disgrace me so, I should kill you!" she exclaimed. "That much I owe myself and my family. And don't speak in that tone to me."

"Save your flower for the Turk," I said. "I had no intention of plucking it."

"I hate you!" she panted, squeezing my arm. "John Angelos, John Angelos, John Angelos!" she repeated, pressing her face hard against my shoulder and breaking into violent sobs.

I took her face between my hands, laughed and kissed her eyes and cheeks, comforting her as if she had been a little girl. I made her sit down, and offered her wine. In a little while she too was smiling.

"I didn't paint my cheeks before I came," she said. "I had that much sense. I know you—you always make me cry, so it would have been a waste of time. Of course I like to seem beautiful to you, but what do you care for that? It's only my eyes you desire. Take them, then," she said, leaning toward me. "You may have them, if only you will leave me in peace."

This was at sunset; outside the light was rosy, and there was dusk in my room.

"How did you manage to come?" I asked.

"The whole city's in an uproar," she answered, laughing. "Everyone is celebrating the coming of the Genoese. Think of it, seven hundred men in plate armor! Our luck has turned. Who could spare a thought for guarding a daughter on a day like this? Even were she to keep company with a Latin she would be forgiven."

"I've never asked you anything about Constantinople before," I said. "Now I should like to. Not that it is of any importance, but for certain reasons I'm curious. Do you know the Megadux, Lukas Notaras?"

She started violently and stared at me in alarm.

"Why do you ask?"

"I only wanted to know what sort of a man he is," I said. And as she still stared I added impatiently, "Would he really choose the Sultan rather than his own Emperor? You heard what he shouted to the people the day we met. Tell me then, if you know him at all: could he really be a traitor?"

"What are you saying?" she whispered. "How dare you say it? You're speaking of the Megadux." She went on vehemently, "I know him well and his family too. He's of an ancient line—proud, ambitious and hot-tempered. His daughter has had an imperial upbringing and it was his intention to marry her to Constantine; but when Constantine became Basileus, a Grand Duke's daughter was no longer good enough. That was an insult difficult to swallow. The Megadux doesn't agree with the Emperor's policy, it's true, but a man who opposes the Union is not necessarily a traitor. No, he's no traitor and never could be; if he were, he would not let his views be so publicly known."

I said, "You know nothing of the passions that sway mankind. Power is a formidable lure. A cunning, ambitious man who disapproves of Constantine's policy might be able to conceive of a Constantinople governed by a megadux in vassalage to the Sultan. There have been agitators and usurpers in the city before now, and even the monk Gennadios openly preaches submission."

She whispered, "You horrify me!"

"But the idea is attractive," I said. "Is it not? A brief tumult, a little bloodshed and the gates may be opened to the Sultan. Better that a few should die than that all be lost, and all your culture and religion perish with the city. Believe me, the right man could justify his action with many valid reasons."

"Who are you?" she asked, drawing away. "Why do you talk like this?"

"Because the right moment has passed," I answered. "Today the Emperor has seven hundred fully armed Latins over and above his own bodyguards, and against them the largest mob would be powerless, even though Gennadios were to bless the revolt and Megadux Notaras were to lead the people against the Palace of Blachernae.

"That is how matters stand," I continued. "The coming of Giovanni Giustiniani has sealed the fate of Constantinople. Its fall is now inevitable and we can heave a sigh of relief. For Sultan Mohammed is not like his father Murad. His word is not to be trusted. Whoever surrenders to him believing in his promises kneels before his executioner."

She said, "I don't understand you. Truly I don't understand you. You speak as if you wanted our city to fall—you speak like the angel of death."

The sunset glow had faded and it was so dark in my room that our faces could be seen only as pale patches in the gloom.

"How do you know I'm not?" I answered. "I have sometimes asked myself that very question. . . . One day, a long time ago, I left the Brotherhood of the Free Spirit," I continued in the darkness. "Their fanaticism was like a cramped stall.

Their intolerance was more intolerant than that of monks and priests. When I had left them I woke early one morning under an old lime tree by the wall of a burial ground. On this wall someone had painted a dance of death, and when I woke, this skeleton-man was the first thing I saw. He was leading a bishop into the dance, an emperor into the dance, a merchant into the dance. He led a beautiful woman into the dance. It was while a nightingale was singing one dewy morning, near the rushing Rhine. In that instant I had a revelation: since that morning, death has been my brother and I have not feared him.

"This city of yours is like an old jewel casket whose precious stones have worked loose and whose corners and edges are dented. But within lies all the loveliness that was. The last of the Greek philosophers, the rapture of faith, the original Church of Christ. Ancient writings, golden mosaics. I don't want it to fall. I love it, painfully, hopelessly, with all my heart—yet the hour of its fall is at hand. Who would willingly surrender his jewel case to a robber? Better that it should be destroyed in blood and soot. This is the last Rome. In you and me a thousand years draw breath. Better, then, the crown of death—Christ's crown of thorns—than the Turkish turban. Do you understand?"

"Who are you?" she whispered. "Why do you talk to me in the dark?"

I had said what I had to say. I kindled a flame and lit the candles. The yellow topazes in her necklace gleamed against her white neck; the yellow topazes of the marksman. They protect their wearer against baseness.

"Who am I?" I said. "A married man, a Latin, an adventurer, as you said yourself. Why do you ask?"

She straightened her collar clumsily.

"Your eyes burn my neck," she complained.

"My loneliness burns you," I said. "My heart burns to ashes when I see your face by candlelight. Your complexion is like silver and your eyes are dark flowers."

"That's in a poem," I said. "I know many words, many beautiful words. I can borrow them from the ancients and from the moderns. Who am I . . .? I am the west and the east, I am the irrevocable past, I am faith without hope. I am the blood of Greece in the veins of the west. Shall I continue?"

"I must go now," she said, and rising she wrapped her mantle about her without waiting for my help.

"I'll fetch a lantern and attend you," I said. "The streets are riotous, and I don't want you to fall among drunken Genoese. There will soon be brawling out there—it is the way of mercenaries. You can't walk alone tonight—the Latins are here!"

She hesitated.

"As you like," she said at last, curtly. Her voice was dead, her face stony. "Nothing matters any more."

I buckled the Turkish saber to my belt. Its edge could cleave a floating feather, or hack a splinter from any western sword. Such weapons are forged for the janissaries.

"This evening," I began, but the words choked me. "This evening," I said again, but could get no further. From the secret springs of my heart there welled a sudden, scalding rage at my disappointment. For many years I had studied under the dervishes; I had avoided meat, I had not wished to harm a single living creature endowed with a spirit. But this evening I desired to strike and slay—to slay a human being, an equal. My Greek blood hated the Latins, and it seemed that something within me had been cleft in two, more violently then ever before. A lust for murder glowed in me, and this I had never felt. It came with love. Love's earthquake had cast up all these secrets from my depths. No, I did not know my own nature any longer.

She gripped my arm, alive once more.

"Don't take your sword," she said. "You would only regret it." A queer, triumphant joy quivered in her voice; she knew me better than I knew myself. It was incredible. The strength went out of me when she touched my arm, and savagely I unbuckled the sword and threw it clashing across the floor.

"As you like," I said, "as you like—just as you like."

We went up the hill. By the harbor the Genoese were reeling and roaring arm in arm in long rows across the street. They snatched at women and greeted passers-by with obscenities in many different languages. But they showed no malice; no one had provoked them and they had left their weapons in barracks. For the two of us they made way without a word. From her carriage and the set of her head they recognized her as a woman of birth, though her face was veiled. As for me, long before Varna the tipsiest of soldiers began to step aside at my approach.

The Greeks had retired into their houses, and when we came up onto the rise everything was quiet. Only the night watchmen patrolled in pairs, lantern in hand, and cautiously announced their approach from afar. In the roadstead the masts of vessels were hung with lanterns, and blaring music echoed over the water. From the wharves came the sound of drums and pipes. Pera's slopes on the other side of the bay twinkled as if alive with glowworms.

But on the silent hill the dome of St. Sophia's rose mute and majestic to the sky. Once more the dark mass of the old imperial palace lay before us. A crescent moon hung above the Hippodrome, whose priceless sculptures Latin crusaders had long ago stolen and minted into coin. Yet in the middle there remained the hissing heads of the Delphic serpents, cast in bronze from the stems of the Persian ships after the battle of Salamis.

I halted.

"If you like you can go on alone from here quite safely," I said. "Keep the lantern; I can find my home way without it."

"I've already said that after this evening nothing matters any more," she answered. "It's not much farther."

A narrow winding lane led us down toward the shores of the Marmora, near the wall. We walked past the mighty arches that support the Hippodrome on the side facing the sea, and approached the disused, ruined harbor called Bucoleon. Near this was a high mound which Greek guides enjoy pointing out to Latins: the heaped bones of crusaders ambushed while returning home through Constantinople. The Greeks lured them unarmed into the passage between the walls and slew them there to the last man, in revenge for extortion, arrogance, robbery and rape. Or so the Greeks say.

Near this grave-mound, by the wall facing the sea, we came upon her home: a beautiful and stately house built of stone. Torches flaring in holders above the iron-studded doors illuminated the narrow bow windows of the upper floor. The ground floor was as windowless as a fortress. She stopped and pointed to the coat of arms carved above the door.

"In case you did not know it before," she said, "I am Anna Notaras—I am Anna Notaras," she repeated, "the only daughter of the Megadux. Now you know."

Her voice was as sharp as glass. Grasping the knocker she struck three thudding blows. Just so do the three shovelfuls of earth thud at last on even the most splendid coffin.

No side door for her, no furtive entry. The door opened. The porter's blue and white coat was heavy with silver embroideries. She turned once more with her head held high, and said as if to a stranger, "I thank you, Master John, for bringing me to my father's house. Go with God."

The door closed behind her. Now I knew.

Her mother is a Serbian princess, the niece of the old despot. Thus she is cousin to the late Sultan's widow. She has two younger brothers. Her father is the Megadux, the Grand Duke, and she was brought up to be the bride of the Emperor; but Constantine broke off the betrothal. Why, why did I have to meet her, of all people?

Anna Notaras. God's dread game of blindman's buff has brought me here; this is what I have been living for. All the tombs of my heart are opened.

My father went to meet the angels, but his son returned, a grown man of forty. Unblinded.

Why should I be so astounded? I had known it from the first moment I saw her; it was just that I refused to accept it. Now the game is over; let grim earnest begin.

1 February 1453

Today after many sleepless nights I went to the forum of Constantine the Great. The marble pavingstones have been ground to powder by cartwheels. The buildings are eroded, and weathered timber houses cling like swallows' nests on the ground by the yellowed marble walls.

I climbed the worn, hollowed spiral stair to the top of the pillar. I was so much exhausted by sleeplessness and fasting that breath failed me; I was dizzy and had to stop several times to lean against the wall. The half-ruined stair is dangerous. Standing at the very top I beheld all Constantinople at my feet.

Formerly this column carried a gigantic equestrian statue of the Emperor. It gleamed in the sun like a golden seamark far over the Marmora—it sparkled gold across to the coast of Asia and pointed eastward with its sword. . . .

Two hundred and fifty years ago, Latin crusaders threw down this statue, after capturing Constantinople. Their rule lasted but a generation—a brief day in the thousand-year history of my city. After that, the pillar was long used as a place of execution. From its towering height traitors were hurled to the pavingstones below. At last a holy monk took the pillar for his dwellingplace, and never left it again until his summer-parched and winter-withered body was lowered thence with ropes. He preached the wrath of God and told his visions to the crowd that used to gather in the square below and gape at him. His hoarse shouts, imprecations and benedictions drowned in the wind, but for a generation he was one of the sights of the city.

Now there was nothing at the top of the pillar—nothing at all. Its stones had begun to loosen. The world's day had reached its fiery evening. Under the pressure of my foot a stone fell over the edge; long afterwards I heard a faint thud as it hit the ground. The square was deserted.

My city too had reached its evening. Gone was the glow of porphyry, the glitter of gold. Gone was the sanctity; the songs of angelic choirs had died away. All that was left was the lust of the flesh and the death of the heart. Coldness, indifference, the greed of commerce, political intrigue. My city was a body breathing its last. The spirit was withdrawing into the stuffy air of monasteries and hiding itself in libraries, in yellowing codices whose pages are turned by hoary old men.

The black pall of night lay over my city; night's shades stretched toward the west.

"Blaze up, my city!" I cried from the abyss of my heart. "Blaze up and burn once more! For the last time. Blaze at the gates of night—kindle thy holy flame! A thousand years have petrified thy soul, but press forth a spirit from the stone, for the last time. Crush from the stone the last drops of thy holy oil. Assume the crown of thorns, put on thy purple for the last time, and so be worthy of thyself!"

Far beneath my feet the ships from the west lay motionless in the long bay. Over the Marmora restless waves pursued one another, and screeching flocks of birds wheeled above the spread nets of the fishermen. At my feet rose the green domes of the churches, and a gray mass of houses stretched from slope to slope between them. And the walls, the invincible, bastioned walls, curved from shore to shore and held my city in their protecting embrace.

No, I did not hurl myself down to the stones of the forum. I resigned myself to my humanity. I resigned myself to my slave-fetters, the fetters of time and space. How should a slave possess anything? I would not if I could. My learning is limited, my words are insufficient, uncertainty is my only certainty. Therefore I had no doubts.

"Farewell, Anna Notaras," I said in my heart. "Farewell, my beloved. You do not know who I am and you shall never know. May your father reign as Pasha of Constantinople and the Sultan's vassal, if that be his choice. It's all one to me. Constantine spurned you, but perhaps Sultan Mohammed will atone for this slight and himself lead you to the nuptial couch, to bind your father to him. He has many consorts, and among them there will be a place for you, Grecian lady."

With peace in my soul again after many waking nights, after the great temptation, my heart dissolved in God's emptiness, and with it all acrimony. My limbs lost their feeling, my heart slackened its beat and I sank down in the posture I had learned, bowed my head and shut my eyes.

"Farewell, my beloved, if we should never meet again," I said in my heart. "There has been no one like you. You are sister to my blood, you are the one star of my bliss. I bless you for having met you. I bless your mortal eyes, your mortal body. Everything of you I bless."

With closed eyes I contemplated the star in my innermost being. The boundaries of time and space melted away, my pulse weakened, my limbs grew chill.

But God is not Cold.

The star within me blazed out in blinding infinity. Burning ecstasy washed over me in vibrant waves.

But God is not Heat.

I melted into the dazzling light—I was clarity of clarity, light of light.

But God is not Light.

And darkness came. Darker than earthly darkness, quieter than all quiet. More merciful than compassion.

But God is not Darkness.

Then there was no longer cold or heat, light or darkness. There was only not-being. God was in me. I in God.

God was.

I held a little stone in my hand; when my fingers relaxed it fell between my knees. The clatter of stone on stone roused me. Only for the instant it took the stone to fall did the timelessness in my rapture last. When man experiences God, a moment to him is the same as a swoon of a day and a night's duration. In God's reality there is no time.

Perhaps I was changed. Perhaps virtue went out of me. Perhaps in that instant I had healed the sick or recalled a dying man to life. But I did not need to do that to prove to myself who I am. To convince oneself is to doubt. Doubt and uncertainty are of men. I did not doubt; I was fellow to the angels. But I turned back from my freedom to the fetters of time and space. And now my slavery was no longer a burden but a gift.

2 February 1453

Having slept until the evening I went to visit Giovanni Giustiniani, the captain-general of the Genoese force. He was not aboard his ship nor in the Palace of Blachernae; I found him at last in the arsenal, near the foundry furnaces. He stood resting on his two-handed sword: a broad-shouldered, florid, paunchy man a head taller than all the others, including myself. His voice was like the rumbling of a barrel as he shouted orders to the Emperor's technicians and foundry workers. Emperor Constantine has already appointed him protostrator, commander-in-chief of the city's defenses. He was in the best of humors, for the Emperor has promised him ducal rank and the island of Lemnos for himself and his heirs in perpetuity if he succeeds in repulsing the Turks. He has confidence in himself and in his profession, as could be seen by his orders and his questions when he was finding out the size and numbers of guns and ballistae the arsenal could produce, if work continued day and night until the Turks came.

"Protostrator," I said, "take me into your service. I have run away from the Turks, and I can wield a sword and bend a bow."

He had hard, pitiless eyes, though there was a smile on his puffy face as he surveyed me.

"You're no ordinary soldier," he said.

"No, I am no ordinary soldier."

"You have a Tuscan accent," he remarked suspiciously, for I had spoken Italian to win his confidence.

"I lived in Florence for some years," I said, "but I was born in Avignon. I speak French and Italian, Latin and Greek,

Turkish and a little Arabic and German. I can draw up lists of supplies. I know a good deal about gunpowder and guns. I can lay a ballista for varying ranges. My name is Jean Ange. I can treat sick dogs and horses, too."

"Jean Ange," he repeated, staring at me with his prominent, bovine eyes. "If all you say is true, you're a miracle. But why have you not had your name entered on the Emperor's rolls? Why seek service with me?"

"You are the protostrator," I replied.

"You're hiding something," he said. "I can see you've tried to enter the Emperor's service, and failed. So you come to me. But why should I trust you, any more than the Basileus?"

"It is not for the sake of the money," I said, to tempt him. "I'm not poor—I don't ask so much as a copper coin from you. It's for Christ's sake, for the sake of Constantinople. I wear a cross on my arm, though you can't see it."

He burst out laughing and slapped his thigh.

"Be damned to that for a tale! A clever fellow of your age isn't after a martyr's crown. Of course, Cardinal Isidor has sworn to me and my men by all he holds sacred that every man who falls on the ramparts in defense of the city will be dragged by St. Peter straight up to heaven by the hair. But it will be heaven enough for me if I get Lemnos, and a ducal coronet instead of the crown of thorns. What is it you're after? Tell me frankly, or go your way and trouble me no more. These are changed times."

"Giovanni Giustiniani," I adjured him, "my father was a Greek. Blood of this city flows in my veins. Should I fall again into the hands of the Turks, Sultan Mohammed will have me spitted on a stake. Why should I not rather sell my life as cheaply as possible?"

But he wouldn't believe me. At last I had to lower my voice, look furtively around and say, "When I escaped from the Sultan, I stole a bag of jewels. I've never dared to tell anyone this. Now perhaps you understand why I'm so loath to fall into his power."

He was a Genoese; he swallowed the bait. A greenish gleam came into his eyes. He in his turn looked about him and then in friendly fashion took me by the arm. Blowing fumes of wine into my face he bent forward and whispered, "If you were to show me those jewels, I might believe you and trust you."

"My house is on the way to the harbor," I said, "and you're still living aboard your ship."

Clumsily he mounted his great charger. Two torchbearers walked ahead to light the way for us, and his bodyguard clattered in the rear. I walked respectfully beside him with a hand on his stirrup.

My servant Manuel opened the door in a fright when the men-at-arms thundered upon it. Giustiniani stumbled over the stone lion and swore. The lantern shook in Manuel's hand.

"Bring cold meat and cucumbers," I said. "Bring wine and my largest cups."

Giustiniani gave a roar of laughter and ordered his men to wait in the street. The stair creaked under his great weight. I lit all the candles before taking the little red leather bag from its hidingplace, and when I turned it inside out, rubies, emeralds and diamonds flashed red, green and white lightnings in the candlelight.

"Holy Mother of God!" whispered Giustiniani, glancing at me, and hesitantly he stretched forward his massive hand, though without touching the stones.

"Take which you like," I said. "It won't bind you to anything. This is just a token of my friendship, not an attempt to buy your favor or your trust."

At first he would not believe me; then he chose a pigeon's

blood ruby—not the largest, but the most beautiful. He had handled precious stones before.

"This is princely of you," he said, admiring the ruby between his fingertips. His voice had changed; he knew not what to make of me.

I said nothing. Once more he surveyed me searchingly with his bright eyes, then lowered them and stroked his worn leather breeches.

"To size men up is part of my profession," he said. "To blow away the chaff and keep the heavy grain. Something tells me that you're no thief, and I feel impelled to trust you. Not only because of the ruby. Such feelings are dangerous."

"Let us drink wine together," I suggested.

Manuel brought in the meat, the wooden tub of cucumbers, the wine and my largest beakers. Giustiniani drank, held out his cup and said, "To your success, prince!"

"Are you trying to make a fool of me?" I asked.

"No indeed. I know what I'm saying—I always do, even in my cups. A simple fellow like me can put a crown on his head, but that won't make a prince of him. Others wear a princely diadem in their hearts. Your brow, your glance, your whole manner shows me what you are. But be easy: I can hold my tongue. What is it you want of me?"

I asked, "Protostrator, do you believe you can defend Constantinople?"

He replied by another question: "Have you a pack of cards?"

I took out a pack printed from woodblocks, such as sailors sell in the harbor. He shuffled them absently and began to lay them out face upwards.

Then he said, "I could never have lived so long or reached the position I hold if I had not been able to play cards. Fate deals us our cards. An experienced man takes his up, examines them carefully and makes up his mind about them before deciding to play. He need not play every round; he can always wait for a better hand. A true player won't let himself be tempted, however big the pool, if he holds bad cards. One can't see an adversary's hand, of course, but one can reckon and guess the probabilities. Besides good cards, skill is necessary, and above all, luck. So far I have had luck, Master Jean Ange.

"Yes, I've had luck at cards," he continued, and emptied his goblet with a few deep draughts. "So far, as I say. Not even a ducal coronet could tempt me into a bad game, but I've examined the city walls. They have withstood the Turks for many generations—why not again? I have been through the arsenals and inspected the Emperor's soldiers, and only after careful consideration am I staking my reputation and my life. From this you will see that I believe I have a playable hand."

"You have also your ships," I remarked.

"Quite so," he admitted, unabashed. "I have the ships. The last card, if the worse comes to the worst. But have no fear: once Giovanni Giustiniani makes up his mind to fight, he fights, as honor and reason require. He fights so long as there is a single chance. But no longer—no longer. Life is a high stake. No one could ask a higher. Not the heaviest breastplate can stop a missile, and a spear can pierce the groin between thigh- and body-armor. In raising one's sword to strike one must expose the armpit. An arrow can penetrate the visor of a helmet, while against liquid fire and molten lead, armor is useless. I know what I'm letting myself in for; it's my profession to know. And I have my honor, which urges me to fight so long as there is a chance. But no longer, no longer than that."

I poured more wine for him.

"Giustiniani, what will you take to scuttle your ships?" I asked him casually.

He started and crossed himself in the Latin manner. "What are you talking about? I would never do such a thing."

"These stones," I remarked, sweeping them into a little heap on the table; "with these you could fit out ten new ships in Genoa."

"That may be," he said, his eyes fascinated by the blood-red luster of the rubies, the blue-white fire of the diamonds between my fingers. "That may be. If I had them in Genoa. No, Jean Ange, we're not in Genoa. If I scuttled my ships those stones might have no value at all for me, and though you offered me ten times—a hundred times—what my vessels are worth I would not sink them."

"So that's the faith you have in your cards!"

He said, "I believe in them and I shall play them. But I have common sense." He stroked his puffy face, smiled and remarked, "Well, well—we must be getting a little fuddled to talk like this."

But it was not true; he could have held a firkin of wine in his bull-like body without any marked effect.

I gathered the stones together in my hands.

"For me these are worthless," I said. "I have scuttled my ships. As worthless as this!" and I flung them from me so that they pattered like hail on walls and floor. "There you are—take them if you like; they're only stones."

"You're drunk," he said. "You don't know what you're doing. Tomorrow morning you'll be clutching your head and bitterly repenting of this."

My throat smarted and I could not speak. I shook my head.

"Take them," I managed to say at last. "They're the price of my blood. Enroll me, let me fight beside your men! I ask no more."

He gaped at me; then a glint of suspicion came into his eyes.

"Are those stones genuine," he asked with a wag of his head, "or are they bits of colored glass, such as Venetians palm off on Negroes?"

I bent down to pick up a big, clumsily cut diamond, walked over to the window and scored a deep line from top to bottom of the green pane, so that the squeak of it set my teeth on edge. Then I threw the diamond away.

"You're a madman," he said, shaking his massive head again. "It would be unfair to take advantage of your muzzy state. Sleep it off, and then we'll talk again."

"Have you ever seen yourself in a vision?" I asked. Perhaps I was a little fuddled, being unused to wine. "I have. Once, in Hungary, before the battle of Varna, I was in an earthquake. Horses shied and broke their traces—birds swirled up in terrified flocks—tents collapsed. The ground shook and rocked and it was then that the angel of death appeared to me for the first time. He was a bloodless, swarthy man—it was my own image. I seemed to see myself coming toward me. He said 'We shall meet again.'

"By the marsh at Varna I saw him for the second time," I went on. "He was standing behind me when the fleeing Hungarians struck down Cardinal Cesarini. When I turned my head, there was the angel of death behind me—my image. 'We shall meet again,' he said, 'we shall meet again at the Gate of St. Romanos.' His words meant nothing to me then, but now I am beginning to understand them.

"I am no thief," I went on. "The Sultan's favor can make a slave wealthier than many a western prince. After the battle I was brought before Sultan Murad, with other prisoners. His victory had hung by a hair, and his flabby cheeks and the pouches under his eyes still quivered from the fear and excitement he had been through. He was a short man—a head shorter than myself—and already heavy and unwieldy from idleness and soft living. Many stretched out their hands to him and cried aloud, offering ransom money for their lives; but in his eyes we were all perjurors and truce breakers. So firm had been his faith in a permanent peace that he had abdicated his throne in favor of Mohammed and retired to the gardens of Magnesia where he meant to spend his old age. Now he bade us choose between Islam and death. The ground was sodden with the blood of those who had knelt in turn before the executioner. Many were afraid when they saw the heads rolling on the ground—they wept, and loudly confessed the God of Islam and his Prophet. Even some of the monks acknowledged that they had lost their faith since God had given the Turks the victory.

"But Murad was weary and prematurely aged," I continued. "His favorite son had been drowned and since then he had not greatly cared to exercise his power. He had taken to drowning his sorrows in wine, in the company of scholars and poets. Bloodshed he did not love. When my turn came he looked at me, liked my face and said, 'You're still young. Why should you taste death? Confess the Prophet!' I answered, 'I am still young, but I am ready to pay the debt owed by all mankind, even as you must pay it one day, great Sultan.' The speech pleased him and he did not insist that I should embrace Islam. 'You're right,' he said. 'The day will come when an unknown hand will level my divine dust with the dust of earth.' He made a sign that my life was to be spared. It was just a whim: my words had brought a line of poetry to flower in his soul. Do you care to hear Sultan Murad's poem after the battle of Varna, Giovanni Giustiniani?"

Giovanni shook his bull's head to show that he did not greatly care for poetry, poured out more wine for himself and began chewing a slice of cold veal. I pushed the cucumber tub toward him and recited the unforgettable poem in Turkish, snapping the beat with my fingers as if I had been plucking the strings of a lute. Then I translated it for him:

"Cup-bearer, pour me again of yesterday's wine;
Music, play on! Forgetfulness bring to my heart.
Brief is our life, though sweet its rest and its mirth,
Soon shall a hand unknown
Level my dust divine with the dust of earth."

"Such was Murad's heart," I said. "He consolidated Turkish power and waged war after war to establish a lasting peace. Twice he relinquished his throne to Mohammed. The first time it was the Christians who compelled him to resume it; the second time Khalil the Grand Vizier called him back after the janissaries had burned the bazaar in Adrianople. Thereafter Murad resigned himself to his continued sovereignty and governed until his death without further wars. Twice a week he caroused with poets and philosophers, and at such times he would confer caftans of honor upon his friends, land, and precious stones. Nor did he ever demand them back next day. Some of these jewels were given me by Sultan Murad. Keep them, Giovanni, if you like. I have no need of them, and I shall not ask for them back tomorrow."

Giustiniani stuck half a cucumber in his mouth, wiped the brine from his hands on his leather breeches, crossed himself devoutly and went clumsily down on all fours at my feet.

"I am a poor man and a simple soldier," he said. "I cannot afford to boast. . . . I willingly humble myself in a good cause."

With that he began to crawl about on the floor picking up the gems, while I held the lantern so that he should not miss any. He puffed and blew as he crawled, but said, "Don't help me, whatever you do. This effort is sweeter to my limbs than wrestling with the fairest woman in the world."

I handed him the leather bag, into which he carefully dropped the collected stones; then rising at last he pulled the pursestrings tight and put it away in his bosom.

"I'm not greedy," he said. "Some of the lesser stones may well have rolled into a crack or under a mat, but your servant will find them when he sweeps the room. My thanks to you." He put his head on one side and contemplated me with a gentler look as he continued, "I have come across holy men at times—seers of spirits and many other madmen—and I should be mad myself not to admit that much happens in this world which is beyond human understanding. My meeting with you is such an event." He put out his broad hand and grasped mine in unfeigned gratitude. "From this day you are my friend, Master Jean Ange," he assured me. "I shall not lend my ear to any gossip I may hear of you. Tomorrow, immediately after reveille, I will have your name entered on my roll, and you must be present. You shall have horse and accouterments—and be sure I shall give you plenty to do, so that you may accustom yourself to my discipline. I drill my men more sternly than the Turks."

He did not thump me on the back or pat my shoulder, as a man of less experience might have done. On the contrary he bowed his head respectfully as he went, and said, "Keep your secret. I am not inquisitive. You would not behave as you do if you intended evil. I trust you."

The Greeks rejected me, a Latin received me. Giovanni Giustiniani understood me better than did the Greeks.

5 February 1453

I have been given armor and a charger. For the first few days Giovanni Giustiniani put me and my capabilities to the test. I accompanied him on an inspection of the walls, and of that part of the defense force which consists of untrained Greek artisans and young monks. He shook his bull's head and laughed at the sight of them.

He has conferred with the Emperor, with Phrantzes, with the Venetian sea captains and those from the Greek islands, with the podesta in Pera and with the Venetian bailo. He talked fully and deliberately to each, recounting many stories of campaigns and sieges in which he has taken part. He can break his way through dissension, envy and prejudice like a broad-beamed ship. People trust him. They must: he is the cornerstone, the foundation upon which the growing defense of the city is based. He drinks a great deal of wine, emptying the largest goblet in two gulps, and the only effect this appears to have upon him is to make him puffier around the eyes.

His slowness and the ceaseless talk behind which he conceals his guile and his knowledge of men irritated me at first, until I began to look at things through his bulbous, bovine eyes. Now I seem to see a machine, devised by a skilled mathematician, being set in motion—squealing and clattering, indeed, and with grinding, grudging cogwheels, yet ever more irresistibly. A machine apt to its purpose, with each part supporting and strengthening the rest.

I am bound to admire him as his own men admire him, and obey each order of his in the certitude that not one is unnecessary.

I too have my usefulness. I have told him about the training of the janissaries, their discipline, arms and methods of fighting. I have told him of Sultan Mohammed's character and of the men closest to him, of the war party and peace party in the seraglio, and of the split between young and old which formed after Sultan Murad's death, and which Sultan Mohammed is deliberately widening and deepening in order to throw down Khalil from his position as Grand Vizier.

"He can never forget how as a young boy he was twice forced to vacate the throne—first at twelve years of age and then at fourteen," I said. "This is the key to his bitterness, his fanaticism and his ambition. The first time, when the crusaders made a surprise advance and approached Varna, he broke down. It was in Adrianople. He wept, shrieked, had convulsions from terror and hid himself in the harem. So the story goes. If old Sultan Murad had not returned from Magnesia and in the course of a few days stamped an army from the soil of Asia, the Turkish Empire would have fallen.

"The second time," I went on, "it was his own people, his veterans, who rebelled. They refused to obey a skinny, nervy boy who was incapable of leading them in battle. They sacked and burned the bazaar in Adrianople, and once more Mohammed was forced to seek refuge in the inviolable harem. Khalil appealed to Murad on his own responsibility; and that is what Mohammed has never been able to forgive him.

"You don't know Mohammed," I said, as I had so often and so vainly said to others. "A boy's wounded pride can swell into a force to crush kingdoms. Remember that it happened twice! Since then Mohammed has served his apprenticeship. His ambition is boundless. To wipe out the insults he has suffered he feels impelled to outshine all his predecessors, and Constantinople is to be the proof. He has been planning its capture for many years, sacrificing the peace of his days and his nights' repose. Even before the death of his father he had learned every detail of the plan of our fortifications, until he could draw any bastion from memory. He found his way about Constantinople blindfold. It's said he was here as a youth and roamed the streets in disguise. He speaks Greek and knows the customs and prayers of the Christians.

"No, you don't know Mohammed," I repeated. "He is not more than twenty-two, but even at the time of his father's death he was a boy no longer. The Prince of Karaman made trouble as usual and by way of a test he occupied one or two Turkish provinces in Asia. He is a kinsman of Mohammed's. Mohammed mustered an army and in two weeks was at the Karaman border with his janissaries. The Prince found it prudent to yield, and rode with a numerous train to meet Mohammed, to whom he laughingly explained that he had merely done it as a joke to put the young Sultan to the test. Mohammed has trained himself to conceal his feelings, and no longer acts impulsively. He can burst out into a foaming fury, but even that is deliberately done to impress an adversary. He is an actor whose like I have never seen."

My words made a certain impression on Giustiniani. He must already have known a good deal of what I told him, but he had never heard it from an eyewitness.

"And the janissaries?" he asked. "I don't mean the rank and file, but the high command."

"The janissaries want war, of course," I told him, "That's their only profession. They are sons of Christians but brought up in Islam, and are therefore more fanatical in the faith than the Turks themselves. They may not marry or leave their cantonments, they may not even learn any trade or craft. Naturally they were enraged when the Prince of Karaman made his submission and thus deprived them of the war they hoped for. Mohammed let them rave and kick their cooking-pots about, while he shut himself up in his tent for three whole days. Some merchants had sold him a Greek slave-girl who had been stolen from one of the islands. She was eighteen and beautiful as the day. Her name was Irene. The Sultan spent three days in her company without showing himself to anyone. The janissaries roared and reviled him outside his tent. They did not want a Sultan who preferred the delights of love to battle and who neglected even his prayers for a slave-girl. The officers no longer exercised any control; perhaps they didn't try."

"I've heard of that incident," said Giustiniani. "It only shows Mohammed's impetuosity and cruelty."

"Cruelty, yes, but not impetuosity," I answered. "It was the deliberate gesture of a great actor. When the janissaries had kicked over their cooking-pots and worked themselves up into a blind rage, he came out of his tent at last, with a rose in his hand. His eyes were heavy with sleep, and his every movement was that of a shamefaced and bewildered youth. The janissaries howled with laughter and threw clods of earth and horse dung, though they were careful not to hit him, and they yelled, 'What manner of Sultan are you, to exchange your sword for a rose?' Mohammed shouted in reply, 'Ah, brothers, brothers, you know not what you say! If you saw her, you wouldn't blame me.' The janissaries waxed even more uproarious and cried, 'Show us your Greek, and perhaps we will believe you.' Mohammed yawned lazily, re-entered the tent and came out dragging the shy, terrified girl who, half-naked and ashamed, tried to hide her face in her hands.

"I shall never forget that scene," I went on. "The shaven heads of the janissaries, each with its one lock of hair—for they had thrown their felt caps on the ground and stamped on them—Mohammed's avid face and yellow-gleaming wild beast's eyes, and the girl more beautiful than the Karaman spring. Mohammed forced aside her hands, tore the last of her garments from her and pushed her toward the janissaries, so that they drew back dazzled by the beauty of her face and the perfection of her limbs. 'Look your fill of her!' cried Mohammed. 'Look, and confess that she is worthy of your Sultan's love!' Then his face darkened with rage, he flung away the rose and commanded, 'Bring me my sword!' The girl knelt upon the ground with bowed head, striving to hide her nakedness with her hands. When Mohammed had grasped his sword, he seized her by the hair and at one stroke severed the head from her shoulders, so that the blood spurted onto the nearest janissaries. They could not believe their eyes, and yelled in dismay. Then they backed blindly among their comrades to get as far as possible from Mohammed. But Mohammed only said, 'My sword can sever even the bonds of love. Trust my sword.' Then he asked, 'Where is your commander?' The janissaries ran to fetch their chief officer, who had hidden himself in his tent. When he came, Mohammed snatched from him the silver ladle, his emblem of office, and in the presence of all struck him so savagely in the face that the bone of his nose was broken, and one eye was put out. But the janissaries were silent and afraid and did nothing to defend their commander.

"The janissaries won't mutiny again," I said. "Mohammed reorganized their corps and increased it by his six thousand irregulars; an act contrary to the ordinances. Janissaries are promoted according to age, and he could not therefore dismiss all their original officers, though he had a number executed that night. But you may be sure he will give them the place of honor at the siege of Constantinople. He will find good use for them. The officers and self-sufficient veterans whom he has marked down will fall before our ramparts.

Mohammed never pardons an affront, but he has learned to bide his time."

I did not know whether to go on, being uncertain whether Giustiniani would understand what I meant. But at length I added, "Mohammed is not human."

Giustiniani wrinkled his forehead and looked at me with bloodshot eyes. His rumbling, good-humored laughter caught his throat.

"Mohammed is not human," I repeated. "Perhaps he is the angel of darkness. Perhaps he is the One who shall come. He bears all the signs. But don't misunderstand me," I added quickly, "if he is a man, then he is the new man—the first of his kind. With him begins a new era, an era which will bring forth men very different from the race we know. Rulers of earth, rulers of night, who in their defiance and arrogance reject heaven and choose the world. They believe nothing but what their eyes and their reason tell them. In their hearts they recognize no laws, whether human or divine; their purpose is their only law. They bring the heat and cold of hell to the earth's surface, and hold the very forces of nature in thrall. They fear neither the boundlessness of the ocean nor the heights of heaven. When they have subjugated land and sea they will build themselves wings in their demented lust for knowledge, that they may fly to the stars and subjugate even them. Mohammed is the first man of this race. How do you imagine you can withstand him?"

Giustiniani clutched his head.

"By the Holy Wounds!" he complained. "Don't we hear enough about the end of the world from the monks of this city, who foam at the mouth with preaching it? Must one of my own officers begin to see visions and spout rubbish? My head will split if you say another word."

But he no longer speaks of Mohammed as a hot-livered

youth about to run his head against a wall. He has grown cautious and has warned his men neither to boast too much in the taverns, nor to underestimate Turkish strength. He has even gone to Latin Mass, confessed and humbly received absolution, although he had already been assured by Cardinal Isidor that his sins were taken from him as soon as he accepted the post of Protostrator of Constantinople. To make doubly sure, he asked that his absolution might be recorded in writing, and this document he always carries on him.

"Now I shall have something to show St. Peter when I come to knock at the Gates of Heaven," he said. "I hear that for some reason the old man has grown stricter with us Genoese. Perhaps the Venetians have been bribing him."

7 February 1453

In Adrianople a shot has been fired which will shake the world.

Orban the Hungarian has kept his promise and has cast the biggest bombard of all time.

When I came home after a strenuous day, my servant Manuel met me; he wrung his hands and his cheeks quivered and twitched as he asked, "Master, is it true that the Turks have a cannon that can flatten the walls of Constantinople with a single shot?"

So quickly do rumors spread in this city! Only this morning Giustiniani received the first detailed reports of the test-shooting.

"It is not true," I said. "No one could make such a cannon. To flatten the walls of Constantinople one would need an earthquake."

"But they say that the ball flew a thousand paces and made a hole as big as a house where it fell," stammered Manuel. "And the earth shook for ten thousand paces round. Many houses in Adrianople collapsed and many women were prematurely delivered."

"Idle gossip, Manuel," I said. "Surely you must see that!"

"But it's true!" he assured me. "Even the cannon that Orban cast for the Sultan's fortress could sink a ship with a single shot. A merchant who has arrived in Pera from Adrianople measured one of the stone balls of the new bombard; he says that not the mightiest man could get his arms around it. He's still deaf from the detonation and shakes like an old man, though he's not yet fifty."

"He shakes from wine, no doubt, not gunfire!" I barked. "He has had too many inquisitive listeners who have filled him up with drink, and the gun has grown a few feet with every cup. Tomorrow it will be as long as a church tower."

Manuel fell on his knees before me. His beard quivered, he groped for my hand to kiss it and said simply, "Master, I am afraid."

He is an old man. His watery eyes reflected the fathomless sorrow of Greek Constantinople, and I understood. The Turks would kill him, for he is too old to be a slave.

"Stand up, fellow—be a man!" I said. "We know the measurements of the gun, and the Emperor's technicians are even now calculating the weight of its missiles and their possible effect on our walls. Certainly it is a terrible weapon which can do a great deal of damage, but it is nothing like as big as rumor has made it. Besides, Orban is an ignorant man, incapable of calculating range and trajectory. The Emperor's craftsmen believe it impossible for him to guess the correct capacity for the chamber in relation to the length of the barrel and the weight of the ball. His bombard may survive a few shots, but sooner or later it's bound to explode and spread worse destruction among the Turks than among ourselves. Orban was once in the Emperor's service; the technicians know him, and know what he can and cannot do. Tell this to your aunts and cousins and your whole family, and tell them to pass it on to others, so that the townspeople may be reassured."

"How should they tell things that mean nothing to them?" sighed Manuel. "What should they know of charges and trajectories? They would rather repeat things they understand—things that sound terrible. A woman here in the city has had a miscarriage merely from hearing about this gun. What will happen when it thunders before our walls and blows them to pieces?"

"Tell them to seek succor from their Panaghia," I said, to be rid of him. But doubt had struck root in Manuel.

"Even the Blessed Virgin will scarcely show herself on the walls now, to frighten the Turks with her blue mantle," he said. "Last time their guns weren't so big. Ones like this bombard would scare the Blessed Virgin herself." His lips trembled as he smiled. "Is there any truth in the story that it's already on its way from Adrianople? That it is drawn by fifty pairs of oxen and that a thousand men are clearing roads and building bridges for it? Is this all exaggeration too?"

"No, Manuel," I admitted, "it's true. The cannon is on its way. Spring is in the air; soon doves will be cooing and flocks of birds will fly northward over the city. When spring is in full blossom the Sultan will be at the gates of Constantinople; no power in the world can prevent it."

"And how long," he asked, "how long shall we last after that?"

Why should I lie to him? He is old. He is a Greek. I am no physician, but a human being—his fellow.

"A month, perhaps," I told him. "Or it may be two . . . Giustiniani is a brilliant soldier. Three months if he matures with his task, as I believe he will. But hardly longer. Hardly longer than that, at best."

Manuel was no longer trembling. He looked me straight in the eye.

"And the countries of the west?" he asked. "The Union?"

"With Constantinople even the western nations will be swallowed up in night. Constantinople is the last lamp, the last hope of Christendom. If they allow it to be quenched they will have deserved their fate."

"And what will be their fate?" he asked. "Forgive me, master, but I am curious to know, so that my heart may prepare itself."

"Flesh without spirit," I said. "Life without hope, the slavery of mankind—a bondage so hopeless that slaves will no longer know they are slaves. Wealth without happiness, abundance without the power to enjoy it. The death of the spirit."

10 February 1453

I have met everyone except the Megadux, Lukas Notaras. It seems as if he purposely dwells as far as possible from the Palace of Blachernae, for his house is at the opposite end of the city in the old quarter, in the shadow of St. Sophia's, the Hippodrome and the old imperial palace. He isolates himself. Both his young sons hold honorary ceremonial appointments at court, but are never seen there. I have watched them playing ball on horseback on the Hippodrome ground. They are fine young men; their features are stamped with the same somber pride as their father's.

As admiral of the fleet the Megadux refuses to co-operate with Giustiniani, and has fitted out the Emperor's five old dromonds at his own expense. Today to everyone's astonishment their oars were laid out and they glided out of the harbor past the great vessels from the west. Once on the Marmora they hoisted new sails, formed into line of battle and stood away for the Asiatic coast. It was a gray, cloudy day, with squalls. The seamen were still unaccustomed to these exercises; the rowers lost their rhythm and the oars continually fouled one another.

Constantinople's last fleet was at sea. Venetian and Greek captains laughed and slapped their knees.

But what can be the object of these maneuvers? It cannot be merely training, for at dusk the dromonds had not yet returned.

Giustiniani rode to the Palace and, defying all ceremony, cuffing bodyguards and eunuchs from his path, marched into the Emperor's private apartments. He made a great show of indignation, though in fact he was merely curious. He has a poor opinion of the Emperor's ships; one heavy western warship could sink them all. But as protostrator he is naturally annoyed that they have not been placed under his command.

Emperor Constantine made this excuse:

"Megadux Notaras is not the man to sit and twiddle his thumbs. The Turks have laid waste the countryside and encircled Selymbria and our other remaining strongholds. Therefore the Megadux is minded to take the offensive and repay them in their own coin, while the sea is still open."

Giustiniani said, "I have cut sally ports in the walls and I have often begged you to attack the scattered bands of Turkish raiders. Their impudence has grown insufferable: they ride within bowshot of the ramparts and shout insults at my men, threatening to geld them all. It is bad for discipline."

The Emperor said, "We cannot afford to lose a single man. The Turkish *asaps* might ambush the troops making the sortie, and annihilate them."

Giustiniani said, "For that reason I have obeyed your command. But Megadux Notaras seems not to heed it."

The Emperor said, "He suddenly announced that he meant to go out on maneuvers; I could hardly order the Venetian and Cretan ships to hinder him. But such highhanded behavior shall not be repeated."

Phrantzes put in conciliatingly, "The Megadux equipped the galleys and paid the crews from his own coffers. We cannot offend him."

But all this was merely talk—they knew it themselves. Giustiniani struck the table with his staff of office and demanded, "How do you know he will return with his ships and men?"

Emperor Constantine bowed his head and said softly, "Perhaps it would be better for us all if he did not."

Afterwards Giustiniani repeated the whole conversation to me, and remarked, "I don't understand these complicated Greek politics. Hitherto the Basileus has strictly avoided offensive action. At each slap in the face from the Sultan he has, with excessive Christian forbearance, turned the other cheek. No doubt by this he seeks to demonstrate to the western world and to posterity that the Sultan is the aggressor and he the man of peace. But why? Everyone of any intelligence knows that already. Now Megadux Notaras has snatched the initiative and begun to make war. He'll come back, believe me, and bring his ships with him—but what he is after I cannot make out. You know the Greeks; perhaps you can explain it."

"I don't know Lukas Notaras," I answered. "Who can guess

what prompts a proud, ambitious man? Perhaps he wants to cleanse some stain from his reputation. Since the uproar at St. Sophia's he has been regarded at the Palace of Blachernae as unreliable and pro-Turk. Perhaps that is why he wants to be the first to show hostility, in contrast to the hesitancy of the Emperor."

"But what good is such a raid on the Turkish coast?" complained Giustiniani. "Now, of all times, when the dervishes are preaching war all over Asia and the Sultan is mobilizing his army? Mohammed could ask nothing better. The man is playing right into his hands."

"You cannot prove that," I said. "We can only judge each incident on its own merits and put the best interpretation on it, until this is disproved by facts."

Giustiniani regarded me with his bulbous eyes, scratched his neck and inquired, "Why are you defending Lukas Notaras? You'd be wiser to hold your tongue," he continued kindly. "Phrantzes drew me aside again as I was going, and urged me to keep an eye on you. You were a dangerous man, he said. You had had free access to the Sultan by day and night. It would do no harm to be careful, he told me."

With that he handed me a copper pencase and appointed me his aide de camp. So from now on I shall be handling his secret papers.

11 February 1453

Last night my servant Manuel woke me in a fright and whispered, "Master, there's trouble in the city!"

Lanterns and torches were moving about the streets, and

people stood at their doors half-dressed. All were looking up at the fiery glow in the sky.

I threw on my fur cloak and walked uphill with the crowds to the Acropolis. Beyond the narrow sea the cloudy night sky was reddened by distant fires. The wind was damp and the moist earth gave forth a strong scent. The darkness was that of spring.

Black-clad women sank down in prayer and men made the sign of the cross before their eyes. Then a whispered name ran from one to another. "Lukas Notaras!" the people muttered. "Lukas Notaras!"

Turkish villages were in flames beyond the sea, but the people did not rejoice. They seemed indeed paralyzed by some dark dread, as if only now fully aware that war had begun. The raw night wind was hard to breathe.

All they that take the sword shall perish with the sword. And the innocent will perish with the guilty.

12 February 1453

Enemy patrols have captured St. Stephen's Tower and executed the garrison for daring to defend itself.

A frightful hailstorm today forced everyone to seek shelter. Many roofs were damaged. At night strange thunderings were heard from the subterranean water cisterns; the very ground shook. Many have seen streaks of lightning cleave the sky without a sound to follow them, and glowing disks flash through space.

Not the great bombard only, but the Sultan's whole artillery is now on the march from Adrianople to Constantinople. Ten thousand cavalry form the escort.

In Adrianople the Sultan has made a great speech before the assembled divan. He has stirred up the young and taken oaths from the elderly and cautious. Both the Venetian bailo and the podesta in Pera have received accurate information as to the tenor of this speech, in which Mohammed proclaimed:

"The power of the Basileus is broken! Only one last effort is needed to wipe out the thousand-year-old empire of Constantine the Great's successor. Constantinople, queen of cities, may now be taken by storm; and success is certain, thanks to our new weapons and the spirit of our army. But we must hasten to strike before Christendom arises and sends its ships to Constantine's relief. Now is the hour! Let it not slip through our fingers."

It is said that before making this speech, the Sultan summoned Grand Vizier Khalil, leader of the peace party, in the middle of the night, to settle accounts with him. At this time at least Khalil dared not open his mouth in the cause of peace.

Since I have had access to the documents in Giustiniani's iron chest I have been able to satisfy myself that Khalil is still in secret communication with Emperor Constantine. Were it not so we should not know all we do about Turkish armaments and the financing of the campaign.

As soon as the fleet had sailed, the Emperor hastened to send a final appeal to Adrianople. He wrote it himself, without consulting Phrantzes. There is a copy of this letter in Giustiniani's box, and I have read it many times. It has moved me deeply and depressed me beyond all words. More than any of his other acts it shows Constantine to be a true Emperor. This is what he wrote to Sultan Mohammed:

It is clear that you desire war rather than peace. Be it then as you wish; I have been unable to convince you of my peace-

ful intentions, although I have shown myself guiltless of treachery and ready to be your vassal in name. I turn now to the Lord and have no refuge but in Him. If it be His will that my city should fall into your hands, how should I oppose it? If He should incline your heart to make peace I would be happy. But I release you herewith from all your pledges, all the agreements we have made with one another. I have shut the gates of my city and will defend my people to the last drop of my blood. May you reign happily until that day when the righteous God, our supreme judge, shall summon us both before Him.

It is a stiff letter, with none of the lofty rhetoric of Greece and nothing of Phrantzes' polished turns of phrase, yet it grips me. It is an Emperor's letter. And vain, so vain. But perhaps Constantine, sitting in his desolate palace, was writing chiefly for posterity, and perhaps in its simplicity it shows more of what he is than the finest accounts of the historians. It is not his fault that he was born under an unlucky star.

13 February 1453

The fleet has returned. Notaras' palace by the sea guards its secrets sullenly. I can no longer endure this uncertainty; more than two weeks have passed since we met and I don't even know whether she is still in the city.

In vain I have ridden through the streets and along the walls. In vain I have sought to drown my dread in feverish work. I cannot be free of her. Her radiant eyes afflict my dreams, her pride and chill defiance sting my heart.

What if she is the daughter of a grand duke and a Serbian

princess? What if her lineage is more ancient than even the Emperor's? I am my father's son.

Forty years—and I thought I had reached the autumn of life. . . .

Why should I not try to meet her? We have only these brief days left; time races past and is lost. Swift as arrows are these days, with their routine, their errands, their lists of stores, their emptiness.

This morning I stepped out of my dim house into brightness. The sun was shining. The sky was stretched like a blue canopy over Constantinople, and a deep rapture filled me as I set forth—not mounted, but on foot like the poorest pilgrim. Far, far in the distance the marble towers of the Golden Gate shimmered in the haze.

I saw again the smooth stone wall, the narrow bow windows of the upper floor, the armorial bearings above the door. I knocked.

"My name is Jean Ange, aide de camp to Protostrator Giovanni Giustiniani."

"The Megadux is at sea, and both his sons are with him. The lady of the house is ill and abed."

"I would like to speak to his daughter, Anna Notaras."

She came, attended by an elderly eunuch, from the locked wing of the house reserved for the women. She has had an imperial upbringing—she is a free Greek. The eunuch was gray, and as wrinkled as an old apple, toothless and hard of hearing. But his raiment was the richer.

She came. Lovelier than ever, and unveiled. She smiled as she came.

"I have been expecting you," she said. "I have been expecting you a long time. But I'm no longer proud that you should have come. Be seated, Jean Ange."

The eunuch shook his head disapprovingly, raised both arms

in protest, hid his face in his hands and sank down in a corner of the room, disclaiming all responsibility.

A servant-girl brought a golden goblet on a silver tray. The cup was of ancient Greek workmanship; round it a satyr pursued fleeing nymphs. A frivolous cup. She set her lips to it and handed it to me.

"To our friendship," she said. "You cannot have come here with evil intent."

I drank of her father's wine.

"To despair," I said. "To oblivion and darkness—to time and space. To our fetters—our sweet fetters, because you exist, Anna Notaras."

Gorgeous carpets of all the colors of the Orient glowed on the porphyry pavement. Outside the narrow bow windows sparkled the Sea of Marmora. Her brown eyes shone, her complexion was gold and ivory. She was still smiling.

"Talk," she said. "Say anything you like. Talk hard, as if you had something very important to tell me. The eunuch cannot hear you, but the faster you talk the more reassured he will feel."

It was hard. I would rather have looked at her.

"The hyacinth scent of your cheeks," I said. "The hyacinth scent of your cheeks."

"Are you beginning all over again?" she said, in a bantering tone.

"Yes, all over again," I said. "Your gown, shimmering with golden threads, is wonderful, but you are far more wonderful. Your clothes guard your beauty all too jealously. Did monks design them? Fashions have changed since my youth. In France, ladies reveal their breasts for men to admire, like King Charles's lovely Agnes Sorel. But here you hide everything, even your faces.

"If only we could journey to the free west one day," I said.

"The first woman who taught me the secrets of physical love I met by the bathing pool at the Fountain of Youth near the Rhine. Earlier that day the nightingale had sung, and my brother Death had danced on the churchyard wall. She was a woman in full flower, older than myself, and she hid nothing of her beauty. She sat naked on the edge of the pool, immersed in a book, while ladies and gentlemen of distinction sported together in the water and ate at floating tables. Her name was Madam Dorothea. She gave me a letter of introduction to Æneus Silvius in Basel, if you know who he is. All this was after I had left the Brotherhood of the Free Spirit. Until then I had loved only under bushes and in the dark. But this fine lady led me to feather pillows and lit candles about the bed, so as to miss nothing."

Anna Notaras reddened and her lips quivered.

"Why do you talk like this to me?" she asked. "It's unlike you. I shouldn't have thought it of you."

"Because I desire you," I said. "The lust of the flesh is not love, perhaps, but there is no love without it. But mind this: I never spoke to you thus when we were alone together and you were in my power. You wouldn't have stabbed me, you know, if I had touched you then. No, no—I can see that in your eyes. But my desire is as clear as a flame. When the time comes you shall offer me your flower; I shall not pluck it by force.

"Anna Notaras," I went on. "Anna Notaras, how dear you are to me! Don't listen, for I don't know what I'm saying. I am just happy. You make me happy.

"The Brotherhood of the Free Spirit," I resumed, "recognize only the four Gospels. They reject Baptism. They own all things in common. They are to be found among the poor and among the rich, and where one would least expect them, and they recognize one another by secret signs. There are some in every country, under various names—even among the dervishes. I owe them my life. That was why I took part in the war in France, for many of them rallied to the Virgin. But when I was twenty-four I dissociated myself from them, for their fanaticism and hatred were worse than any other bigotry. After that I traveled many roads."

"And then you dissociated yourself from everything, and married," she teased me. "That I know already. Tell me about your marriage and about how happy you were then. Even happier perhaps than with the naked woman in the bathing pool? Tell me. Don't be shy."

I remembered Florence in summer heat, the yellow waters of the river and the parched hills. My lighthearted happiness melted away.

"I must have told you about Florence and Ferrara, surely?" I asked. "And of how the most learned men of our age disputed for two whole years about three letters of the alphabet?"

"Why these evasions, John Angelos?" she interrupted. "Does it hurt you so much to recall your marriage? What joy it is to hurt you as you have hurt me!"

"Why must we always talk about me?" I countered obstinately. "Why can't we talk about you?"

She raised her head and her brown eyes flashed.

"I am Anna Notaras," she said. "That is enough. There is no more to say of me."

She was right. She had lived her life in the shelter of the palace walls and the gardens by the Bosporus. She had been carried in a litter so that the mire of the streets might not soil her shoes. Venerable philosophers had taught her. Absently she had turned the pages of great folios and looked at the glowing paintings in gold, blue and vermillion. She was Anna Notaras. She was brought up to be the Emperor's consort. What else is there to say of her?

"She was called Madam Ghita," I began. "She lived in an alley leading to the Franciscan monastery. In the gray wall of her house there was one grilled window and an iron-studded door. Behind the grille she dwelt in a room as meager as a nun's cell. All day long she shouted prayers, sang hymns and reviled passers-by shrilly through her window. Her face was frightening: she had suffered a disease which left it pock-marked and lifeless. It was like an ugly mask. Only her eyes were alive.

"To pass the time she often went shopping in the city, and she would then be attended by a black slave-woman who carried the basket," I continued. "At such times she wore a mantle made of colored patches sewn together, and this as well as her headdress was so thickly hung with tiny images of saints and holy medals that the jingling of them could be heard at some distance. She tittered and mumbled to herself as she walked, but of anyone stopped and looked at her she flew into a rage and poured forth frightful abuse. She called herself God's Fool. The Franciscans protected her because she was rich. Her family let her live as she would, for she was a widow and her fortune was safely invested in their wool- and banking-business. Every one in Florence knew her except myself; I was a stranger.

"I knew nothing whatever about her when we first met. She saw me one day on the Ponte Vecchio and began following me. I thought she was mad. She wanted to force a present on me—a little ivory statuette that I had admired on some counter. But you couldn't understand. How can I explain what happened between us?

"I was still young. I was twenty-five, on the threshold of my prime. But by then I hoped for nothing. Disappointment had made me loathe the black cloaks and bearded faces of the Greeks. I hated Bessarion's round head and massive body.

Where I lodged I woke every morning to the stench of sweat, dirt and ordure. It was a scorching summer. In Ferrara I had been through pestilence and love, and now I believed in nothing any more. I hated even myself. Slavery, fetters, the prison of the flesh. Can you understand?

"She invited me to her home. In her cell there was a wooden bench where she slept, an earthenware jar of water and the stinking remains of food on the floor. But behind this cell she had many beautiful and splendidly furnished rooms, and a walled garden with rippling water, green trees and cages of singing-birds. In the same way, behind all her babbling and tittering there was revealed an intelligent, despairing woman who through anguish had made herself God's fool.

"In her youth she had been very beautiful, a rich and happy woman. But her husband and both children had died within a few days of each other, and the same disease had ruined her beauty. She had come face to face with the uncertainty of human life and the terrifying insecurity looming behind all outward happiness. As if in mockery God had struck her to the ground and pressed her face into the mire. Probably for a time her mind had been unhinged, but even after she recovered she continued to behave in the same way in public, from despair and in defiance of God and man. She blasphemed when she prayed: she prayed when she blasphemed; and the look in her eyes was piercing and tormented. No, I doubt if you can really understand. She was no more than thirty-five, but her face made her look like a withered old woman. Her lips were cracked and there was froth at the sore corners of her mouth when she talked. But her eyes . . ."

Anna Notaras had lowered her gaze and she crushed her folded hands tightly together as she listened. Daylight glowed in the black and red pattern of the carpets. In the corner the eunuch poked forward his gray, wrinkled face, looking from one to the other, muttering and trying to read the words on my lips. I went on.

"She gave me food and drink. Her eyes devoured my face. When I had visited her a few times and talked with her, unutterable compassion awoke in my heart. Compassion is not love, Anna Notaras, but sometimes love can be compassion, as when by his mere presence one human being takes pity on another. Remember that at that time I did not know she was rich; I merely guessed that she was well-to-do, since the Franciscans protected her. She wanted to give me new clothes; she had them sent to the place where I lived and with them came a purse full of silver. But I did not want to accept her presents—even to please her.

"Then one day she showed me a portrait of herself when young. I saw what she had once been, and understood at last. God had smashed her happiness and then locked her up in the hell of her own body. When she caught sight of me on the bridge she had fallen blindly in love with me, and desired me, though at first she would not admit it even to herself.

"Well, there it was!" I exclaimed, hot with embarrassment. "I lay with her; I took pity on her with my body, because this was something I set no value on. I shared her hell and fancied I was doing good. For three nights. Then I sold all I possessed, my clerk's clothes, even my Homer, distributed my money among the poor and fled from Florence.

"God's judgment caught up with me that autumn on the mountain road to Assisi," I ended. "Madam Ghita had followed my trail in her litter, and with her was a Franciscan and an able lawyer. I was bearded, dirty and unkempt; she made me wash and shave and put on new clothes, and we were married in Assisi. I had got her with child, and she regarded this as a miracle. Only then did I discover who she was and realize the snare in which the Lord had caught me. Never in my life before had I been so thunderstruck."

I could sit still no longer. I rose and looked out though the greenish window at the menacing crenelations of the seawall and at the sparkling Marmora beyond.

"I've been warned against having any communication with this house," I said. "Perhaps I shall be locked up in the marble tower as a result of this visit—perhaps not even my appointment under Giustiniani will save me. But you have me in your power already, for this part of my life is unknown to any one else. You see, Anna Notaras, Madam Ghita belonged to the family of the Bardi, and when I married her I became one of the wealthiest men in Florence. The mere name could make every money-changer from Antwerp to Cairo, from Damascus to Toledo, bow down before me.

"How much she had to pay the monks and the Pope himself to secure her fortune and herself from her relatives, and establish the validity of our marriage, I never wanted to know. I had not even a name. The documents relating to my father and my origins were with Gerolamo the goldsmith in Avignon, and he denied ever having received them. But the lawyer managed everything, and I was given a new name. Jean Ange was forgotten. At first we settled down in her house in Fiesole—that is, until our son was born. When I let my beard grow and curled my hair, and dressed myself like a nobleman with a rapier at my side, no one could have recognized the poor French clerk from the synod. I stood it for four years. I had all my heart could desire: hawks, coursers, books; merry company and learned acquaintance. Even the Medicis tolerated me, But not for my own sake; I was only my father's son. My son was a Bardi.

"Madam Ghita grew tranquil; after the birth of our son she was a different woman. She became devout, she blasphemed no longer, she built a church. No doubt she loved me, but above all she loved our son.

"For four years I endured it. Then I took the Cross, to attend Giulio Cesarini to Hungary. I left a letter for my wife and fled secretly—a thing I have often done. She and my son believe I fell at the battle of Varna."

But I had not told everything. I did not say that before going to Hungary I had gone to Avignon, taken Gerolamo by the beard and set a knife to his throat. This I did not speak of, nor did I ever mean to; it is a secret between God and myself. For Gerolamo could not read Greek and dared not show the documents to anyone who could.

What was there left to say?

"My marriage was God's judgment upon me," I went on. "I had to experience stupendous wealth with its attendant glories in order to renounce it. Bars of gold are even harder to force than the prison bars of books, reason and philosophy. As a child I was immured in a dark tower in Avignon; since then my life has been a flight from prison to prison. Now only one is left: the prison of my body—of my knowledge, will and heart. But I know that I shall soon be released from this one too; little time remains."

Anna Notaras shook her head slightly.

"You're a strange man," she said. "I don't understand you; you frighten me."

"Fear is but another prison," I said. "From fear, too, there is release. One can say thank you, and take one's leave, in the certainty that one has nothing to lose but one's chains. Fear is the fear of losing something—and what does a slave possess?"

"And I?" she asked softly. "Why have you come to me?"

"The choice is yours," I said, "not mine. It is as simple as that."

She clasped her hands tightly with a vehement shake of her head replied, "No, no. You can't mean what you say."

I shrugged my shoulders.

"Why do you suppose I have told you so much about myself? To pass the time, perhaps, or to make myself interesting in your eyes? I thought you knew me better. No. I wanted to show you that nothing means what you think it means, or what you have been brought up to believe. Riches and poverty, power and fear, honor and shame, wisdom and stupidity, ugliness and beauty, good and evil—nothing has any significance in itself. The only thing that has significance is what we make of ourselves and what we desire to be. The only real sin is treachery: to know a truth and be false to it. I have stripped myself of everything. I am nothing. And for me this is the highest that mortals can attain—this tranquil sense of my dominion and my power. I have nothing else to offer. The choice is yours."

She was agitated. Her mouth narrowed and lost its color, and a cold hatred came into her eyes; she was not even beautiful now.

"And I?" she asked again. "What is it you really want of me?"

"When I saw your eyes, I knew that every human being does after all need a fellow-human. Don't deceive yourself—you know that too. Such a thing happens only once, and to some it never happens at all. I have told you about myself to show that everything you have had hitherto—everything you thought you possessed—is unstable and illusory. You would lose nothing by renouncing it. When the Turks come you will be forced to lose a great deal. For your sake I could wish that in your heart you might already have bidden farewell to everything which sooner or later you must give up."

"Words!" she cried beginning to tremble. "Words, words—nothing but words."

"I've had enough of words too," I said, "but I can't take you in my arms with your eunuch looking on. You know that with my arms around you, you would understand everything; we should need no words then."

"You're mad," she said, and drew back. But our eyes met, just as at St. Sophia's. Our eyes exchanged naked looks.

"Anna, my beloved," I urged her. "Our time is dwindling; the sands are running out to no purpose. When I saw you for the first time I recognized you; it had to happen. Perhaps we were born into the world before and met in a former life. But of that we can know nothing—only one thing is sure: we have met now, and it had to happen. Yet this may be our only opportunity—the only place and hour in the universe at which we may meet. Why do you hesitate? Why do you deceive yourself?"

She raised her hand and laid it over her eyes; she turned back—home to her carpets, her windows, her porphyry pavements, to her own time. To her upbringing and the things she knew.

"Father stands between us," she said in a low voice.

I had lost. I, too, came back into time.

"He took ship," I said. "Why?"

"Why?" she flared up. "You ask that? Because he's weary of an incompetent Emperor's feeble policy! Because he will not bow before the Sultan as Constantine does. He makes war, since war it is to be. Why, you ask. Because he is the only real man in the city, the only true Greek. He will not lean on Latin aid. He relies on himself and his dromonds."

What could I reply? Rightly or wrongly she loves her father; she is Anna Notaras.

"So you have chosen," I said. "You will tell your father about me."

"Yes," she said. "I shall tell my father about you."

I had walked into the trap of my own free will. I said no more; I would not even look at her. Yet even this was preordained.

15 February 1453

The fleet returned yesterday, all five dromonds. Pennants fluttered, seamen beat drums and blew pipes and the little bronze cannon fired a salute. The townspeople raced down to the harbor or waved white cloths from the walls.

Today Turkish slaves were on sale in the market. Fishermen, old fellows with long beards, lean boys, weeping women who tried to hide their faces in their threadbare garments. Truly a brilliant victory this, that Notaras has won over the Turks.

He was able to make a surprise raid on a couple of villages on the Asiatic coast and take the inhabitants prisoner. The people of other villages fled but he burned their houses. He sailed as far as Gallipoli and succeeded in sinking a Turkish cargo vessel. When the Turkish war galleys rowed out to his encounter, he returned to port.

What rejoicing! How the Greek seamen have been feted! How the crowds cheered the Megadux as he rode to his house! Giustiniani and the Latins have been put in the shade, and Lukas Notaras has been the hero of Constantinople for a whole day.

Yet at the slave market no one was anxious to bid for the

Turkish prisoners. No one mocked or reviled them, and curious onlookers soon dispersed. People dropped their eyes in shame before these miserable wretches, who clung to each other and murmured verses from the Koran to keep up their courage.

18 February 1453

From Adrianople echo has replied. Sultan Mohammed has had Emperor Constantine's letter publicly read, as evidence of Greek treachery, and then trampled underfoot. His iron-shod runners have brought word of it to every Turkish city. Dervishes and priests preach vengeance and the peace party has been silenced. Mohammed takes even the west to witness:

Time after time the Greeks have broken their oaths and treaties, as soon as opportunity offered. When Emperor Constantine surrendered his Church to the Pope, he broke the last ties of friendship between Turks and Greeks. His only aim is to inflame the western nations against the Turks. With deceitful words and feigned candor he still seeks to conceal his plots, but the Osmanli villages now in flames along the Marmora coast have illumined and revealed his savage schemes. Byzantium's lust for conquest is a threat to our very existence; the cunning and cruelty of the Greeks cries out for vengeance. To put an end to this constant menace, to liberate our realm from the lurking peril of the Greeks, it is the duty of every believer to rise up and wage the holy war. He who would still excuse the Greeks reveals himself as an enemy to his nation. The chastising sword of the Sultan must be raised to avenge those of the faithful who have been murdered, tortured, burned alive or enslaved.

To sweep away the last vestiges of indecision the Sultan has caused the names of the slaughtered Turks to be read aloud in all the mosques at Friday worship.

The naval action has given Mohammed the one weapon he needed to crush the peace party and the resistance of Grand Vizier Khalil. Anyone now opposing the siege does so at the peril of his head. Not even Khalil is safe, Grand Vizier though he be, and kinsman to two others.

21 February 1453

Miracles are happening at the Pantokrator monastery. On damp mornings mist condenses into drops on the holy icons, and the monks say that the saints are sweating in anguish. A nun has sworn that she saw the Holy Virgin of the Blachernae weeping tears of blood, and the people believe her, although the Emperor has invited Cardinal Isidor and the puppet Patriarch Gregorios—and with them, learned philosophers—to examine the image, and they found no trace of blood upon it. The people will not believe apostates, and their ignorant, fanatical adherence to the original creed is stronger than ever.

Young monks, artisans, burgesses and merchants, who but lately could not tell one end of a sword from the other, are now drilling in platoons of tens and hundreds under the direction of Giustiniani's tested warriors. They desire to fight for their faith; they burn with eagerness to prove themselves equal to the Latins, if need be. They mean to hold their city.

They can bend a bow, perhaps, but the arrows fly at random. They level their lances and charge with enthusiasm at suspended sacks of hay, but their want of practice makes them clumsy. One or two have gashed their own legs in tripping over their cloaks. Yet there are some stout men among them. They will be best fitted to hurl stones from the walls when the Turks make their assault.

Volunteers and those called to arms by the Emperor will not all be given helmets, or even leather jerkins. Those who have received helmets take them off at the first opportunity, complaining that they pinch the head and chafe it. The straps of their harness constrict them, they say, and with leg-armor they can hardly move.

I do not blame them. They are doing their best. They have been nurtured in peaceful occupations, fully trusting to their walls and to the Emperor's mercenaries. In a pitched battle one janissary could dispatch ten of these volunteers in a twinkling.

I have looked at the fine white hands that can so exquisitely carve a piece of ivory; I have seen eyes that have been sharpened by the work of engraving images of saints in cornelian. Men who can read and write; men who with brushes like hairs illuminate the initials in liturgical manuscripts, in vermilion and gold.

They must now learn to thrust swords into unprotected groins, to aim lances at a man's face, to shoot arrows into eyes that behold heaven and earth.

What a mad world—what a mad age!

Light swivel guns for the walls have been fetched from the arsenal, also heavy wrought-iron cannon, for the Emperor has not the means to have them cast in bronze. The raw recruits fear cannon more than they fear the Turks, and throw themselves down with their hands over their ears whenever they are fired. They complain that the noise deafens them and the flash from the muzzle blinds them. Most unluckily a small iron cannon exploded on the first day, maiming two men.

24 February 1453

Giustiniani has completed his scheme of defense. He has divided the Latins according to nationality and placed them at the most exposed points along the wall, and at the gates. Venetians and Genoese will compete with one another for glory; even from Pera young men have come to be enrolled under Giustiniani. Their conscience would not abide the disgrace of inactivity in this war which, ultimately, will determine the fate of the west.

Giustiniani places his reliance only on the Latins and on the Emperor's artillerymen and technicians. The rest of the Greeks are to be stopgaps on the walls. But they are necessary. The landward wall alone—the largest—measures ten thousand paces and has a hundred towers. The sea- and harbor-walls in the huge triangle of defense are equally long, but will hardly be as severely threatened. The harbor is protected by the western warships, which are far superior to those of the Turks; while the wall facing the sea is unlikely to be endangered—Greek fire can set the light Turkish craft ablaze at a bow-shot's distance. For this purpose the Emperor's technicians have special projectiles resembling little flying cannon. But they guard their secrets jealously and will not divulge them to the Latins.

In any event, Giustiniani expects the real battle to be fought out along the landward wall. At the center of this is the Gate of St. Romanos, in the vale of Lykos, the defense of which he has reserved to himself and his iron-clad Genoese. From there too he can most swiftly send reinforcements to exposed points along the wall. But the final disposition of the defense forces will depend on the Sultan's plan of attack.

The worst of the rush of preparation is over. The walls are still being strengthened, but everything is progressing methodically and each man knows exactly what he has to do from hour to hour of the day. Martial exercises go forward in the same way, though the dinner interval is greatly protracted owing to the huge area of the city: volunteers must return home for their meals.

Giustiniani has discarded his worn leather breeches, he has had his hair elegantly dressed and waved in the Greek manner, dyed his beard red and braided it with threads of gold; and although he does not paint the corners of his eyes blue and his mouth red, like the young officers in the Emperor's bodyguard, he flaunts a quantity of gold chains around his neck and has begun to feel at home in Greek company. The ladies of the Palace of Blachernae pay him flattering attention.

He is a powerful, burly man, a head taller than most Greeks. He burnishes his cuirass to the brightness of a mirror, and in the evenings exchanges the protostrator's chain, which the Emperor gave him, for a chain of amethysts, in the hope that these stones will prevent him from getting drunk.

The Emperor has confirmed with a chrysobull his promise of the dukedom of Lemnos, if Giustiniani succeeds in repulsing the Turks. The seal alone is worth many bezants, and with his own hand the Emperor had drawn his triple cross upon the document.

Since the naval action, Megadux Notaras has remained in retirement in his house, and the Emperor, on Giustiniani's advice, has strictly forbidden him to take his dromonds to sea again. Notaras insists with equal firmness that he acted rightly, and accuses the Emperor of cowardice and truckling to the Latins.

He has let it be understood that he expects Giustiniani to confer with him about the defense of the city and the disposition of the troops. As megadux and commander of the imperial fleet he regards himself as at least the equal of Giustiniani, despite the latter's rank of protostrator. Above all, of course, he is curious to know what position Giustiniani has allotted him in his scheme of defense. He cannot be disregarded; he is far too highly placed and influential a man for that. Nevertheless the Latin sea captains exercise full command over their ships and take their orders directly from the Emperor; in fact, therefore, Notaras controls only those five sluggish, dropsical dromonds—and even these are nominally the Emperor's, albeit the Megadux has repaired and equipped them at his own expense.

Despite the popular favor he has won, Lukas Notaras is a very lonely man these days—at least as far as the Palace of Blachernae is concerned.

Giustiniani is letting him wait. Giustiniani is an adventurer exalted to protostrator, and is therefore perhaps more rank-conscious than a hereditary grand duke. Is the same disturbingly childish duel to prevail here too, inducing the two men to measure their thrones with a foot-rule?

In actual fact the city is wholly under the control of the Latins, and the Greeks have no power, although the Emperor seems not to have realized this. The harbor is held by Latin vessels, while the key-points of the city and its walls are manned by the iron-clad troops of Giustiniani and the Venetians.

Is it possible that Giustiniani can be making secret political plans? He has made contacts, sometimes through the distaff side, with the most influential of the Latin-minded Greeks. Should the Turkish attempt fail and Sultan Mohammed sustain a defeat—should the fleets of Venice and the Pope, with their Latin auxiliaries, arrive in time—Constantinople would reveal itself as no more than a Latin base for the capture of the Black Sea trade and for the subjugation of a divided Turkish state. The Union has already been proclaimed. Might the Empire become Latin once more, with the Greek puppet-Emperor allowed to retain his throne?

Would the victor remain content with vassalage in Lemnos?

My Greek blood no longer believes that anything is what it seems. It is a doubting blood, the blood of a thousand years of political intrigue. Daily the Latin part of me shreds away. I am my father's son; my blood is turning homeward.

25 February 1453

Fear and dread have spread throughout the city. The townsfolk have fallen silent and they eye each other mistrustfully. Many are praying in the churches. The rich are packing their chests and burying their valuables, or hiding them in wells. Cellars are being walled up. The hands of many an archon are swollen with unaccustomed labor; there is a guilty look in these men's eyes and telltale specks of mortar on their sleeves.

"Something is happening," my servant Manuel said today. "I can see it, hear it, smell it—but what it is, I don't know. Tell me, master."

I too can feel something strange in the air. There is unrest in the harbor and much rowing to and fro between the ships. The Venetian Council of Twelve meets behind locked doors.

26 February 1453

I had already undressed when my servant Manuel announced that a young Greek was asking for me. I did not trouble to get out of bed; I was tired.

The boy came in without bowing and looked inquisitively around, wrinkling his nose at the smell of leather, paper, sealing wax and metal polish. I recognized him; I had seen him on horseback at the Hippodrome. He was Anna Notaras' younger brother.

My mood was chilled. The violent gusts of wind made the shutters rattle.

"It's dark outside," the boy said. "The sky is overcast. One can hardly see a hand before one's face."

He is seventeen and a handsome youth, very conscious of his beauty and rank, yet charmingly so. He seemed curious about me.

"You escaped from the Turks," he said. "You're much talked of in the city. You were pointed out to me once as you rode by. My father would like to meet you, if it wouldn't give you too much trouble." He looked away. "As I said, it's a dark night. One can't see at all."

"I don't like going out in the dark," I said, "but of course I cannot fail to comply with any order from your father."

"It's not an order," he protested. "How should my father give you orders? You have enrolled under Giustiniani. It's not as a soldier he wants to meet you; you're to be his guest—perhaps his friend. You may have valuable information to give him, and he wonders why you have avoided him; he's curious about you. But naturally he would bear you no ill-will, should you deem it best not to come."

He talked cheerfully and volubly to conceal his embarrassment at the task he had been given. He was a frank, attractive boy—and he did not like going out in the dark either. Why was his father keeping this invitation so secret that he was unwilling to confide in a servant, but sent his own son?

A lamb to the slaughter, I thought. A well-grown ram on the altar of ambition. He is willing, then, to sacrifice his own son if necessary.

He was the brother of Anna Notaras. I smiled at him cordially and when I was dressed I brushed his shoulder lightly with my hand. He started and blushed, but smiled in return: evidently he did not regard me as a man of low birth.

The north wind roared through the night, snatched away our breath and pressed our clothes tight against our bodies. It was pitch dark. Between the scurrying clouds the black sky flashed its stars at us now and then. The yellow dog followed me out, although I ordered it to stay at home. But it slunk away in the darkness. I took the lantern from Manuel and handed it to the boy; this he found hard to stomach, yet he carried it without protest. Whom did he take me for? The dog followed us the whole way, as if to guard me even against my will.

It was dark in Notaras' palace. We entered it through a back door in a corner against the sea wall. No one was to be seen, and yet the night seemed full of hidden eyes. The soughing, sighing wind spoke to me, but I could not distinguish the words. There was a roaring even in my head, as if the gale had confused my wits.

It was deathly silent in the corridor. Warm air came to meet us. We went upstairs. In the room to which I was taken there was a writing desk with quill pens and paper, and big, beautifully bound books. Before the icon of the Magi burned a lamp of scented oil.

His head was bowed as if in heavy thought. He did not smile, and received my greeting as a natural mark of respect. To his son he said only, "I shan't want you again." The boy was hurt, but tried not to show it. He had been very curious to hear what we should say to one another, but now he bent his comely head submissively, wished me good night and went out.

As soon as he had gone Lukas Notaras became more animated, and looking at me intently he said, "I know all about you, John Angelos, and so I shall speak frankly."

I realized that he knew of my Greek origin; this fact in itself was not surprising, and yet it affected me unpleasantly.

"You're going to speak frankly," I remarked. "A man says that only when he means to hide his thoughts. Dare you be frank even to yourself?"

"You were Sultan Mohammed's trusted adviser," he said. "You escaped from his camp last autumn. A man who has attained that position does not act thus without some object."

"It is your intentions which are now in question, Megadux," I said evasively, "not mine. You would not have summoned me secretly unless you thought I could be of service in carrying them out."

He made a gesture of impatience. His signet ring too was the size of a baby's hand. The sleeves of his green outer mantle reached to his elbows, and the undersleeves were of purple silk embroidered with gold, like the Emperor's.

"And yet from the beginning you have sought to get in touch with me," he said. "You have been very cautious. That was understandable and right, both from your point of view and mine. It was very ingenious of you to make the acquaintance of my daughter, seemingly by chance. Then you accompanied her home one day when she had lost her attendant. When I was away at sea you dared to visit my house in broad daylight. It was my daughter you wanted to meet. That was very cunning."

"She promised to tell you about me," I admitted.

"My daughter is fond of you." He smiled. "She doesn't know who you are and guesses nothing of your purpose. She is sensitive and proud—she knows nothing. You understand."

"She is very beautiful," I said. The Megadux once more waved away my words.

"You are above that sort of temptation. My daughter is not for you."

"I wouldn't be too sure of that, Megadux," I said.

For the first time he allowed himself to look surprised.

"Sufficient unto the day," he said. "Your game is too difficult and dangerous for you to bring a woman into it. For appearance's sake, perhaps; not otherwise. You're walking on a knife edge, John Angelos; you cannot afford to stumble."

"You know a great deal, Megadux," I remarked, "but you don't know me."

"I know a great deal," he assented. "More than you think. Not even your Sultan's tent is a safe place to converse in. There are ears there too. I know that you did not part from the Sultan in anger; I know that he gave you a princely present of precious stones. Unfortunately the Basileus and Phrantzes the keeper of his seal know it too. Therefore your every step has been watched since you came to Constantinople. I don't want to know how much you paid to be entered on Giustiniani's roll; all Latins can be bought. But not even Giustiniani can save you if you make the smallest mistake."

He threw out his hand again.

"It's ridiculous," he said. "Sultan Mohammed's authority is your only protection here in Constantinople, so low has the

Second Rome fallen. They dare not raise a hand against you, because they have not yet discovered your intentions."

"You are quite right," I said. "Truly it is ridiculous. Even now that I have run away from the Sultan and betrayed him, his power it is that protects me; this fact has been borne in upon me every hour. We live in a mad world."

He smiled with narrowing lips.

"I am not so mad as to think you would dare to reveal your plans even to me. I am a Greek, after all. Nor is it necessary. Common sense tells me that after the capture of the city you will attain an even higher position in the service of the Sultan—if not publicly, then in secret. Therefore a mutual understanding, or even co-operation within certain limits, might profit us both."

He regarded me questioningly.

"It was you who said it," I returned cautiously.

"There are only two possibilities," he continued. "Either the siege will be successful and the Sultan will take Constantinople by storm; or it will fail, and then we shall be a vassal state to the Latins for all time."

He rose, straightened his back and raised his voice. "We have experienced Latin rule before. It lasted for one generation, and after three hundred years Constantinople has not recovered from it. The Latins are robbers, less merciful even than the Turks, and they have falsified the true faith. The Turks at least allow us to retain our faith and our traditions. Therefore Panaghia herself is now on the side of the Turks, though she weeps blood over our weakness."

"You are not addressing the mob, Megadux," I reminded him.

He replied with emphasis, "Don't misunderstand me. Whatever you do, don't misunderstand me. I'm a Greek: I will fight for my city so long as any hope of independence remains. But I will never let it fall into the power of the Latins; that would result in nothing but incessant slaughter for tens of years, with Constantinople as a Latin outpost of Europe—and so the last of our strength would drain away. We are weary of Europe, we have had enough of Latins. Beside those barbarians even the Turks are cultured people, thanks to their Arabian and Persian heritage. The Sultan's power will raise Constantinople to a fresh flowering. At the frontier of east and west, Constantinople shall once more rule the world. The Sultan does not demand that we should betray our religion, only that we should dwell in amity with the Turks. Why should we not conquer the world with him and let our ancient Greek culture be the leaven for their more robust civilization? Let the Third Rome be born! A Sultan's Rome, where Greeks and Turks are brothers and respect each other's faith."

"Yours is an inspiring dream," I said. "I would not for the world throw cold water on your glowing heart—but dreams are only dreams. Let us stick to reality. You don't know Mohammed; yet you hope that your city may be captured and fall into his power."

"I don't hope for it," he said. "I *know* that Constantinople will fall. I'm not a strategist for nothing.

"A live dog is better than a dead lion," he went on. "Emperor Constantine has chosen his destiny, for otherwise he could not act. Without doubt he will seek death on the ramparts when he sees that all is lost. But how can a dead patriot help his people? If it be my fate to fall, I shall fall on the walls of Constantinople—but I would rather preserve my life, and work for the good of my people. The Palaeologos era is at an end; the Sultan will be the only Emperor. But to control the Greeks and manage Greek affairs he will need Greek men. After the capture of the city this will be inevitable; he will have to fill the higher appointments with those who are familiar with court ceremonial and the work of administration. Therefore Constantinople has need of patriots who love their countrymen—who love their heritage from Ancient Greece more than their own reputation. If I can serve my people like a dog I ask no lion's death. I have only to persuade the Sultan of my good will, and when the cry runs round the walls—'The city is lost!'—the hour will have come for me to take my people's destiny in my hands and guide it aright."

He fell silent and looked at me expectantly.

"Your speech was long, beautiful, persuasive and it does you great honor," I said. "It's true that the ancient Greek heritage you spoke of includes Leonidas and Thermopylae, but I know what you mean. You wish to persuade the Sultan of your good will—but have you not made that sufficiently clear? You led the opponents of the Union, you fanned the hatred against the Latins, and other conflicts within the city, and thus weakened its defense. You took ship and by a pointless raid gave the Sultan the provocation he needed. Well and good. Then why do you not write directly to the Sultan and offer him your services?"

He replied, "You know very well that a man in my position cannot do such a thing. I am Greek. I must fight for my city, albeit I know the battle will be in vain. But I reserve the right to act according to circumstances for the good of my people. Why should my countrymen die or be dragged away into slavery if I can prevent it?"

"You do not know Mohammed," I repeated. My contrariness seemed to trouble him.

"I am no traitor," he said. "I am a politician. Both you and the Sultan must understand that. Before my people and my conscience, before the judgment seat of God, I will answer for my thoughts and actions, heedless of calumniators. My political sense tells me that a man like myself will be needed at the fateful hour. My motives are pure and unself-seeking. Better that my countrymen should in some sort survive than go under altogether. The spirit of Greece, its culture and faith, mean not merely the city walls, the Emperors' palace, the forum, the senate and the archons; these are but outward forms—and though forms change with time, the spirit endures."

I said, "Political wisdom and divine wisdom are two different things."

He corrected me. "If God has given man the power to think politically, it is surely His intention that we shall use that power."

"You have spoken plainly enough, Megadux Lukas Notaras," I said bitterly. "When Constantinople has fallen it will be men of your kind who will rule the world. I can assure you that Sultan Mohammed knows your views and estimates your unselfish motives at their true worth. Doubtless he will at some suitable time convey his wishes to you, and tell you in what way you can best serve him during the siege."

He bent his head slightly, as if acknowledging me as Sultan Mohammed's envoy and my words as a message from him. To such an extent can a man be enslaved by his own wishes.

His tension relaxed and he made a friendly gesture with both hands as I was about to take my leave.

"Don't go yet," he begged me. "We have had a most formal conversation, but I also want to win your friendship. You serve a master whose resolution and far-sightedness I wholeheartedly respect, for all his youth."

He walked quickly to a table, poured wine into two cups and offered one to me. I did not take it.

"I have already drunk of your wine," I said. "In the company of your beautiful daughter I tasted a cup of it. Permit me this time to keep my head cool. I am unused to wine."

He smiled, misinterpreting my refusal.

"The commandments of the Koran have their good points," he said easily. "I have no doubt that Mohammed was a great prophet. In our day every thinking person acknowledges the good in other religions, while yet adhering to his own. I can well understand Christians who of their own free will have embraced Islam; for in matters of faith I respect all honest convictions."

"I have not been converted to Islam," I said. "I will maintain my Christian faith at the sword's point. I am not circumcised. Nevertheless I prefer to keep my head cool."

His face darkened again.

"Moreover I have assured you, and I repeat my assurance, that I have left the Sultan's service," I added lightly. "I came to Constantinople to die for the city. I have no other aims. I thank you for your confidence and will not abuse it. Everyone has the right to make political calculations in his head; no one can blame you for that, so long as they remain there. Emperor Constantine and his advisers have doubtless taken into account the possibility of such calculations. Be careful, then—as careful as you have been hitherto."

He set down his wine untasted.

"You do not trust me," he complained. "You have of course your own mission, and tasks which do not concern me. Be you careful too, therefore. You may wish to get in touch with me again when you deem the time ripe. You know my views. You know what to expect from me—and what not to expect. I'm a Greek. I shall fight for my city."

"Like myself," I said. "At least we have that in common. We both mean to put up a fight, although we know that Constantinople must fall; we no longer hope for miracles."

"Time is old," he replied. "The age of miracles is past. God no longer intervenes. But He is a witness to our thoughts and deeds."

He turned toward the Magi and the scented lamp, and raised his hand as he pronounced this oath:

"By the Lord God and His only begotten Son, by the Mother of God and all the saints, I swear that my motives are selfless and that I aim only at my people's good. I do not strive after power. It is a heavy trial that I am undergoing, yet for the future of my line, my kinsmen and my city I must act as I have resolved to act."

He swore this oath with so convincing a solemnity that I had to believe him. He is not merely a calculating politician: he really believes that he is acting rightly. He has endured abuse, his tender pride has been wounded, he hates the Latins and he has been thrust aside. Therefore he has conceived his vision and believes in it.

"Your daughter Anna Notaras," I said. "Will you still permit me to see her?"

"What is the point of that now?" he demanded in surprise. "It would only attract unnecessary attention. How could she show herself in the company of a man whom all suspect to be the secret envoy of the Sultan?"

"I'm not yet in the marble tower," I said. "If Giustiniani may amuse himself with the ladies of the Blachernae, why should not I pay my respects to the Megadux's daughter?"

"My daughter must guard her reputation." His voice was cold and discouraging.

"Times are changing," I persisted. "With the Latins come the freer customs of the west. Your daughter is full-grown and knows her own mind. Why should you not allow singers and musicians to entertain her? Why should I not ride beside her litter to church? Why should I not invite her for a row in the harbor some sunny day? Your house is gloomy. Why begrudge her a little joy and laughter before the days of trial begin? What have you against it, Megadux?"

He threw out his hand.

"Too late," he said. "I am sending my daughter out of the city."

I looked down to hide my face. I had known of this; it was no unexpected news, yet I seethed with bitterness at my loss.

"As you will," I said. "Nevertheless I intend to see your daughter once more before she goes."

He shot me a swift glance, and his large brilliant eyes assumed an absent look, as if for an instant he were envisaging possibilities which he had not previously taken into account. Then he waved his hand, dismissing them, and looked toward the window as if to peer across the dark sea, through glass and rattling shutter.

"Too late," he repeated. "I am sorry, but I believe the ship has already sailed. The wind tonight is most favorable. This afternoon she was rowed secretly out to a Cretan ship with her baggage and servants."

I turned and went blindly out, snatched my lantern from the hook by the entry, fumbled open the door and rushed from the house into the darkness. The wind howled, the sea thundered beyond the wall, and waves beat upon the embankment. The gale wound my mantle tightly about my body and pressed the breath out of me. I lost all self-control: I slung the flickering lantern away and it flew in an arc through the darkness, crashed and went out.

It saved my life. My angel was on guard—and the dog. From behind me a knife drove in under my left arm and glanced off my ribs. Then my assailant tripped over the dog, yelled as it bit him, and slashed blindly about with his knife.

A pitiful howl told me that the dog had received a mortal wound, and fury blazed up within me. I caught a slippery neck in a wrestler's hold I had learned from the Turks—I smelled the garlic in the panting breath and the stench of filthy rags. Then I pressed the neck to the ground and drove my dagger into a struggling body. The man uttered a frightful screech as the blade cut into his flesh. Then I bent over the dog, which tried to lick my hand. Its head fell to one side.

"Why did you follow me when I forbade you?" I said softly. "It was not you but my guardian angel that saved me. You died for me in vain, good friend."

It was just a stray yellow dog. It had attached itself to me of its own free will, had known me, and had now paid for that acquaintance with its life.

A light gleamed in one of the windows of the palace and the door was noisily unbarred. I started running, but being blinded with tears I rushed straight into a wall and scraped my face against it. I wiped away the blood and began groping my way toward the Hippodrome. My left side was wet with blood. Between flying clouds I glimpsed now and then a cluster of stars, and gradually my eyes grew accustomed to the darkness. In my stunned head one thought was hammering: "Phrantzes, not Constantine. Phrantzes, not Constantine."

Did they then esteem me so dangerous a man that they preferred to assassinate me rather than immure me in the marble tower? Phrantzes had warned me against Notaras' house.

But these unprofitable speculations vanished from my thoughts as I rounded the Hippodrome and came up onto the hill. I staggered past the gigantic dome of St. Sophia and down toward the harbor, with my hand pressed to my side. My pulse beat out: "She is gone, she is gone. . . ."

Anna Notaras had left the city. She had made her choice.

She was her father's obedient daughter. What else had I imagined? Without a message, without farewell.

My servant Manuel had sat up waiting for me and kept the lamp burning in my room. He was not surprised to see my grazed face and the blood on my clothes. In a moment he had fetched clean water, bandages and ointment. He helped me to undress and washed the wound which ran from my shoulder blade down my left side. It smarted most painfully, yet the sting of it did my soul good.

I gave him a surgeon's needle and silken thread and showed him how to stitch the gash. I bade him wash it in strong wine and collect spiders' webs and mildew to prevent wound-fever. Not until he had bandaged me and helped me into bed did I begin to shiver. I shivered until the bed creaked.

"Dog," I said in a quavering voice. "Thin yellow dog—I wonder who you were."

I lay long awake. I was alone again, then. But I did not pray for mercy. Anna Notaras had made her choice, and who was I to judge her?

Yet on the day of my death I will fall asleep in the hyacinth scent of your cheeks. That you cannot prevent.

28 February 1453

During last night's northerly gale a number of vessels fled the harbor: the great ships of Piero Davenzo the Venetian and six fully laden Cretan vessels. The oath, the kissing of the cross, and the threat of fines were therefore insufficient to keep them here. The captains have saved twelve hundred cases of soda, copper, indigo, wax, mastic and spices for Venice and the owners in Crete.

Over and above this they rescued hundreds of rich refugees who paid whatever they were asked for their passage. It seems that for several days this exodus has been an open secret in the harbor.

Not one shot did the Turks in Gallipoli fire at these ships, not one war-galley did they send to attack them. This too, then, was prearranged through neutral agents in Pera. And after all, why should the Sultan trouble his head about a few cases of copper and spice, when in this way he can diminish the number of ships available to the Emperor and thus impair the defenses of the harbor?

The Megadux, commander of the fleet, must also have been aware of the flight and sent his own daughter to safety with these vessels. But the ladies of the imperial family have gone too, though no one knows when they sailed.

From the sea captains still remaining the Emperor has demanded fresh oaths, and their assurance that they will not leave port without his permission. What else can he do? The Venetians refuse to unload their valuable cargoes, which would be the only certain way of keeping them here.

1 March 1453

Giustiniani has been to visit me, as I do not yet care to show myself out of doors. My wounds smart, my whole face feels on fire and I am feverish.

As he dismounted from his great charger a crowd instantly gathered about him. The Greeks admire him, for all he's a Latin. Boys respectfully fingered bridle and reins. The Emperor has presented him with a gold-mounted saddle and jeweled harness. His visit was a great honor for me. We had a long conversation, and I expounded my philosophy to him—the ideas of my teacher Dr. Cusanus, that right and wrong, truth and lies, good and evil, do not cancel one another out. That there is no absolute right or wrong, good or evil, truth or falsehood—that everything is relative in a limited world, and in timelessness is reconciled. But this he did not understand.

He wagged his head and clicked his tongue delightedly when he came in and saw my sore forehead and skinless nose.

"Just a tavern brawl," I told him.

"But you held your own?"

"I hit back and then got out."

"If that's true you shall be spared punishment," he said. "At least no one so far has complained that you've been drunk to the prejudice of good order. May I see your wound?"

He made Manuel undo the bandage and poked clumsily with his thick forefinger at the swollen edges of the gash.

"A stab in the back," he said. "A finger's breadth from death. This was dealt in no tavern brawl, though your face suggests something of the kind."

"I haven't many friends in this city," I owned.

"You should wear a coat of mail," he said. "Light chain mail would break the tip of a sword and prevent even the thinnest dagger from penetrating too far."

"I don't need it," I said. "I'm hard enough, if only I can keep my wits about me."

He was curious.

"Are you really hard?" he asked. "Have you a talisman? Have you caused a spell to be laid upon you, or do you carry vervain in your pouch? All ways are good, so long as you believe in them."

I took a long silver pin from the table by my bed.

"See here," I said, and muttering an Arabic formula of the Torlak dervishes, I thrust the pin swiftly through the muscle of my arm so that the point stuck out the other side. Not a single drop of blood appeared. He wagged his great head again.

"Then why has your wound given you a fever?" he asked doubtfully. "Why does it not heal of itself and grow together, if you're as hard as you say?"

"Because I was excited and forgot myself," I said. "Don't be uneasy; the wound will heal. The day after tomorrow I shall be fit for duty."

Then he went, and the heavy hoofs of his charger rang hollowly on the paved street. The heavy hoofs of Time's charger are trampling my heart to rags.

2 March 1453

There is warmth in the sun. In gardens and at street corners people are burning rubbish. Pale green blades of grass thrust out from the cracks in the yellow marble, and the slopes of the Acropolis are bright with spring flowers. In the harbor the racketing and carousing goes on far into the night, and through the stillness of evening the music can be heard even from my house. Never, never have I seen such radiant sunsets as these, when the cupolas seem on fire and the bay lies black as ink between the hillocks and the high ground. On the other side, the walls and towers of Pera glow crimson and are mirrored in the dark waters.

As I sat staring at the sunset, my heart embittered with my loss, my servant Manuel approached, to discharge upon me a flood of eloquence.

"Master, spring has come but not the Turks. The birds, wild with spring fever, chase each other madly, and the cooing of pigeons disturbs men's rest. In the patriarch's stables the jackasses bray so terribly that everyone who hears them goes mad too. Master, it is not good for man to be alone."

"What's this?" I exclaimed in amazement. "Surely you're not thinking of marriage—you with your gray beard? Or are you trying to mulct me of a contribution to the dowry of one of your cousins' daughters?"

"Master, I'm thinking only of your own good," he said, hurt. "I know you, I know your rank, and understand what is fitting for you to do and what unfitting. But spring can stir the blood of even the most exalted man, and in this there is no difference between emperor and goatherd. I do not want to see you staggering home again with blood on your clothes, to terrify me out of my wits. Believe me, dark gateways and walled courts are dangerous in this city."

He rubbed his hands together and avoided my eye as he sought suitable phrases.

"But everything can be arranged," he went on meaningly. "You're downcast and sleep badly at night, and it grieves me. Of course I am not one to ferret among your affairs; I know my place. Yet I could not avoid noticing that for a long time now you have not had a visit from that welcome guest who made your face light up with joy. Far from it: you came home bloody from head to foot, from which I deduce that all has been discovered and that you are suffering the pangs of enforced separation. But time heals all wounds; for all wounds there are soothing salves—even for those of the heart."

"Enough," I said. "Were it not that the sunset has made me sick with melancholy I should by now have struck you on the mouth."

"Do not misunderstand me, master, I beg," he hastened to

reply. "But a man of your age needs a woman, unless he be a monk or in some other way dedicated to pious abstinence. It is a law of nature. Why should you not enjoy life during the short time remaining? I have a suggestion to make—even two, if only you will not misunderstand me."

He drew back warily and making himself even smaller than before, he continued, "A cousin of mine has a daughter—a young widow in her prime who lost her husband so soon that she is practically a maiden. She has seen you riding about the city and has fallen so much in love with you that she pesters me continually to let her into the house and make her known to you. She is a personable, decorous girl; you would make her happy and do all our family the greatest honor if you would show her your favor for a night or two. She asks no more than that, and you shall give her whatever you think fit when you have tired of her. In this way you would be doing a kind action and at the same time giving your body the peace it needs."

"Manuel," I said, "I appreciate your good intentions, but if I were to yield to the enticement of every woman who follows me with her eyes I should never be free of them. From my youth up I have suffered the curse of being desired more than I desire. Yet every time I myself have longed for something, the other has not longed for the same thing. Such is my punishment. Believe me, I should only cause your cousin's daughter sorrow and pain were I to take her to my bed to warm me, without desiring her."

Manuel assented at once.

"That's what I tried to get into her head, but you know what women are—obstinacy itself. But I have another proposal. One of my aunts has an acquaintance—a honorable man of perfect discretion—who gladly helps both high and low in their troubles. For this purpose he has built a house near the

Palace of Blachernae—an outwardly modest house, but within most tastefully arranged and furnished. In this house there are young slave-girls from many different countries and one may obtain hot baths and massage. Even used-up and impotent old archons have left this house well pleased with the services rendered them there, and afterwards shown their gratitude to their benefactor in many ways. The house is worthy of your rank, and you would lose nothing by trying the varied possibilities there offered."

He noted my expression and looked abashed, as he hastened to explain. "Not that I would imply for a moment that you were used-up or impotent, master. On the contrary, you're a man in the prime of life. In this house one may meet, with perfect secrecy and discretion, distinguished ladies who need a change or who by reason of their husbands' meanness welcome a little pin-money. You may not believe me, but even ladies from the Palace of Blachernae have visited this house without disagreeable consequences. On the contrary: my aunt's honorable friend has a wide and profound knowledge of men, and is most understanding. He sifts his clientele with the utmost discrimination."

"I will do nothing to help the deterioration of morals in this dying city," I answered. "No, Manuel. You don't understand."

Manuel seemed deeply hurt.

"How can you talk of deterioration of morals, master, when it's a question of freely frequenting the company of cultured, sensitive people of the same level of society? Does it seem to you more natural and less decadent to climb walls on dark nights, or whisper shameful suggestions to fine ladies on the sly? If one must sin, then why not do it gaily, aristocratically and with a good conscience? You must be very Latin not to understand that."

"It isn't sin I miss, Manuel," I said. "I miss only the love I have lost."

Manuel shook his head and his manner became once more submissively melancholy.

"Sin is always sin, in whatever guise it may appear, and whether one calls it love or pleasure. The result is the same. You do but weary yourself, master, by inflaming your feelings thus. Not the most alluring sin is worth the necessity of sewing up one's own hide with needle and thread. You disappoint me, master; I thought you had more sense. But common sense is not given one as a christening present, even when one's born with purple boots."

At the same instant I seized him by the back of the neck and forced him to his knees in the dust of the court. My dagger flashed red in the sunset—but I controlled myself.

"What was that you said?" I demanded. "Repeat it if you dare!"

Manuel was very frightened, and his lean neck quailed in my grasp. Yet it seemed as if after the first shock he accepted my violence as an honor. Lifting his watery gaze and dusty beard with a look of shrewd obstinacy, he assured me, "I never meant to wound you, master. I did not think you would be angered by a jest."

But he had phrased his words too cunningly for me to believe this. At the very end of his long rigmarole he had set a bait for me, to see if I would snap at it. What had become of my self-control? Where was my calm? I slapped the dagger back into its sheath.

"You don't know what you're saying, Manuel," I told him. "For a moment the angel of death stood at your back."

He remained on his knees before me as if enjoying this humiliating posture.

"Master!" he cried. His eyes shone and his gray cheeks

slowly reddened. "You have laid your hand on my head and my earache has gone. My knees no longer hurt me, though I kneel here on the damp ground. Master, is that not proof enough of who you are?"

"You're raving," I said. "You were afraid of my dagger. A sudden fright drives other pains away."

He hung his head, picked up a handful of earth and let it fall again. His voice was so low that I could barely catch the words. "When I was a little boy I saw the Emperor Manuel many times," he whispered. "Master, I will never fail you." He raised his hand as if he would have touched my hip, and stared at my feet as if bewitched. "Purple boots," he whispered to himself. "You laid your hand on my head and the pains of my decrepitude are gone."

The last blood-red reflection of the sunset faded, and evening brought dusk and chill. I could no longer distinguish Manuel's face. I said nothing. I was very much alone. I turned and regained the warmth of my house.

Ink and paper. Formerly I loved the sweet smell of ink and the dry rustle of paper; now I hate them. Words are only similes, as are all temporal things—only clumsy symbols of things spiritual which everyone interprets as he chooses, according to his mind and nature. No words can express the infinite.

There are still ships in the harbor, and with good luck a western vessel can still sail unmolested through the Dardanelles and out into the Aegean. There is no Latin who cannot be bought. But it was my heart's fever that made me fling the jewels at Giustiniani—my heart's fever that made me strip off my riches once more, like a tight garment. Now I'm too poor to bribe a ship's captain and sail in pursuit. Was that what I feared? Was that why I threw away my precious stones? Nothing comes about by chance—nothing. All things follow an appointed pattern and no one can escape his fate. Man makes his fate come true as surely as a sleepwalker, once he has made his choice.

Did I fear myself? Mistrust myself? Did Mohammed know me better than I did when he thrust the leather bag into my hand as a bait, at our parting? Was it because of that, that I had to free myself from his gift?

Sultan Mohammed the conqueror! I have only to take the ferry across to Pera and enter the house with a dovecot in its courtyard—and betray. Betray again.

So fathomless a despair as this I have never known. The choice is never done with, but presents itself hourly until the last breath is drawn. The door stands ever open: the door of flight, betrayal and self-deception.

By the marsh at Varna the angel of death said to me, "We shall meet at the Gate of St. Romanos." Hitherto these words have been my comfort. But he did not say which side of the gate. He did not say.

Nor need he. All my life I have broken out of one prison into another. From this last prison I will not escape—not this one, whose walls are the walls of Constantinople. I am the son of my father; this prison is my only home.

7 March 1453

Early in the morning, before sunrise, a crowd of black-clad monks, nuns and poor women, carrying lit tapers, made their way to the church of the Khora convent, near the Palace of Blachernae and the Kharisios Gate. They sang, but their chant was swallowed up in the silence of the city and the dusk of dawn. I went with them. The roof and walls of the church are one vast mosaic: the colored stones blazed from a golden ground in the light of countless wax candles, and there was a smell of incense. The glowing devotion of the worshipers was balm to my heart.

Why did I go with them? Why did I kneel by their side? I have seen plenty of monks and nuns before; they go in couples from house to house with their begging-bowls, collecting alms for the poor refugees who have been pouring into the city in flight from the Turks.

All nuns look alike and it is impossible to distinguish one from another. There are both aristocratic and base-born women among them: solitary women of well-to-families who have bought themselves a place in some convent, or lay sisters who offer up the lowly work of their hands without taking the veil. They enjoy greater freedom than nuns in the west. Greeks also allow their priests to marry and to wear beards.

All nuns are alike: they wear the same black cloak which hides the curves of their figure, and the same veil which conceals the face up to the eyes. Yet unconsciously, without looking, I noticed one nun who followed me in the street and stopped when I turned around. She passed my house with her companion, and paused beside the little stone lion to look at my windows. But she did not knock to ask for alms.

Since then I have carefully scrutinized every nun I meet. Something in the carriage of the head, in the walk, and in the hands that hide themselves in the wide sleeves would make her known to me among all the rest.

I dream dreams and see visions. Despair has made me blind and I believe the impossible. A hope that I dare not own scorches my mind like the flame of a candle.

10 March 1453

These last days I have been living in dreams and delirium. This morning the two nuns again passed my house and halted to look up at my windows as if expecting me to come out. I tore downstairs, flung open the door and stood panting before them, unable to speak. They drew back and bowed their heads. One of them held out her wooden dish and murmured the usual prayer.

"Enter my house, sisters," I said. "My purse is within."

Hidden behind the older nun she kept her head bent, that I might not see her eyes, and both women tried to withdraw. Self-restraint deserted me; I seized her by the arm and she could not resist. Manuel came running out aghast.

"Master, are you out of your mind?" he shouted. "You'll be stoned by the mob if you assault a nun."

The older woman struck me in the face with her bony fist and began thumping my head with the wooden dish, but she dared not scream.

"Come in," I said. "We're attracting attention."

"Your commanding officer will have you hanged," said the elder nun threateningly, yet she turned as if in doubt and looked at her companion. The companion nodded; she could not do otherwise, for I was holding her arm.

When Manuel had locked the door behind us I said, "I recognized you—I recognized you among thousands! Is it really you? How is this possible?"

Trembling she tore herself free and said hastily to the other, "There is some mistake or misunderstanding. I must clear it up. Please stay here."

From this I realized that she was no true nun—she had taken no vows, or she could not have remained alone with me. I led her into my room and bolted the door. I tore the veil from her face and took her in my arms.

Took her in my arms.

Only then did I too begin to tremble, and to weep. So terrible had been my despair, my desire and my doubt. Now all was released. I am forty, on the threshold of autumn. But I was shaken by convulsive sobbing, like a child returning from a nightmare to the security of its home.

"My beloved," I said. "How could you do it to me?"

She let her hood slip from her head and threw off the black cloak as if ashamed of it. She was very pale. She had not had her hair cropped. She was no longer trembling. Her eyes were a clear gold, proud and curious. She stroked my cheek with her fingertips and looked at them as if wondering why they were wet.

"What is the matter, John Angelos?" she asked. "Are you weeping? Have I been unkind?"

Words failed me; I could only look at her, knowing that my face was alight as in the days of my youth. She cast down her brown eyes beneath my gaze.

"I really thought I was rid of you." She tried to go on, but the words caught in her throat and a flush mounted to her neck and cheeks. She turned her back on me, and surrendered. I laid my hand on her shoulders; my hands slid down to her breast, and breathlessly I felt her loveliness and the quivering awakening of her body. I drew her to me and her proud head leaned on my shoulder. I kissed her mouth and it was as if she uttered her whole soul in that kiss. A fresh, vibrant joy flooded through me, and there was no darkness left. My desire was as limpid as a spring, as pure as a flame.

I said, "You came back to me."

"Let me go," she entreated. "My knees are trembling. I can't stand on my feet."

She sank into a chair, rested her elbows on the table and her forehead in her hands. After a while she raised her eyes. So familiar, so naked, the brown eyes looked into mine.

"I'm better now," she said in a voice that shook. "For a moment I was afraid that I should die in your arms. I didn't know—I couldn't guess that it would feel like that.

"Or perhaps I did know," she went on, looking at me as if she could not gaze her fill, "and that's why I stayed in the city, although I had sworn never to see you again. I swore, so that I might dare to stay. I was childish enough to think I could hoodwink myself."

She shook her head. Her hair was of gold, her skin of ivory. The high blue arches of her brows, the golden-brown tenderness in her eyes. . . .

"I avoided you, I wanted to shun you—but I had at least to see you sometimes, if only at a distance. Soon I expect I should have come to you of my own accord. As a nun I have more liberty than ever in my life before. I can move freely about, talk freely with poor people, feel the dust of the street under my feet, hold out a wooden dish and receive alms in return for a blessing. John Angelos, I've learned much during these days. I have been preparing myself for you, all unawares."

She put out her bare foot. The leather sole of the sandal was fastened with leather straps about her ankle, and the straps had chafed her white skin. Her foot was dusty from the street; it was the living foot of a living being. She was no longer a painted idol; she was changed.

"But how is it possible?" I asked. "I saw your father that night. He sent for me, and he told me that you had sailed."

"Father doesn't know," she said simply. "He still thinks I went. I bought myself a place in a convent where noble ladies sometimes make a retreat. There I am just a paying guest called Anna; no one asks me my name or family. It would mean trouble for the convent if I were to be discovered, so my secret is their secret too. If I wanted to stay there for the rest of my life I should be given a new name—I should be born again and no one need ever know who I once was. You alone know—and that could not be helped."

"You surely don't mean to stay in the convent for good!" I exclaimed aghast.

She looked at me guilelessly through her eyelashes. "I have committed a great sin," she said, affecting an air of guilt. "I have deceived my father. Perhaps I must do penance."

I still did not understand how one so jealously guarded as she was could have made her escape. She told me her father wanted to send her to Crete, to prevent her capture by Turks or Latins. But her mother still lay ill and could not go, and so the whole plan was repugnant to her from the beginning. She was rowed out to the ship with baggage and servants under cover of darkness, to find it full of fugitives who had paid dizzy sums for their passage. In the general confusion she had crept back to the boat and made the boatmen take her ashore. When the moorings were cast off the servants still believed her to be aboard, and it would be long before her father learned of her disappearance.

"I am free," she said. "They are welcome to think I fell overboard and drowned, for it would be a greater sorrow to my father to know I had deceived him. I dare not even think of that."

For a long time we sat silently looking at one another. It was enough. I felt as if the least thing more than that—a smile, or a touch—would have burst my heart. I understood what she meant by saying she was afraid she might die in my arms.

Then bony knuckles beat upon the door, and the harsh voice of the elder nun cried in agitation, "Are you still there, Sister Anna?"

I heard Manuel trying in vain to calm her.

"I'm just coming," cried Anna in reply; then turned to me, touched my cheek and said with a radiant look, "Now I must go."

But she could not go at once. She rose on tiptoe to see better into my eyes, and asked softly, "Are you happy, John Angelos?"

I answered, "I am happy. And you, Anna Notaras—are you happy too?"

She said, "I am very, very happy."

She opened the door and the elder nun rushed in brandishing the wooden dish. Anna slipped her hand soothingly under her arm and led her away. I took Manuel's head between my hands and kissed him on both cheeks.

"The Lord bless you and keep you," I said.

"You also, and may He be gracious to your soul," he returned when he had recovered from his astonishment. "A nun!" he said with laughter in his eyes, and he shook his head. "A nun in your room! Does this mean you're forsaking the Latins at last and embracing the only true faith?"

15 March 1453

Spring has blossomed everywhere in the city. Barefooted children sell flowers at street-corners and boys play reed pipes among the ruins. There is no sound more beautiful and plaintive than this music. I bless every day that glides by—I bless every day I am allowed to live.

The elder nun is called Khariklea; her father was a shoemaker and could read. But her face does not match her name, says my servant Manuel. At meals she readily unveils her face before him, he tells me. She likes to eat meat and drink wine. She is only a lay sister and is glad to get her alms-dish filled with so little trouble. Manuel has explained to her that before the Turks come I desire to renounce my false Latin doctrine, that I may receive the Body of Christ in leavened bread and recite the only true creed without interpolations. To this end, he says, I am receiving instruction from Sister Anna.

I don't know what she thinks about us, but she has taken Sister Anna under her wing and regards her as a learned and distinguished lady, whose conduct it would ill become a lay sister to comment upon.

Today Giustiniani sent me to the Golden Gate to supervise the military exercises, and Anna and Khariklea brought me a basket of food. This attracted no attention: many others had their noon meal brought to them, for it is a long way in to the city from the marble towers of the Gate. The young monks are allowed to eat at St. John the Baptist's monastery; they are dispensed from fasting and have grown sunburned and sturdy from their exercises. Readily they roll their sleeves and kilt up their black habits as they listen to the bragging of their instructors. During rest intervals they sing Greek hymns in parts. It is very beautiful.

Only imperial triumphal processions may pass through the Golden Gate; it has not been opened within the memory of man. Now it has been walled up for the duration of the siege. We sat on the grass in the shadow of the ramparts; we broke bread, ate and drank together. Khariklea grew drowsy; she moved a little apart and lay down to sleep with her veil over her face. Anna took off her sandals—the hard leather had chafed her feet until they bled—and plunged her white toes into the grass.

"I've not been so free and so happy as this since my childhood," she said.

A hawk circled high up in the radiant blue spring sky. Sometimes the Emperor's falconers send up their birds to chase Egyptian pigeons. As if that were any use. Slowly, searchingly, the hawk wheeled overhead.

Anna drew her slender forefinger through the grass and said without looking at me, "I have learned compassion for poor people." After a little while she went on. "People trust the nun's habit. They confide their troubles and fears to me—they talk as to an equal, which is something quite new for me. 'What is the good of all this?' they say. 'The Sultan's warriors are beyond counting. His artillery can flatten the mightiest walls with a single shot. Emperor Constantine is an apostate and has delivered himself into the hands of the Pope. He has sold his birthright and his city for a mess of pottage. And to what end? The Sultan does not threaten our religion; in his cities Greek priests are free to serve their Christian communities. It's only church and monastery bells that he forbids. Under the Sultan's protection our faith would be secure from Latin heretics. Turks never molest poor folk, so long as they pay their dues—and the taxes imposed by the Sultan are much less severe than the Emperor's. Why should a people perish or be enslaved just for the benefit of the Emperor and the Latins? Only the rich and noble have reason to dread the Turks.' Thus freely do many troubled people talk."

Still she did not look at me, and I stiffened. What did she want of me—why was she talking like this?

"Must our city either be sacked or become a vassal state to the Latins?" she asked. "All these little people only want to live—to work with their clever hands, bring children into the

world and cherish their religion. Is any cause great enough to be worth dying for? They have only this one life—this one little mortal life. I am sorry for them."

"You talk like a woman," I said.

It was for her to stiffen now.

"I am a woman—and what then?" she demanded. "Even women may have wisdom and sense. There have been times when this city was governed by women, and those times were better than most. If women were in control today we should send away the Latins with their guns and galleys, and the Emperor with them."

"Better the Turkish turban than the Papal miter," I suggested maliciously. "Do you speak with your father's tongue?" As I looked at her I had an alarming suspicion.

"Anna," I said, "I thought I knew you, but perhaps I was mistaken. Is it true that you stayed in the city without your father's knowledge? Will you swear to it?"

"That's an insult!" she cried. "Why should I swear? Is my word not good enough? If I speak with my father's tongue it's because I've come to understand him better than before. He is a greater statesman than the Emperor, and loves his people more than those who for the sake of the Latins are ready to lay the city in ruins and let the people perish. He is my father. No one else would dare to defy the Emperor and proclaim his convictions aloud, as he did the day you and I met. Allow me to be proud of my father."

My face felt stiff; even my lips were cold and rigid.

"That was a cheap, demagogue's trick," I said softly. "Unworthy angling for popular favor. He defied no one. On the contrary, he chose to drift with the current. He won a temporal advantage at the expense of his soul; for it was no impulse; it was a deliberate attempt to stir up the people."

Anna stared at me incredulously.

"Are you a supporter of the Union, then?" she demanded. "Are you a Latin at heart, and is your Greek blood a lie?"

"And if it were so," I said, "which would you choose, your father or me?"

Her cheeks were white and the corners of her mouth were so tense that she looked ugly. For a moment I thought she would strike me; but she let her hand fall and made an awkward gesture with it.

"I don't believe you: you're no Latin. But what have you against my father?"

My self-restraint was swept away by jealous doubt and fury.

"Is he asking the question or are you?" I demanded roughly. "Is it he who has sent you to try me, because he was unable to win me over to his side?"

Anna sprang up and brushed a few blades of grass violently from her hands, as if wanting to shake herself free of me. The contempt in her brown eyes burned into my soul. She was near tears.

"I shall never forgive you this!" she cried, and rushed blindly away, forgetful of her sandals; she struck her bare foot against a stone, fell and broke out sobbing. I did not hurry to her; I felt no sympathy with her tears. Suspicion was seething within me in cloudy, troubled eddies, and rose like gall into my throat. Perhaps she was acting. Perhaps she hoped I would relent and stoop to dry her deceiving tears.

After a moment she rose, hanging her head and wiping her face with her sleeve. Khariklea sat up and looked at us in amazement.

"I forgot my sandals," Anna said tonelessly, and stooped to pick them up. I set my foot on them. Her feet were bleeding and I turned away my eyes.

"Wait," I said. "We must discuss this further. You know me,

but you don't know everything about me and never can. I have the right to mistrust everyone—even you."

"It was my own choice," she said through clenched teeth, trying to pull away her sandals. "Fool that I am, it was my own choice. I fancied you loved me."

I took her head between my hands and forced her to stand up before me, though she resisted. She is stronger than I thought, but I made her turn her face to me. She closed her eyes so as not to see me, so bitterly did she hate me at that moment. No doubt she would have spat in my face if she had not been so well brought up.

"We must get to the bottom of this," I said. "So you don't trust me, Anna Notaras."

She hissed at me impotently, as the tears escaped from between the closed lids and rolled down her cheeks. But she managed to utter, "How can I trust you when you don't trust me? I should never have believed this of you."

"Why did you say what you did just now?" I retorted. "Perhaps you weren't speaking for your father; I take that back, and beg your pardon. But do you yourself in your inmost heart believe that I am still in the Sultan's service? As your father—as everyone believes? All except Giustiniani, that is, who is sharper than any of you. You must, or you would never have said that to me. You wanted to test me."

She relented very slightly.

"What I said was sensible enough," she said. "I wanted to sort out my own thoughts—and perhaps I wanted to know yours. I meant no harm by it. It's what the people are saying, at any rate; you can't alter that."

I released her, regretting my violence. She did not pick up her sandals.

"Talk like that must stop," I said vehemently. "A man who speaks so is a traitor, even though an unconscious one. It benefits no one but the Sultan—and he knows no mercy. I don't doubt he's generous with hints and promises, and lets his envoys spread them abroad, but he has no intention of standing by more of them than may suit his plans. Courage is the only thing he respects. Compliance he regards as cowardice, and for the weak and cowardly there is no room in his Empire. The man who talks of submission or pins his faith on the Sultan digs his own grave.

"Can't you see, beloved?" I cried, shaking her by the shoulders. "He means to make Constantinople his capital—to make it a Turkish city and transform its churches into mosques! In his Constantinople there will be no room for Greeks, except as slaves, and so he will have to raze the Greek state to its foundations. That is what he wants to do, and he won't be content with less—and why should he? Here he can rule both east and west. Therefore we have no choice but to fight—fight to the last drop of our blood—fight even after all hope has fled. If the Empire of a thousand years is to fall, then let it be with honor! That is the only truth. It would be better for the mothers in this city to dash their children's heads against the stones than to talk of submission. Whoever bows to the Sultan bows to the headsman's sword, whether he be rich or poor. Believe me, beloved—do believe me! I know Sultan Mohammed, and I would rather seek death among you here than follow him. I do not want to survive Greek Constantinople."

She shook her head, tears of anger and humiliation still glistening in her eyes. Her cheeks were flaming. She was like a young girl who has been undeservedly scolded by her teacher.

"I believe you," she said. "I must. But I don't understand."

She pointed: far away above the vast conglomeration of gray and yellow houses rose the gigantic Dome of St. Sophia. She carried her hand around: beyond the fields of ruins many other domes dominated the sea of buildings. And close beside us soared the great sunlit ramparts, golden-brown with age, higher than the highest stone-built house, running northward across hills and hollows until they vanished, with the whole huge city in their protecting embrace.

"I don't understand," she repeated. "This city is far too big, far too ancient, far too rich even in its poverty and decline, to be sacked and wiped out. Hundreds of thousands of people have their homes here; they cannot all be slain or sold into slavery. Constantinople is far too big to be filled with Turks. A hundred, two hundred years ago they were robbers and shepherds; they need us to build up an enduring Empire. The Sultan is an enlightened man who speaks both Greek and Latin. Why should he wish us harm if he succeeds in capturing the city? Why should he slay his own subjects? I don't understand. We're no longer living in the days of Genghis Khan or Tamerlane."

"You don't know Mohammed." There was nothing else I could say, futile though it might sound. "He has read all about Alexander the Great, he has studied Greek histories and Arabian tales. The Gordian knot was too complex to be untied. Constantinople is the Gordian knot of the Turks: a tangled skein of east and west, Greek and Latin, hatred and mistrust, public and private intrigue, treaties broken and honored—all the tortuous, centuries-old politics of Byzantium. That knot can be loosed only by a blow of the sword. There are no innocent or guilty—there is only a people under the shadow of the sword."

I remembered Mohammed's glowing face and the glint in his eyes as he read the Greek story of the Gordian knot and from time to time asked me the meaning of some word he did not understand. At that time Sultan Murad was still alive: a fat, melancholy little man with blue lips and cheeks, swollen with drink and very short of breath. He died at the festive board among his beloved poets and scholars. He was just and merciful, and pardoned even his enemies, being weary of war. He had conquered Thessalonica, he had been compelled to besiege Constantinople, he had been victorious at Varna; yet he had never wanted war. War was repugnant to him. But he had begotten a wild beast to succeed him, and during his last years he was conscious of this. He found it hard to meet his son's eyes, so alien was he.

But how could I have explained all this, which had become a part of my experience in the course of seven years?

"Sultan Murad had no belief in power," I said. "In his eyes a ruler was little more than a blind man set to lead other blind men. An instrument, a means to serve developing forces and pressures, a tool which could neither steer nor stave off events. He enjoyed the beauty of life, he loved women, poems and wine. In his old age he used to wander about with a rose in his hand and his head muzzy with wine, and then even beauty seemed but vanity in his eyes. He believed that he was nothing but dust. He believed that the universe was but a grain of dust in the vortex of the infinite. Nevertheless he performed his devotions, honored Islam and its teachers, built mosques and founded a university in Adrianople. His contemporaries looked up to him as a devout man and a builder of the state. But he only smiled sadly when men praised his victories and his statesmanship.

"Murad had no belief in power," I repeated. "In his eyes, life—even a ruler's life—was no more than a spark blown by the wind into the darkness, and extinguished. But Mohammed believes in power. He believes that with his will he can rule events. He has more intelligence and intuition than Murad. He knows. For him there is neither right nor wrong, neither truth nor lies. He is ready to wade through blood if it suits his schemes.

"And he is wise," I went on with lowered voice. "He is right. The suffering and death of a hundred, a thousand, a hundred thousand people is no more than that of one. Numbers measure finite things—they are merely arithmetic. The only measure for suffering and death is Man, the chalice that holds an ocean. That is why Christ with His suffering and death could redeem the sins of the world. In the realm of Christ it matters not whether one Greek or two hundred thousand Greeks perish by the sword. Numbers and figures are significant only for him who would rule the finite world: for such a man people are only numbers seen in relation to other numbers; they are not human beings."

Anna raised her head.

"What are you trying to prove?" she asked impatiently.

"Beloved," I said. "I am only trying by means of feeble, inadequate words to tell you that I love you more than anything in the world. I love you despairingly, inconsolably. You are my Greece. You are my Constantinople. In the fullness of time Constantinople must fall, just as your body will one day be dissolved. That is why earthly love is so comfortless. When we love we are more acutely the prisoners of time and space than at any other moment. Within you dwells the desperate longing of all temporal things—the longing to endure.

"Beloved," I said. "When I look at you I can perceive the skull through your cheeks. Through your soft flesh I see the skeleton, just as when in my youth I was awakened by the nightingale, beside the churchyard wall. Love is a slow death. When I take you in my arms, when I kiss your mouth, it is death I am kissing. So madly, so terribly, do I love you."

But she didn't understand.

So I said, "You have hurt your foot because of me. I bring you nothing but pain and suffering. Let me help you."

I picked up her sandals; she leaned on my arm and I led her away to the great water-cistern. It was hard for her to walk, and the thistles pricked the tender soles of her feet. I supported her and she trusted me—her body trusted me, albeit her proud, defiant thoughts rebelled.

I helped her to sit comfortably on the edge of the leaky cistern, and washed her feet. I washed the blood from her wounded feet. I bathed her bare feet—until suddenly she turned pale as from some inward pang, and drew away.

"Don't do that," she said. "Don't—I can't bear it."

She was in my power. Somewhere in the distance a goatherd was playing his reed pipe; the thin, shrill notes cut me to the heart. The sun blazed down. I touched the calf of her leg; its white skin was alive and warm. If I had pressed her to me then and kissed her she could not have withstood me, even if she had wanted to. But she was not afraid of me. She looked at me with that direct, brown gaze of hers.

"Stand up," I said. "Lean against me while I fasten your sandals."

"My face is burning," she said. "It will be burned red because I haven't veiled it from you. My feet are red now, through going unshod in all weathers."

I bless every day I am allowed to live.

When she had gone and the training-exercises were resumed, we fired off a heavy cannon from the top of the wall. Giustiniani wanted to accustom the recruits to the noise, flash and smoke, to prove to them that gunfire is more alarming than dangerous, as he himself believes. One of the Emperor's technicians had mounted the gun as firmly as possible on the wall; it fired according to calculations, hurling a stone ball the size of a man's head in a high arc over the outer wall and the ditch, and fell, shaking the ground. But the great wall shook more. A long crack ran up it and big stones fell to the ground; and although no one was hurt, the incident confirmed what Giustiniani had said: that cannon are more dangerous for those who use them than for the enemy. It had a depressing effect, and monks and artisans stared at the fissure unwilling to believe their eyes, for it showed them how illusory was the impregnability of that massive wall.

Beyond the ramparts the countryside lies waste as far as the eye can see. Trees have been felled to give a clear view, and the stumps of cypresses and plane trees gleam white against the brown and green of the earth. Even the fruit trees have been cut down, and all houses have been demolished so as to leave neither cover nor materials for the besiegers. Somewhere far away beyond the horizon a black pillar of smoke rose against the sky as if from a burning building; otherwise there was no sign of life in all that desolate land.

The drawbridge has not yet been destroyed, so I ordered the partly blocked gate to be opened, and sent a few men out to fetch the cannon ball. Even the most able stonemason needs at least a day to shape hard stone into a ball of given diameter. I placed archers on the turrets and behind the crenelations of the outer wall, just as if we were making a real sortie. The men I sent out felt unprotected, and glanced about in fear as soon as they left the shelter of the ramparts. But they soon plucked up courage, went out and dug up the ball, and brought it back with them.

Some of them took a refreshing swim in the moat; as this has only recently been finished, the water is still clean. This ditch is a good thirty paces wide and of equal depth, and is kept supplied by cleverly built underground conduits from the sea and from big reservoirs at different points in the city.

It is dammed at intervals, so that it cannot run dry, and lies like a string of pools between the city and the surrounding country. Before the Palace of Blachernae it comes to an end, for here the ground falls steeply away to the bay. Instead, walls and bastions are more massive at this point, and the palace buildings are incorporated in the *enceinte* to form a continuous fortress all the way down to the shore.

But the great wall was cracked today by the firing of a single cannon from the battlements.

18 March 1453

We do not talk politics any longer, she and I; we keep our thoughts to ourselves. Her body believes me, her heart does not.

I felt it my duty to tell Giustiniani what the townsfolk think. It left him quite unmoved. He looked at me as if I were an idiot.

"Of course no one in his senses wants war," he said, "It's natural for women to want to keep their children and their men, their homes and belongings. If I were a merchant or a peasant, an ivory carver or a weaver of silk, nothing would induce me to start a war. I've seen enough of it. But when it comes to the point, the people don't matter. Ten men in plate armor can control up to a thousand civilians; the Romans taught us that. The people are of no importance; they'll shout what they're told to shout, they're like oxen led blindfold to the slaughter.

"The first thing I did when I received the protostrator's staff," he went on, "was to collect and register all weapons in the city. This order applied to rich and poor alike. The sons of archons had to hand in their fine crossbows, all inlaid with ivory, and the butchers their cleavers. Now arms must be handed in each day after the exercises, and only sentries may keep their equipment. Everyone may practice with his chosen weapons, but may not take them home. An unarmed population is not dangerous. In coming here I came to a place seething with hatred and mistrust of the Latins, and I have transformed it into a quiet and orderly city, whose inhabitants are doggedly learning to defend themselves under Latin tuition. That in itself is a military feat, is it not? No, have no concern about the townsfolk, Jean Ange. They will fight for their lives and I shall see to it that once battle is joined no one will think of treachery.

"Our own seamen, kept idle, are a far greater peril," he continued. "Their headstrong violence does damage, and annoys both Latins and Greeks." He gave me an amused look and rubbed his big hands. "I had a great deal of trouble in persuading the Emperor to set them to work. Why should he hire idlers at three thousand ducats a month? The Greek laborers demand payment for every stone they drag to the walls and every basketful of earth they carry from one place to another. That's only right and natural; they are poor men who must support themselves and their families. But every thrust of the spade costs the Emperor money, while the sailors do nothing but play their flutes and caper about the deck all day long. The Emperor is loath to fall foul of the Venetian skippers, and on their part they shield their men from all labor not directly benefiting the vessels. But at last I had contrived to have Aloisio Diedo put in command of the fleet.

"In command of the whole fleet and the harbor," he repeated with emphasis. "This means that early on Monday morning all the big galleys will be rowed into the Golden

Horn and drop anchor by the Blachernae, in Kynegion harbor. There picks, shovels and earth-baskets lie in readiness. It will be the task of the ship's companies to dig a ditch from the Wood Gate to the Tower of Anemas, where the ground is level. It would be mad to let the Turks crawl on their bellies so near the harbor, almost to the Blachernae walls, perhaps mining beneath the palace. I have heard that the Sultan has summoned not only Serbian cavalry but also Serbian miners."

It is evident that Giustiniani had had other information about the Sultan's plans, since he deems it necessary to embark, at the eleventh hour, on so formidable a task as the digging of a new ditch. But I paid little heed to this; the most startling piece of news was the thrusting aside of Lukas Notaras. Naturally the Latin shipowners and captains do not acknowledge Greek authority, but I marveled that the Emperor dared at this stage to offer the Grand Duke so grievous an affront.

"Week after week Lukas Notaras has been expecting you to confer with him," I said, "and now without asking him you have set him aside. How dare you do it?"

Giustiniani threw out his hands and cried eagerly, "Far from it, far from it! Emperor Constantine, his advisers and I were quite at one in deciding that so noted and experienced a strategist as Lukas Notaras should bear a worthier part in the city's defense. What can he do with his worm-eaten dromonds, since the Latins are resolved to retain command of their own vessels? No, he has been promoted. He will have a considerable stretch of wall to defend."

I could hardly believe my ears.

"Are you all mad?" I cried. "Why do you lead him into that temptation? It's unfair both to him and to the city. He has openly declared that he would rather submit to the Sultan than to the Pope."

Giustiniani eyed me merrily.

"That cannot be helped," he said. "It's a perfectly voluntary and unanimous decision. Lukas Notaras is to command a good quarter of the perimeter. Who are we to reject anyone for his honest convictions? Away with mutual mistrust! We extend a brotherly hand to him—we shall stand shoulder to shoulder in the defense of this superb city."

"Are you drunk?" I demanded. "Has Emperor Constantine finally taken leave of his senses?"

Giustiniani pretended to wipe a tear from his eye. He found it hard to contain himself.

"This promotion will help Megadux Notaras to swallow the loss of his dromonds," he continued, still grimacing. "Aloisio Diedo's first step to insure the safety of the harbor was to remove all small and unserviceable craft; the Emperor's galleys will therefore be unrigged and beached. Their crews will form a welcome reinforcement for Notaras, since I hardly think I can spare him any of my men.

"Don't be uneasy," he went on. "Many other vessels are to be either scuttled or beached; for if they were to break loose from their moorings or catch fire during the fighting they might damage the warships. Moreover, once they are rendered useless they can offer no temptation of escape for anyone, should events take a bad turn. In this way all will be plain sailing. Aloisio Diedo is a clever fellow, for all he's a Venetian."

"So in fact you're driving the Megadux into the Sultan's arms," I remarked. "You're tempting him along a path which as a Greek and a patriot he might nevertheless have hesitated to tread. You take the harbor from him—you take away the ships which he has fitted out at his own charges. You are still further embittering an embittered man. I do not understand this policy—yours and the Emperor's."

"We're not taking the harbor from him," Giustiniani returned, with an air of injured innocence. "On the contrary, it's the harbor wall that he is to defend. His sector extends from the Venetian concession to the Palace of Blachernae—the whole length of the inner harbor wall: at least five thousand paces. I am contenting myself with a modest thousand paces of the landward wall."

I had no need to consult a map to understand. With the Latin vessels guarding the entrance to the harbor, no assault could threaten the inner wall along the Golden Horn; a handful of sentries would suffice to guard the whole of it, and to keep an eye on the shipping in the harbor. This part of the perimeter would be the safest of any, unless the Turks grew wings, and command of it would be an empty honor.

When at last I saw the point, Giustiniani burst into a roar of laughter; he squirmed, groaned and thumped his knees with both fists.

"Now do you see?" he stuttered, wiping away the tears. "It's a huge sector—much longer than any other officer has under his command. Notaras will be obliged to put a good face on the matter, even if he sees what it means. And of course he sees; he's not a fool."

"You've thrown your distrust of him in his face, thinly disguised as a mark of distinction," I remarked. "Perhaps you're wise. Perhaps."

Giustiniani stopped laughing and regarded me inquiringly. "We're depriving Notaras of an opportunity for treachery," he said gravely. "Once the siege has begun he will be tied to his wall, unable to stab us in the back even if he wished. Why aren't you pleased? It was you who warned me about him."

Logically he is right. Logically he has hit on the most discreet way of rendering Notaras harmless. Then why am I dissatisfied?

19 March 1453

Today the great galleys were rowed into Kynegion harbor, with pennants fluttering, horns bellowing and drums rumbling. Seamen and soldiers came ashore in good order, and having been given picks, shovels and baskets, were marched off in parties under their own standards; they passed out through the wall by the Hebdomon Palace. Here Emperor Constantine, dressed in purple and gold, awaited them on horseback and bade them welcome.

The ditch, which is to be a good hundred paces long, was already measured and marked out, and the ships' captains thrust their standards into the ground at the points allotted them. It was to be eight feet wide and eight feet deep: an easy enough task for close to two thousand men. At a sign from the Emperor, waiting servants broached scores of wine-jars, whereupon each man might go and pour himself a measure of wine. Little wonder, then, if they set to work singing and vied with one another in digging and in filling the baskets, which others carried off at the run for the reinforcement of the outer wall. It was a fine sight, and many people gathered to watch. The presence of the Emperor spurred even captains, mates and shipowners to bear a hand.

By sunset the work was nearly complete, and only a little piece of undug ground separated the end of the ditch from the water. Certainly this ditch is not to be compared with the great ditch or moat whose walls are bricked, though the sides of this one too are to be revetted with stones and timber, to resist the undermining action of the water.

25 March 1453

The day before yesterday the Sultan marched from Adrianople. Now it is only a question of days.

26 March 1453

Today Anna Notaras said, "This cannot go on."

We don't quarrel now; the clouds of fate loom too darkly over us. Expectation catches everyone by the throat and weighs upon all hearts like a stone. Just so, long ago, did I await death's footsteps, chained to a stone wall. Then I had nothing to lose, nothing to grieve for. Now I may lose her.

"No, it cannot go on," I agreed. "Someone might begin to suspect. You might be recognized. The street has eyes and pillars have ears, and your father may fetch you home."

"I'm not afraid of father," she said. "My nun's habit protects me. That was not what I meant."

We had walked out onto the Point, in the shade of the plane trees of the Acropolis, and were lying in the sun, on the steps of yellowed marble. A lizard scuttled over a stone. Below us the Sea of Marmora glittered like silver, and the Bosporus opened out before us like a dark blue ribbon between heights green with spring. On the other side of the harbor rose the walls of Pera. The cross of Genoa floated from the tower.

Khariklea was not with us; she was washing clothes in my

house and volubly entertaining Manuel with pious legends of the saints. A great deal of wine has been consumed at home lately.

But Anna and I were ill at ease in my room; restlessness drove us out under the open sky. We trusted to luck, despite the risk of detection.

"No, that was not what I meant," she repeated. "You know very well what I do mean."

The sun had reddened her forehead; she stretched out her legs and curled her toes in the grass. Her cheeks flushed and her mouth smiled, but her brown eyes were sad.

"This habit is only a disguise," she said. "I'm no nun. Now that I have left behind me my home, my customs, my family and my upbringing I am better and happier than ever before. Food tastes good. I have never known the wind to fill my lungs so gloriously. I live. I exist. I have a body—and the body troubles me."

"I have respected your religious habit," I said stiffly.

"Yes, indeed—too well," she said in reproach. "You're afraid of committing desecration, and dare not touch me."

"You're enough for me as you are," I said. "We're together. I am forty. I love you. There is no love without desire, but my desire is a clear flame. I do not need to touch you."

She fingered her sleeve.

"No love without desire," she repeated. "I haven't your age and experience. You may be right: perhaps it isn't worth it. But my shameless body tells me that it is. When you lay your hand on my knee I tremble all over. Why do you not do it any more?"

"I'm no angel," I answered. "Never think that."

"You have great self-control," she said. "I don't tempt you, then?"

She drew up one leg and stroked her bare knee, regarding

me the while under lowered lids. Yet if I had touched her she would have torn herself free—I knew it. She spoke thus only to torment me.

"I committed a great sin when I betrayed my father's trust," she said. "I thought I might expiate it by assuming the habit of a nun and sharing in the convent prayers. I meant never to see you again. I toyed with the idea of cutting my hair off later on, and taking the veil. Tell me, beloved, do people always lie to themselves to get what they want?"

"Human beings are incurable liars," I told her. "They believe what they hope for and persuade themselves that what they desire is right. But in his heart of hearts no one can deceive himself."

"John Angelos," she said thoughtfully, "I think it might be better for both of us if you would marry me." She laid a silencing hand upon my mouth. "It's true that you were married according to the rites of the Latin church, and that your wife is still alive. But what of that? If you will renounce your heresy and recite the only true creed, you may receive baptism a second time. There are any number of priests who in that case would readily regard your earlier marriage as invalid and marry us, if only to vex the Latins."

"But what significance would it have?" I asked. "In my heart I am married to Ghita. I will not break the sacrament. Not even the Pope could release my heart from wedlock entered into of my own free will."

Anna looked at me with hatred under her lowered lashes.

"Then she means more to you than I do," she said. "Is it my fault if you have dissipated your life in the arms of strange women, and then wearied of it? You can't even laugh; if you could, you would marry me. Why do you grudge me my peace of conscience? Your own conscience will never know any peace, whatever you may do."

"Nor would yours," I answered. "A marriage like that would mean nothing. It would be undertaken without your parents' consent and under a false or incomplete name. It could be contested at any time, whether by temporal or ecclesiastical law."

"Contested, yes," she said. "But it would be a legal quibble. Why shouldn't we marry in good faith, even secretly? I could move to your house. In the mornings I should wake naked under the same coverlet. Wouldn't that be worth a little stretching of your absurdly rigid conscience?"

I stared at her.

"You're my sin," I said. "And my sin will be but the greater for breaking the sacrament on your account. In my heart I commit adultery just by looking at you or touching your hand. When first I saw your eyes I recognized you and opened my heart to sin. Why won't you understand me?"

"Why can't you be content to be human, and bargain a little with your conscience?" she retorted obstinately. Yet at the same time her blush grew deeper and deeper and spread over her neck. "It's true that every time I look at you I love you," she confessed. "It's true. In my heart I have sinned with you already, though according to worldly laws I have done no wrong. Don't you see that I want safety for you and me, so that no one can lawfully accuse us if—if anything should happen between us?"

"God be good to us!" I exclaimed. "Our sin will be neither more nor less for our lying together, be our union blessed or unblessed. This is a matter between you and me—we're responsible only to each other. But have I ever once tried to tempt you? That at least you cannot accuse me of."

"You have," she declared. "With your eyes. With your hands. And anyhow this argument is foolish and unnecessary, since we're talking about different things. You're getting on your high horse, as men will, and talking of principles, while I, like a practical woman, am talking about how best to arrange the matter without offending against virtue and decorum more than is necessary."

I could only stare at her.

"So you think it's a foregone conclusion?" I asked.

"Why, of course," she said, eying me through her lashes as if wholeheartedly enjoying my agitation.

"In that case," I said, "what the devil have virtue and decorum to do with it? We're grown people. Soon the Turks will be at the gate—soon the guns will roar. Then come terror and death. In the face of death it is surely a matter of indifference whether or not we're formally married."

"Thank you, my darling, thank you!" she said with feigned delight. "If it really is all the same to you, then as a woman I will of course choose marriage."

I snatched at her, but she threw herself to one side and dragged me down with her onto the grass. Her eyes mocked and she laughed aloud as she resisted me with all her strength. When I pressed her to the ground she tensed her whole body, thrust her head against my breast and with closed eyes whispered, "No, John Angelos, never in this life. You will never win me by force—not until you have renounced your Latin heresy and we have been blessed by a Greek priest."

Sweet was our struggle, and it enflamed us. Then all at once she lay still, pale and rigid—she opened her eyes and stared with dilated pupils. Like a flash she sank her teeth in my arm and bit as if she meant to tear away a piece of flesh. I cried out in pain and released her.

"There!" she muttered. "Now do you believe me? Now will you stop plaguing me?"

She sat up, smoothed her hair and remained motionless, with both hands pressed to her cheeks. "Is this I?" she murmured, staring straight before her. "Can this be Anna Notaras —rolling in the grass under a Latin like a tavern wench in a stable? Never, never could I have believed it of myself."

She shook her head. Suddenly she slapped my face and stood up. I understood. The fault was mine.

"I never, never want to see you again," she said between clenched teeth. "I hate you more than anything in the world. I hate your eyes and your mouth and your hands. But more than anything I hate your conscience, and your 'clear flame'! How can you allow yourself to talk such disgraceful nonsense?"

I straightened my clothes in silence.

"You're right, Anna," I owned at last. "We cannot go on like this."

Did I say we never quarreled now?

31 March 1453

The last day of this month. Soon all will be over.

The Emperor dared delay no longer, and today the sailors dug the remainder of their ditch and let in the water. Perhaps the piles and the stone revetment will withstand the wear of the water as long as may be necessary.

As they worked, the men often glanced up at the hills. No flutes or drums could be heard now, and the flags were gone. The Emperor, arrayed in silver armor, rode up onto one of the hills with his guard. But no Turks were to be seen. Their army is huge and marches slowly.

Today the Venetians, headed by the Council of Twelve, walked in procession to the Imperial Palace. The Emperor has entrusted to them the defense of the four gates of the Blachernae, of which he has given them the keys. Constantine himself is nominally in charge of the Gate of St. Romanos, though in fact Giustiniani is responsible both for that and for the Vale of Lykos as far as the Kharisios Gate. Today we have attained the final stage of readiness, and the sentries have been reinforced by many times their original number. Nevertheless, most of the troops are still quartered in the city itself.

After our last meeting, Anna Notaras did not leave the convent for three days. I hardly know whether it was herself or me she wanted to punish. On the third day Khariklea came alone with the alms-dish, and making herself quite at home at the kitchen table she began lamenting the capriciousness of young women. Manuel fetched food for her from the tavern opposite, and after voluble protest she ate it with relish. She seemed to feel that she was abusing my hospitality by coming without Anna, and so I poured wine for her myself to show that she was welcome. She threw out her hands in deprecation, crossed herself and drank three big gobletfuls.

"Sister Anna is praying for guidance," she said. "Sister Anna is afraid of falling into temptation in your house."

"When one is afraid of that one is already in temptation," I replied. "It grieves me to hear this, Sister Khariklea. Tell her that I am far from wishing to tempt or ruin anyone; tell her that as far as I am concerned she is welcome to stay away from my house."

"A-rrh!" exclaimed Sister Khariklea, for this was not at all to her taste. "It's only a whim. What woman ever knows what she wants? It is our lot to withstand many kinds of temptation and seduction in this world. Better then to meet them boldly with one's head held high, rather than dodge them like a coward."

Khariklea's father told her all the Greek stories and myths

he knew. She has a lively imagination and her soul delights in spinning the continued story of Anna and myself. Like all women she is at heart a born procuress. But it is with the best intentions.

I don't know what she may have said to Anna, but next day Anna came with her. As soon as she stepped into my room she tossed her head and threw off her nun's cloak; she had dressed herself once more like a worldly woman of rank. She had painted her lips and cheeks, and colored her brows and lashes blue. Her air was haughty and she addressed me like a stranger.

"Sister Khariklea told me that you were grieved by my absence," she said coldly. "She said you had grown thin and pale in a couple of days, and that your eyes had a wild, feverish look. Naturally I don't want you to fall sick on my account."

"She lied, then," I replied with equal coldness. "I have lacked for nothing. On the contrary, I have known peace and quiet for the first time for many a long day. I have been spared stinging words and the needless pain they cause."

"True, true," she said, clenching her teeth. "What have I to do here? Nothing ails you, it seems. I had better go: I only wanted to assure myself that you were not ill."

"Don't go yet," I said hastily. "Manuel has saved jam and pastry for Khariklea. Let the poor woman eat it. Convent fare is meager enough—you yourself are hollow-cheeked and look as if you have had no sleep."

She went quickly over to my Venetian mirror.

"I can see nothing wrong with my face," she said.

"Your eyes are so bright," I went on. "You're not feverish? Let me feel your neck."

She drew back.

"Certainly not! I'll slap you if you try."

Then she was in my arms. We kissed and caressed one another in unquenchable thirst. We kissed until flames seemed to be shooting through the roof to the very sky. In a delirium of burning desire we kissed until we forgot time and space. She wore no habit to protect her now. Panting, glowing, she kissed me, stroked my head and my shoulders, threw her arms about my waist. But my desire burned in vain: her will and her maidenhood kept watch even when her eyes were closed. Only when I began to tire did she open them, push me away and say in proud triumph, "There, you see—I can at least torment you, if nothing else."

"You torment yourself as much," I answered, my eyes still wet with tears of passion.

"Don't think it," she said. "So long as I know that I can turn your joy to pain I shall feel only delight. You shall see which is the stronger of us two. At first I was bewildered, through inexperience; now I have learned something of your western ways."

With trembling hands she began to smooth her dress and hair before the mirror.

"Don't think I'm so innocent that you can do what you like with me," she said with a defiant smile. "I made that mistake at first and you played upon me as upon a cithara. Now it's my turn to play upon you. We shall see how long you can stand it. I'm a woman of breeding—and grown up too, as you have often pointed out. I'm not to be seduced like any tavern trull."

She seemed transformed. Her very voice was sharp and scornful. I was still trembling; I could make no reply, but only look at her. She shot me a coquettish glance over her shoulder. Ah, her slender white neck, the blue arches of her brows . . . her head rose like a flower from the rich gown; the hyacinth of her cheeks still clung to my palms.

"I don't recognize you," I said at last.

"I hardly recognize myself," she admitted, candid for a moment. "I never knew there were so many sides to me; you seem to have turned me into a woman, Master Jean Ange."

She ran up to me, seized me by the hair with both hands, shook my head violently and kissed me on the mouth—then as suddenly released me.

"It's you who have made me like this," she said softly. "You arouse my evil qualities. But the awakening is not unpleasant; I'm curious to know myself."

She took my limp hand and began abstractedly playing with it, stroking it with her soft fingertips.

"I've heard about western customs," she said. "You told me of some—you told me that even wellborn men and women may bathe and play together in public. That beautiful ladies leave their breasts uncovered and permit their male friends to drop a kiss on the nipple, in courteous greeting. That gay revelers enjoy themselves in couples, to the accompaniment of wine and flutes, and that even married men allow their wives to lie with some good friend and be caressed, so long as nothing worse ensues."

"You have a strange notion of the west," I said. "In every country there are rakes and debauchees and they have their own customs, whether they be Christians or Turks, in Venice or in Constantinople. That is why such people like to journey from place to place under different pretexts. Even pilgrimage is with some merely a pretext, in perplexed and degenerate times, when religion is dead and only its husk remains. The more eagerly a man seeks pleasure, the harder it becomes for him to find fresh delights. In such things there is a limit to man's invention and he is forced to be content with the maddeningly restricted world of the senses. A man without other desires must remain eternally unsatisfied.

"You have a strange notion of the west," I repeated. "I

have met holy men—rich men who distribute their wealth among the poor and enter monasteries, men of rank who renounce their position to live on alms, scholars who ruin their sight in deciphering ancient writings, princes who pay fortunes for a rat-gnawed manuscript, astrologers who spend their lives calculating the course of the heavenly bodies and their influence on men's destiny, merchants who have invented bookkeeping by double entry so that at any moment they can make a complete assessment of their property. In every country there are witless singers and strummers, too. It is only the form of intercourse between men and women that varies."

She seemed hardly to hear. She was turning and twisting in front of the mirror, and now unfastened a brooch in her gown, which she drew down over her shoulders until her breasts were bare. She examined her image critically with her head on one side.

"No," she said, "no, my modesty forbids me to go about like this in front of men. At least I should have to see other women doing it first. Perhaps one would soon get used to it, and then of course there would be no harm."

"You tempt me," I said, and my throat was dry.

"Not in the least," she retorted affectedly, and quickly drew up her gown. "How could I? You who are so hard and clear! How could an inexperienced woman like myself tempt you? You said yourself that you needed fresh diversions. What variety have I to offer?"

Her malice exasperated me, though I had been determined to keep my temper.

"I never said that!" I exclaimed. "I was not talking of myself. On the contrary, I have always avoided women rather than been attracted to them—they only cloud my ideas and dim my vision, and that is why I have kept away. I have begun to loathe their bright eyes and stifling caresses."

Anna Notaras turned and put her hands behind her.

"Stifling caresses!" she repeated. "I hate you!"

"I didn't mean you!" I cried aghast. "Dear God, of course I never meant you."

"You—you profligate Latin! You sapless twig!" She snatched her cloak and wrapped it around her, pulled up the hood and dropped the veil before her face.

"Farewell," she said. "My thanks for all the good counsel. Next time I shall know better."

She was not angry with me; I knew this, though she deliberately clawed my heart across and across with these words of hers. She went her way, not in wrath but in joy, with head erect. She had said "Next time." And I, poor wretch, had thought I knew her as if she had been a part of myself.

1 April 1453

From early morning the bells of church and cloister called the people to prayers of intercession for the city. It has been a radiantly beautiful day—far too beautiful. The mighty harbor boom is completed: the timbers have been renewed and the links repaired and strengthened. It lies in curves along the shore and reaches from the tower of Eugenios to that of St. Mark.

After the service many Sunday strollers went down to the harbor to look at the boom. The round-hewn timbers that are to keep the chain at surface level are so massive that a grown man cannot get his arms around some of them. The links are made of iron as thick as my calf, and if placed on end would reach halfway up my thigh. The balks of timber are fastened end to end with huge hooks. The famous boom placed by the Knights of St. John across the entrance to Rhodes harbor is a toy to this. Not the mightiest vessel could break through it. Parents were showing it to their children, who could easily creep through the links. Even the Emperor rode down with his suite to inspect it. One end is riveted fast to the rock by the Eugenios Tower.

In the afternoon both nuns came hand in hand to my house. The prayers, and the sight of the boom, had imbued Khariklea with fresh courage. She prattled ceaselessly, and told Manuel how the Mother of God and many other saints had shielded Constantinople for generations and sent Turks and other assailants flying. She declared that ever since the Turks built their fortress on the Bosporus, Michael himself, the archangel-strategist with his flaming sword, had left the Bosporus for Constantinople. Many trustworthy witnesses had seen him in the clouds above the Church of the Apostles. His raiment was so dazzling that the beholders were obliged to cover their faces and turn away.

"How many pairs of wings had he?" demanded Manuel eagerly, hoping for an authoritative answer to an old and controversial question.

"No one had time to count them," snapped Khariklea. "The flaming sword dazzled everyone, so that for a long while they could see nothing but glowing disks flying all over the sky."

Thus they chattered on, and from time to time I joined in the conversation, for it was Sunday and fine weather and Anna resolutely refused to enter my room. She sat silent and was again quite changed; she was now enveloped from head to foot in the black habit. She kept even her face covered, and her hands were hidden in the wide sleeves. Whenever I asked her a question she merely shook her head slightly as if she had taken a vow of silence. From the little I could glimpse of her face I saw that she was pale. Her brown eyes gazed at me, large and reproachful; they were ringed with blue shadows and the lids were swollen as if she had wept. In a word, she was doing her best to awaken my sympathy and my self-reproach. When I sought to take her hand she withdrew it, offended. I suspected that she had used white powder and painted blue shadows 'round her eyes, so unnaturally wretched did she look.

When Sister Khariklea had had more wine she glanced sideways at Anna now and then and could not restrain her titters. Anna returned furious looks, which made Khariklea cover her mouth with her hand; but soon she was sniggering again.

At last I could stand it no longer. I dashed forward to Anna, seized her wrists, dragged her to her feet and asked roughly, "Why are you play-acting? What's the meaning of this mummery?"

She pretended to be frightened, and putting a finger to her lips she said, "Hush, the servants will hear you."

As if submitting to the inevitable she shrugged her shoulders and followed me to the stairs, though she still refused to enter my room.

"No, I'm not going to commit that foolishness again," she said. "I must guard my reputation. What will your servant think of me?

"And talking of servants," she went on with mounting vehemence, "you insult me in front of them as if we were already married. And it's unseemly of you to talk nonsense to that foolish woman who misunderstands every word one says. Or is it I who have misunderstood? Perhaps you're in love with her, and I merely provide you with a pretext for meeting her—for giving her wine and making her the victim of your lust when she can no longer defend herself? That is why I did not dare to let her come here alone, although for my own part I never want to see this house again."

"Oh, Anna!" I said beseechingly. "Why do you behave like this? What am I to make of you? Have you gone mad, or am I the imbecile?"

"Well done! Revile me, call me an imbecile!" said Anna relentlessly. "It's my own fault for forsaking home and family, and delivering myself into your hands. I cannot remember when I last had a kind word from you. Nothing pleases you: if I dress according to my rank and breeding you treat me like a harlot. If I try to please you, and behave with modesty and reserve, you curse and insult me, hurt me with your hard hands and drag me to your room as if to assault me. Revile me, by all means, but first pluck the beam from your own eye."

"God pity me for having entangled myself in the toils of such a woman!" I replied, weary and despairing. "I must be a Latin at heart after all, and shall never understand a Greek."

She softened very slightly, opened wide her wonderful eyes and answered, "Don't blame the Greeks; it's women you don't understand. It may be that you're not a rake and a seducer after all, but a quite inexperienced man who knows no better—and therefore no doubt I shall have to forgive you."

"Forgive me!" I exclaimed in a rage. "Which of us is it who has something to forgive? But certainly, certainly—forgive me by all means. I will humbly beg your pardon if only you will make an end of this dodging and doubling. I can stand no more of it. Why do you treat me so?"

Shyly she cast down her eyes, but watched me furtively through her lashes.

"Because I love you, Master John Angelos," she said softly. "Because I love you so terribly that I could weep—and because you're such a child. It may be just that which makes me love you so."

I stared at her incredulously, uncomprehendingly.

"A queer sort of love," I said. She patted my cheek kindly.

"My dear, my only beloved," she said tenderly. "Why are you so obstinate?"

"Obstinate? I?" I was choking with rage, and had to swallow before I could go on. "At least I'm not capricious—all fits and starts, like you!"

"Capricious?" she repeated in a questioning tone, as if seriously considering the word. "Am I really? Certainly I'm not as simple as you in these things. Women are usually rather more complex."

"What is it you want of me?" I asked. "Tell be, once and for all."

"As legal a marriage as is possible under present conditions," she replied, clearly and simply, stressing every word. "I have to consider my reputation, my future, my family and my father."

I clenched my fists until the nails dug into my palms.

"There is no future," I said with forced calm. "Do try to understand, once and for all, that your birth, your father's palace, your reputation and everything else will soon be meaningless. The Turkish cannon are already within five thousand paces of the city; there are so many that no one has been able to count them. We have no future—none, none. . . . Do you understand?"

"Why must you be so stubborn?" she said, forcing herself to be as calm as myself. "If indeed we have nothing to look forward to—if nothing means anything any more—then why in God's name won't you humor me in this trifle?"

"The churches are united," I said. "Try to understand that. The Union has been proclaimed. A Latin marriage is as valid as a Greek one, and I should be breaking the sacrament if I went through another form of marriage. It's a question of principle. I have never denied my faith even at the sword's point; it would be shameful to do it for a woman's whim."

"In most churches the creed is still recited without interpolations," she returned obdurately. "Weddings and funerals, baptism and communion are all celebrated according to the ancient rites; Gregorios Mammas is a puppet patriarch and has been ejected by the Holy Synod. The Pope can bestow no preferment on him—he is a shadow appointed by the Emperor. The true Church of Greece is eclipsed by that shadow, but will one day stand forth again, when the time is ripe. Join it, and your former marriage will become invalid, as if it had never been."

I smote my breast and tore my hair.

"Why was I born into this doomed world?" I cried bitterly. "Why may I not live as I will and as my conscience enjoins? What curse is this? Would you too set priests and lawyers at my heels, though I've never so much as touched you?"

"And you never shall touch me—never in life were I to die for it," she exlaimed. "It shall be a question of principle for me too—the principles you keep harping on. By all means do as your conscience bids you—and live and die alone. We're living here and now, not in the millennium. A man who would dwell among his fellow men must give and take a little, and adapt himself. I have left father and home for your sake, and you must renounce something too, or I shall conclude that we're not suited to each other. We have a choice to make, you once said. Well and good. Choose; it's your turn now. And that is my last word."

Blinded by tears of rage I dashed into my room, buckled on my sword, pulled on my boots and snatched my coat of mail.

"Farewell, Anna," I cried as I ran past her on the stairs. "Henceforth you will find me on the ramparts. You hold an apple in your hand which you dare not bite into, for fear of a worm within."

"Take your apple!" she shouted in reply, hurling at me the first object she could lay her hands on; it chanced to be my precious glass lamp. The glass smashed against my head, cutting my hand and neck—yet at the time I never noticed it. I slammed the outer door behind me so that the din of it resounded through the house.

She ran to open it again and called after me anxiously, "You haven't hurt yourself, have you?"

I did not turn. I rushed away up the street with my armor rattling under my arm, as if the devil himself were after me. So far beyond all reason did I love her.

4 April 1453

On Monday the boom was laid out, and it now bars the harbor mouth from the Eugenios Tower to the Galata Tower in Pera. The port is closed and no vessel can sail from it. The chain winds like a huge serpent from shore to shore.

At nightfall the whole northwest horizon was lit by the glow of Turkish campfires.

On leaving my house I made for Giustiniani's quarters, by the Gate of St. Romanos. The Latins lie idly in turret and guardhouse, stewing mutton in their cooking-pots, playing cards and drinking wine. The Greeks chant psalms in harmony, and pray. Sentries stand guard upon the ramparts. Now and then one of them fancies he sees a shadow moving in the darkness, and throws a blazing torch or shoots a fiery arrow across the ditch. But beyond the walls there is only emptiness.

Soon there'll be an end of cooking, and the cauldrons will be filled with molten lead and seething pitch.

Numbers of culverins have been placed on the battlements; also some heavy bombards, which spew forth their mighty stone balls in a lofty arch. But the bombards have not yet been tested; the powder is being saved for the muskets and swivel guns which fire leaden bullets. The Emperor's technicians have also erected old-fashioned ballistae and catapults. These hurl great boulders far across the ditch, though the missiles travel more slowly than those of the bombards.

Where there is a choice between hand-gun and crossbow, only one man in fifty will choose the gun. The crossbow is both surer and safer.

The sky glows red in the northwest and the Latins are laying wagers with one another as to whether the Turks will be at our gates by morning. Suspense has put everyone on edge and robs them of sleep. The professional soldiers swear a great deal, which offends the Greeks. The Greeks hold themselves aloof from the Latins.

Bitterness and doubt creep into my mind as I keep watch with the others; I cannot help thinking of Anna Notaras. I cannot help it. Surely it is not destiny alone which drives me so relentlessly along this path! Why is she so determined to bind herself to me with legal bonds? She should understand that I have good reason for refusing. For I have—I have!

If I ignored the Union and allowed myself to be wedded to Anna Notaras it would simply be a further step toward temptation.

Why did she cross my path again? Can it have been planned deliberately? Does her father really not know that she is in the city? Or are they acting in collusion, father and daughter—in secret league together? But Lukas Notaras cannot know who I am.

Why, why did she cross my path at St. Sophia's? My way lay plain before me. Now the spirit within me is stirred up and cloudy, and my thoughts seethe. Shall I let my spirit yield to the temptation of the flesh? But my love is as much spirit as flesh. So I believe. So I believed.

A man, not an angel. Yet Manuel's knee was healed when I laid my hand upon his neck.

All this that I may see God.

All this that for a woman I may hurl myself into the burning grave of my lust.

Should I not hate her? For I love her.

5 April 1453

Shortly after sunrise a cloud of dust began rising from all the roads and tracks leading to the city. Through it appeared the first scattered Turkish troops. When they saw our walls they began calling upon God and the Prophet and brandishing their weapons. Spear points and scimitars flashed redly through the dust.

Giustiniani sent for me. He and the Emperor sat their horses at the Kharisios Gate. A hundred young Greek noblemen were waiting on either side and had the greatest difficulty in controlling their restless chargers, which champed and pawed the ground. It was these same young men who had jeered during the Emperor's speech to the Latins—these who played ball on horseback at the Hippodrome: handsome, proud youths who deemed it beneath their dignity even to talk to Latins.

"You can ride, Jean Ange," said Giustiniani. "Can you also wind a horn?"

I nodded.

"You wanted to fight, I believe? Good; you shall. But see to it that the battle doesn't last too long and that you don't get cut off. Tell these damned blockheads in Greek that I'll hang every one of them who doesn't obey the trumpet signal and turn when the retreat is sounded. We must not lose a single man. This is a demonstration, not a sortie; you need not do more than flurry the Turkish columns. Keep an eye on the tower: I'll signal with the flag if you're in danger of being outflanked."

I took the trumpet and sounded a call: its note was clear and true. The mettlesome horses reared and I shouted to the lads that I had not come to force myself upon them and share their glory. By order of the protostrator I was to follow them and in due time give the signal to retire. I mentioned that I was older than they were, and that I had been in cavalry charges even before Varna.

Giustiniani spoke kindly to his great charger and explained the situation to him before handing me the reins.

"My horse will be a better protection than your sword," he said. "He will cut a way through the worst melee with his hoofs, and at a pinch he can bite a Turk in two."

It was indeed a fierce and terrible stallion—a war horse of European strain—heavier and clumsier than the Greek thoroughbreds. Fortunately animals respect me, or I should have been more in dread of this stallion than of the Turks themselves. Giustiniani is tall and his stirrup leathers did not suit me, but I had no time to shorten them. The drawbridge was already being lowered, with much rumbling and din, and dozens of men were heaving open the gates.

In well-dressed ranks the Greeks rode forth, but while yet

on the drawbridge they set spurs to their mounts and tore off at full gallop, each striving to be first. I followed over the thundering ground. My great steed was furious at being left behind, accustomed as he was to careering ahead of all the rest; he did his utmost, therefore, and I felt as safe as if I had been on the back of a war elephant, in a timber howdah.

We rode straight at a detachment of infantry who were approaching along the road from Adrianople. When these troops saw us they opened out on either side of the road; then the first of the arrows sang toward us. The young Greeks also deployed, as if they had been playing ball, each of them aiming at a Turkish head. Then my charger trod the first corpse underfoot. Far away on one flank a troop of Turkish spahis in fluttering red cloaks were advancing at a gallop.

The first of the Turks had thrown away their weapons in their fright, so as to be able to run more swiftly; these were scattered men from the vanguard. Then a group closed their ranks, lowered their pikes and thrust them into the ground to halt our horses. The Greeks swerved to encircle the troop, but my stallion blundered straight in among the spears, snapped them off like sticks against his breastplate and trampled the terrified Turks underfoot.

I had come to fight, and fight I must. But these men had not even buff jerkins. They shouted "Allah, Allah!" and I heard myself shouting "Allah, Allah!" too, as if I were entreating their God to have mercy upon them.

The field was strewn with bundles of ragged clothes. My horse put his ears back and sank his teeth in the belly of a young Turk, shook the life out of him and tossed him aside.

The Turkish columns had halted in disorder. The Greeks swung their horses' heads about and rode off, until they came to rising ground and had to slacken speed. Arrows were still whistling among us, though as yet no one had fallen from the saddle.

I glanced toward the city. Giustiniani's flag with the cross upon it was being madly hoisted and dipped. I sounded the retreat—not once but many times—but the Greeks feigned not to hear. If the ever-steepening slope had not forced them to move more slowly they might have ridden all the way to Adrianople.

At last I managed to gather up my troop and we turned back toward the city. As we rode past wounded Turks writhing on the ground with their hands to their heads, one or another of the young Greeks, by way of practice, bent and delivered the *coup-de-grâce*. The air was heavy with the stench of blood and excrements. From some way off the spahis approached us in wild career, invoking Allah and brandishing their scimitars in flashing arcs. They rolled toward us like a red, tempestuous wave, and more and more of our young men looked behind them and furtively spurred on their steeds.

I did not look around. I kept my gaze fixed upon the walls and bastions of Constantinople rising before me. I tried to see them through Turkish eyes, and could not wonder that their infantry had halted at the sight of them. They extended as far as the eye could reach, those yellow and brown, castellated, turreted ramparts. First came the ditch with its counterscarp; beyond it the first low outworks, then the outer wall with its towers, garrison and artillery, this wall alone being mightier than any city wall I had ever seen in Europe. Yet behind that again, loftier than the tallest house, rose the great wall of Constantinople with its massive bastions. Outworks, outer wall and great wall looked like three gigantic steps. Even should the enemy surmount the first two, they would still be penned in a death-trap between the second and third.

As I beheld these towering steps I felt for the first time a glimmer of hope. Nothing short of an earthquake could breach those walls, I thought.

Then my horse was trotting across the resounding drawbridge. The line of spahis with their plumes, breastplates and floating cloaks had halted a bowshot to our rear. Hardly had we regained the city before the engineers raced out to tear down the bridge, while masons stood ready with bricks and mortar to wall up the gateway. In the same way the four last drawbridges were demolished and the last gateways bricked up. All that remained were the narrow sally ports in the great wall. The Emperor has entrusted the keys of these to the Latins.

From all directions the Turks continued their advance, deployed and halted out of range. Great herds of cattle were driven along behind them. On the other side of the Horn too, on the hills beyond Pera, endless marching columns appeared. By evening the Turks were massed so densely from the inner end of the Horn to the Marmora that not a hare could have slipped through them. But they halted at a distance of two thousand paces, and from the walls they looked the size of ants.

Small indeed does man appear before this gigantic, thousand-year-old wall. But time engulfs everything. Even the mightiest rampart must one day fall—one era gives place to another.

6 April 1453

It is Friday, the holy day of Islam. This morning Sultan Mohammed rode forth, parallel to our walls, in the bright sunshine, with a retinue of many hundreds. He kept out of range and his face could not be distinguished, yet I recognized him by his lofty bearing. I also recognized, by their clothes and headdresses, some of the eminent members of his suite.

Not an arrow, not a single shot was discharged on either side. By now the Turks had carried away the bodies of those cut down during the sortie. When the Sultan had ridden the length of the wall he turned and mounted the hill opposite the Gate of St. Romanos, where his great silk tent with its baldaquins already awaited him, and where countless sappers were busy fortifying the mound with trenches and palisades.

Without dismounting, the Sultan dispatched a herald to our gate, under a flag of truce. In a chanting voice this envoy called upon Emperor Constantine and offered him peace. His Greek was faulty, but no one laughed. The Emperor mounted one of the towers of the great wall and showed himself to the herald. He wore the golden hooped crown and was attended by a ceremonial suite.

Sultan Mohammed, in accordance with the precepts of the Koran, offered peace and pledged his word that the lives of all should be spared if the city surrendered without resistance. This was the last opportunity for Grand Vizier Khalil and the peace party to bring about negotiation, and I believe that Mohammed, sitting there motionless in his saddle, feared more than anyone that his offer might be accepted.

Emperor Constantine caused Phrantzes to repeat the message which the Sultan had already received from him in Adrianople. Phrantzes' thin, courtier's voice did not carry far; the Latins soon wearied of listening and began yelling insults at the herald, after the manner of soldiers. The Greeks too began to shout, and a concerted howl of defiance rose along the whole wall. The Greeks plucked up courage at the sound of their own voices; their eyes gleamed and their faces flushed, while some of the arbalestiers began eagerly winding up their weapons. But Emperor Constantine raised his hand and sternly forbade them to shoot at the Sultan's messenger, who came under a flag of truce.

The herald departed, and by the time he reached the Sultan the sun was high in the sky. It was the hour of the noon prayer. Sultan Mohammed dismounted; a prayer mat was unrolled before him and a spear thrust into the ground so as to point in the direction of Mecca. The Sultan grasped his left wrist and bowed his head, fell on his knees and pressed his forehead to the ground. He omitted the customary ablutions, since he was on a campaign and the water would not have sufficed for all his warriors. Many were his prostrations, and all his army, from the shores of the Marmora to the innermost end of the Horn, bowed themselves down in time with him. A huge, living carpet seemed to cover the earth to the very horizon.

As if in response, bells began pealing in all the churches of the city, and those of the monasteries chimed in. The clanging and din carried confidence to the townsfolk and floated over the fields to the Turks, to vex their devotions.

After repeating many verses, Mohammed stretched forth his hands and proclaimed a state of siege. Those who heard him loudly took up the cry, which spread through the ranks like the roar of the sea. "The siege has begun!" cried the Turks, and upon the instant the entire army charged with brandished weapons towards the wall, as if to storm it without delay. The bright battalions rolled forward until they were near enough for us to make out a sea of gaping, howling faces. So bloodcurdling was the sight that the raw Greeks started back from their posts, and even the Latins bent their bows and drew their swords.

But the Turks halted in good order at a distance from us

of about a thousand paces, beyond the range of our artillery, where they began digging a trench, carrying stones and raising palisades to protect their camp. A few janissaries ran up to our ditch and challenged the Greeks to single combat. The officers of the Emperor's guard eagerly begged leave to go down and display their skill in arms, and among Giustiniani's men too there were some who would gladly have matched the western two-handed sword against the short, curved blades of the janissaries; but Giustiniani sternly forbade rashness.

"The age of tournaments is past," he said. "A stout soldier serves no good purpose by risking his life in a foolish contest of honor. I was summoned here to wage war, not to play games."

He ordered his best marksmen to take aim with harquebus and crossbow, and fire a volley. Five janissaries fell, struck by bullets and bolts. The rest, enraged by this breach of honorable convention, foamed at the mouth and cursed the Greeks and Latins for cowardly wretches who dared not tackle brave men save from the shelter of their walls. After two more had fallen, the remainder came to their senses and tried to carry back their comrades' bodies. By now firing was general all along the wall, and many fell. But fresh janissaries came in unbroken succession, heedless of missiles, to remove the corpses. Not one body was left by the ditch; nothing remained but a few bloodstains on the grass.

While the Turkish army were digging and pile-driving, Giustiniani rode along the outer wall and tried to estimate their numbers. The janissaries, who are encamped round about the Sultan's tent, opposite the Gate of St. Romanos, number twelve thousand, as we already knew. Of spahis, the regular cavalry, there are at least as many. Giustiniani believes that the relatively well-equipped infantry, in half-armor, may amount to one hundred thousand. To this must be added an equal number of irregulars: poor men who at the Sultan's summons joined the army from religious zeal and lust for plunder, and who are clad in rags and armed with swords or slings. A few of them carry small, leather-covered wooden shields. Only about a quarter of the Sultan's men wear padded leather jerkins.

The Turkish numbers are alarmingly high, but Giustiniani believes the light troops to be of little value. He was not in the least cast down after his ride; he simply wondered what had become of the Sultan's much talked-of artillery.

To hearten the defenders, Emperor Constantine arranged with Aloisio Diedo for the Venetian galley crews to parade with flying colors along the outer wall, from one end to the other. Pipes and drums sounded, and the lion banner of St. Mark flew in the wind. This was without doubt a shrewd stroke of diplomacy, inasmuch as it showed the Sultan that he was at war with Venice too.

Before evening it was evident at what price this demonstration had been made. Emperor Constantine moved with his bodyguard from the Palace of Blachernae and pitched camp beside Giustiniani's lines at the center of the wall. Into the deserted palace marched the Venetian bailo at the head of the Venetian garrison and volunteers. By evening the Lion of St. Mark was floating beside the imperial standard. Thus the whole of the strongly fortified Blachernae sector lies in the hands of the Venetians. Should the city after all succeed in repulsing the Turks, the Venetian occupation of the palace might well acquire a sinister significance.

But Giustiniani and his iron-clad men-at-arms hold the post of honor opposite the janissaries, by the Gate of St. Romanos. Here he has assembled at least three thousand of his best men.

And the total number of defenders? Only the Emperor and Giustiniani know that. But Giustiniani has allowed it to be understood that half the garrison is stationed between the Romanos and Kharisios gates. From this it seems that our entire defense force, including monks and artisans, amounts to no more than six thousand. I cannot believe this. The Venetian seamen alone account for two thousand, though of these a number must be kept back to guard the harbor and the ships. Therefore I believe that we have at least ten thousand men on the walls, albeit only a thousand—apart from Giustiniani's six hundred—are fully equipped.

Let us say ten thousand against two hundred thousand. But as yet the Sultan's artillery has not arrived, nor has his fleet been sighted.

During the afternoon there came from the Selymbria direction an occasional rumbling as of thunder, though the sky was clear. From the blue islands in the Marmora a mighty pillar of smoke is rising to the sky.

7 April 1453

Last night the naked, mutilated bodies of those who defended Selymbria were all impaled on stakes outside the Selymbrian Gate. There are forty stakes and forty bodies.

According to a rumor from Pera, the Sultan's fleet had for two days been vainly trying to storm this last island stronghold. Yesterday, by order of the Turkish admiral, wood was stacked around the tower and set alight, and the garrison was burned alive inside.

The Greeks know how to die for the last inch of their crumbling Empire.

Barbarians in the east, barbarians in the west. On the borders of the two worlds Christ's last city is fighting for its life —without hope of help, without claim to glory. Naked, mutilated corpses pierced with stakes, swarming with flies. . . .

Clad in iron from head to foot, a head taller than all the rest, goes Giustiniani, laughing: a walking tower, with puffy face and hard eyes. Today, after seeing the defenders of Selymbria, I hated him.

We fight without hope, without a future. Even should we defeat the Sultan, Constantinople would be but a dead city under barbarian, Latin rule.

All my life I have loathed and avoided spite and fanaticism. Now in my heart they burn with a bright flame.

9 April 1453

After a quiet Sunday the nine largest galleys moved up to the boom and made ready to defend it. The Turkish fleet is expected.

Big teams of oxen are dragging up the great bronze guns of the enemy. Behind the Turkish lines, herds of cattle stir up dust clouds and their lowing carries as far as our walls.

Our defense is prepared; each man knows his place and task. Emperor Constantine has been riding along our ramparts all day, talking to the commanders of the different sectors, encouraging the Greeks and making fresh promises to the Latins.

11 April 1453

In small groups parallel with the landward wall the Sultan has set up hundreds of small cannon and mortars. His heavy artillery is massed at four points: before the St. Romanos Gate the Kharisios Gate and the Kaligari Gate in the Blachernae sector, where the walls are thickest but where there is no ditch. There are also three big guns in front of the Selymbrian Gate.

These pieces have been dragged so close to the walls that a sharp-eyed observer can distinguish the faces of the artillerymen, swarms of whom are busy lashing down the guns to massive beds of timber and stone. The guns lie clumsy and helpless on their bellies, but when one compares their gaping muzzles with the men beside them one appreciates their formidable size. Each one of the balls which are being stacked beside them stands as high as a man's thigh.

The guns are protected by ditches and palisades. None of the Latins had ever seen such mighty pieces of ordnance before. They will devour boatloads of powder and kill hundreds of Turks when they explode—or so says Giustiniani to hearten his own men.

The biggest bombard, cast by Orban in Adrianople and talked of as long ago as January, has been placed opposite the Kaligari Gate, where the wall is thickest. The Sultan evidently believes that his artillery will take effect on any wall whatsoever. Giustiniani was curious to see this piece, and since all was quiet he allowed me to go with him. He also wanted to know how the Venetians were settling down in the Palace of

Blachernae and at the Kharisios Gate, whence the road runs to Adrianople.

Many of the garrison had left their posts and gathered in big groups to look at the giant bombard, while townspeople too had climbed onto palace roofs and towers for a better view of the monster.

Some pointed, and shouted that they recognized Orban, although he was wearing a Turkish kaftan of honor and the headdress of Master of the Ordnance. The Greeks showered curses and abuse, and the Emperor's technicians took aim with swivel gun and harquebus, firing several rounds to disturb the Turks at their laborious task of raising and mounting the great gun. Many of the Greeks turned pale and covered their ears when these little shots cracked out from the wall.

Minotto, the Venetian bailo, called his men to order and advanced to greet Giustiniani. With him came his son, who despite his youth, commands a Venetian galley. The Emperor's technician Johann Grant also joined us. It was the first time I had met this remarkable man, of whose skill and attainments I had heard so much. He is middle-aged with a black beard; his forehead is furrowed with thought and his gaze restless and searching. He was pleased to find that I knew a few words of German, though he speaks fluent Latin and has already learned a good deal of Greek. The Emperor took him into his service as a successor to Orban, and pays him the salary which Orban begged for in vain.

Grant said, "This gun is a marvel of the founder's art, exceeding anything we believed possible. A piece larger than that would be more than any man could control, and did I not know that they have already tested it in Adrianople, I would never believe it could withstand the pressure of the charge. Not for a hundred ducats would I stand near it when it's fired."

Giustiniani said, "I, poor wretch, accepted the defense of the St. Romanos Gate, when all others were silent. But now I don't regret my choice at all, and heartily wish the Venetians joy."

The Venetian bailo, unpleasantly affected by this remark, said, "We can hardly expect anyone to remain on the wall or in the tower when that gun is fired. We are only merchant-volunteers, and many of us are fat. I myself become breathless when I mount the wall, and I suffer from heart trouble."

Giustiniani said, "You must expect to pay something for the Palace of Blachernae. But if you like I will gladly exchange my uncomfortable tower for the Emperor's bed, and promise to mount the wall early tomorrow morning. Change with me; I have no objection."

The ruddy-faced bailo regarded Giustiniani with suspicion, measured the huge bastions of the Blachernae with his eye and compared it with the rest of the landward wall. Then he replied shortly, "You're joking."

Johann Grant the German burst out laughing and observed, "The Emperor's technicians and I have worked out and proved, for our own amusement, that so large a cannon cannot be cast satisfactorily—and that if one could cast it, it would not hold together. And supposing even that it could be fired, it would only spit the ball a few yards. That can all be proved by figures. Tomorrow I ought really to make a shield and buckler of my reckoning-tablets, and take up my position on the wall opposite the gun."

Afterwards Giustiniani took me aside and said, "Jean Ange, my friend, no one can know what will happen tomorrow, for the world has never before seen such guns as these. It is conceivable that they may breach the walls with a few rounds, though I don't believe it. Stay here and keep an eye upon the great bombard—take up quarters in the Blachernae, if the

Venetians will let you. I would like to have a dependable man here until we have seen what damage the gun can do."

Johann Grant took me under his wing, since we are both strangers among Latins and Greeks. He is taciturn, and when he does speak is inclined to sarcasm. He showed me the empty workshops by the Kaligari Gate, where a handful of elderly Greek shoemakers, with their hearts in their mouths, were still sitting and pegging soldiers' boots. All the young men, down to the apprentices, have been sent to the walls. We wandered through the halls and galleries of the imperial palace too, where the Venetian volunteers have installed themselves. Bailo Minotto has taken the Emperor's sleeping-apartment for himself, and spends his nights on down pillows beneath a purple coverlet.

The heating system of the palace, consisting of hot-air channels under the floors, devours colossal quantities of fuel, and therefore quite early in the spring the Emperor forbade any heating of the palace, though the nights were still cold. He wanted to save all wood in the city for bread-baking and other essentials—above all for repairing the walls, should the Turks really succeed in breaching them.

At nightfall I beheld the Venetian guards lighting a fire on the polished marble pavement of the great ceremonial hall. The marble is cracking, and smoke blackens the priceless mosaics of the ceiling.

12 April 1453

I rose at dawn. Not many slept soundly last night. The Greeks prayed. The Latins drank too much. When I went out into the chill morning air my feet slipped on their spewings in the galleries of the palace.

The sun rose more radiantly than ever beyond the Bosporus. The coasts of Asia gleamed golden-yellow and a gentle breeze floated in from the Marmora.

From the battlements I could see the Turkish soldiers performing their devotions. My thoughts followed the thoughts of Sultan Mohammed: he would scarcely have slept much either. If the whole city was heavy with expectancy, so surely was he.

But the morning hours passed without incident. Then a rumor spread from man to man along the wall that the Turkish fleet had appeared. Hundreds of sails, it was said, covered the sea. In the harbor, ships' bells sounded the alarm and were heard as far as the Blachernae.

Then we saw the Sultan on his snow-white horse riding up onto the hill opposite us, surrounded by his highest officers and a retinue of green-clad *tsaushes.* The horsehair switches of pashas and viziers floated from their staffs. Mohammed was coming to inspect his largest cannon, but halted prudently at a distance from it of five hundred paces. All the horses were then led away.

When the Turkish gunners fled from the great bombard, leaving only a half-naked slave waving the smoldering match on a long linstock to make it blaze, the bailo lost his equanimity and ordered the evacuation of the threatened part of the wall. This welcome command sent even the boldest scuttling like terrified sheep.

Then came a flash, and a roar more frightful than the loudest thunderclap. The wall shook as if from an earthquake; I lost my balance and fell, like many others. A mighty smoke cloud, black as gunpowder, hid the bombard from us. I heard later that in nearby houses plates had fallen from the tables and water in the jars slopped over. Even the ships in the harbor trembled.

As soon as the wind had borne away the smoke and the dust from the wall I saw the Turkish gunners running up to look, and to point out to each other the effect of the shot—I saw them shout and wave their arms, but heard nothing; the din had deafened me. I shouted myself, but no one heard. Only by pulling at the sleeves of one or two dazed arbalestiers could I get them to draw their crossbows. But in their agitation they shot wildly; not one Turk was injured, though many of our men were firing at them from loopholes and embrasures. The enemy gunners were so spellbound that they cast only vague, fleeting glances at the arrows that were stabbing into the ground about them as they slowly returned to their gun, conversing and shaking their heads, seemingly dissatisfied with what they had seen.

The mighty stone ball had merely made a hollow in the wall, hardly as big as a small room, and had naturally been smashed into a thousand pieces. But the foundations of the wall remained unshaken.

Over by the bombard I saw Orban swinging his club of office and bawling orders. A group of soldiers swarmed round the gun, wrapping it in thick woolen blankets, that the metal might not cool too quickly, and pouring oil by the barrelful into its vast maw to ease its recovery after the terrific strain of the discharge.

Farther away, from the Kharisios and Romanos gates, another alarming roar was heard. I could see flashes and clouds of smoke, though the report sounded only faintly in my dulled ears.

Sultan Mohammed alone remained erect when all his suite and the *tsaushes* flung themselves on the ground at the detonation. He was standing motionless now, staring at the ramparts while his officers brushed the dust from their clothes. He stood still because he did not wish to betray his feelings. Perhaps in his own mind he had half fancied that a single shot from so mighty a weapon could indeed bring down a twenty-foot wall.

When Orban had seen to it that the great gun was snugly covered, the other two cannon on either side were discharged. They are powerful enough, yet they look like piglets beside the great mother sow. The gunner touched them off without seeking cover.

Nevertheless the two flashes following close upon one another dazzled me for a moment, and then the view was hidden by the pitchy clouds of smoke that billowed up and followed the missiles. The stone balls struck at almost the same point as the first, sending a tremor through the wall, and through the rising dust cloud whirled a rain of stone splinters. A Venetian was wounded by some of these. Yet when we went down to view the damage we found it to be less than we could have expected. The Blachernae wall had stood the test.

Bailo Minotto laughed aloud in his relief and cried cheerfully to his men, "Now by the Holy Spirit, we need not fear—we may take heart! The Sultan may shoot such peas at us all day long and the wall will be none the worse for it."

But while the Turks tended their guns as if they had been sick cattle, Johann Grant set the whole garrison to work. Knowing now on what point the enemy guns were trained, he caused huge leather bags stuffed with wool, cotton and grass to be lowered, to protect the holes in the outer face of the wall. He too was cheerful and was of the opinion that the damage could easily be made good during the night.

Soon fresh rumblings were to be heard and the wall quaked under my feet, for now the Sultan's hundreds of slender culverins and serpentines opened fire, and his short, stocky mortars hurled their stones in lofty arcs. Many of the missiles flew over the walls into the city and brought down a few houses before the gunners learned to estimate the correct charge and to lay the guns at the proper angle. The air was filled with incessant din, and scattered parties of Turks began to advance toward the ditch, clashing brass plates together and praising Allah at the tops of their voices. But up on the walls the defenders were growing accustomed to the firing and took good aim, so that many Turks fell by the moat and their comrades suffered losses as they retired with the dead.

I set off for the parapet of the outer wall near the Gate of St. Romanos to tell Giustiniani that so far the great gun had proved less formidable than had been expected. Now and then I had to run a few steps to gain the shelter of the next merlon, against the whining arrows and shot.

Along that sector of the outer wall which lies between the Porphyrogenetos Palace and the Kharisios Gate the defenders were looking glum. The first rounds from four big cannon had torn whole merlons from the crenelated wall and crushed three men to a bloody pulp. A dozen others had been wounded by stone splinters and had to be dragged into the city through a postern in the great wall to receive attention. They left pools of blood behind them on the rampart. The defenders peered uneasily at the cannon into which the Turks had already put fresh charges. The gunners were just ramming home chunks of wood with clubs, to tamp the charge, and throwing in wet clay to exclude all air before rolling the stone ball down the barrel.

This part of the wall is defended by the three Guacchardi brothers, young Venetian adventurers who pay their own men and have taken service under the Emperor. They walked to and fro along the wall encouraging the novices, slapping them on the shoulder and assuring them that the danger was not so great as they fancied. They were curious to hear an account of the damage caused by the great bombard, and I stayed with them for a while to observe the effect of the firing on this part of the wall. They offered me wine in the tower which they have chosen for their quarters, and which they have furnished with costly carpets, draperies and soft cushions from the Palace of Blachernae.

As we awaited the next shots they spoke robustly of their experiences with Greek girls in Constantinople, and questioned me as to the customs of Turkish women. They are all three under thirty, and from the way they talked it was evident that they are simply boys thirsting for adventure, glory and gain. They seem unconcernedly prepared to stand before their God at any moment, with their heads full of wine and their hearts full of memories of fair women. They have of course received full absolution for sins past and to come. I have no wish to judge them; on the contrary, in their company I was conscious of something like envy of their sparkling youth, which no philosophy has yet embittered.

Meanwhile the Turks had loosened the wedges under the guns and trained them lower, toward the foot of the wall. From the battlements men shouted that the gunners were swinging their matches, and the brothers Guacchardi hastily threw dice to decide which of them should have the honor of showing himself on the wall as an example to the defenders. The youngest threw sixes, and elated by his good fortune sprang to the battlements, his eyes alight with fervor and wine. He stepped forth at an embrasure immediately opposite the cannon, waved his steel-clad arms to attract the attention of the besiegers and began shouting a torrent of obscenities in Turkish, so that I was ashamed for him. But when the matches were set to the touch-holes, he prudently dodged behind a merlon and clung fast.

The three pieces went off almost simultaneously, momentarily deafening us and shaking the wall beneath our feet. When the smoke and dust had cleared away we saw young Guacchardi still standing sturdily with his feet apart, unharmed. But the balls had skimmed the ditch, sweeping part of the outworks with them and tearing great holes in the outer wall. It was clear that in time this bombardment will cause severe damage, and slowly but surely gnaw the wall away.

From the guns, cries of lamentation reached us, and we now saw that the cannon on the left had burst its lashings and bounced off its bed: timber and stone had been hurled for a great distance, crushing at least two of the gunners. The rest paid no heed to their comrades but dashed forward to wrap the guns in blankets and give them olive oil to drink, for they were of more value than human lives.

As I continued my way along the wall the Turks kept up an uninterrupted fire with cannon and harquebus; they clashed cymbals, blew trumpets, beat drums or dashed forward in small parties to the ditch in an attempt to reach some of the defenders with their arrows. Giustiniani's men, being in plate armor, did not trouble to dodge these but let them clash and break against buckler and cuirass.

Just as I reached Giustiniani's sector the great guns opposite the Gate of St. Romanos were fired; part of the battlements of the outer wall collapsed and countless splinters sang through the air. Lime dust choked me and the poisonous smoke blackened my hands and face. In front of me I heard curses and cries and Greek voices invoking the Holy Mother of God. Close beside me a hapless workman, carrying stone for the walls, fell headlong, blood pouring from his torn side.

"Jesus Christ, Son of God, have mercy upon me!" he moaned, and gave up the ghost without further suffering.

Giustiniani came hurrying toward me in his clashing armor to inspect the damage; he thrust up his visor and his round ox-eyes blazed green with the lust of battle. Staring at me as if he had never seen me before he shouted, "The fight has begun! Have you ever known a more glorious day?"

He drew a deep breath to savor the smell of smoke and carnage until the straps of his great breastplate cracked again. He was transformed—a different being from the stolid, deliberate commander I had known. It was as if he had only now entered his proper element, and was enjoying deep draughts of the tumult and the din.

Again the walls trembled under our feet, a roar shook heaven and earth, and the air was darkened. The bombard by the Kaligari Gate had been fired a second time. No other noise can compare with it. The sun glowed like a red ball through the cloud of dust and smoke. I estimated that it had taken about two hours to cool, swab, lay and load this great gun.

"You've heard that the Turkish fleet has come?" Giustiniani said. "Three hundred sail have been counted, but most of these are merchantmen, and the war galleys are light and narrow compared with the Latin vessels. The Venetians were lying in wait for them at the boom with their hearts in their mouths, but they sailed past and anchored in the Bosporus, in the Port of Pillars beyond Pera."

He talked freely and gaily, as if all his cares had been swept away; yet two rounds from the heavy Turkish guns had demolished the breastworks and damaged the outer wall. Indeed, at one or two points it was cracked from top to bottom. He roared at the frightened Greek workmen to carry away their comrade's body. These peaceful artisans, who had never bargained to fight for Latins, were crouching in the passage between the outer and main walls, crying to be let into the city through the sally port. At last two of them crawled up onto the outer wall, knelt by the body and wept to see the wounds inflicted upon it by the stone splinters. With dirty, clumsy hands they brushed the lime dust from the dead man's face and beard, and felt his chilling limbs as if unable to believe that a man could die so suddenly.

They then demanded a silver coin from Giustiniani for carrying the body into the city. Giustiniani swore and said, "Jean Ange, it's for such mean wretches as these that I'm defending Christendom."

My Greek blood protested as I beheld those helpless old men, who had not so much as a helmet or a leather jerkin between them—nothing but their stained working-clothes.

"It's their city," I replied. "You undertook the defense of this part of the wall. The Emperor pays you for it, and you must pay the Greek workmen unless you want your own fellows to repair the wall unaided. That was the agreement. You yourself are mean to try and force these defenseless men to work for nothing. They must eat, and buy food for their families. The Emperor does nothing for them."

And I added, "A small silver coin means as much to them as a ducal coronet to you. You're no better than they are. You've sold yourself to the Emperor out of greed and lust for glory."

Giustiniani, intoxicated by the battle now beginning, was not angered.

"One would think you were a Greek, to hear you twist straightforward facts," he growled; yet he threw a silver piece to the workmen. They quickly took up their comrade's body and bore him down from the wall, his blood dripping upon the worn steps as they went.

13 April 1453

An unquiet night. Not many in the city have slept. At midnight the ground shook again from the detonation of the great gun, and the mighty flash from its muzzle lit the sky. All night men worked at repairing the cracks in the wall, and facing the threatened points with sacks of wool and hay.

The Turkish fleet has remained in the Port of Pillars, where great quantities of timber and stone are being unloaded from the vessels for use in the siege. The Venetian galleys are still lying by the boom and have been prepared for an attack during the night.

In the daylight hours the heavy Turkish cannon have time to fire six times each. The wall by the Kaligari Gate seems likely to stand up best to the bombardment, although it faces the great gun. The Venetians quartered in the Palace of Blachernae now regard the Holy Virgin there with reverence, and have begun to believe the Greeks, who affirm that the miracle-working Panaghia is guardian of the palace walls.

Not a single Latin has yet fallen, though two are severely wounded. Their armor protects them well. Of the artisans and monks who have been called to arms, many have died in the sector between the Golden Gate and the Rhesias Gate. This has convinced the rest that it is wisest to wear the uncomfortable helmet and not to complain of the constricting harness straps.

The townsfolk are becoming seasoned in battle. Hatred for the Turks increases with every casualty. Many women and old men come out onto the walls to dip their garments in the blood of the slain, whom they hail as martyrs for the faith.

Human beings adapt themselves easily. There is perhaps nothing they cannot force themselves to accept. Yesterday it seemed even to me that the din of the great gun, the quaking of the ground, the crumbling of the walls and the whirling of splinters through the air could never seem anything but terrifying. Yet today the pressure at the pit of my stomach has eased and my breathing is quieter.

14 April 1453

Today one of the great Turkish cannon exploded, and smoke poured from cracks in the barrel. The bombardment has slackened. The Turks have set up forges beside the gun emplacements and are strengthening the weapons with bands of iron. Orban has established a foundry on the hillside behind the Turkish camp, and at night a red glow mounts from it into the sky. Tin and copper smelting continues throughout the twenty-four hours. A Jewish peddler who came by the Pera road said he saw hundreds of slaves at work around the huge pits in which the molds for the cannon are sunk. The weather is fine and the sky clear. The Greeks have every reason to pray for rain, says Grant the German, for should water reach the molds they would burst when the molten metal was poured in.

He is a queer, mystical man, caring neither for wine nor women. The Emperor's technicians have erected many old-fashioned ballistae and catapults on the outer wall, but their range is restricted and they will be useless until the Turks attempt to take our defenses by storm. Grant has made drawings to show how these engines could be improved and lightened, for they have been built to the same pattern since the days of Alexander. Whenever he has time he visits the Emperor's library to study the writings of the ancients.

The Emperor's white-haired librarian guards his volumes jealously; he will not lend them and allows neither candle nor lamp to be lit in the reading-room. The codices may be read only by daylight. He hides the catalogues from the Latins. When Grant asked for the works of Archimedes, he shook his head vehemently. They were not in the library, he said. If Grant had asked, even once, for the Fathers of the Church or the Greek philosophers he might have been more warmly received. But Grant reads only technical and mathematical works, and is therefore despised as a barbarian.

As we talked of this, Grant said, "Archimedes and Pythagoras could have built engines to change the world. Those old fellows knew the art of making water and steam do the work of men; but no one wanted such things in their day, and they never troubled to develop them. Instead, they turned their thoughts to the Arcana and Plato's ideas. They deemed the supernatural world more worthy than the tangible. Yet in their forgotten writings one may come upon hints by which even the artists of today might profit."

I said, "If they were wise men, wiser than we are, why don't you believe them and follow their example? What can it profit a man to have all nature at his feet, and harm his own soul?"

Grant surveyed me with his restless, searching eyes. His soft beard is coal-black and his face furrowed with thought and wakeful nights. He is a majestic and awe-inspiring figure. The thunder of the great gun made the walls of the library shake, and little clouds of dust flew from the cracks in the ceiling, to float in the sunbeam from the narrow window.

"Aren't you afraid of death, John Angelos?" he asked.

"My body fears it," I answered. "My body fears disintegration, and so the roar of cannon causes my knees to fail me. But my spirit is not afraid."

"If you were more experienced you would fear more," he declared. "If you had seen more of war and death, even your spirit would be afraid. Only the raw warrior is without fear. Conquest of fear, not absence of it, is the true heroism."

He pointed at the thousand golden figures and vermilion texts on the walls, and at the great folios which with their silver-mounted, jeweled bindings lay chained to the reading-desks.

"I am afraid of death," he said. "But knowledge is greater than fear. My knowledge relates to earthly things, for knowledge of heavenly things has no practical value. That is why it cuts me to the heart to see this place. Here lie buried the last, irreplaceable remnants of the ancient wisdom. For centuries no one has troubled to make an inventory of all that is here. Rats have gnawed away the manuscripts in the vaults. Philosophers and Fathers of the Church are revered, but mathematics and engineering have been left to feed the rats. And that greedy old man over there won't understand that he has nothing to lose by letting me rummage in the cellars and light a candle to seek the priceless, despised knowledge of which he is the custodian. When the Turks come, this building will go up in flames like the rest, and the manuscripts will be shoveled out to feed the cooking-fires."

"When the Turks come, you say," I put in. "Then you don't believe we shall keep them out?"

He smiled.

"I measure with an earthly yardstick," he said. "With the

yardstick of common sense. I don't care to cherish a vain hope, as perhaps a younger and less experienced man might do."

"But," I said, wondering, "in that case even you should find greater use for knowledge of God and of the reality which stands above temporal things, than for any mathematical or technical science. Of what use are the most marvelous engines, if you must die in any event?"

He said, "You forget that we must all die. Therefore I don't at all regret that curiosity drove me to Constantinople and into the Emperor's service. I have already beheld the largest cannon ever cast by human hands. That alone was worth coming to see. And I would cheerfully exchange all the holy writings of the Fathers for two pages of a forgotten manuscript by Archimedes."

"You're mad," I said with repugnance. "Your obsession makes you madder than Sultan Mohammed."

He stretched forth his arm to the sunbeam as if he would have weighed the dancing motes in his hand.

"Do you not see?" he said. "In these particles of dust the eyes of a lovely maiden regard you—a maiden whose smile death has long ago erased. In these particles dance a philosopher's heart, his liver and brain. In another thousand years I myself as a grain of dust may greet a stranger in the streets of Constantinople. In that sense your learning and mine are of equal value. Let me therefore keep the knowledge I have and do not despise it. How do you know that in my heart I do not despise yours?"

I was trembling through and through, but I strove to keep my voice calm as I returned, "You're fighting on the wrong side, Johann Grant! Sultan Mohammed would hail you as his fellow, if he knew you."

He said, "No, no. I belong to the west—to Europe. I fight for the freedom of man, not his bondage."

"And what is the freedom of man?" I asked him.

He looked at me with his restless eyes, pondered for a while, and answered, "The right to choose."

"Just so," I whispered. "That is man's terrible freedom—the freedom of Prometheus, the freedom of our original sin."

He smiled, laid his hand upon my shoulder and sighed. "Ah, you Greeks!"

I feel alien to him; I wanted to shun him, and yet in spite of all, I suspect that our minds are akin. We stand on common ground, he and I. But he has chosen the kingdom of death and I the reality of God.

I was born on the borders of two worlds. In the west as in the east the tree of death is in bud. Let posterity taste its fruit; I will not.

Is that it? Is that how I have chosen?

Guns roar, walls split, the mighty drum of death sets heaven and earth a-trembling. But I am hard and cold—no, I am a glowing fire and think only of you, my beloved! Why have you pierced my flesh with thorns? Why would you not let me fight and die in peace, once I had made my choice?

Now I desire only you. And through you my part in the holy mysteries. A renegade's return to the house of his fathers.

15 April 1453

Sunday again. Church bells ring jubilantly in the clear morning air, but the green of spring is already covered in soot and dust. Like ants, weary men labor at repairing the wall under cover of temporary barricades. During the night stakes were driven into the ground in front of the gaping holes in the outer wall, and these are now being filled up with earth, osiers, bushes and hay. The citizens have had to give up their mattresses; these, lashed to the face of the wall, take up the deadly shock of the cannon balls. Over them have been stretched oxhides which are constantly soused in water to protect the materials beneath from fiery arrows.

I know and feel, not least from my own experience, how a war of despair such as this transforms us and stirs us to our very depths.

Fatigue, fear and sleeplessness inflame a man until he is drunk and no longer responsible for his actions or thoughts. He puts faith in the wildest rumors. Silent men become voluble; gentle natures dance with joy to see a Turk fall to the ground, an arrow through his throat. War is a perilous intoxication; its changes of mood, its plungings between hope and despair, are violent and abrupt. Only a seasoned soldier can keep a cool head, and most of the defenders of Constantinople are raw, unpracticed laymen. For this reason Giustiniani feels it necessary to spread hopeful rumors about the city—though for the most part they are false.

The Sultan's army contains twice as many Christians as there are armed men in the city: auxiliaries from Serbia, Macedonia and Bulgaria, as well as Greeks from Asia Minor. By the Kharisios Gate a Turkish arrow has been found with a note attached to it, written by a Serbian cavalryman. It ran: *So far as it depends on us, Constantinople shall never fall into Turkish hands.*

Grand Vizier Khalil also is secretly working against the Sultan. For the present he can do little; his hour will come as soon as the Sultan meets with reverses.

The nights are cold. So vast is the Sultan's army that only a small proportion of the men have tents. Most of them sleep under the open sky; unlike the janissaries they are not used to this, and so, during the silent hours, a continual sound of coughing and sneezing reaches us from the Turkish camp.

But our people cough, too, as they work at the damaged walls in the darkness. Towers and vaults are dank, and all wood is needed for defense works. Firewood and brushwood may be used only for cooking and for heating the cauldrons of lead and pitch. Therefore many of the Latins have bad chills, although they wear thick clothes beneath their cold armor.

17 April 1453

My servant Manuel came to the Palace of Blachernae today with clean clothes and fresh writing materials for me. Food I have no lack of, for the Venetians will make room for me at their hospitable table for as long as I may lodge at the palace. Cardinal Isidor has given them dispensation from fasting for the duration of the siege. But Emperor Constantine watches and fasts so fervently that in a short time he has grown thin and pale.

I could not refrain from asking Manuel whether anyone had inquired for me at home. He shook his head. I took him up onto the wall and showed him the great gun. The Turks had just finished loading it. The din made Manuel clutch his head, but he could satisfy himself that the wall still stood.

The cannon gave him less of a shock, however, than the sight of what the Venetians had done to the palace. He said, "The Latins keep to their old ways. When they captured Constantinople two hundred and fifty years ago they used the sanctuary in St. Sophia's as their stable, lit fires on the floor and left their ordure in the corners."

The Latin serving men are allowed to move freely about the Blachernae, and so Manuel asked me to take him to the Porphyrogenetos Palace. Glancing at me slyly he said, "No plebeian foot can have sullied its floors before, but still mine are Greek feet and therefore holier than the feet of Latin stable boys."

We climbed up the old marble staircase to the upper floor and stepped into the room whose walls are faced with polished porphyry. The carved golden bed with the double eagle still stood there, but everything movable had been stolen. As I beheld the bare, plundered room I realized that no emperor would ever be born in Constantinople again.

Manuel inquisitively opened a narrow door and stepped out onto a stone balcony.

"Ten times have I stood humbly down there among the crowd, awaiting news of the Empress' delivery," he told me. "Old Emperor Manuel had ten children. Constantine is the eighth. Only three of those sons survive, and not one has a son of his own. That is the will and judgment of God."

He was looking sideways at me the whole time with those red-rimmed eyes under their matted brows; he stroked his beard and looked mysterious.

"What has that to do with me?" I said coldly.

"Little did I think I should ever stand up here," Manuel went on, ignoring my words. "But Roman porphyry alone cannot make an emperor. That is pure superstition. Yet one has heard of forsaken women who have clutched a piece of porphyry for comfort."

He pointed to a dark corner, and I saw that in several places pieces of the wall-facing had been broken away. For an instant I was a child again: a little boy in wall-girdled Avignon, with the sun of Provence beating hot upon my head. I held a piece of crimson porphyry that I had found in my father's chest.

"Were you seeing ghosts, master?" asked Manuel softly. He had dropped on his knees as if to examine the corner, yet at the same time he was kneeling before me and turning his old man's face up to mine. His gray cheeks were quivering as if from tense excitement or imminent tears.

"I was remembering my father," I replied curtly. I no longer wondered why my father had been blinded; perhaps he had been too trusting in a world of cruelty and fear.

Manuel whispered, "Master, my eyes are dim because I am old. Perhaps it is this purple light which deceives them. Permit me to touch your feet."

He stretched forth his hand and reverently touched my legs. "The purple boots," he said. "The purple boots."

But so frightening was the silence of the Emperor's birthplace that he looked around in a scared way, as if afraid of eavesdroppers.

"You've been drinking again," I said roughly.

"Blood never denies its origin," he whispered. "It returns to it, though it may have journeyed far—aye, though it may have passed from one body to another. One day it must return."

"Manuel," I said, "believe me, that time is past. My kingdom is not of this world."

He bowed his head and kissed my feet, and I had to shove him away with my knee.

"I'm just an old fellow babbling from too much wine," he said. "My head is full of old tales. I see visions. I mean no harm."

"May such visions and tales be buried beneath our crumbling ramparts," I said, "and may some stranger find them one day, when our dust whirls up under his feet and he steps upon a stone fallen from these walls."

When Manuel had gone, I returned to the battlements and Giustiniani. It is alarming to see how much of the outer wall has collapsed during these few days, on both sides of the St. Romanos Gate. A great earthwork has been thrown up and huge crates and barrels full of soil have been placed along the top to form a parapet. All day long small parties of Turks charge up to the ditch to throw stones, timbers and faggots into it, while fire from their fieldpieces and the shafts of the bowmen force our defenders to take cover. Giustiniani's Genoese have already suffered losses despite their armor, and each one of them is worth ten, nay fifty, untrained Greeks. Each one is irreplaceable.

18 April 1453

No one could have guessed that the Turks would make their first assault last night. It was clear that their object was to storm the outer wall opposite the Gate of St. Romanos. The attack started unnoticed two hours after sunset. Under cover of darkness the Turks crept forward to the ditch and laid scaling-ladders across it. If the garrison had not been at work repairing the day's damage the attack might have succeeded. But now the alarm was given in time; trumpets sounded on the walls, pitch torches were lighted and bells in the city began to ring.

After the failure of this surprise attack, drums great and small thundered in the Turkish lines and the assailants raised a fearful yell which could be heard across the city. With long hooks they began pulling down the temporary breastworks and destroying what they could, and at the same time they tried to set fire to the sacks of hay and wool hanging along the wall. The battle lasted four hours without a break. The Turks approached the walls at other points as well, but the main attack was directed at Giustiniani's sector.

In the night-darkness the noise and tumult seemed doubly terrible, and people in the city fled half-naked from their houses. As I hastened from the Blachernae to join Giustiniani I caught sight of Emperor Constantine. He was weeping—weeping in mortal terror because he fancied the city already lost.

In fact, only a few Turks came even as far as the top of the outer wall. There they were at once cut down by Giustiniani's men who, like a living, moving wall of iron barred their way. The scaling-ladders were thrust off with long poles as soon as raised, while seething pitch and molten lead were slopped from great ladles upon the assailants below. The enemy suffered heavy losses and by morning their dead lay in heaps in front of the wall. Among these were only a few janissaries, from which it was evident that for this attempt the Sultan had sent in only the less efficient of his light troops.

Nevertheless, when the Turks retired, many of Giustiniani's men were so exhausted that they sank down where they stood, and slept. Emperor Constantine, who inspected the wall shortly after the battle, had to shake many of the sentries with his own hand, to rouse them. Giustiniani forced the Greek workmen to descend into the ditch and clear it of all the material with which the Turks had sought to fill it. Many went to their deaths in this way, when the enemy in revenge for their failure discharged their cannon in the dark.

In the morning thirty of the Turkish galleys rowed from the Port of Pillars up the boom. But no fighting ensued between them and the towering Venetians. A few shots were exchanged, and then the Turks returned to their harbor. In the course of the day the Sultan had a couple of heavy bombards set up on the hill behind Pera; their first shot struck a Genoese vessel at the quayside, sinking her and her whole cargo, to the value of fifteen thousand ducats. The Genoese of Pera protested at this violation of their neutrality. The bombards stand on their territory, and one or two other missiles hit roofs and killed a woman in the city. The Sultan promised to pay compensation after the siege for any damage the Genoese might have sustained, and assured them of his friendship.

But he gained his object: the Venetian galleys were forced to withdraw from the boom, some to the quay and some to the sheltered area below the bastions and harbor-wall of Pera, where no shot could reach them. Many people gathered to watch this strange bombardment. For the most part the balls fell into the harbor, sending up huge columns of water.

In spite of all this the mood of the townsfolk is one of hope and enthusiasm, for the successful repulse has cheered us all. And Giustiniani has spread exaggerated accounts of the Turkish losses. But to me he said bluntly, "We must not be puffed up over a victory that was no victory. The attack was an ordinary reconnaissance to test the strength of the wall. A thousand men at most took part in it, as I've learned from our prisoners. But custom requires me, as protostrator, to issue a communiqué. So, when I put it about that we have beaten off a heavy attack—that the Turks have lost ten thousand men killed and as many wounded, while our own losses are confined to one man killed and a sprained ankle—every seasoned soldier knows what it means and pays no heed. But on the city's morale it will have an excellent effect." He looked at me with a smile and added, "You fought bravely and well, Jean Ange."

"Did I? There was such confusion that I hardly knew what I was doing."

This was true. This morning I found my sword sticky with blood, but the events of the night I recalled only as a muddled nightmare.

In the course of the day the Sultan had fifty pairs of oxen driven up to the great bombard. It was removed from its bed and, with the help of hundreds of men, was dragged to a new position opposite the Gate of St. Romanos. The Blachernae wall has proved too strong for it, then, and the Sultan is making ready for a prolonged siege.

I have visited the wounded, who lie on straw in empty stables and sheds near the wall. The experienced Latin warriors have set aside money for surgeons and are therefore receiving expert care, but the Greeks are tended only by a few trained nuns, who do it purely out of charity. Among them I recognized to my amazement Khariklea, who had removed her veil and rolled up her sleeves and was skillfully washing and dressing the very worst wounds. She greeted me warmly and I could not resist telling her that I was living at the Blachernae. So weak was I—and I believe she read my thoughts. At least she hastened to say, without any question from me, that she had not seen Sister Anna for many days.

The wounded aver with one voice that the Turks, against all decency and custom, use poisoned arrows; for even the slightly hurt fall grievously ill within a few days and succumb in convulsions. In one corner I beheld a corpse which had stiffened in a bow, its face fixed in a ghastly grin, so that it was terrible to see. The muscles felt as hard as wood. Many of the wounded are therefore asking to be carried into the open air or to their own homes. I spoke to Giustiniani about them, but he will not allow any of his men to leave the walls and help them.

When I reproved him for his lack of charity he replied, "Experience has taught me that the recovery of the sick is in God's hands. One man receives attention from a surgeon and dies, another recovers with no care at all. One gets a cut on his little finger and dies of blood poisoning, while another loses a whole arm and lives. Abundant food and comfortable beds only soften a sick man and do harm. Such has been my experience. So don't meddle with things you don't understand."

19 April 1453

Jesus Christ, Son of God, have mercy upon me a sinner!

Having written so much yesterday I hoped I might at last get some sleep. I have had little lately. To smother my heart's uneasiness I have walked about, or sat down to write these vain words.

But as I lay with wide-open eyes in the darkness of my cold room in the Blachernae, enjoying my solitude and tormented by it, she came to me. She came. She herself, of her own free will. Anna Notaras, my beloved.

I recognized her light step, her breathing.

"John Angelos," she whispered, "are you asleep?"

She put her cold hands in mine, she lay down beside me; her nose and lips felt cold, but her cheek was hot against my cheek.

"Forgive me," she said. "Forgive me, my beloved. I didn't know what I was doing—I didn't know what I wanted. You're alive!"

"Of course I'm alive," I said. "I'm tough. Ill weeds thrive."

"The earth quakes," she said, "and the walls are split. Death roars for nights on end, and with a thousand voices. No one can know what war is until they have seen it. When the Turks attacked last night I prayed for you as I've never prayed before—I vowed to stifle all my selfishness, my malice and pride, if only I might see you again alive."

"Do you love me, then?" I asked doubtingly, though her hands, cheeks and mouth assured me of it. "You told me you hated me."

"I hated you for days—perhaps a week," she said. "Not until the cannon began thundering, rocking the convent walls, did I understand. I had resolved, I had vowed in my heart, never to see you again. Or if I did see you, that I would not speak a word—or at least only to put you in your place. Well, and here I am. At night, in the dark, alone with you. And I have kissed you. Alas for me, and for you!"

"And I had made the same resolve," I said, shaking her by the shoulders. Her shoulders were round and soft under her clothes. I smelled the hyacinth scent of her cheeks. In relief after her tension and fear she began giggling—she laughed like a little girl, and couldn't stop, though she pressed both hands to her mouth.

"Why are you laughing?" I asked suspiciously. In the pain of my love I thought she might be fooling me still, and reveling in my humiliation.

"Because I'm happy," she laughed, and vainly pressed her fingers to her mouth. "So terribly happy—and I can't help laughing to think how funny you looked when you ran away from me with your armor under your arm."

"It wasn't you I ran away from," I said. "It was myself. But I can't escape. Neither on the ramparts, nor in the Blachernae, neither waking nor sleeping. At every hour you have stood invisibly beside me."

Her soft mouth opened under mine, and panting she breathed out her love. In her fire—yes, and in her pain—she but pressed the closer to me, stroking my shoulders and back as if she would keep the memory of my living body forever in her hands.

Afterwards I rested beside her, empty, tranquil, cold. I had plucked her flower. She had permitted it. From that moment she was a woman without honor. But I loved her, I loved her as she was. I loved even her willfulness.

After a long time she whispered softly in my ear, "John Angelos, is this not best?"

"It is best," I answered, feeling intensely sleepy.

She laughed silently and whispered, "So simple, so easy, so straightforward. It's you who make things difficult and complicated for yourself. But now I'm happy."

"You have no regrets?" I asked drowsily, simply for something to say.

She was astonished. "What should I regret? Now you can never run away from me. And I have known joy. Why, even if you married me now, it would be no safeguard—you've already left one wife in the lurch. But now that this has happened, your conscience will never allow you to do the same to me. That much of you I know already, hard though you may think yourself. My beloved!"

I was full of tranquillity and peace, and in no mood for thinking. She breathed on my arm, her lips touched my ear, her hair caressed my neck and I smelled the hyacinth of her cheeks. I laid my hand on her bare breast and fell deeply asleep. It was very long since I had slept thus without dreaming.

I slept late. I did not wake when she left me. I did not even wake when the great gun roared at dawn and summoned the Turks to their morning prayer. The sun was high in the sky when I awoke. I had rested; I was renewed and happy.

She had gone while I slept. It was best. I did not want her to be discovered and I knew that I should see her again. More cheerful, more relaxed than ever before in my life, I went and ate an abundant breakfast. I put on no armor, nor even buckled on my sword. In my plain Latin dress, humble as a pilgrim, I turned my steps toward the Pantokrator monastery.

There I had to wait an hour or two while the monk Gennadios performed his pious exercises, and meanwhile I knelt and prayed before the holy icons in the monastery church. I prayed for forgiveness of my sins. I plunged into the mystic reality of the heart; I knew that before God our sins are weighed in other scales than those of men.

At sight of me Gennadios the monk knitted his brows and stared at me with his glowing eyes.

"What do you want of me, Latin?" he demanded.

I said, "In my youth I met many men in the monastery of Mount Athos who had abandoned their Roman faith and turned to the true Greek Church to dedicate their lives to God, and be partakers of the holy mysteries in the original manner of the Church of Christ. My father died while I was yet a child, but from his papers I learned that my grandfather was a Greek of Constantinople. He forsook his faith, married a Venetian and accompanied the Pope to Avignon. My father lived in Avignon and received a pension from the Papal treasury until he died. I was born there. But all this was error. Now that I have come to Constantinople to die on the walls, fighting for Christ against the Turks, I desire to return to the faith of my fathers."

His zeal blinded him, so that he did not listen overattentively to my words; and for this I was thankful, not wishing to answer the suspicious questions which might have formed on the tongue of a more reflective man.

He merely cried out accusingly, "Then why do you fight with Latins against the Turks? Even the Sultan is better than the Emperor, who has acknowledged the Pope."

"Let us not argue about that," I begged him. "Fulfill your task. Be the shepherd bringing the strayed lamb back to the fold upon his shoulder. Remember, you too signed, after due consideration. My sin is no greater than yours."

With his left hand he raised his right, which I now saw was paralyzed, and said triumphantly, "Day and night have I prayed that in token of His forgiveness God might wither the hand that signed the Act of Union in Florence. And when the guns roared for the first time the Lord heard my prayer. Now the Holy Spirit dwells within me."

Bidding a lay brother attend us, he led me to the pool in the courtyard and ordered me to undress. He then thrust me down into the water, pressed my head beneath the surface and baptized me afresh. For some reason he gave me the name of Zacharias. When I had come up out of the water I made my confession in the usual manner to him and the lay brother, and he laid only a few light penances upon me because I had shown good will. His face was radiant and he softened noticeably, prayed for me and invoked a blessing.

"Now you're a true Greek," he said. "Remember, this is the time of fulfillment, and the Last Day is at hand. Constantinople must perish. The longer it resists, the greater will be the fury of the Turks and the more bitter the sufferings that will overtake even the innocent. If it be God's will that the city should fall into Turkish hands, who can hinder it? He who fights against the Sultan, fights in his blindness against the will of God. But he who drives the Latins from Constantinople is pleasing to God."

"Who has given you authority to speak thus?" I asked sorrowfully.

"My repentance, my suffering, my fears for my city—these have given me authority," he replied vehemently. "It is not I, Gennadios the monk, who speak it, but the Spirit within me."

Glancing around he caught sight of the gray fish darting in their fright through the muddied water of the pool.

"The day of affliction is at hand," he cried, pointing at the fish with his left hand. "On that day those fish shall turn red as blood from terror, so that even the faithless must believe. Let that be the sign! If you are still alive upon that day, you shall behold it. The Spirit of God, the Lord of all Worlds, speaks through my mouth."

He declared this with such solemn fervor that I had to believe him. Then, wearying, he fell silent. When the lay brother had gone, I put on my clothes again.

"Father, I am a sinner," I said, "and have offended against the law, as you have just heard. I have lain with a Greek woman and robbed her of her innocence. Is it in any way possible for me to atone for my sin by marrying her, although I have a wife in Florence whom I married according to law and the rites of the Roman Church?"

He pondered, and then with the glint of a one-time politician in his eyes he said, "The Pope and his cardinals have so bitterly reviled and persecuted our Church, our patriarchs—ay, and our creed—that there can be no sin in causing the Papal Church what vexation I may. Now, after this baptism, your previous marriage is invalid. I declare it invalid, since in our present straits we have no legitimate patriarch to make this pronouncement. There is only the apostate Gregorios Mammas, judgment be upon him. Bring the woman here and I will make you man and wife beneath a consecrated roof."

I said doubtfully, "This is a delicate matter which must be

kept secret. You may recognize her. The wrath of an exalted man will be upon your head if you marry us."

He said, "It is in God's hand. Sin must be expiated, and what father would be so unnatural as to prevent his daughter's atonement? Should I fear noblemen and archons, I who fear not the Emperor himself?"

No doubt he believed that I had seduced the daughter of some Latin-minded courtier, and was therefore well content with the proposal. He promised to keep the matter secret if I would bring the woman to him that evening. I do not know enough about the Greek Church to decide whether such a marriage as this is valid. For my heart it suffices.

I hastened home to my house by the harbor, and I had guessed aright: she was there. She had already sent to the convent for her clothes-chest; she had rearranged everything, so that nothing of mine was in its proper place, and ordered Manuel to scrub the floors.

"Master," said Manuel meekly, wringing dirty water from a rag into a bucket, "I was just thinking of going out in search of you. Do you really intend this headstrong woman to move in here and turn everything upside down? My knees are sore and my back aches. Were we not very well as we were, without a woman in the house?"

"She stays," I said. "Don't whisper a word of it to anyone. Should the neighbors be inquisitive, tell them that she is a Latin woman, a friend of your master's, and that she is to lodge here for the duration of the siege."

"Have you well reflected, master?" asked Manuel cautiously. "It's easier to hang a woman round your neck than to shake her off." He added slyly, "She has been poking among your books and papers, too."

I did not stop to argue with him. With fever in every limb I ran up the stairs like a boy. Anna had dressed herself like a simple Greek woman, but her face, her complexion and her whole bearing betrayed her birth.

"Why have you been running—why are you so breathless?" she asked in feigned alarm. "You can't mean to chase me from the house, as Manuel threatened? He's a disagreeable, self-willed old man who doesn't know what's good for him." Throwing a guilty glance around at the disorder in my room, she added hastily, "I've only shifted a few things to make it more comfortable for you. And it was dirty here, too. I will buy new curtains if you'll let me have the money. And a man in your position can't sleep in that lumpy, shabby old bed."

"Money!" I repeated vaguely, and realized in some dismay that I had little money left. Such things had long been indifferent to me.

"Of course!" she said. "I've heard that men do all they can to force money on the women they've seduced. Or are you going to be mean now that you've got what you want?"

I burst out laughing in spite of myself.

"You should be ashamed to talk of money now," I said, "just when I've come to make an honest woman of you. That's why I've been running."

She forgot her teasing and regarded me gravely for a long time. I saw her brown eyes as nakedly as on that first day by the church. I recognized her across the centuries as if we had already lived many lives together, though the sleep of death and our rebirths had made us forget them and dropped a veil between us.

"Anna," I said, "would you not like to marry me after all? That's what I came to ask you. Let a holy mystery unite our souls as our flesh has already been united."

She bent her head; a few tears escaped from under her closed lids and rolled down her cheeks.

"You do love me, then, after all? You really love me?" she asked hesitantly.

"Did you doubt it?" I returned.

She looked at me.

"I don't know," she admitted frankly. "I thought to myself that nothing had any value if you did not love me. I thought I would offer you my maidenhood to see if that was all you wanted—and I think I should have lost nothing if I had found it to be true. I should have left you, I think, and never wanted to see you again. I was only playing here, pretending we had our own house."

She threw her arms around my neck and pressed her head against my shoulder.

"You see, I've never had a home of my own. Our house is simply the home of my mother and father. I never had anything to look after there, and I envied one of our servants who married and could go and buy cheap household things for herself. I envied ordinary people their happiness, believing that I was not born to know anything like it. But now I have it, if you will really marry me."

"No," I objected, "we have nothing. Nothing. Just a short time. But be you my earthly home so long as I have to live. And don't hold me back when our time has run out. Promise me that! You will promise, won't you?"

She made no answer, only raised her head a little and shot me a glance from under lowered lids.

"Imagine it!" she said. "I, who was to be the consort of an Emperor! Sometimes I have borne a grudge against Constantine because he went back on his word, but now I am glad I escaped marriage with him— Now I'm happy to wed a Frank who has deserted his wife." She looked at me again, and said with an artless smile, "Truly it is lucky that I am not the Emperor's consort, for I suppose I should have deceived him with you, if we had met. And then he would have had your eyes put out and shut me up in a convent for the rest of my life. And that would have been hard for you."

Hourly the cannon roared outside the city walls, and our light timber house trembled and creaked at the joints. But we enjoyed our brief happiness and forgot the time. In the evening I sent Manuel to hire a litter, and we set off together for the monastery of the All-Ruler. Gennadios was startled to recognize Anna Notaras, but he kept his promise. Manuel and the monks held the sacred canopy over our heads while we were made man and wife. Afterwards Gennadios blessed our marriage and made out the certificate, which he sealed with the great seal of the monastery.

As he handed it to me he gave me a strangely significant glance and said, "I don't know who you are, but the Spirit tells me that there is a purpose behind this. If so, may all turn out for the best, for our city and our faith."

When he said this I felt with a chill conviction that nothing has happened by my will. Since I escaped from the Sultan's camp I have followed step by step, surely as a sleepwalker, the path marked out for me by fate. Why else should I have met, out of all the women in the world, Anna Notaras, and recognized her by her eyes?

20 April 1453

I awoke in my house. She was sleeping naked by my side. She was unutterably lovely. Her mortal body was like ivory and gold. So fair, so virginal was she, in spite of all, that I felt a stab in my throat at the sight of her.

Just then the church bells pealed the alarm, drowning the din of the guns. Crowds of people came running past the house, and their steps rattled the vessels on the table. I sprang out of bed, reminded of my duties. She awoke and sat up in alarm, covering her nakedness with the bedclothes.

I dressed hastily. I had not even my sword. Then with a hasty kiss of farewell I dashed downstairs. Manuel was standing beside the stone lion, detaining some of the hurrying people to inquire what was afoot. His face was lit by incredulous wonder.

"Master!" he cried. "A miracle has happened! This is a blessed day. The Papal fleet is coming; the first ships are already in sight."

I ran with the others all the way up to the Acropolis. There, high above the wall facing the sea, I stood amid a group of breathless, waving, shouting townsfolk and beheld four western ships which with bellying canvas were standing steadily in over the heavy swell toward the Acropolis, amid a turmoil of Turkish galleys. Three of the vessels flew the Genoese flag while the fourth, a big merchantman, had hoisted the purple pendant of the Emperor. No other Christian ships were to be seen.

The vessels were already so near that the wind carried to us the noise of battle—shouts, oaths and shots. The Turkish flagship had rammed the largest vessel amidships and was fast in her side. To each of the others Turkish galleys had made fast with hooks and grapnels, so that the mighty ships trailed a bunch of light craft along with them.

All about me excitedly yelling people were telling how the battle had started far out to sea. The Sultan himself had ridden out into the shallow water near the marble tower to call orders to his vessels and urge the sea captains to destroy the Christian fleet.

The whole length of the sea wall was black with people. Rumors and news spread from mouth to mouth. It was said that the Sultan had bared his teeth like a dog and foamed at the mouth. It may well be true; I myself have seen Mohammed in the grip of one of his rages, though since then he has learned to control himself.

Slowly but steadily the wind drove the great ships toward the harbor and safety, dragging the Turkish galleys with them as a bear drags hounds clinging to its coat. There were so many of the enemy craft that they often collided with one another, and the great waves were topped with bloody foam. Now and then one of the galleys gave up the struggle, cast off and pulled away to make room for another. Far out to sea drifted a single foundering galley.

The air was full of the din of drums and horns, hideous shrieks and dying howls. In the water floated corpses and wreckage. On their lofty decks Christian marines in plate armor, wielding axes, swords and pikes, fought off the Turks that continually swarmed up the steep sides of the ships. The Turkish admiral stood on the quarter-deck of his galley with a speaking-trumpet, roaring his orders.

Suddenly the crowd began shouting with one accord: "Phlaktanellas, Phlaktanellas!" and the cry was borne jubilantly all over the city. Someone had recognized the captain of the ship that flew the imperial pendant. This vessel had sailed for Sicily before the siege, to fetch grain. On board of her could be plainly seen a giant of a man who grimaced, laughed, brandished a bloodstained battle-axe and pointed out to his archers the enemy perched aloft in the rigging of the galleys.

The Genoese had wetted their sails, that the fiery arrows

might not set them alight. But across the deck of an enemy galley there suddenly spurted a stream of fire, and the shrieks of the burnt Turks for a moment drowned the noise of battle. The damaged vessel withdrew from the conflict, leaving behind her a blazing wake.

It was an incredible sight to see these four Christian ships cutting their way irresistibly toward the harbor, surrounded by at least forty Turkish war galleys. The jubilation of the crowd is not to be described. Again and again they yelled that the Papal fleet was on its way and that these were but the forerunners. Constantinople was saved!

The reeking, seething hurly-burly of craft passed Acropolis Point, and here the ships were compelled to alter course to larboard, to make the boom and the Golden Horn. By this they lost their following wind and their steerage way. Under the lee of the high hill the sails hung slack and it was clear that the vessels no longer answered to the helm. A shout of triumph rose from the Turkish galleys and the watching crowds fell silent. From the hills on the further shore, beyond the walls of Pera, a triumphant yell reached us against the wind. There stood dense masses of Turkish onlookers praising Allah.

Fighting incessantly, the Christian ships closed up; they would not abandon one another, though the Turkish flagship still had her bows fast in the hull of the largest Genoese and hampered her movements. Grappled to one another, side by side, the four vessels rocked in the swell like a conglomerate fortress, spewing forth stones, round-shot, arrows and molten lead over the Turks. In hissing arches Greek fire spurted across the enemy decks and kept the crews busy extinguishing it.

"Phlaktanellas, Phlaktanellas!" came the shout again from the crowds on the sea wall. The ships were now so near that the faces of the fighting men could be plainly distinguished, but no one could help them. Behind the harbor-boom the Venetians were cleared for action, but the chain prevented them from coming out in support.

As I watched the fantastic efforts of the Genoese ships I forgave Pera all its huckstering and sharp practice. I saw the discipline, seamanship and seaworthiness demanded by such an action; I understood how it was that for centuries Genoa had vied with Venice herself as ruler of the seas. Infinitely slowly, inch by inch, this fire-spitting fortress of ships glided toward the boom, laboriously impelled by the sea swell and a few mighty oars.

Along the wall and on the hills of the city the people fell on their knees to pray. The suspense was now unendurable, so formidable was the Turkish superiority, so doggedly did the galleys relieve one another and come fresh to the fray. Their admiral was hoarse from shouting, and blood poured down his cheek. With severed wrists the turbaned boarders fell into the sea and drowned, while their hands remained clinging convulsively to the rails of the Christian ships.

"Panaghia, Panaghia! Holy Virgin, protect thy city!" prayed the people. Greeks were praying for Latins, fired by the endurance and heroism of the sailors. Perhaps it is not heroism to fight for one's life, but heroic it certainly was of these four ships to cling so loyally together, and fight their slow way through vastly superior forces to the relief of Constantinople.

And suddenly—suddenly it was as if a blue puff of wind passed across the sky. Through the air swept a fold of the Virgin's blue robe. A miracle came to pass: the wind changed! The heavy wet sails filled once more and the floating mass moved nearer to the boom. At the last moment the Turkish admiral ordered his crew to hack away the bows of the flagship, so that only her stem remained wedged in the hull of the Christian. With blood pouring from the scuppers, he turned his galley and rowed away. Limping, with smashed oars, smothered in smoke from the unquenchable Greek fire, the rest of the Turkish craft followed their commander, and the continuous cheering of the people of Constantinople shook the very heavens.

I know little of miracles; but that the wind should change just at that decisive moment seemed little less. There was something holy in the event, something which the human senses could not grasp. Nor was its strangeness dimmed by the shrieks of the wounded or by the seamen's hoarse oaths as with exhausted voices they hailed the harbor, asking for the boom to be opened. To unfasten the great chain is a difficult and dangerous task, and not until the Turkish vessels had vanished up the Bosporus did Aloisio Diedo allow it to be done; and the four ships staggered into port amid salutes in honor of the Emperor.

That same afternoon the ships' companies paraded with their colors, led by their officers and followed by rejoicing crowds, through the city to the Khora monastery, there to render thanks to the Panaghia of Constantinople for their preservation. All the wounded who could walk came too, and some of the others were carried on stretchers to the church in the hope of miraculous healing. Thus the Latins thanked and praised the Holy Virgin of the Greeks, and their eyes were dazzled by the gold mosaics in the Khora church.

But for the more reflective of the citizens, the general rejoicing lost something of its luster when it was learned that these three Genoese ships formed no part of any united Christian navy, but had simply brought cargoes of arms which the Emperor had ordered and paid for last autumn. The Sultan's attack upon them was a barefaced breach of neutrality, since in fact the vessels were bound for Pera. The captains had resisted only because their cargo was contraband and they feared to lose their ships. Now that they had come safely to port they and the owners were rich men. Whether they will be able to keep their wealth and ships for themselves, on the grounds of Pera's neutrality, is another matter.

My enthusiasm was over. I had to return to the Blachernae and report to Giustiniani. With my thoughts already elsewhere I kissed my bride farewell and forbade her to go into the city lest she be recognized. I also ordered Manuel to obey her and promised to return home as soon as my duties allowed.

By the Gate of St. Romanos not only the outer wall but the great wall itself had been damaged by bombardment. At dusk timber, earth, faggots and hides were dragged in an unending stream to the outer wall to strengthen it. Anyone may go through the great wall to the outer one, but to return is more difficult. Giustiniani has posted sentries who seize everyone attempting to come back, and force all visitors to stay and do a whole night's work. Giustiniani's Latins are exhausted by the gunfire, which has continued throughout the twenty-four hours, and by the many minor assaults on the breach, where the Turks are doing their best to hinder the work of repair. Most of the defenders have not removed their armor for many days and nights.

I described the sea battle to Giustiniani and said, "The Venetians in the Blachernae are furious at the Genoese victory, since their own ships have reaped little honor by lying at the boom or rowing out of reach of the Sultan's bombards."

"Victory," said Giustiniani, and was suddenly grave. "Our only victory has been in holding the city for nearly two weeks. The arrival of these vessels is our sharpest reverse. Hitherto we have at least been able to hope that the Pope's crusading fleet might arrive in time to relieve us. But now we know that the Aegean lies empty and that no navies are assembled even in Italian harbors. Christendom has forsaken us."

I protested. "But such an enterprise would have to be kept secret up to the last possible moment."

"Rubbish!" he said. "No one could fit out a big fleet without the Genoese captains catching some hint of it." Then he glared at me with menace in his ox-eyes and demanded, "Where have you been? I've not seen you at the Blachernae for twenty-four hours."

I said, "It was a quiet day and I had private business to attend to. Don't you trust me?"

He said accusingly, "You're on my rolls and I must know what you're doing." Suddenly he thrust his face close to mine, his cheeks swelled and there was a green glow in his eyes as he burst out, "You've been seen in the Turkish camp!"

"Are you mad?" I cried. "That is a shameless lie, and must come from someone who seeks my life. How could I have got there and back in the time?"

He replied, "Every night boats ply between us and Pera, as you well know. One has only to fee the podesta—and the guards on the gate are poor men who don't say no to a little extra income. You needn't think I don't know what goes on round the Sultan. I have eyes over there, just as he has eyes here."

"Giustiniani," I said, "for our friendship's sake you must believe me. It was a quiet day yesterday and I married a Greek woman. But in God's name keep this to yourself, or I shall lose her."

Giustiniani burst into thunderous laughter and slapped my shoulder with his broad hand as of yore.

"I never heard of anything crazier," he said. "Is this the moment to think of marriage?"

He believed me. Perhaps he had only wanted to scare me

into telling him what I did when I was out of his sight. But I was depressed and filled with foreboding. All night new fires have been burning in the Turkish camp and the big cannon are discharged every other hour, although hitherto the enemy has been content to fire once only in the course of the night.

21 April 1453

A hellish day. During the night the Turks dragged up more guns and reinforced their batteries. Their new method of aiming at separate points along the wall has already proved successful. In the afternoon one of the towers near the Gate of St. Romanos collapsed, and with it a large portion of the main wall itself. The breach is considerable. If the attacking force had been stronger they might perhaps have penetrated the city, for at the corresponding point in the outer wall there remains only the temporary palisade which has to be renewed every night. But fortunately the Turks have been sending detachments not more than a couple of hundred strong to test different points along the wall. These have now no time to carry off their dead, and so many corpses lie by the outer wall and where the ditch has fallen in that the stench of them poisons the air.

Skirmishes continued all day until late in the evening. The Sultan has tested the ramparts at every point. On the high ground behind Pera he has set up more cannon in an attempt to bombard the ships in the harbor. At least a hundred and fifty cannon balls have fallen there. When the Venetian vessels rowed away from the boom to avoid them, the Sultan's galleys tried to break the chain, but the alarm was given in time for the Venetians to return and defend it; they were also able to inflict such damage on the enemy galleys that these made off. During this action the Turks could not fire from behind Pera for fear of hitting their own ships. Three times the Sultan's fleet tried in vain to break through the boom.

It is as if the Sultan were moving heaven and earth to avenge yesterday's disgraceful defeat at sea. They say that last night he rode out to the Port of Pillars and with his own hand belabored his admiral on breast and shoulders with the iron club of an emir. Admiral Baltoglu was already severely wounded and had lost an eye in the fighting, and two hundred men aboard his flagship had perished, so that it was all he could do to withdraw from the battle unaided. Without doubt he is a brave man, albeit incapable of commanding a whole fleet; this is evident from yesterday's turmoil.

The Sultan meant to impale him, but the seamen and their officers pleaded for him on the grounds of his personal valor; therefore Mohammed confined himself to having him flogged. The man was made to lie face downwards on the ground in front of the whole fleet, and was thrashed with rods until he lost consciousness. All his property has been confiscated and he has been dismissed from the Sultan's camp. Since he has lost eye, honor and property in the service, it is understandable that a willing successor should have proved hard to find. However, the Turkish fleet has now cast off its lethargy and has been active all day, though without noticeable result.

The Venetians fear that this activity and the constant scuffles with reconnaissance patrols presage an imminent general assault. Our men have stood to arms all day; no one may leave the wall, no one may remove his armor even at night. Yesterday's triumph has been followed by gloom throughout the city. No one troubles to count the cannon shots now, so constant is the roar of the guns. Smoke darkens the sky and blackens the houses.

Every day fresh troops and volunteers arrive at the Sultan's camp, tempted by the prospect of plunder. Among them are both Christian and Jewish merchants, who make good money by selling victuals to the troops and who mean to invest their profits in loot when the Turks have reduced the city. It is said that carts and sledges, draft animals, asses and camels have all risen greatly in price owing to the expected demand for means of conveying stolen treasure out of Constantinople. The poorer people count on there being enough slaves available in the city to carry the booty away into Asia on their shoulders.

All these things indicate an approaching climax. Already the Sultan's batteries have learned to train their pieces on three special points in the outer wall, so that a large portion of it may collapse simultaneously and fill the ditch. Here and there, both in the city and on the ramparts, signs of panic may be observed.

Men of Notaras' reserve ride through the streets, ruthlessly dragging every fit man to the walls. Only women, old men and children may stay at home. Even the sick are torn from their beds, since many feign sickness in sheer terror. Others maintain that this war concerns the Latins and the Emperor alone, and feel disinclined to fight the Latins' battles. Many have found hidingplaces in cellars, underground vaults and dry wells, where they may take refuge if the Turks succeed in entering the city.

22 April 1453

A Sunday of horror. This morning the church bells fell silent and on the wall overlooking the harbor great numbers of townsfolk assembled, rubbing their eyes in mute amazement. There was scared talk of sorcery and of dervishes who could walk on the water and use their mantles as sails. Directly opposite the Church of St. Nicholas and the Gate of St. Theodosias the Pera harbor is crammed with Turkish galleys. No one could imagine how these vessels had crossed the boom so as to lie as they now do in the rear of ours. Many rubbed their eyes again and vowed that the ships were a hallucination. But the Pera shore was swarming with Turks, who were throwing up earthworks, raising palisades and laying cannon to protect their vessels.

Then a shout went up. On the high ground above, a galley suddenly appeared and began gliding downhill with all sails set, amid the music of drums and trumpets. She seemed to be sailing on dry land. Hauled by hundreds of men along a timber slipway, she moved down to the shore, splashed into the water and freed herself from the timber cradle that had supported her, to be rowed away to join the other ships, of which there was a row of at least fifty. None of these are large, however; they carry eighteen or twenty oars and are between fifty and seventy feet long.

The Sultan and his new admiral contrived this surprise maneuver in the course of only twenty-four hours. Later it was known that the Genoese in Pera had supplied the Sultan with a vast quantity of timber, rope, rollers, and lard for greasing the slipway. Then with the help of wind machines, oxen and laborers the Turks hauled the ships from the Bosporus up the steep hill behind Pera, that they might glide down the other side to the Golden Horn.

The Genoese of Pera say in their own defense that everything happened so swiftly and secretly that until dawn this morning they had no inkling of these preparations. As for selling such enormous quantities of lard, their excuse is that to preserve their neutrality they are obliged to trade as much with the Sultan as with the city. And even if they had known what was going on they could not have prevented it, for tens of thousands of Turkish warriors are posted on the hill to guard the galleys.

Aloisio Diedo hastily summoned the Venetian Council to confer with the Emperor and Giustiniani in St. Mary's Church. Meanwhile fresh ships came gliding down the hill past Pera, their sails set. Helmsmen thumped their drums and the crews cheered and brandished their oars, rejoicing like children at this cruise on dry land. Our fleet lay ready for battle but was powerless.

The conference was held in secret, and Aloisio Diedo did not invite the Genoese sea captains, who are consequently more embittered than ever against the Venetians. As evidence of how difficult it is to keep anything secret in this city I may mention that this evening many in the Blachernae are already acquainted with the course of the discussion.

Some of the Venetians proposed taking the offensive immediately, so that their large ships and heavy armament might destroy the Turkish craft while these still lay alongshore. They could scarcely offer strong resistance, it was thought, despite their numbers. But the more cautious members of the Council, among them the bailo, have a wholesome respect for the cannon which the Sultan has placed to defend his ships, and opposed a risky enterprise which might result in the sinking or disabling of their own precious vessels.

It was also proposed to make a surprise landing by night from a couple of light galleys, but to this Giustiniani refused to agree. Turkish strength in Pera was far too formidable, he said, and we could not afford to lose a single man.

Emperor Constantine vetoed both these plans on political grounds. The Turkish galleys are anchored on the Pera side of the Golden Horn. The foreshore belongs to Pera, therefore we should not and could not make any sort of attack upon it without first consulting the Genoese. For although the Sultan has blatantly violated Pera's neutrality by occupying the beach, Constantinople is not thereby entitled to commit a similar offense. Phrantzes supported the Emperor in this and said that Constantinople could not afford a clash with the Genoese, whatever the Sultan might choose to do.

The Venetians shouted with many oaths that one might as well communicate the plan of attack directly to the Sultan as to the Genoese, who were traitors to Christendom. The Sultan, they said, could never have moved his ships overland to the Golden Horn without their connivance.

At this Giustiniani drew his two-handed sword and bellowed that he was ready to defend the honor of Genoa against one, two, or the whole Council of Twelve at once. It would be shameful and unjust, he cried, to draw up any plan of attack without first hearing the Genoese sea captains. Their vessels were exposed to the same perils as the Venetians and took an equal share in the defense. It was absurd of the Venetians to attempt to patch their ragged honor by such an enterprise. The Emperor had to stand before him with arms outstretched, to pacify him, and then sought with tears in his eyes to soothe the indignant Venetians.

At last the Venetian captain Jacomo Coco spoke up—he

who came here from Trebizond last autumn and by guile sailed straight down the Bosporus past the Turkish vessels without the loss of a single man. He is a cross-grained fellow who prefers action to speech, but there is a twinkle in his eye sometimes; his men adore him and tell countless tales of his seamanship and resource.

"Too many cooks spoil the broth," he said. "If anything is to be done it must be done at once, by stealth, and without letting too many into the secret. We need no more than one galley, protected with sacks of wool and cotton. Under cover of that we can send over several rowing-boats and set fire to the Turkish vessels before anyone has an inkling of what is happening. I will gladly take command of the galley, but only on condition that we stop talking and act tonight."

His proposal was certainly sound, but the Emperor was afraid of offending the neutral people of Pera. Coco's plan was therefore adopted in principle, but it was agreed to postpone the operation for some days and plan it in consultation with the Genoese. Jacomo Coco shrugged his shoulders and laughed. "I have had more than my share of luck, but we must not expect the impossible. However, this will give me time to repent of my sins and make my communion. The enterprise spells death to me if it be not undertaken at once."

Giustiniani did not tell me all this. He said only, "It will be for the fleet to take the necessary steps. The Turkish galleys in the Horn constitute no threat to the Venetians. The most they can do is to row across one dark night and set fire to a few Christian ships. What is far worse is that the harbor wall must be entirely remanned. Hitherto I have had a mere handful of sentries posted along it, but henceforth we must be strong enough to prevent any attempt at landing from across the bay."

He went on: "By last night's work the Sultan has doubtless

won himself the name and fame of Alexander, and surpassed the exploits of the Persian King Xerxes in these waters. Ships have indeed been dragged overland before now, but never in such great numbers and under such difficult conditions. Let the Venetians boast of their vessels; I think more of Mohammed's military genius. By threat alone, without a shot fired, he has forced me to regroup the defense and spread my forces."

Glancing sideways at me he added, "Did I tell you? The Emperor and I are agreed that Megadux Notaras, by his contribution toward the city's defense, has proved himself worthy of a new task. Tomorrow he is to be given command of the reserves, in the center of the city by the Church of the Apostles. I shall entrust the defense of the harbor to someone else when I send the fresh troops there."

"Giustiniani," I said, "he will never forgive you this. Through him you insult the entire Greek population—the churches and cloisters, priests and monks—the whole spirit of Greece."

Giustiniani eyed me.

"I can put up with even that for the sake of a dukedom," he said. "I could never forgive myself if one dark night the spirit of Greece went and opened the harbor gates and let in the Turks." He muttered something to himself and repeated, "The spirit of Greece—aye, that was the right term: the spirit of Greece. That's something we must all beware of—the Emperor too!"

I was hot with anger, though I could understand.

Our only joy on this Sunday of sorrows has been that one of the great Turkish cannon exploded with an appalling noise, killing many of its team and throwing all those nearest it into confusion. It was nearly four hours before the guns in that sector could start firing again.

Many of the defenders are suffering from fever and pains in the stomach. The Guacchardi brothers have hanged a Greek workman who had deliberately cut off his fingers to escape work on the wall.

Is this really the Latins' war, then, and not the Greeks'? I am afraid of my heart. I am afraid of my own thoughts. In time of war not the coolest intellect can remain unclouded.

25 April 1453

Last night at about midnight Jacomo Coco had two galleys and many small craft ready to attack and set fire to the Turkish ships below the Pera hill. But the Genoese forestalled the action by promising to share in it with larger forces as soon as the assault has been more thoroughly planned.

I wonder how they can hope that this secret will be kept, now that almost everyone in the fleet knows of it and people everywhere seem to be discussing the possibility of a surprise attack on Pera.

The bombardment continues. Losses mount. What is repaired at night is smashed by stone balls next day. In the Guacchardis' sector of the great wall two towers have fallen.

28 April 1453

This morning while it was yet dark Giustiniani came and shook me awake, as if to assure himself that I was at my post in the Blachernae. Then he curtly ordered me to go with him. Dawn was still some time off, and my mood was chilled by the night air. Dogs were barking in the Turkish camp, but for the rest all was still.

We mounted the ramparts opposite the Turkish anchorage. A couple of hours before sunrise a signal fire suddenly flared up from the lofty tower in Pera.

"God Almighty!" said Giustiniani. "Why was I born a Genoese? Their right hand knows not what their left hand does."

The night was dreadfully still. From the Turkish shore no sound was to be heard. The waters of the harbor lay black and shining below us, while up on Galata Tower blazed the bright flame. Summoning up all my powers of vision I seemed to discern the shadows of ships gliding across the water. Then the night erupted. Flashes from the guns opposite dazzled my eyes. Stone balls smashed into oaken hulls, and in an instant the night was filled with mighty clamor. Torches flared, Greek fire spurted over the water and drifted upon it in blazing pools. I could now see that the Venetians had sent a whole squadron across to destroy the Turkish galleys. Nearest the shore moved two large ships, shapeless from the stuffed sacks lashed fast along their sides. But one was on the point of foundering. Cannon balls crashed incessantly into the barges and brigantines which had been rowing under cover of the big vessels.

The entire Turkish fleet seemed on the alert, and were rowing to meet the Christians. Soon these were ramming one another in the utmost confusion, and the frantic orders of their captains echoed across the water. From time to time dense smoke clouds obliterated everything, and only a red glow told of yet another galley set alight. The Christians kindled their fire ships, set them adrift and leaped overboard to swim to other vessels.

The battle continued until dawn, when the Venetian galleys were able to disengage themselves and return. One of them, under Trevisano's command, would have gone to the bottom had not her crew stopped the leaks with their cloaks. The first galley, commanded by Coco, sank in a few minutes, though some of her crew swam ashore on the Pera side.

When the sun rose we could see that the surprise attack had been an utter failure. One Turkish galley was in flames and presently sank. Other fires were being extinguished one by one.

It was the son of the Venetian bailo who commanded the remaining galley. As he rowed back past Pera he fired his guns and we saw the balls throw up a cloud of dust at the foot of the city wall. The beacon which had been lit on the tower at the moment when the Venetians put out was so clear a proof of Genoese treachery that not even Giustiniani attempted to dispute it.

"Right or wrong, Genoa is my birthplace," he said. "The Venetian fleet is far too strong in comparison with the Genoese. A little bloodletting is wholesome, and will restore the balance in the harbor."

We were already on our way from the wall when I threw a last glance across at the reeking Pera shore and seized Giustiniani by the arm. There was the Sultan on his white charger, and the rising sun struck fires from the jewels in his turban. He had ridden onto a hillock by the shore, and a string of stripped and plundered captives were being led up to him, their hands bound behind them. These were the seamen who had swum ashore from the foundered galley. People near us were pointing, and crying that they recognized Jacomo Coco among the prisoners.

At this moment a group of Venetians came running from the Blachernae, having left their posts on the wall. Giustiniani ordered them to return, but they said that they took orders only from their bailo, who had ridden to the harbor to meet his son and bidden them attend him fully armed.

But the dispute was interrupted as, aghast and breathless, we turned our eyes again toward Pera. There the Turks were forcing their captives to their knees while a headsman brandished his sword. Heads fell, blood spurted—yet even this was not enough. Pointed stakes were driven into the ground in a row and the beheaded corpses were spitted on them. Then the heads with their grinning, distorted faces were impaled at the top of the stakes. Many among us hid our faces at this grisly spectacle. The Venetians wept with rage. A woman vomited and tottered from the wall.

The victims were so numerous that the first were already hanging blood-drenched from their stakes while the last awaited their execution. The Sultan spared none. By the time it was full daylight, forty crimson corpses hung there, their heads crying for vengeance though their mouths were dumb.

Giustiniani said, "There cannot be many Venetians left who are anxious to visit the Turks."

Rowing-boats were approaching from the ships, packed with men whose weapons flashed in the sunlight. Giustiniani surveyed them with knitted brows.

"What's this?" he said suspiciously.

Behind us we heard the clatter of hoofs. The Venetian bailo rode past at a wild gallop, heedless of age and girth. After him came his son, with drawn sword and armor still stained with blood. "Follow us, Venetians!" they cried. "To the captives!"

Giustiniani shouted in vain for a horse; then recollecting himself he said, "All the same, I can't withdraw my men from the Romanos Gate. Let this shame be upon the Venetians' heads. You saw how they forsook two of their ships and fled in panic."

It was not long before the furious Venetians returned, soldiers and sailors higgledy-piggledy, dragging and kicking and cuffing the Turkish prisoners they had brought from tower and dungeon. Some had been taken in the city after the siege began, but most of them had been caught during the Turkish reconnaissance raids near the Gate of St. Romanos and elsewhere. Many were wounded and could hardly walk. Within an hour over two hundred captives had been assembled by the harbor wall. The Venetians thronged about them; every now and then someone would step up and hit them in the face, kick them in the belly or slash among them at random with a sword. Many of the prisoners fell and lay prostrate; others attempted to pray and to call upon Allah in their mortal distress.

Giustiniani shouted to the Venetians, "I shall appeal to the Emperor. These are my prisoners."

The Venetians retorted, "Hold your tongue, you damned Genoese, or we'll hang you too."

The Venetians numbered many hundreds and were all fully armed. Giustiniani saw that he could do nothing and that his own life was in danger. He approached the bailo and attempted to negotiate, saying, "I dissociate myself from what the Genoese of Pera have done. Here we all fight to the glory of God and for the survival of Christendom. You will gain no honor by hanging these poor men, of whom many are brave warriors who did not fall into our hands until after they had been wounded. Moreover it would be foolish, for afterwards no Turk would ever surrender, but would rather fight on to his last breath."

The bailo cried with foaming lips, "The blood of our brothers and kinsmen yet reeks over there—yet you, you filthy

Genoese, are not ashamed to speak in defense of the Turks. Are you trying to get ransom for them? Ha! A Genoese would sell his own mother if he could get enough for her. Come, we'll buy your prisoners at the current price. Take it!"

Tearing his purse from its strap he flung it contemptuously at Giustiniani's feet. Giustiniani turned pale but controlled himself and went, beckoning me to follow.

The Venetians now began hanging the Turkish captives one by one, from the battlements and from the tower immediately opposite the Sultan's place of execution. They hanged the wounded too; in all, two hundred and fifty prisoners, six for every Venetian beheaded. The seamen were not ashamed to play the executioner; even the bailo's son hanged one of the wounded.

As soon as we were out of sight of the Venetians, Giustiniani hastened his steps. We met two mounted patrols from the reserve. Giustiniani ordered both the Greeks to dismount and commandeered their horses, and so we quickly reached the Emperor's quarters. He had shut himself up in his tower and was kneeling before an icon. His excuse was that he had been compelled to comply with the Venetian demand and approve the execution, or they would have taken the prisoners by force, defying his authority.

Giustiniani said, "I wash my hands of it. I can do nothing. I cannot take any of my men from the breach, no matter how many Venetians may have left their posts without permission. Keep the reserves in readiness, for otherwise I cannot answer for what may happen."

But having regained his own position and observed the Turkish camp for a while, he did nevertheless return to the harbor that afternoon with a score of men. The Venetians had tasted blood in hanging the helpless Turks. Many indeed returned to the wall, and the bailo shut himself up in the Blachernae to mourn Jacomo Coco's dishonored death. But the remainder roamed in scattered bands about the harbor, crying "treachery" and "death to the Genoese." When any Genoese crossed their path they knocked him down, rolled him in the dirt and kicked him mercilessly in the ribs.

When they began breaking in the doors and windows of a Genoese merchant's house, Giustiniani ordered his men to advance in line and clear the streets of the Venetian rabble. General uproar followed. Soon there was fighting in all the streets of the harbor quarter; swords clashed and blood flowed. The watch sounded the alarm and Lukas Notaras came riding down the hill at the head of a troop of Greek horse. These began charging at Venetians and Genoese impartially and with the best will in the world. Greeks who had taken refuge in neighboring houses plucked up courage, hurled stones from roofs and windows and belabored passing Latins with long sticks.

When the battle had been raging for about two hours and the sun was low in the sky, Emperor Constantine himself rode down to the harbor arrayed in his brocade mantle of imperial green, with the purple tunic and boots and golden hooped crown. Beside him rode the Venetian bailo, also wearing the outward symbols of his dignity. The bailo hailed Giustiniani and with quivering cheeks begged his pardon for the abuse he had hurled at him earlier in the day. The Emperor shed tears and appealed to the Latins for the love of Christ to forget their internal quarrels in this hour of common peril. Though some of the Genoese in Pera had been guilty of treachery, all Genoese were not therefore culpable.

His appeal brought about some sort of reconciliation, in which Lukas Notaras also shared, offering his hand both to the bailo and to Giustiniani, embracing them and calling them his brothers. All old grudges must be buried, he said, now that each and every one was risking his life to save the city from the Turks. I believe that at that moment Notaras was perfectly sincere, since in moments of enthusiasm the Greek spirit is easily roused to noble behavior and self-abnegation. But both Giustiniani and Minotto, bred in the political schools of their own cities, believe Notaras to have been playing a part because he deemed the moment favorable for strengthening ties of friendship with the Latins.

At any rate, everyone dismounted from his charger. Notaras' men surrounded the harbor quarter, while the Emperor, Giustiniani, Minotto and Notaras walked through it, each urging his men in Christ's name to keep the peace and forget their squabbles. The Emperor's ceremonial splendor deterred even the most impudent Latin from raising his voice. The seamen straggled back to their boats and were soon aboard ship again. The only men left in the streets were a few Venetian sailors who in their grief for Coco had drunk themselves insensible. Three Genoese and two Venetians had lost their lives, but at the Emperor's desire this fact was suppressed and the dead secretly buried during the night.

The rioting had raged round my house too, and when all was quiet, therefore, I asked Giustiniani's leave to call there. He replied kindly that he had nothing against a cup of wine himself, after a day of such grief and shame. But I fancy he was only curious to see my wife.

Manuel unlocked the door. In a voice trembling with eager pride he told us that he had hit a Venetian carpenter in the face with a stone and felled him to the ground. Manuel was an honest, clever fellow, Giustiniani told him good-humoredly. Wearied by his heavy armor he tumbled into a chair, shaking the house; then stretching out his legs, he asked in God's name for wine.

I left Manuel to serve him and hastened to Anna, who had

withdrawn into the innermost room. Would she like to meet the renowned Giustiniani, I asked her, or did she prefer to remain apart in the Greek manner? When she had assured herself that I was unharmed from the rioting, she gave me a reproachful look and said, "If you're ashamed of me and my appearance, and unwilling to present me to your friends, I shall of course remain in my room."

I answered that on the contrary I was proud of her and would like her to be seen. Giustiniani would certainly not know her by sight, and in any case had promised to keep our marriage secret. She might therefore safely show herself.

I caught her hand eagerly to lead her in to him, but she snatched it away and snapped, "If ever you want to show me off to your friends again, I hope you will let me know beforehand, so that I may comb my hair and put on a suitable gown. I can't be seen looking like this, happy though I should be to meet so famous a man as Giustiniani."

In my innocence I exclaimed, "You're beautiful as you are—to me you're the most beautiful woman in the world. I don't know how you can talk of hair and clothes on such a day of shame. No one heeds such things, anyway."

"Indeed!" she retorted hotly. "You know little of the world. But of this matter at least I know more than you, being a woman. Allow me, if you please, to be a woman. That was after all the reason you married me, I suppose?"

Her behavior baffled me; I could not think what whim had hold of her to make her so prickly. I shrugged my shoulders and said, "You must do as you like. Stay in your room if you think it best; I will explain to Giustiniani."

She caught my arm and said hastily, "Don't be ridiculous. I shall be ready in a twinkling. Go down and entertain him meanwhile, so that he may not run away."

When I left her she already had her ivory comb in her hand

and was loosening her hair. In my confusion I drained a cup of wine at a gulp, which is not my habit, and Giustiniani readily followed my example. Anna was no doubt right: women are unlike men in very many ways, and attach importance to different things. I began to see that I know little about her yet, close to me though she is. Even when she lies in my arms her thoughts follow other paths than mine and I can never quite reach her.

Fortunately Giustiniani thought it quite natural that Anna should delay her coming, and made no remark. My house felt snug and safe. Through the window we caught now and then a reddish glint from the gun flashes reflected in the water of the harbor. Shortly afterward the roar would reach us with a tremor that set the wine quivering in the jar. But this was very different from the ramparts. Filled with a restful weariness we half-lay in our chairs, and the wine swam so agreeably in my head that I quite forgot my displeasure over Anna's caprices.

Then the door opened. Giustiniani at first glanced towards it carelessly, but then his face changed; he sprang to his feet with a clash of accouterments and bent his head respectfully.

Anna was standing in the doorway. She had put on what seemed to me a perfectly plain white silk gown, caught at the shoulder by a jeweled clasp. A gold-mounted, jeweled girdle set off the slenderness of her waist, and her arms and legs were bare. She was shod with gilt sandals and had painted her toenails red. On her head she wore a little round hood which sparkled with the same stones as the clasp and girdle. Her transparent veil had been allowed to fall round her neck, and she held it to her chin, smiling shyly. Her face was paler, her mouth redder and her eyes larger than ever. She was to me unutterably beautiful as she stood there, raising her thin, arched, deep blue eyebrows in surprise.

"Oh!" she said. "Oh, forgive me—you have a visitor."

In pretty confusion she extended her fingers and Giustiniani bent his bull-neck, kissed her hand, and still holding it surveyed her face in delight.

"Jean Ange," he said, when he had recovered from his astonishment, "I wonder no longer why you were in such a hurry. If she were not your lawful wedded wife I should strive with you for her favor. As it is I can do no more than pray to heaven that she may have a twin sister whose acquaintance I may make."

Anna said, "I am proud to meet the great Giustiniani, whose glorious fame is the pride of Christendom. Forgive my simple gown. If I had had a hint of this I would have dressed myself more fittingly." Putting her head on one side she gazed at Giustiniani through her eyelashes. "Oh," she said softly. "Perhaps after all I was too hasty in yielding to John Angelos. I hadn't seen you then."

"Don't believe him, Anna," I said hastily. "He has a wife in Genoa already and another in Kaffa, and girls in every port in Greece."

"What a beard!" whispered Anna, brushing Giustiniani's henna-dyed beard with her fingertips as if unable to resist the temptation. She poured wine into a goblet, sipped it and handed it to him, looking him steadfastly in the eyes with an alluring smile. I felt sick with rage and hurt pride.

"If I'm in the way here I'll go into the courtyard," I said stiffly. "I seem to hear more noise than usual from the walls."

Anna glanced at me with so mischievous a wink that my heart turned to water and I realized that these blandishments were all in fun, to charm Giustiniani and win his good will. Reassured, I smiled back. As they continued their playful conversation I could not look my fill of Anna, and passion blazed up in me as I saw how easily she beguiled him.

We ate together, and when Giustiniani rose reluctantly to take his leave, he looked at me and with a sweeping movement lifted from his shoulders the weighty chain of the protostrator with its enameled breastplate.

"Let this be my wedding present to you," he said. He hung the chain about Anna's neck and slyly brushed her bare shoulders with his heavy paws. "My men call me invincible, but before you I am vanquished. This chain and breastplate will open doors which neither cannon nor sword can force."

He could afford to make this gesture, being a vain man with a great collection of chains to choose from, as I knew; but I was not at all pleased at his hint that Anna would be welcome at his command post whenever she chose to come. But Anna thanked him delightedly, threw her arms about his neck, kissed him on both cheeks and even brushed his fleshy lips with her mouth.

Giustiniani, touched by his own munificence, wiped a tear from his eye and said, "I would gladly give your husband the staff of a protostrator and take his place here with you. But since that may not be I will give him furlough for tonight, and in future I shall look the other way if he's absent from his post—so long as there's no fighting in progress. Some temptations a man can resist, but your husband is no man if he can resist such a one as yourself."

He went and I followed him out politely. Seeing my impatience he loitered just to tease me, and prattled on though I never took in a word of what he was saying. When at last he climbed onto his charger I tore upstairs, caught Anna in my arms and kissed and caressed her so vehemently that my love seemed more like wrath. She glowed, kindled, smiled and laughed in my arms and was more beautiful than ever. Even in bed she wanted to keep on Giustiniani's chain as a trophy and would not part with it even when I tried to take it away by force.

Afterwards she lay motionless, staring at the ceiling with a dark look which I did not know or understand.

"What are you thinking about, beloved?" I asked her.

She moved her head slightly. "I live, I exist," she said. "That's all."

Tired, empty, cooled, I regarded her enchanting beauty and remembered the men whose bodies were impaled on stakes on the Pera shore, and the Turks hanging along the harbor all with blackened faces and stretched necks. Away in the night the cannon roared. The stars looked down unconcernedly upon the earth. Earthly beauty lived and breathed beside me, with darkness in its look. Each breath drove the fetters of time and space more deeply into my flesh.

1 May 1453

Our position is becoming desperate. The Sultan's troops are building a floating bridge mounted on huge casks straight across the Horn to the Pera shore. Hitherto the men on the Pera hills have had to maintain communication with the main force by way of a detour around the bay. The bridge is protected by mighty anchored rafts on which guns are mounted; these prevent our ships from hampering the work of construction. As soon as the bridge is completed the Turkish galleys will be able to bombard our harbor wall under cover of the floating cannon.

Bombardment and assault on the temporary barricades we have thrown across the breaches cause daily losses. Our defense is weakening, while to the Sultan's camp fresh flocks of volunteers from Asia pour in daily.

Our wine is running short, and the price of food in the open market has risen beyond the reach of the poor. Today, therefore, the Emperor has requisitioned all bread, that it may be fairly distributed. The elders of each quarter of the city are responsible for supplying the families of the garrison with their barest needs as well as the fighting men themselves and the laborers on the walls; no one therefore need leave his post to find food for himself or his dependents.

The commander of the reserves has the duty of making a daily tour of inspection along the walls and calling the roll at various points. This concerns the Greeks only, not the Latins.

By the Kharisios Gate the great wall has collapsed in several places. The outer wall is in a bad state, but nowhere have the Turks succeeded in crossing it. So far our men have contrived to clear the ditch every night, and the timber and fascines of the Turks have been of good service in our breastworks and palisades.

Along the outer wall the air is full of the stench of carrion, and many of our men have become deaf through gunfire.

4 May 1453

At about midnight, in the teeth of fresh contrary winds and in pitch darkness, a brigantine with twelve volunteers on board crept from the harbor. The men were in Turkish dress and they flew the Sultan's pendant so as to slink out through the Dardanelles. Our observers on the tower in Pera have studied the flag signals of the Turkish fleet on both incoming and outgoing vessels, and so there is hope that the brigantine may get through. She sails on an important mission: namely, to find the Venetian ships under Loredano's command, which the bailo has assured us are on their way to our relief.

But this fleet from the Greek archipelago would have reached Constantinople long ago if it had so wished. Perhaps the Grand Signoria are afraid that their ships will be sailing into a trap if they come here. And without the protection of that fleet the Venetian trading posts on the Greek islands will fall an easy prey to the Turks. There would not be a single Venetian here now had not the Emperor by means of forced treaties and threats of fines compelled the ships from the Black Sea to remain and take part in the defense of the city.

There are cheering rumors of a relieving naval force already on the way, and of the mobilization of a Hungarian army to attack the Turks in the rear. If only it were so! But the west has clearly forsaken us.

5 May 1453

It is easy to think, it is easy to write, when one is alone. It is doubtless easy to die, too, when one stands alone upon the ramparts and the drum of death beats all about. The ground before the walls is black and scorched by gunfire as far as the eye can reach. The halls of the Blachernae tremble, and great, glassy-smooth slabs of marble loosen and fall from the walls. It is easy to wander alone through the Emperor's apartments waiting for death, while the irrevocable past echoes in its own emptiness.

But today I have been home again. I need only catch a glimpse of her limpid brown eyes—only touch her with the tips of my fingers and feel the living warmth of her skin, her transient loveliness—for the fire and desire in my blood to sweep all thought aside and transform everything.

It is well when we lie in one another's arms—when for one quivering instant my mouth receives her sobbing, panting breath. But afterwards, when she opens her lips to talk, we no longer understand one another. Only in the closeness of our bodies is there mutual comprehension—only then do we know things I never knew before. The body's knowledge is full of beauty and of awe. But our thoughts follow different paths. At times we wound one another with a single word, and glare like enemies. Alien strangeness, cold contempt, are mirrored in her widened pupils, though her cheeks yet glow with love.

She cannot understand why I must die, when I might live on if I wished.

"Honor!" she said today. "The most hateful of all men's words—an imbecile word. Is Sultan Mohammed in all his glory without honor? Does he not most highly honor those Christians whom he keeps about him, who have abjured their faith and taken the turban? What is honor to a vanquished man? He is disgraced in any case. Honor is for the victor alone."

I said, "We're talking of different things and will never understand one another."

But she is obstinate. She drove her nails into my arm as if to force me to her way of thinking and said, "I can understand your fighting—you're a Greek. But where's the sense of dying when the walls cave in and the Turks pour into the city? You're only half a Greek if you don't see that then everyone is his own nearest neighbor."

I said, "You don't understand me because you don't know

me. But you're right: I alone am nearest to myself. I can only obey myself."

"And I?" she demanded for the hundredth time. "You don't love me, then."

"I can resist the temptation of you," I said, "but don't drive me to despair. My beloved, my only beloved, don't make me despair."

She pressed her hands to my temples—she panted, her mouth on mine. She stared at me with eyes glittering with hate and whispered, "If only I could open your forehead—if only I could uncover the thoughts hidden in your skull! You're not the man I thought. Then who are you? I have embraced only your body—never yourself. And so I hate you—oh, how I hate you."

"Give me just these brief days, these few moments," I said. "Perhaps centuries will pass before I meet your eyes and find you again. What harm have I done you that you should torment me so?"

"There is no past and less future," she said. "That is all dreams and imagination—a fool's philosophy. I care nothing for such lies. It is this life I want, and you in this life. That's why I must torment you to the last—and I shall never forgive you. Neither you nor myself."

Exhausted, I said, "My crown is heavy to bear."

But she did not understand.

6 May 1453

Disturbances all day. The bombardment is incessant, shaking heaven and earth. Every two hours the great gun is fired, drowning all other noises, and the wall seems to quiver to its foundations all the way from the harbor to the Sea of Marmora.

The Turks are moving. Ceaseless noise comes from their camp, and the roll of drums, and the dervishes are working themselves into such a frenzy that their hoarse shrieks can be heard from here. Many of them approach the wall, dancing and whirling, and get as far as the ditch before being pierced with arrows; but they continue spinning on their heels as if insensible to pain. The Greeks are aghast at the sight and call upon priests and monks to drive away the devil.

No one has been able to leave the ramparts. At all four points under fire from the big guns, the original outer wall has been swept away and the main wall badly breached. The firing prevents all repair work during the day, but as soon as darkness falls an earthen rampart springs up to fill the gaps.

Grant the German declares that the Turkish cannon are showing signs of wear, for many of their balls fly wide of the target, some even soaring over the wall into the city without doing any real damage. But beyond the hill rises the glow from Orban's foundry furnaces, and every day one can hear the mighty hiss of the molten metal plunging into the huge molds.

In the city there is a shortage of cooking oil. The poor suffer most from this. But from Pera, cartloads of oil are carried daily to the Turkish camp. After each shot the hot mouths of the cannon swallow jars of the precious fluid. No siege in history can have been as costly as this one. But Mohammed draws unsparingly on the wealth of his viziers and generals. There are bankers from every country in his camp, Jews and Greeks as well, and his credit is still unlimited. It is said that even the Genoese in Pera are anxious to take up his bills of exchange, as the safest possible investment.

7 May 1453

Hell broke loose shortly after midnight, when at least ten thousand men took part in the storming of the breaches. The heaviest assault was directed at Giustiniani's force by the Gate of St. Romanos, where the great bombard has caused the most damage in both walls. The assault troops advanced under cover of darkness in good order and without noise, and had time to fill in the ditch at several points before the alarm was sounded. Dozens of scaling-ladders were raised at the same moment. Our work people took to their heels and only Giustiniani's presence of mind saved the situation. Bellowing like a bull he hurled himself into the hottest of the fray and with his two-handed sword cut down the foremost Turks. These had already reached the summit of the earthen rampart. At the same time torches and flares were lit and all was as bright as day.

Giustiniani's roars overtopped the shrieks and drumbeats of the Turks, and as soon as he saw that this was to be a full-scale attack he sent word to the reserves. But when the battle had raged for two hours, we had to draw further reinforcements from other parts of the wall on either side of the Romanos Gate. After the first attack the Turks returned in regular waves of a thousand at a time. They had dragged their fieldpieces right up to the ditch. While the shock troops went in, archers and artillery tried to force the defenders to take cover, but, protected by their plate armor, Giustiniani's men formed a living wall of iron along the top of the outer rampart. Ladders were thrown down and the Turks who had pressed forward under movable penthouses to the foot of the wall were showered with boiling pitch and lead until they scattered, exposing themselves to the bolts from our crossbows.

It is hard to estimate the Turkish casualties. Giustiniani launched rumors in the city that at dawn the heaps of the fallen had risen to the height of the outer wall, but this of course is nonsense calculated to put heart into the townsfolk. However many Turks may have been slain, they cannot make up for the Latins who fell with their armor pierced or were dragged down from the walls by Turkish grapnels.

Compared with this attack all others have been child's play. Last night the Sultan was in earnest and a considerable part of his army took part. At the Blachernae, however, the danger was slight: the scaling-ladders would not reach so high. The bailo therefore detached a company of his soldiers and bade me take them to Giustiniani, that the Venetians might win their share of glory.

Just as we arrived a gigantic janissary had by sheer bodily strength scrambled up on the wall, and with a yell of triumph he called his comrades as he dashed off in pursuit of Giustiniani, the men in armor giving way before him. Giustiniani was fighting in the breach a little lower down and would have fared ill had not one of the workmen—an ordinary Greek without armor—taken a bold leap from the battlements and hewn off one of the janissary's feet with his broad battle-axe. It was then an easy matter for Giustiniani to dispatch him. Giustiniani gave his rescuer a handsome reward, but said he would rather have dealt with his assailant singlehanded.

I witnessed this scene by the light of torches and fire-arrows, amid shrieks and the clash of shields. Then I had no time to think of anything, for the pressure of the attack was so formidable that we had to support one another three deep to withstand it. Today my sword is blunt. When at dawn the

Turks began their withdrawal I was so mortally weary that I could hardly lift an arm. Every limb ached and my body was covered with bruises and tender swellings. But I was unwounded and in that respect luckier than many. Giustiniani had been gashed in the armpit by a spear, but his armor had prevented fatal harm.

It is said that a Greek by the Selymbrian Gate has slain a Turkish governor of horsetail rank.

When Giustiniani saw the state I was in he gave me friendly counsel.

"In the heat and excitement of battle it's not unusual for a man to put forth strength far exceeding his normal capacity. But nothing is so dangerous as to slack off during a lull in the fighting, for one is apt to sink down in exhaustion. After that one can hardly struggle to one's knees. For this reason an experienced fighter never exerts all his powers, even in the hottest fray, but keeps something in reserve. It may be the saving of his life if fighting starts again." He regarded me merrily with his pop eyes and added, "He can at least run away."

He was in a good humor and was not put out by having to dilute his wine with water as an example to his men. The wine is almost exhausted.

"Well, well, Jean Ange," he said. "We're beginning to get a taste of war. The Sultan is warming up and soon we shall have real attacks to beat off."

I stared at him sceptically.

"What is a real attack, then?" I asked. "I've never seen a worse one than this, and can't imagine it. The janissaries fought like wild beasts and I thought I had turned into a wild beast myself."

"You have plenty to see yet, Jean Ange," said Giustiniani kindly. "Greet your beautiful wife for me. Women like to smell blood on a man's clothes, and I have never found such delight in a woman's body as on a day when I've sent many men to heaven with my sword, and am bruised and exhausted. I envy you the experience, Jean Ange, if you've not yet had it."

Downcast and disgusted I paid no heed to his talk. The chill morning air was foul with steam from the heaps of newly-dead. How could I touch my wife while my eyes were yet glazed with horror—when there was blood on my clothes and hands and when my head was full of wild, whirling scenes from the battle? I dreaded lest I should wake shrieking as soon as I had closed my eyes, though I longed for nothing so much as sleep.

But Giustiniani was right. He was dreadfully right. I availed myself of his permission to go home and rest after the fighting; and never before had my bruised and battered body been so full of fire as it was that morning. My sleep was deep. My sleep was deep as death when I rested with my head on Anna Notaras' white shoulder.

8 May 1453

Late last night the Council of Twelve met in secret. The recent assault had clearly shown how inadequate were our defense forces. The mighty bridge which the Sultan has thrown across the Horn threatens above all the Palace of Blachernae. The Venetians therefore decided after long argument to evacuate Trevisano's three great ships and thus release two thousand men for the ramparts. The cargo is to be stored in the Emperor's arsenal, while the ships' companies and their soldiers man the Blachernae.

Trevisano protested on behalf of the owners and captains,

pointing out that if the cargoes, valued at tens of thousands of ducats, are brought ashore there will be no hope of saving them if the Turks capture the city. Besides this, the ships will be lost and most likely the crews as well.

Nevertheless the Council of Twelve decided to have the ships unloaded. The crews on hearing of this offered armed resistance, led by their officers, and refused to disembark. This is still the position today; the Council of Twelve has not been able to budge the seamen, though the Emperor himself with tears in his eyes has appealed to their conscience.

12 May 1453

The seamen will not give in and all negotiations have broken down. But the Council of Twelve has succeeded in winning Trevisano and Aloisio Diedo over to their side. The sea captains have received presents of money. The Venetians are anxious to retain the Palace of Blachernae at all costs.

There is no doubt that the Blachernae area is gravely threatened, but quite apart from its defense the Venetians wish to increase their garrison as much as possible so as to control the city should the Sultan be forced to raise the siege. For this reason they deem it necessary to transfer the ships' companies to the walls. And in addition to the sailors there are four hundred iron-clad men-at-arms on board the vessels from Tana.

Meanwhile the Greeks shed their blood hourly, and die upon the walls. Notaras is right. Both at the Golden Gate and on either side of the Selymbrian Gate the Greeks have repulsed all attacks unaided. It is true that the walls there are less badly damaged than at the Romanos and Kharisios gates, yet most of the defenders are artisans and monks, barely trained in the use of arms. There are weaklings among them who take to their heels when the Turks attack, but by far the greater number are of the stuff that fought at Thermopylae and Marathon.

War brings out the best in men, and the worst. The longer the siege lasts, the more do the bad qualities prevail. Time is working not for us but against us.

While the Latins, fat, florid and gleaming with grease, squabble among themselves, the Greeks grow daily thinner. They lack oil and bread. A drop of the cheapest, sourest wine is all they may draw from the Emperor's stores. Their wives and children weep from hunger as they walk in devotional processions to the churches. From morning till night and night till morning the ardent prayers of the humble and unhappy rise to God's heaven. If prayers could save the city, Constantinople would endure till Judgment Day.

While the Latins confer in the Church of the Holy Virgin in the Blachernae, the Emperor has summoned the Greeks to a service and a council of war this evening in the Church of St. Sophia. Giustiniani is sending me in his stead, not wishing to be so long absent from the walls.

13 May 1453

The council of war began in an atmosphere of tension, and was cut short almost at once by alarm signals from the ramparts. Outside the church we were met by an express messenger who reported that the enemy was attacking the Blachernae both from the shore and at the Kaligari Gate. But the fiercest assault was being made at the breach by the Kharisios Gate.

Alarm bells pealed into the night, lights were lit in the houses and half-clad people rushed terrified into the streets. In the harbor the ships were rowed out to the boom as if an attack were to be expected there too. It was midnight. In the still air the tumult of battle at the Blachernae could be heard all over the vast city as far as the Hippodrome. The Turkish camp fires burned brightly in an unbroken semicircle around the city.

Setting spurs to our horses we galloped by the light of torches through the streets. As we approached the Kharisios Gate we encountered a crowd of fugitives, among them men with weapons in their hands. The Emperor reined in his horse and adjured them loudly in the name of Christ to return to the ramparts; but the men were blind with terror and paid no heed. Our bodyguards were compelled to ride straight at them and cut many of them down, before the rest halted, staring round them as if ignorant of where they were, and then slowly and slackly made their way back to the wall.

The Emperor did not wait for them. Our troop arrived in the nick of time. Next to the Kharisios Gate the great wall had been breached to half its height. It was here that the defenders had yielded, and many Turks were already running through the neighboring streets, howling hoarsely and cutting down all who came in their way. Our troop of horse swept them aside like chaff, and it soon appeared that they were the remnants of a wave of attack. The defenders had let them through, but had had time to man the walls again before the next wave broke. Giustiniani had arrived and we saw him organizing his defense at the top of the wall.

This incident shows what a hairsbreadth divides the city

from disaster. However, at other points the Turks have not had the same success.

At dawn the assault ebbed away. This was no general attack after all, since the Turkish fleet made no move. Giustiniani estimated that about forty thousand men had taken part in the night's engagement.

"The Sultan is simply wearing us down," he said. "Don't think that this has been a victory for us. We have sustained heavy losses. I won't tell even you how many of our men have fallen. But I freely own that tonight the Venetians too have somewhat cleansed their tarnished honor."

By sunrise the ground was strewn with Turkish dead from the shore to the Gate of St. Romanos. The bodies of those who had forced their way into the city were thrown from the outer wall; they numbered over four hundred.

Now that Trevisano's seamen have seen and heard their compatriots fighting for their lives they have at last withdrawn their resistance. During the day they unloaded their ships and in the evening the four hundred men-at-arms with Trevisano at their head reported to the bailo at the Blachernae. They were allotted the most exposed and honorable position: the northern tip of the city by Kynegion harbor where the sea- and landward-walls meet. The sailors have promised to follow in the morning and hazard their lives in Christ's name.

This reinforcement is necessary, for without it the city could not withstand another night attack. All day small companies of Turks have been active at different points, with the sole aim of keeping the garrison busy and preventing it from getting any rest. Our men have therefore been divided into watches. But this morning when the Emperor inspected the walls he found many sentries sleeping like the dead. With his own hands he shook them awake and comforted those who wept from sheer exhaustion. He forbade the officers to punish any found sleeping at their posts—and indeed what punishment remains to give? The meager rations allow of no further diminution, the wine is at an end, and to stand upon the walls is in itself punishment enough for anyone.

When the morning sun hung red above the hills of Pera I saw the Guacchardi brothers beheading the bodies of Turks who had reached the wall and fallen there. The armor of the three men was splashed with blood from helmet to greaves, and they were hurling Turkish heads at one another, shouting and laughing, as if playing some singular ball game. They had made bets as to who should find the longest beard, and already brown, black and gray ones were floating from their belts. Their game was a refusal to give in to fatigue after the night's fighting, and they defied it in this unseemly sport.

Amid the blood, soot and rubble from the ramparts, a few yellow flowers had blossomed in the earth of the great wall.

Last night I was spared the worst of the fighting, my task having chiefly been to convey Giustiniani's orders to different points along the wall. Nevertheless I was reeling with exhaustion, and everything appeared as unreal as a dream. Once more the Turkish artillery began flashing, and the wall trembled under the impact of the stone balls, yet all noises came to my ears like distant echoes. The hills of Pera were dyed red by the sun, and red too was the armor of the Guacchardis playing ball with Turkish heads. This morning hour was engraved unforgettably in my heart. Heaven and earth and all their colors, the soot and the blood—all was unutterably beautiful in my sight just then, while the blank eyes of the dead around me stared into vacancy.

Equally unreal, equally incredible and of just such unearthly beauty had the world about me appeared once before. It was in Ferrara when I was sickening for the plague, though still unaware of it. The light of a cloudy November day pressed in through the painted windows of the chapel, censers exhaled their bitter scent of purifying herbs and the quill pens rasped as always; yet as I sat there everything slid far away and only a rushing sound filled my ears. I saw everything more clearly, more truly than before. I saw Emperor John's grudging face in shifting hues of sulphur-yellow and green as he sat with a black and white dog at his feet, on a throne which had been made exactly the same height as the throne of Pope Eugenios. I saw Bessarion's big, beaming face alter and become insensitive and cold. And the Latin and Greek words ringing through the greenish light of the chapel receded and sounded as meaningless as the baying of distant hounds.

In that hour I experienced God for the first time—as I was sickening for the plague.

In a lightning flash of truth I now sensed that that moment had contained this morning within itself, as bark contains the wood. Had I been more percipient I might even then have experienced and seen what I saw today. Both occurred within me and within eternity at one and the same instant. Thus are moments of clear vision contained in one another, and the sequence of time between them is but illusion. Weeks, months, years, are measures invented by man; they have nothing to do with true time, God's time.

In this hour I knew also that I should be born into the world again in accordance with God's inscrutable purpose. And when this happens I shall bear this hour in my heart still, contained in the visions of my new life. Again I shall behold the headless corpses on the ruined walls that tremble in the firing of the great gun. The little yellow flowers will gleam out amid soot and blood, and the Guacchardi brothers in bloody armor will play merrily at ball with the heads of the enemy.

But this experience awoke neither ecstasy nor even joy

within me, only unspeakable woe that I am and shall be only a man—a spark blown by the winds of God from one darkness into another. More keenly than my bodily pain and weariness I was aware of my heart's longing for the ineffable repose of oblivion. But there is no oblivion.

There is no oblivion.

15 May 1453

Today I have had a stab to the heart. I had been aware of its coming. Man loses what he must lose and not even the greatest happiness endures forever. Looking back, it seems a miracle that we have been able to hide as long as we have. For many a day now everyone in the city has been subject to visits by the Emperor's patrols, who have the right to enter even the houses of the great without warning, and search larders and cellars for deserters, hoarded provisions and coin for the Emperor's treasury. The poor man's painfully saved handful of flour is confiscated as ruthlessly as the rich man's wheat sack or jar of oil.

At nightfall I was visited on the walls of the Blachernae by my servant Manuel. He had tears in his eyes and someone had torn his beard so that his bluish cheeks were speckled with blood.

"Master," he panted, his hand over his heart, "there has been a misfortune."

He had run through the city, and reeled where he stood. Such was his agitation that he took no care to see whether anyone was listening. He told me that military police had searched my house that morning. They had found nothing, but one of the men had looked attentively at Anna and evidently knew her, for that afternoon the men returned, this time under the command of one of Notaras' sons. He had at once recognized his sister, and Anna had gone with them unresisting; what could she have done? Manuel had tried to defend her on the grounds that I was not at home, but they had torn his beard, knocked him down and kicked him. Forgetful of his rank Anna's brother had even struck him in the face.

As soon as Manuel had recovered he followed them at a distance and saw them take her to Megadux Notaras' house.

"Because she's his daughter," he said in a matter-of-fact tone. "I've known that almost from the beginning, though as you wished to keep it a secret I said nothing. But that's neither here nor there. Master, you must fly, for without doubt Megadux Notaras will seek you out and kill you, and his chargers are swifter than my legs."

"And whither should I fly?" I asked. "There is nowhere in the city where he could not find me if he wished."

Manuel so far forgot himself as to shake me by the arm.

"It will soon be dark," he said urgently. "It's quiet on the wall just now; you can let yourself down by a rope and escape to the Sultan's camp. You will feel quite at home there—many others have done it. If you like I will lower you myself and coil up the rope again so that you will leave no trace. In return, remember me when you enter the city with the conquerors."

"Talk sense, old fool!" I said. "The Sultan would set up my head on a stake if he caught me."

"Yes, of course, of course," said Manuel, peering at me sideways with his red-rimmed eyes. "That's the story you stick to and it's not for me to judge. But believe me, from now on you will be safer in the Sultan's camp than in Constantinople, and perhaps you could put in a word for us poor Greeks."

"Manuel," I began, but could not go on. How was I to penetrate the armor of his prejudice? He thrust at my breast with his forefinger.

"Of course you were sent here by the Sultan," he said. "Did you really think you could fool an old Greek? You can deceive the Latins as much as you like, but not us. Why else do you suppose that everyone draws aside from you so respectfully and blesses your path? Not a hair of your head has been harmed. That is proof enough. No one dares touch you because the Sultan is your shield. And it is no shame for a man to serve his own master; even Emperors have allied themselves with Turks in time of need, and made use of them."

"Hold your tongue, fool!" I said warningly, and looked around. A Venetian soldier had approached and was watching the excited old man with amusement. At that moment a gun went off and the stone ball struck the wall quite near us, so that it trembled under our feet. Manuel caught me by the arm and only now threw a glance over the blackened, fire-spewing ground below us.

"We're not in a dangerous place, are we?" he asked anxiously.

"Your thoughtless words are far more dangerous for me than the Turkish artillery," I said wrathfully. "In the name of God, Manuel, believe me! Whatever I may be, I shall live and die for this city. I have no other future, I desire neither power nor purple. Power is dead. I will answer to God for myself alone. Get this into your head, once and for all: I am alone, entirely alone. What is hidden in my heart dies with my heart, when the Turks come."

I spoke so gravely and convincingly that Manuel stared at me astounded. He was compelled to believe me. Then he burst into tears of disappointment and said, "In that case it is you who are the fool and not I."

When he had wept for some time he wiped his nose and said resignedly, "So be it! We have had mad Emperors before now, and no one regarded it as a real misfortune. There was only a certain Andronikos who was so cruel in his madness that at last the people hanged him in the Hippodrome and thrust a sword up him from vent to throat. But you are not cruel; you are indeed gentle in your madness, and therefore it is my duty to follow you even along the path of folly, having once known you for what you are." He looked round and sighed deeply as he added, "It is bad enough here, but I can't return to your house. I am too much afraid of Megadux Notaras. I would rather take a cleaver in my hand and meet a raging Turk than encounter the Megadux after helping you to steal his daughter. You see, unless I am much mistaken, Anna Notaras has long been destined for the Sultan's harem."

Once more I marveled at how much information an ordinary man of the people like Manuel could pick up. What after all would suit Lukas Notaras' plans better than to marry his daughter to the Sultan, and so strengthen their alliance? Perhaps the only reason he wanted to send her to Crete and safety was because that would put him in a stronger position for bargaining. Mohammed is omnivorous in his desires, and in this too resembles his model, Alexander the Great. A woman of the most eminent family in Constantinople would gratify his colossal arrogance.

"Where do you find out all you think you know?" I could not resist asking.

"It's in the air," he said, throwing out his hands. "I'm a Greek—I have politics in my blood. But I don't wish to be mixed up in the affair between you and your father-in-law; I would rather look on from outside, if you will allow me."

I realized that he really was safer on the ramparts than in my house. If Lukas Notaras means to kill me either with his own hand or by that of an assassin, he would find it safer to remove all witnesses to my marariage at the same time. I therefore allowed Manuel to join the Greek workmen whom the Venetians have posted here, and told him to look after himself.

My first idea when I heard that I had lost Anna was to gallop straight to her father's house and demand her return, since she is my wife. But what good would that do? It would be easy for Notaras to have a solitary stranger murdered.

Behind lock and grille in Notaras' house Anna is beyond my reach. She is my wife; therefore I must beware of Notaras. The simplest way for him to annul our marriage would be to slay me, and I do not want to die at Greek hands.

I have stayed up to write. From time to time I have closed my eyes and rested my hot forehead on my hands. But sleep will not take pity on me now. Through eyelids gritty from weariness I see her beauty—her mouth—her eyes. How her cheeks burn at the touch of my hand—how dazzling a flame shoots through me when I stroke her naked loins. Never have I longed so madly for her as now, when I know that I have lost her.

16 May 1453

I could not sleep, therefore, though my position would have permitted me the luxury. Solitude and sleep are the two greatest boons in war. The stars were still twinkling like fine silver needles when I came out, driven by my own restlessness.

The night was still and icy cold during these last hours before daybreak.

Near the Kaligari Gate I stopped and listened. It was not only the beating of my heart. I seemed to hear a muffled thudding far beneath my feet. Then I saw Grant the German advancing with a torch in his hand. Tubs of water were ranged behind the wall and he was going from one to another, pausing at each. At first I thought he was out of his mind, or practicing exorcism, for it was some way from the wall and no fire threatened us here.

He greeted me in the name of Christ, shone the light of his flare on the water in one of the tubs and bade me look. At short intervals the dark surface was ruffled by swift, tremulous rings, though the night was still and the guns silent.

"The ground is trembling," I said. "Does even the soil of the city quake in mortal terror?"

Grant laughed, though his face was somber.

"Don't you understand what your eyes tell you, Jean Ange?" he said. "If you knew what this meant, cold sweat would break out on the back of your neck as it did on mine just now. Help me to move the tubs, for my assistants have wearied and lain down to sleep."

Between us we shifted the tub a few paces to one side, and Grant thrust a stick into the ground to mark where it had stood. When we had moved it a few more times the surface of the water was again ruffled. I was seized by a superstitious dread as if I were witnessing some black art. Grant, if anyone, should know such mysteries; his face betrays it.

He pointed to the winding line of sticks that he had planted in the ground.

"The soil is rocky," he said. "As you see, they're having to twist and turn like moles. It will be exciting to watch how far they get before they dare break to the surface."

"They?" I said, mystified.

"The Turks," he said. "They're working under our feet. Didn't you understand?"

"How is that possible!" I exclaimed. But at the same moment I remembered the Sultan's Serbian miners. In former sieges the Turks had sometimes attempted to tunnel under the walls, but had always failed because of the rocky ground. Consequently we had given no thought to this danger, though our sentries have been ordered to look out for suspicious heaps of soil outside the walls. But no trace of sapping could be detected and the matter was forgotten.

For a time I forgot my own cares and was as eager as Grant.

"How cunning they are!" I cried. "They must have begun digging under cover of that nearest mound, more than five hundred paces away. And this is the best place they could have chosen, as there is no outer wall in front of the Blachernae. They have already passed the great wall. What are we to do?"

"Wait," said Grant calmly. "There's no danger now that I know how their tunnel runs. It's still far below us. Time enough to act when they turn upwards." He looked at me grimly. "I've dug mines myself. It is a terrible task. Never enough air, and constant fear. Death in a mole-run, by fire or water, is a ghastly death indeed."

Leaving his tubs he took me with him on a walk along the wall. He had put drums in a number of vaults, with peas on the parchment, but the place where I had seen the water quivering was the only one where he had noticed anything.

"A tunnel is only dangerous if discovered too late," he explained. "Luckily the Turks have attempted to penetrate the city itself. If they had been content to undermine an area under the wall only, propped it with timbers and then set fire to the props, they might have succeeded in bringing down a big stretch of it. But no doubt the ground is unsuitable."

As the stars paled he told me how to lay a countermine furnished with a movable grille, and how fumes of burning sulphur are introduced into the enemy saps.

"There are many methods," he said. "We can let in water from a cistern and drown them like rats. A flooded tunnel is useless. An even better way is to roast them with Greek fire, for this sets their props alight at the same time and the tunnel falls in. But the most exciting thing is to dig one's own tunnel and lie in wait behind a thin wall to snatch away the diggers. By torturing them one can discover whether other mines have been dug, and if so where."

His cold-blooded words shocked me. I thought of the men beneath our feet, panting, sweating, blinded by falling earth, toiling like beasts of burden and never guessing that every stroke of the pick brought them nearer a pitiless death. If they were indeed Serbs they were my brother-Christians, although in accordance with the treaty signed by their aging despot they were compelled to serve the Sultan. But Grant surveyed me uncomprehendingly with his dark, restless eyes.

"Cruelty is foreign to me," he said. "For me all this is mathematics: an absorbing problem which offers the opportunity for many different calculations."

But as he stood there beside his tub he looked like nothing so much as a black cat watching a rathole.

The sky over us grew pale. The hills of Pera were tinged with red. The great gun thundered out and called the Turks to morning prayer. From the Blachernae buildings and from vaults below the walls sleepy men-at-arms crawled out to ease themselves. Some of them came up and gaped first at us and then at Grant's water tubs. The sulkiest angrily buckled on their harness and went silently up onto the ramparts to relieve the guard.

Then with swift steps, wearing a mantle of imperial green,

came the Megadux Lukas Notaras. Behind him walked his two sons, grave-faced, with their hands on their sword hilts. He had no other attendants. I withdrew a step and stood beside Grant, so that I had the tub in front of me. Notaras halted: his dignity would not allow him to play catch-as-catch-can with me round a bucket; nor could he order the guards to seize me, since the Blachernae is under Venetian control and he had no men of his own with him.

"I wish to speak to you, John Angelos," he said. "Alone."

"I have no secrets," I answered. His dark, proud visage was inscrutable and I felt no inclination to follow him like a lamb to the slaughter.

He opened his mouth to make a sharp rejoinder, but at that instant caught sight of the surface of the water in the tub. The cannon were still firing now and then, but even in the intervals the water trembled into rings. He stared, frowned, and glanced at Johann Grant; his keen mind had at once grasped the situation and instantly his political sense was at work. Without another word he turned and walked away as rapidly as he had come. His sons cast a surprised look at me, but obediently followed their father.

The mine had been discovered; he could therefore not harm the Turks by reporting it to the Emperor. He would reap the honor of the discovery and win the Emperor's confidence. It was not long before Constantine came riding toward us, attended by his most confidential advisers.

"The Megadux has stolen your glory," I said to Grant.

"I didn't come here for glory," he retorted in a surly tone. "All I want is to increase my knowledge."

But Notaras hastened up to him at once, laid his right hand on his shoulder as a token of favor and addressing the Emperor praised Grant's resourcefulness and observation, referring to him condescendingly as a sound fellow and an honest

German. The Emperor too showed him favor, promised him a present of money and bade him, under Notaras' direction, trace and destroy all the Turkish tunnels. For this purpose he should have at his disposal the necessary men from the garrison, and also the Emperor's technicians.

I had seen to it that Giustiniani too should get word of the discovery, and he soon arrived on horseback to share in the general rejoicing. Grant at once took steps on his own account and secretly sent for anyone in the city or on the walls who had any knowledge of mining. At the same time he chose men to watch the tubs and drums, but these gave many false alarms before they became familiar with the task. Each time the nearest guns were fired the water quivered and the peas danced, so that the watchers with their hair on end dashed to report that the Turks were breaking to the surface.

When Grant had set his men to work he turned to the Emperor and said, "I did not enter your service to gain money or honor, but to study the knowledge of the Greeks. Give me leave, then, to look through the catalogues in your library and read the manuscripts hidden in the cellars, and also to borrow the writings of the Pythagoreans. I know that there are works there both by the Pythagoreans and by Archimedes, but your librarian guards them like a mad dog and won't allow anyone to light a candle or a lamp in the whole building."

The Emperor was ill-pleased by this request. A worried look came into his emaciated face and he avoided Grant's eyes as he replied, "My librarian is only doing his duty. His appointment is hereditary and its obligations are laid down in detail, so that not even he can modify them. You would displease God if in the city's hour of need you were to seek after the writings of pagan philosophers. Only One is needful, as you should know. Neither Pythagoras nor Archimedes can help you, but only Jesus Christ, who gave His life that our sins might be forgiven, and rose from the dead for our salvation."

Grant muttered, "If only One is needful, it is useless for me to waste my discoveries and calculations on keeping the Turks out of the city."

The Emperor flung out his hand in annoyance and said, "Greek philosophy is our heritage in perpetuity, and we do not lend its treasured writings to be mishandled by barbarians."

Giustiniani coughed loudly, and even the bailo, who had now arrived, rolled his bloodshot eyes in resentment. As soon as Grant had gone the Emperor said conciliatingly that the word "barbarians" was in no way directed at the Latins. But Grant was a German, and thus a barbarian by birth.

The bombardment continued all day as usual, or perhaps even more violently. The great wall itself has now collapsed at several points. Women, children and old men have volunteered to help in the work of repair. Fear and dread lend them superhuman strength, so that together they shift stones and carry gabions which even a strong man would find too heavy. They say, "We would rather die with our husbands, our fathers and sons, than be slaves of the Turks."

Horrible weariness has dulled the defenders' fear, so that many expose themselves to enemy arrows if thereby they can save themselves a few steps. Unprotected men with eyes smarting from lack of sleep stagger as far as the ditch to fish up Turkish timber and brushwood with hooks. From the wall there is not a single bush or tree to be seen; the Turks have cut them all down in their efforts to fill in the ditch. The Pera hills too and the Asiatic coast on the other side of the Bosporus have been stripped.

17 May 1453

Today the Turkish fleet approached the boom, but hove to while still at some distance away. Our vessels fired at least a hundred rounds, but inflicted little damage upon them. The Venetian sailors brag of their victory. "If every man on the walls did his duty as boldly as we do," they say, "Constantinople would be in no danger."

Yet it is clear that the Sultan only wants to keep our ships busy, so that no further reinforcements can be spared from them for the walls.

Many have asked for employment at Grant's water tubs, but he has wisely chosen the old and infirm for this task, provided their sight is good. I should have liked to procure some such light duty for Manuel, because of his age and his feeble legs. But when I found him he had already released himself from work on the walls and found favor with the Venetians. He is familiar with the city, knows where the best brothels are situated and can find women willing to exchange their chastity for the preserved fruits and fresh bread of the Venetians. Even half-grown girls wait outside the gates of the Blachernae to offer themselves.

I ran into Manuel as he was on his way into the city, bent double under a sack of forbidden victuals. He had obtained a Venetian pass to present to the police patrols, and boasted that if only the siege might last a little longer he would be a rich man.

When I reproved hem he was offended and said, "Everyone is his own nearest neighbor. Private trading is going on all over the city, with the aid of Venetian and Genoese passes. Few have smarted for it, and many have grown rich. Where there's demand, there's supply—that's the way of the world. If I don't go after the profits, someone else will. Better, surely, that the Venetians' delicacies should find their way to Greek mouths rather than to their own greedy bellies. And is it my fault if lusty young men are full of base desires and crave women or boys to solace them between battles?"

Working himself into yet greater vehemence he shouted, "The Venetians are our friends. They're sacrificing their blood and their lives for our city. Is it wrong, then, for a poor girl to sell her maidenhood, to please them and earn a piece of bread for her parents? Is it wrong even for a respectable married woman to lie on her back for a moment in return for a pot of jam whose sweetness her body has long been deprived of? All this is coming to pass to the glory of God and as a blessing to Christendom, as the Venctians say. Master, you should not meddle with the way of the world, which you can do nothing to alter. We are but poor sinners, every one of us."

Why should he not be right? Who am I to judge him? Each of us must fulfill his destiny in accordance with circumstance.

I have been vainly expecting Lukas Notaras to seek me out again. Today I had a few glimpses of him, but he did no more than send me a baleful glance as he hurried by. From Anna I have received not the slightest sign.

In the feverish daze in which I now exist, I resolved at least to try to perform one good action. It may be that Johann Grant is to be a slave in the coming era, under the sign of the beast; yet I like him, with his restless look and furrowed brow. Why should he not be happy in his fashion, while he may? Today therefore I visited the library and spoke to the toothless, deaf librarian who, unconcerned by the tumult of the siege, puts on his ceremonial dress every day, with its chain and other insignia.

I pointed out to him the direction of the Turkish tunnel and convinced him that the enemy were on their way to the subterranean vaults of the library, through which they intended to make their way into the city. He is so full of his own importance that he believed me blindly as soon as he grasped what I was telling him.

"Ha!" he exclaimed aghast. "This must not be. They might trample on the books and damage them, and perhaps be careless with their torches and set fire to the whole library. It would be an irreparable loss to the world."

I advised him to seek the aid of Grant. In his extremity he humbled himself and led Grant into the cellar, showing him every hidingplace. Grant placed buckets of water down there and promised to come and look at them whenever he had time. He also received permission to light a lamp so that he might observe the surface of the water. The librarian unearthed a rusty sword and swore valiantly that only over his dead body should the Turks reach his shelves.

Fortunately he has not yet discovered that the Venetians long ago began using the sacred books in the palace for kindling and for gun wadding.

But Grant had not long to study. Shortly after nightfall he was summoned to the Kaligari Gate where this time the Turks seemed to be working close under the great wall. Here Grant had already countermined, and his tunnel was now put into use, so that the Turks suddenly found themselves trapped and were suffocated by poisonous sulphur fumes. Only a couple of men escaped. Grant pierced holes for draft at suitable places, and soon the props in the Turkish mine were one thunderous sea of flame, until the whole passage fell in. But it lay too deep to affect the wall above. Five hundred paces away, beyond the hillock, black stifling smoke belched up for a long time before the Turks were able to block the opening.

18 May 1453

The end is near. Nothing can stop it now. And none of our previous experiences can compare with the horror we have known today.

When dawn broke we beheld a monstrous marvel looming before the wall near the Gate of St. Romanos. During the hours of darkness the Turks had built, with incredible speed and seemingly by the aid of evil spirits, a gigantic traveling siege-tower of wood. It stood on the very brink of the ditch, only thirty paces from the remains of the outer wall on which the defenders had been toiling all night. How it was done no one knows.

This fort, which can be moved by means of huge wooden rollers, is three stories high and overtops the outer wall. The timbers are everywhere protected from fire by many thicknesses of camel-and ox-hide. The walls are double and packed with earth, so that our small cannon cannot harm them. Arrows whine from the loopholes, and from the topmost platform a mighty mangonel hurls massive blocks of stone to demolish our temporary earthworks. From the Turkish camp a covered way five hundred paces long leads into the tower, enabling its crew to come and go freely.

While the mangonel hurls its rocks, while arrows fly and small ballistae sling fire pots at the palisade and gabions of the outer wall, ports on the bottom story open and shut, discharging earth, stones, fascines and timbers into the ditch. When we had gathered horrorstricken to behold this tower which rocks and works without a single man being visible, like some miracle of live machinery, a huge shutter in front of the middle platform opened with a great rumbling and a drawbridge shot out toward the outer wall. Fortunately the distance was too great for it to reach us.

Even Grant hastened up to survey this engine whose like has never been seen. He measured its dimensions with his eye, noted them down and remarked, "Although the tower must have been constructed beforehand and put together by sections on the spot, the mere erecting of it in one night is a marvel of skill and organization. In itself the tower is no novelty—siege-towers have been used as long as walls. It's only the size which is remarkable—it exceeds any measurements noted by the Greeks and Romans. Were it not for the ditch the Turks could wheel it right up to the wall and use it as a ram."

Having gazed at the tower for a time he turned and went, for he saw nothing new about its pattern. But Giustiniani ground his teeth and shook his head. It touched his honor that the tower should have been erected unobserved opposite his section of the wall.

"Let us wait until tonight," he said. "What man can build he can also destroy."

But this fort that spews fire, arrows, cannon balls and stones, and thunders with its own might, is so formidable that no one believes Giustiniani. The Emperor is at his wits' end; he wept to see many Greek workmen stretched lifeless between the walls by the flying boulders. As long as our outer wall is dominated by this engine, repairs are out of the question.

In the afternoon one of the big enemy guns succeeded in shooting away one of the towers on the great wall almost opposite the siege-engine; part of the wall itself collapsed, burying beneath it a number of Latins and Greeks.

While the chief officers were debating what was to be done to meet this latest and greatest peril, Giustiniani burst into wrathful speech against Notaras, demanding that he should hand over the two large guns which still stand on the harbor wall and are now and then ineffectually discharged at the Turkish galleys on the farther side of the Horn.

"I need powder and guns to defend the city," he said. "All too much valuable powder has been wasted in the harbor already."

Notaras answered coldly, "The guns are mine and I pay for the powder myself. I have already sunk one galley and damaged many others. If you wish, I will save powder, but the guns are needed at the harbor to keep the enemy vessels at a distance. You know yourself that the wall by the inner harbor is the weakest point in the city."

Giustiniani shrieked, "Then what in hell is the use of the Venetian ships, if they can't control the Turks even in the harbor? Yours are not reasons but pretexts—wind! What you hope to do is to weaken the defense at the most exposed point, which is here. I know you—your heart is as black as the Sultan's beard!"

The Emperor sought to mediate between them.

"In the name of Christ, dear brothers, do not make matters worse by quarreling. You're both acting from the best of motives. Megadux Notaras saved the city from destruction when the Turks attempted to undermine our walls, and if he believes that the cannon are needed at the harbor we are bound to defer to his judgment. Embrace each other in brotherly fashion, therefore, for we are all fighting in a common cause."

Giustiniani said roughly, "I'll embrace the devil himself,

if he'll give me guns and powder. But Megadux Notaras gives me neither."

Lukas Notaras in his turn showed no inclination to embrace Giustiniani, but withdrew hurt, leaving the Emperor and Giustiniani to continue the discussion alone. But I, seeing that the end was near, pocketed my pride and hastening after Lukas Notaras, stopped him and said, "You wanted to speak to me alone. Had you forgotten?" To my amazement he smiled cordially, and laying his hand on my shoulder replied, "You have dragged the honor of my family in the mire and induced a daughter to rebel against her father, John Angelos. But we live in evil times and I can no longer afford to quarrel. My daughter is dear to me and her entreaties have caused me to relent. Whether I can forgive your Latin conduct in this matter depends on you."

Hardly believing my ears I asked, "Will you really give me leave to meet your daughter Anna again . . . my wife?"

His face darkened.

"Don't call her your wife yet. But you may see her and speak with her. Yes, it will be better for her to put my terms before you. She is her father's daughter and I rely on her good sense, although because of you her heart eclipsed it for a time."

"May God bless you, Lukas Notaras!" I cried from a full heart. "I misjudged you and your aims. You are after all a true Greek."

He smiled uneasily and said, "Yes, indeed. I am a true Greek, and so I hope will you be."

"When and where may I meet her?" I asked, the breath catching in my throat at the mere thought.

"You may take my horse and ride to my house now, if you choose," he said kindly, and he laughed aloud. "I fancy my daughter has been expecting you impatiently for a couple of days, but I thought a little delay would do you both good, and tame you somewhat."

I should have been suspicious of so much good will. But forgetful of guns and Turks, of the Blachernae and my duties, I swung myself up onto his coal-black charger and careered with slack reins through the city to the Marmora. I shouted aloud for joy as I galloped. This month of May sparkled about me, a heaven of blue and gold, though wall and harbor lay enveloped in black smoke.

Once at the house, so noble in its simplicity of line, I barely gave myself time to tether the horse. Swiftly as a lover to his first, sweet assignation I raced up to thunder on the door. Only then did I think of my appearance; I tried to wipe the dust and soot from my face, spat in my hands and burnished my cuirass.

A servant in blue and white livery opened the door, but I did not spare him a glance. Through the entrance hall Anna Notaras was hastening toward me, slender and beautiful, her eyes radiant with joy. So young and lovely was she in her own surroundings that I dared not take her in my arms, but only looked at her, my breath caught in my throat. Her neck was bare. She had painted her lips and eyebrows. The sweet scent of hyacinths enveloped her, as when we met for the first time.

"At last!" she whispered eagerly. She took my head in her hands and kissed me on the mouth. Her cheeks were glowing.

No one guarded her. No one had shut her up in the women's wing. I could not understand it.

She took my hand. It was enough. Hand in hand we went up to the great hall on the floor above. Through the narrow windows glittered the silver waves of the Marmora.

"The end is near, Anna," I said. "You don't know what is happening now on the wall. I thank God for His grace in allowing me to see you again and look into your eyes."

"Just to look into my eyes?" she smiled. "Is that all you want? Yet I am your wife."

No, I could not understand; it all seemed a dream. Perhaps I was already dead. Perhaps a cannon ball had crushed me so suddenly that my soul still lingered on earth, bound by its earthly desires.

"Drink," whispered my wife Anna Notaras, and poured out a goblet of tawny wine. I saw that she had mixed amber with it, in the Turkish manner. Why should she inflame me? I longed for her keenly enough as it was.

Her lips were to me a sweeter cup. The sweetest and loveliest chalice in the world to me is her body. But when I would have touched her she restrained me. Her pupils widened and darkened and she said, "No, not yet. Sit down, beloved. First we must talk."

"Say nothing," I begged in my disappointment. "Say nothing, my dearest one. Speech ends only in quarrels and hard words and pain. It is not through words that we understand one another best, but in a different way altogether."

She looked at the floor and said reproachfully, "Is it only bed you want—nothing else? Am I no more than a body to you?"

"You yourself would have it so," I answered, with an ache in my throat.

She looked up and blinked until her eyes sparkled with tears.

"Be reasonable," she urged. "You have met my father. He is ready to forgive me, and you too, if only you will let him. For the first time he has spoken to me as to a grown person—he has explained his ideas and hopes and aims. For the first time I have understood him, and so must you. He has a plan."

A chill descended on me, but Anna went on, tenderly stroking my sooty hand with both of hers.

"He's my father. My father can do no wrong. Next to the Emperor he is the most eminent man in Constantinople. When the Emperor betrays his people and his faith and sells the city to the Latins, it is my father who bears the responsibility for the people's fate. It is his duty and he cannot shirk it, however heavy and humiliating it may seem. That you can well understand."

"Go on," I said bitterly. "Go on. I seem to have heard this before."

Anna flared up. "Father is no traitor. He would never stoop to treachery. He is a statesman who must save what can be saved from the ruins of our city."

Through her eyelashes she regarded me curiously. No more tears could be seen in her eyes, however rapidly she blinked. On the contrary she seemed to be secretly enjoying herself as she continued: "After the fall of the city I was to have been Sultan Mohammed's consort, and through this alliance the Sultan would have made a treaty with the Greek people. My father took it exceedingly ill that a whim of mine should have upset this plan. Yet how could I have known? He never said a word of it to me."

"What a lot you've missed," I sneered. "First you were to be Basilissa, and then one of the countless wives of the future ruler of the world. You have been unfortunate, and I can well understand your regrets. But don't be too distressed: I haven't many days left to live and then you will be free again."

"How can you talk to me in that tone?" she cried hotly. "You know I love you! And you're wrong to speak of dying. Both you and I have many years before us. You shall see—if only you will take my father's advice."

"Let us hear this advice, then, that he hasn't dared to offer me himself," I retorted bitterly. "But hurry. I must get back to the wall."

She seized me with both hands as if to prevent my departure.

"You shan't go back there," she exclaimed. "This very night you're to return to the Sultan's camp. You need not give him any information about the city's defenses, if that goes against your honor. You have only to carry a secret message from my father. The Sultan knows you and believes in you. Any other Greek he would suspect."

"And what is this message?" I asked.

"Father cannot write it down," Anna explained eagerly. "Even though he trusts you and the Sultan, a written message would be far too dangerous. There are people even among the Sultan's entourage who are working against him and stirring up Greek resistance. Perhaps you know that. But you're to tell the Sultan that there is a strong peace party in this city who disapprove of the Emperor and who are prepared to collaborate with the Turks on the Sultan's own terms. Say to him: 'We are thirty high-ranking and influential men'—my father will tell you which they are—'who realize that the future of the Greeks in Constantinople is bound up with their understanding of and friendship for the Sultan. Our honor will not allow us to interfere directly on his behalf, so long as the city is able to defend itself. But in secret we're working for him, and when the city falls there will be found within it a complete administration in which the people have confidence. We thirty therefore put ourselves under the Sultan's protection, humbly requesting that our persons, families and property may be spared when he enters the city.' "

Anna looked at me.

"Is there any harm in that?" she asked. "Is that not a lawful and honorable proposal? We stand between Turks and Latins as between the hammer and the anvil. Only by deposing the Emperor and laying down our arms as unanimously as possible can we safeguard the future of the city. We are not delivering ourselves into his hands; on the contrary, his political sense will tell him that this solution is the best one for himself. You're no Latin—why should you fight for the Latin cause?"

Since I remained silent in my bitterness and dejection, she thought I was pondering the matter and went on. "It's only a question of days before the city falls, my father says. So you must make haste. When the Sultan has beaten down the Latin resistance you will march in with the victors and bring me home as your wife. You will be connected now with the house of Notaras, and you surely realize what that means."

She pointed to the marble walls, the carpets, the costly furniture that surrounded us, and added even more vehemently, "Isn't this better than the wretched little wooden house you brought me to? Who knows, perhaps one day we shall live in the Palace of Blachernae! If you will support my father you shall belong to the most distinguished society in Constantinople."

She fell silent, her cheeks glowing with enthusiasm. I had to say something.

"Anna, you are your father's daughter, and that is as it should be. But I do not mean to run errands to the Sultan for your father. Let him choose someone with more political sense than I have."

Her face hardened.

"Are you afraid?" she asked coldly.

I seized the helmet that lay in my lap and hurled it to the floor with a crash.

"In a good cause I would go to the Sultan, though he were to impale me on the spot!" I cried. "That is beside the point. Believe me, Anna, your father's lust for power has blinded him. In trusting to the Sultan he digs his own grave. He doesn't know Mohammed. I do.

"If these were the old days," I went on, "there might be some sense in his schemes. But the Sultan's great bombard has ushered in a new era. An era when no one can trust his neighbor, and when man is the defenseless tool of power. Though the Sultan were to swear by his Prophet and all the angels, with his hand on the Koran, he would still be laughing in his heart; he believes neither in the Prophet nor the angels. He would clear your father out of the way as soon as he had no further use for him. But it's waste of time for me to warn Notaras. He would never believe me.

"And even if one could trust the Sultan," I pursued, "I would never go back to him, though you begged me on your knees. This is my city. While it fights I fight with it. When its walls crumble I perish with them. That is my last word, Anna. Torment me no longer. Torment yourself no longer."

Anna stared at me, pale with wrath and disappointment.

"You do not love me, then," she said again.

"No, I don't love you," I said. "It was error and delusion. I thought you were someone else. But forgive me for that; you will soon be free of me. If you ask him prettily, the Sultan may yet consent to take you into his harem. Follow your father's counsel: he will arrange everything for the best."

I rose and picked up my helmet from the floor. The waves of the Sea of Marmora glittered like molten silver. The polished marble of the walls reflected my image. So irrevocably had I lost her that at that moment I was as cold as ice.

"Anna," I said, but my voice broke. "If you want to see me again you will find me on the wall."

She made no answer. I left her and went my way. But on the staircase she caught up with me and cried, reddening in humiliation, "Farewell, then, accursed Latin! We shall not meet again. I will pray to God hourly that you may die and I be rid of you. And if I should see your dead body I will kick it in the face to be free at last!"

With her curse ringing in my ears I went out, my lips trembling, and put on my helmet. Notaras' coal-black charger lifted his head and snorted. I did not scorn to mount him; I climbed into the saddle and drove my heels into his sides.

Now it is midnight. Tonight I long for death as I have never longed for anything before. Giustiniani has given me leave to court death, since I know Turkish and can help him in his task. Jesus Christ, Son of God, have mercy upon me.

Because I love. Because I love her senselessly, hopelessly. Farewell, Anna Notaras, my dearest.

19 May 1453

It seems then that I am to drain the cup of destruction and death to the very dregs.

I was not allowed to die last night.

Once, to impress Giustiniani, I told him that I was hard, immune. I meant only that it is possible for the spirit to master the body and its sensations. But I am not hard. And my body no longer obeys my spirit.

The professional soldiers say enviously, "You're lucky, Jean Ange!"

It's not luck. I perceive more keenly and painfully than ever that no one dies before his appointed hour. Wildly though death may rage against the walls of my city both day and night, every ball follows a path traced by God.

Last night we burned down the Turks' siege-tower. In the

opinion of many this was a greater marvel than the erection of it in a single night.

During the darkest hours I lay at its foot clad in Turkish dress. I heard their password. Someone trod on me in the darkness, but as I never moved a muscle he took me for a corpse.

Two hours before daybreak we forced our way into the tower, smashed open the ports and succeeded in throwing in a few earthenware pots filled with gunpowder. Without these we could never have set it alight. My hair and eyebrows have been singed away and my hands are covered with blisters. Giustiniani did not recognize me when I came crawling back. Of those who entered the tower I am the only survivor.

Some of the Turkish occupants escaped. This morning the Sultan had them executed and impaled their heads on stakes.

The bombardment roars in my ears and the floor trembles under my feet.

Worse than the smarting of face or hands is the searing bitterness in my heart.

After the earthquake in Hungary; that was the first time. Then at Varna. He said then: "We shall meet again at the Gate of St. Romanos." Tonight I awaited him there, but he never came.

20 May 1453

During the night the Turks brought up more siege-towers, though none of them as big and menacing as the one we burned.

Every day their fleet moves up to the boom to detain the Venetian ships and men. But I hear all this from others, being still unfit to dress and go to the wall.

21 May 1453

Grant the German came to see me today, to show that he too had singed his beard and hands. The Turks have now learned how to wage war underground and defend their tunnels. Grant's men, who had countermined near the Kaligari Gate, were met today by a shower of floating fire, and the relief team was held up by a wall of spears and poisonous smoke. Grant had to crawl underground to hearten his men. They managed to destroy the Turkish mine but suffered severe losses. These subterranean battles arouse superstitious dread in the city.

Grant's eyes were swollen and red-rimmed from sulphur fumes and lack of sleep. He told me, "I have found a manuscript by Pythagoras himself, but the letters dance like flies before my eyes. I can't see to read any more."

His face was distorted with impotent rage, he shook his fists and yelled, "What is this blind spot in the eyes of even the wisest Greek mathematicians and craftsmen? They might have deflected the world from its course, as Archimedes promised, but when I thought I had found fresh knowledge I read only that spirits dwell in trees and stones. Pythagoras too! He might have built machines to harness the forces of nature—but that he judged to be of trifling value. He fled to the soul, to the innermost self, to God."

I said, "Then why not believe these Greek sages, since you

do not accept the evidence of the Bible and of the Fathers of the Church?"

"I don't know, I don't know," he whispered, rubbing his eyes. "Perhaps I haven't all my wits about me just now. Sleepless nights, unending strain and tension have thrown me into a fever. My thoughts wheel past each other like birds in the air, and I can't control their flight. What is this dreadful path that leads into man, but not out of him, and ends in darkness? Pythagoras could build the universe of numbers, but even he was brought up short before man, who cannot be built of numbers. Can the darkness of mankind be after all something more fundamental than the light of nature and science?"

I said, "The Spirit of God has swept over the earth. The Spirit of God has descended like tongues of fire upon us mortals. That you cannot doubt."

He laughed harshly, thumped his temples and cried, "Unquenchable fire can consume human flesh. Human reason flashes from the mouths of cannon. I believe in man's freedom —in the freedom of knowledge. In nothing else."

"You're on the wrong side," I told him again. "You would find realization for yourself in serving the Sultan rather than the Last Rome."

"No," he said stubbornly. "I serve Europe and the freedom of the human intellect. Not power."

22 May 1453

Two mine tunnels were discovered this morning near the Kaligari Gate. One was demolished only after savage fighting. The other fell in of itself, having been unskillfully shored up.

Grant believes that most of the expert miners have perished, so that the Sultan has been obliged to employ unskilled men.

Shortly before midnight a glowing disk sped across the night sky. No one could explain it. The Emperor said, "The prophecies are being fulfilled. Soon the Empire of a thousand years will be at an end. It was founded by the first Constantine and perishes with the last. I was born under an unlucky star."

23 May 1453

Today our last hope has faded. The Emperor was right. Prepared as he is through fasting, watching and praying he is more sensitive than the rest of us to the last slow pulse beats of his realm.

The brigantine which had been dispatched in search of the Venetian fleet returned at dawn with her mission unaccomplished. By a combination of great good fortune, good seamanship and gallantry, the vessel slipped unharmed through the Dardanelles and past the Turkish guardships.

Twelve men sailed, twelve returned. Six of them are Venetians and the rest Greeks. They have cruised for twenty days in the Aegean without a glimpse of a Christian ship, in hourly peril of being sighted by a Turkish patrol.

When they saw that their search was vain they conferred together. Some said: "We have done our duty. More we cannot do. Why should we return to hell? The fall of the city is certain."

Others said: "The Emperor sent us. To the Emperor we

must make our report, vain though our efforts have been. But let us vote."

They met each other's eyes, burst out laughing and with one accord agreed to sail the brigantine back to Constantinople.

I met two of these men in the Palace of Blachernae. They still laughed heartily as they told of their fruitless voyage, while the Venetians poured wine for them and slapped them on the back. But their eyes—haunted by danger and the sea—did not smile.

"How did you find the courage to return to certain death?" I asked them. They turned their weatherbeaten faces to me in surprise and answered with one voice, "We're Venetian seamen."

That was enough, perhaps. Venice, queen of the sea, greedy, cruel and calculating though she may be, has yet bred up her sons to live and die in defense of her honor.

But six of the twelve were Greeks. They have shown that a Greek too can be faithful to a lost cause, until death.

24 May 1453

This afternoon a number of Turks moved in brilliant procession toward the ramparts by the Gate of St. Romanos. They waved flags, blew trumpets and requested that an envoy from the Sultan might be admitted into the city to negotiate with Basileus Constantine. At the same time their artillery ceased firing and all their fighting men returned to camp.

Giustiniani suspected a trick and was unwilling to let the Turkish spokesman see how badly the wall is damaged and how flimsy the temporary barricade. But when Emperor Constantine mounted the battlements he recognized the envoy as his personal friend, the Emir of Sinope, Ismail Hamza. This man's family has for many generations maintained friendly relations with the Emperors of Constantinople, though old Murad shortly before his death made a treaty with him by letting Mohammed marry Ismail Hamza's daughter. Constantine greeted him cordially, nevertheless, and asked that he might be helped across the barricade. He entered the city through the sally port.

As soon as the Venetian bailo heard that an envoy had arrived he summoned his Council of Twelve, withdrew a number of Venetians from the walls and marched at the head of two hundred soldiers to the Emperor's headquarters. Giustiniani, on his part, having distributed provisions and the last of the wine among his men, went from one to another threatening each with his fist and bawling, "Laugh, damn you, laugh—or I'll wring your necks!"

As Ismail Hamza looked keenly about him, stroking his beard, he saw nothing but laughing men in armor chewing pieces of meat and carelessly throwing away the scraps. The Emperor gave him his hand to kiss and regretted that they should meet in such unhappy circumstances.

The Emir of Sinope spoke up loudly and clearly, that his words might be heard by the soldiers too: "May this day be a day of blessing, for Sultan Mohammed has sent me to offer you peace on honorable terms!"

At this Giustiniani's Genoese burst out into yet heartier peals of laughter than before, though many were at the weeping point from exhaustion. Giustiniani had taken his dagger between thumb and forefinger and, going behind his men, he furtively pricked the thigh of any who failed to laugh loudly enough.

Ismail Hamza begged to speak to the Emperor in private. Without hesitating, Constantine showed him into his headquarters and, heedless of his counselors' warnings, shut himself up with him in a small room alone. Meanwhile the Venetian bailo, having thrown a cordon of men around the tower, approached at the head of the Council of Twelve and begged that the Emperor might be informed of the Venetians' refusal to countenance any separate negotiations with the Turks.

The Emperor replied that he had never considered making any decisions behind the backs of his allies; he then summoned his own counselors and made known to them the Sultan's peace terms.

Ismail Hamza said gravely, "For your own sake and for the sake of your people I beg you to accept these conditions, which are the best that could possibly be offered. Your walls are in ruins and in several places are level with the ground. Your city is in a desperate situation, your defenders are few and famished and the townspeople are in despair. This is your last chance. If you do not surrender now the Sultan will slay every man, sell the women and children as slaves and sack the city."

The Venetians cried, "For God's sake do not trust the treacherous Sultan! What can he promise you? The Turks have broken their word before now. Have we then shed our blood in vain—have our best men sacrificed their lives on the ramparts for nothing, to uphold your throne? No, no—the Sultan wavers, uncertain of his victory. Why else should he seek to ensnare the city by wily offers of peace?"

Ismail Hamza took this very ill and said, "If you had any sense in your heads you would see that Constantinople's position is hopeless. From sheer humanity—from the desire to spare you all the horrors of a capture by storm—the Sultan offers to let the Emperor depart unmolested, together with his treasury, his entourage and his personal attendants. Those inhabitants who wish to accompany him may take their property with them. Those who remain are promised life and goods by the Sultan. As the Sultan's ally the Emperor may retain the Morea, and the Sultan will defend his rights there against all aggressors."

At this the Venetians began shouting and beating on their shields to drown his voice. But the Basileus bowed his head and said, "Your terms are humiliating and unjust. It would not consist with my dignity as Basileus to accept them, even if I could. But I cannot, for to surrender the city is not in my power, nor in the power of any here. We are prepared to die, and we will sacrifice our lives without complaint."

Dejected and contemptuous he surveyed the yelling Venetians, who were so ready to fight to the last Greek. Have they not their great vessels lying in the harbor: a chance of escape when all is lost?

The Sultan must have known very well that Constantine would not accept such terms as these. But for the sake of the peace party—and of the army which is displeased at its reverses—he was compelled to resort to this plan in order to demonstrate to his subjects the obduracy of the Greeks. He is but human, and at heart he is weak.

If our city is now the prey of a consuming despondency and dread, Sultan Mohammed's uncertainty must be at least as hard to bear. He has staked everything, and has no choice but to conquer or be crushed. He has not only the city against him, but also men in his own camp.

For this reason Sultan Mohammed is now the loneliest of the lonely; lonelier even than Emperor Constantine, whose decision is made.

For this reason I am now linked with Sultan Mohammed in secret brotherhood; I miss him, I desire once more to see that inaccessible face, that obstinate jaw, those wild beast's eyes with their golden glint. I want to talk to him and assure myself once again that I do not wish to live on into an age when he and his like will rule the world.

He is the future. He will win. But the future with him is not worth having.

"Laugh, laugh!" Giustiniani ordered his Genoese. And when the Emir of Sinope departed, they could not stop—those men with their emaciated faces, dented armor and bloodstained bandages. They laughed, they laughed with all their hearts, hating Giustiniani for constantly goading them to superhuman efforts. They hate him, but they love him. Somewhere at the back of their minds floats the dream of a vineyard and a white house on the slopes of Lemnos. Of Greek slave-laborers in fertile fields. Of the seigneur's right to the maidenhood of pretty peasant girls and of banquets for his warriors.

With tears of weariness in their eyes they whooped in helpless laughter and reeled back to the wall, while the Turks rode away with floating banners and braying trumpets. When hundreds of guns were once more thundering against us, Giustiniani himself bent and picked up a knuckle bone from the ground. There was still some meat on it, and he brushed off the sand and gnawed it clean.

"My ducal coronet is proving expensive," he remarked. "I've lost twenty pounds of my own flesh and blood, and still there's no sign of victory.

"No, I see no sign of victory," he repeated with a glance at the great breach, now over a thousand feet wide and protected only by a bank of earth, timber, fascines and heaps of stones, in place of the outer wall, with gabions to shelter the archers.

Today is Thursday, and tomorrow will be the holy day of

Islam. Next Thursday, perhaps, I shall not see. Mohammed has now obeyed the precepts of the Koran and offered peace, before taking the city by storm. Time has ripened for Islam's great assault: "That army is mightiest, that prince greatest among princes, who shall capture Constantinople."

We are the gate to the west. The last western outpost against the east. When our walls have crumbled our living bodies will be the last, the only barricade.

25 May 1453

Basileus Constantine summoned the senate early this morning, with his advisers and representatives of the Church. He did so, knowing that the patriarch Gregorios Mammas had resigned his office. Nor did Cardinal Isidor attend the meeting; he stays in the tower that he has undertaken to defend.

This was a final attempt to reconcile the supporters and opponents of the Union. But this too stuck half-way. We have been freed from an old man whom Greeks hate and Latins despise, but the Church is now without a patriarch altogether. From his monastic cell in the Pantokrator the unseen, unyielding spirit of Gennadios the monk rules over church and cloister, prophesying disaster.

The Sultan has proclaimed a general fast throughout his camp and adjured all the faithful to perform the ablutions and devotions prescribed. Exacerbated by hunger and thirst the Turks have been attacking all day, howling like a pack of hounds each time they see a Christian fall. Sometimes they shout in chorus: "Allah is God and Mohammed is his Prophet." Their mournful yet triumphant cries have a depressing effect on both Greeks and Latins. Many simple-minded Latins have taken to discussing the matter. "Could God ever permit the Turks to win?" they ask. "If so, does it not prove that their God is more powerful than ours and their Prophet mightier than Christ, who let Himself be crucified?"

Minotto, the Venetian bailo, has turned pious and received the means of grace. He intends to compete with Giustiniani and prove that a Venetian is equal to any Genoese. The Venetian marine-soldiers have displayed incomparable valor in defending the northern tip of the Blachernae, the Pentapyrgion fortress. Not a single Turk has reached the top of the wall there.

At dusk bonfires were lit in the Turkish camp. Drums rolled and trumpets blared so fiendishly that many on the walls fancied a fire had broken out. But this is all part of the Turkish fast. At nightfall they may eat and drink, and abstinence is resumed at dawn as soon as a white thread may be distinguished from a black. In the glow of their huge fires the camp was as bright as day.

The nearer the decisive hour approaches, the more sternly do the Venetians regard me. They declare that I am spying upon them on Giustiniani's behalf, and their constraint shows that they have something to conceal. Presumably they have now decided how best to turn the victory to account for Venice, should the attack fail and the siege be raised. The advantages are great enough to make it worth their while to attempt the impossible. Moreover the wall around the Blachernae is still so strong that as long as the Venetians defend it the Turks can never break into the city from that direction.

Where the outer and main walls adjoin that of the Blachernae at right angles, there is a half-sunken sally port in the great wall leading from the street. Many generations ago it was used as a short cut to a circus built outside the city, and for this reason is known as the Kerkoporta, though it was afterwards walled up. Now it has been opened again, like all the other posterns. Through it one may conveniently pass from the Porphyrogenetos Palace to the Guacchardi brothers' sector by the Kharisios Gate, and thence further between the walls to Giustiniani's area.

By the Kerkoporta the wall is undamaged, and the Turks have never tried to attack here, as the right-angled wall exposes the assailant to severe cross-fire. By this sheltered way, therefore, reinforcements may most swiftly be sent to the Kharisios Gate, where the ramparts have collapsed almost as completely as by the Gate of St. Romanos. The Venetians have formed a special troop of reserves which at need may be detached and sent in support of the Guacchardis. At this quiet Kerkoporta section the inner and outer walls are manned by only a handful of Greeks. In justice to the Latins it must be admitted that they have readily accepted the posts of greatest danger.

Shortly before midnight, Manuel came to me. He was badly frightened, and said, "The great church is on fire!"

We went up onto the roof of the palace, where already numbers of onlookers were gathered. The Turkish fires still burned high, but in the center of the dark city the gigantic dome of St. Sophia's was lit by a strange, unearthly glow. It was not so much fire as a vivid blue shimmer. Latins beholding this whispered to each other, declaring it to be an ill omen.

That strange luminosity hovered over the dome, now fainter, now brighter. I set off into the city in the direction of the church, and I was not alone. In the darkness around me murmured an agitated crowd; all were making for the same place. I heard the sobbing of women and the chanting of monks. Near the church the blue light was so strong that no one dared approach very near. People fell on their knees on the damp ground and began to pray. God was giving us a sign. The unearthly was taking earthly shape. Now that I have beheld this with my own eyes I can no longer doubt that the Christian era is at an end and that the time of the wild beast is come.

The dome glimmered and shone for over an hour. Then the brightness suddenly dimmed; it quivered for a time and went out. The sky was so heavily overcast that all at once the night hung pitch-black about us. The Turkish fires too went out and their glow ceased to illuminate the clouds overhead. The air was heavy with moisture and filled with the smell of earth and decomposition, so that one seemed to be walking through a churchyard among newly opened graves.

In the darkness a slender, hot hand was slipped into mine. Perhaps I deceived myself in thinking I recognized it. I dared not touch her or speak to her. Perhaps it was just a child who had strayed from its parents and sought safety with me; or a woman, overwrought by darkness and fear, and craving the company of a man. Yet I recognized her hand. Hot and helpless it was: a wordless message of reconciliation before death.

She said nothing. We breathed in the darkness and our hands met. Our pulses thudded painfully together in silent testimony to our mutual need. All was well. It was best so. In this way we understood each other, at a moment when words would have broken the link between us.

So simple, self-evident—so small, pitiful and helpless. A fevered hand in the darkness, amid the heavy odor of mold. Across the graves, across death, we stretched forth our hands in reconciliation. Then she was gone.

Even if it were fancy, an illusion, yet it has reconciled me to much within myself. As I groped my way back like a sleepwalker to the Palace of Blachernae, no bitterness now corroded my spirit. I was free; the mists had cleared. I had witnessed a miracle and felt a human being's hand in mine.

26 May 1453

The nocturnal miracle at St. Sophia's has thrown the city into such a ferment that early this morning a crowd, led by monks and nuns, surged into the Blachernae to fetch the miracle-working icon of the Virgin from the church there and carry it to the walls. With her narrow, unutterably sad face, set about with gold and precious stones, the Blessed Virgin looked upon her people. Many saw her countenance quicken and her eyes shed tears. All desired to touch the image, and in the press of people it fell to the ground. At that moment raindrops the size of pigeons' eggs began falling from the low-hanging clouds; in a moment the shower had turned into a cloudburst, the air was darkened and water gushed along the streets. The miracle-working icon became as heavy as lead as it lay in the wet, so that only the brawniest monks with their united strength could raise it and carry it to safety in the Khora convent.

We hoped that the sudden rain would soak the Turkish gunpowder, but it was a vain hope. Even during the storm the guns roared now and again, and when it ceased and left the ground steaming, they began a savage bombardment, as if to make up for lost time.

The Turks are still fasting. From the battlements later in the day I saw the Turkish commanders assembling on the hill by the Sultan's tent. The council of war lasted all the afternoon. Then Mohammed's green-clad *tsaushes* galloped off to all parts of the camp to make known his commands. The roars and yells that arose, the jubilant clang and clamor of instruments and voices surpassed all we had yet heard, and increased towards evening to an incessant thunder, like that of a mighty ocean. It was not difficult to guess that the Sultan has fixed the day and the hour for his final assault.

When I saw that the Sultan had summoned the great divan, I set off to the Gate of St. Romanos and sought out Giustiniani, who was on the wall directing the ceaseless labor on the barricades.

"The Palace of Blachernae is in good shape," I said. "The assault will be made at any moment. Let me fight beside you at the Romanos Gate. I made a rendezvous here nine years ago, at Varna. I don't want to be like the merchant of Samarra when the time comes."

He thrust his big arm cordially under mine, raised the visor of his helmet and looked at me with a smile in his bloodshot ox-eyes. He seemed to be laughing secretly at something unknown to me.

"Many are reporting here today," he said. "I feel flattered, for it shows that this is the place of honor. Sultan Mohammed himself has favored me with his notice," he went on, pointing to a balk of timber projecting from the earthworks. From the end of it, heels brushing the ground, dangled the body of a bristly-bearded peddler, his worn apron still upon him.

"The Sultan sent me word that he admired my courage and military skill. He required no treachery of me, being unwilling to tarnish my honor. But if I and my men would retire from the wall and go on board the vessels in the harbor, he promised to make me a rich man and give me command of the janissaries. He would also allow me to keep my religion, for he has Christians in his service already. In token of my agreement I was to strike my colors. Instead, I hoisted his messenger. That was my answer and I hope he can see it, though I cannot at present trouble my men to build me a proper gallows."

He rubbed his face, which was smarting with sweat and dust, and added, "A message like that brings a crumb of hope with it. The fate of the city rests upon our swords. The Emperor is sending the pick of his guard here, and his noblest knights. Of my own men more than three hundred are still fit for battle. We will show the Sultan that a living wall of iron is ever stronger than one of stone.

"Yet I mistrust everything and everyone," he said, looking at me now with disfavor. "It is a specially suspicious circumstance that you, of all people, should wish to return here today, of all days. With his last gasp that huckster threatened me, saying that the Sultan has many other ways of getting rid of me. Therefore I'm not overanxious to have at my back a man who once escaped from the Sultan's camp, good friends though we may be, Jean Ange."

The rejoicings in the Turkish camp surged over to us in tempestuous waves of sound.

"Once Sultan Mohammed has decided on a plan, he will use any means to carry it out," I agreed. "If you stood in his way he would never hesitate to hire an assassin."

"You'll understand, then, that I don't want strange people swarming around me," said Giustiniani benevolently. "But some people one cannot refuse if one has a kind heart. Besides, it is part of my duty as protostrator to keep an eye upon you and prevent your doing anything rash. Keep within sight of me when the attack begins, or my last task shall be to send a headsman to you."

Just then we espied Megadux Notaras approaching at a walk on his black charger, surrounded by a troop of military police. He dismounted by the sally port and evidently intended to make for Giustiniani's sector. Giustiniani funneled his hands about his mouth and roared to his men not to admit the Grand Duke to the ramparts. Notaras' face darkened with wrath. He shouted, "I must pass freely everywhere on the Emperor's business. There are escaped smugglers and felons among the Greek workmen on the walls."

Giustiniani slid down the shattered wall and landed with a jump at Notaras' feet.

"You shan't come spying on my wall," he cried. "Here *I* am king. Rather give me back my two bombards, for now if ever do I need them."

Notaras gave a sneering laugh. "Do you intend the Greeks to defend the harbor with their bare hands? Now if ever the guns are needed to keep the Turkish ships at a distance."

Giustiniani ground his teeth until his jaws cracked, and he bellowed, "Ah, why don't I run my sword through you, you accursed traitor!"

Notaras turned gray in the face, looked around and felt for his sword; but he was wise enough not to tackle a man of Giustiniani's size. He retired a couple of paces until his back was protected by his men, tried to smile and with forced calmness replied, "God may judge which of us is the traitor, the Emperor or I. Do you not carry about you a written promise, sealed with the triple seal, that you shall receive Lemnos as a dukedom if you're successful in defending the city?"

"What then?" asked Giustiniani, staring hard at Notaras to detect any sign of falsehood. But Notaras' voice was all too sincere as he continued, "You damned fool of a Latin! Do you not know, then, that before the siege began the Emperor promised Lemnos to the King of Catalonia in return for ships and auxiliaries? The ships never came, but the Catalonians long ago occupied Lemnos. You'll have to fight another war for it, if you survive this one."

Giustiniani's body began to twitch and he broke into terrible laughter.

"Greeks will be Greeks!" he panted. "Are you prepared to kiss the cross on what you say?"

Notaras drew his sword and kissed the cross of the hilt.

"As truly as God shall judge every man according to his works, so truly did Emperor Constantine confirm with a chrysobull the Catalonians' title to Lemnos. A fool's cap is what you deserve, Giustiniani, and no dukedom."

Can ever so venomous an arrow have struck a man to the heart at a more fateful moment? Notaras, well content, mounted his horse and rode away. I went out through the sally port and rejoined Giustiniani. Seeing me, he laid his heavy hand on my shoulder as if for support and said, "Treachery and deceit lurk everywhere among men. Perhaps my own heart is not altogether free from it; I have fought for Genoa rather than for the Emperor. But in this hour I swear to fight to the uttermost, as long as hope remains, for my own immortal glory, that I and the city of my birth may be spoken of so long as a single stone of these walls remains."

Tears of bitterness streamed from his eyes, and crossing himself several times he prayed, "God be merciful to me a sinner, and if it be Thy will, give this city rather to the Turks than to the Venetians. May worms consume the timbers of their ships, may their sails be blown to tatters. The Greeks I will not even trouble to curse. Let the Turks deal with them."

After his prayer he bade his men haul down the Emperor's purple pendant and leave his own standard floating alone above the heap of rubble, which is here all that remains of the great wall.

The night is dark again, and the Turkish fires blaze to the clouds. I cannot but marvel at the human heart and at the mirage called honor which impels even a toughened professional soldier like Giustiniani to set aside his own advantage and hazard his life for the sake of honor alone. Now that in his extremity the Emperor has tried to purchase assistance by breaking his word, Giustiniani might justly cancel his part of the bargain and embark his men. The Sultan would shower him with horsetails and kaftans of honor were he to enter Turkish service after the siege.

There must after all be something more in man than selfishness and political ambition.

Is there perhaps something even in Lukas Notaras beyond mere lust for power?

My servant Manuel is counting his money. He looks about him uneasily and is in sore distress, for he does not know where to hide it from the Turks.

28 May 1453

Today the enemy have been preparing their assault and through the darkness can be heard a low, unbroken murmur as they bring forward their scaling-ladders, beams, bridges and fascines. Their fires were lit only for a short time, and were extinguished when the Sultan allowed his men a few hours' rest before the attack.

But how can I sleep on such a night as this? Volunteers have been pouring out from the center of the city to help, at the eleventh hour, in carrying stones and earth to the breaches. Giustiniani therefore has allowed his own fit men to rest. Tonight and tomorrow everyone will need the last ounce of his strength. But how can I sleep on my city's deathbed?

Today there has been no stint of firewood and victuals. The

Emperor has ordered all stores to be emptied, and anything remaining has been distributed: even the Latins had their share.

It is strange to feel that this night will be my last, the night I have been awaiting, the night for which my whole life has been but the preparation. I don't know myself well enough, but I hope I shall keep my courage. I know that death is not so very painful; I have seen much of it these last weeks.

I am humble tonight. Tranquil. Silent. Happier than ever before.

Perhaps it is wrong to feel happiness on such a night. But on my own account I neither blame nor judge anyone. I can look on unconcerned at the Venetians as they stock their holds from the Emperor's stores and row boatloads of costly furniture, carpets and plate to their ships. I do not reproach the rich, the noble and the wise who at the eleventh hour purchase life and a passage on board, for themselves and their families.

Each one acts as his conscience bids him. Lukas Notaras too, and Gennadios. Emperor Constantine. Giustiniani.

The Guacchardi brothers throw dice, sing Italian lovesongs and drink sparingly, in the only tower left standing by the Kharisios Gate.

How fair, serene, resolved is this hour! Never has paper felt so smooth and pure beneath my fingers; never has ink gleamed so black. My senses seem sharpened, and their perception is keener than before. Thus, then, do the dying behold for the last time the vanity of life.

Why am I so happy? Why do I smile at death tonight?

Early this morning I reported to Giustiniani. He was still asleep, in his casemate under the great wall, though the place was trembling under the first bombardment of the day. He was in full equipment, and beside him lay a Greek youth in bright new armor. I assumed he was one of the young bloods whom the Emperor promised Giustiniani as reinforcements. They have sworn an oath to meet death at the Gate of St. Romanos.

The boy awoke and sat up yawning, rubbed his eyes with grimy fists and smoothed his tousled hair. He gave me a haughty look and I took him for one of Lukas Notaras' sons. He resembled his father. I felt a little envious of the favor Giustiniani was showing him and therefore did not meet his eye. When at that moment Giustiniani awoke and stretched his great body, I asked sarcastically, "I trust you've not been obliged to relapse into the old Italian vice, Giustiniani? Are there no women in the city to delight you?"

Giustiniani burst out laughing, ruffled the boy's hair and clapped him on the back.

"Up with you, lazybones, and attend to your duties," he said.

The boy rose, eying me askance, went over to a wine jar and filled a goblet which he offered Giustiniani on one knee.

I sneered. "That boy couldn't even guard your rear in a tight place, he's far too puny. And he seems to be dressed for parade rather than for battle. Kick him out and let me take his place beside you. The bailo has no further need of me at the Blachernae."

Giustiniani shook his bull's head and gave me an amused stare. "Are you blind? Don't you recognize this noble youth?"

At that instant my eyes were opened; I caught sight of Giustiniani's chain of office around her neck.

"Great God!" I exclaimed, shaken to my very depths. "Is it you, Anna? How did you get here?"

Giustanini said, "She came yesterday and placed herself under my protection. The guards let her through, as she was wearing my chain. But as to what we're to do with her, that must be for you to decide."

I looked at Giustiniani; he stepped back and crossed himself three times, swearing by Christ's wounds that he had passed the night chastely and that his honor would never have allowed him to approach his friend's wife with any shameful motive.

"Though indeed the temptation was strong." He sighed. "But I'm all too weary from sleepless nights and fighting and my heavy responsibility to think of women these days. There's a time for everything."

Anna said shamelessly, "Speaking as one soldier to another, I can well understand the Maid of France, who wore breeches so as to live more safely among the fighting men."

She threw her arms around my neck, kissed my cheeks, pressed her head to my breast and said with a sob, "Am I so ugly, then, that you never recognized me? But I was compelled to cut off my hair or I should never have got the helmet on."

She rested in my arms. She was close to me, she hated me no longer.

"Why did you leave your father?" I asked. "And was it you who put a hand in mine, the night the great church was illumined?"

Giustiniani cleared his throat, rubbed his side where the armor galled it and said discreetly, "I must go up and inspect the guard. Eat and drink anything you can find—and by the way, you can lock the door if you want to display your affection for one another and are not afraid of gunfire."

He went, closing the massive door behind him. I saw from his face that he was greatly charmed by Anna and envious of me. Anna peered slyly up at me, but I hadn't the courage to go over and lock the door. With an absent-minded air she went herself and drew the bolt.

"Beloved," she said. "Can you ever forgive me for being so stubborn and selfish, and for not understanding you?"

"Beloved," I answered, "forgive me for not being the man you hoped I was. But you can't stay here," I added, with a pang at my heart. "You must go back to your father's house. There you're as safe as anyone can be in this city when the assault begins. I fancy that the Sultan will take him under his protection after the capture."

"He is sure to," she said. "I've heard that the first thing the Sultan will do is to send *tsaushes* to guard us. But I also know why, and therefore I won't go back."

"What has happened?" I asked, full of dark forebodings.

She came up to me, laid her hands on my hips and looked at me with the deepest gravity in her brown eyes.

"Do not ask," she said. "I am my father's daughter. I cannot betray him. Isn't it enough that I have come to you? That I have cut off my hair and donned my brother's armor to die with you on the wall, since it is God's will?"

"You shan't die," I said. "You must not die. That cannot be intended for you. Both your determination and your dress are outrageous."

She said, "This is not the first time in these last thousand years that a woman has grasped a sword in defense of our city. You know that very well. Even a Basilissa has been known to don armor when the Emperor fell."

"You can't," I said. "The first Turk you meet will knock you down and cut off your lovely head—and what good would that do?"

She looked at me in deadly earnest and said, "What good will our whole resistance do? The Sultan will win. The wall is down. They are too many, we are too few. Thousands of people will die in vain before dawn tomorrow. If you thought only of what was useful you wouldn't be here either. Let me think as you do—at last!"

She squeezed my arms, and her face was pale beneath the cropped, tangled hair.

"I'm your wife," she said. "For us there can be no future, but I have at least the right to die with you. It's you I love; what could life mean to me if you fell? I would rather win the martyr's crown."

A great stone ball tore away a piece of the battlements somewhere overhead and we heard the crash of falling masonry. Mortar and sand fell from the roof. She raised her face to mine, folded her arms and said, "My mind is made up. Why should we waste what time we have together?"

With unaccustomed hands she began unbuckling the straps of her harness; then laughing she said, "Dearest, help me with these terrible hooks at the back. It takes a man to invent this sort of thing."

My throat was dry as I told her, "You may thank your stars that you're not wearing proper knight's armor, with secret fastenings from head to heel. There are such cunning locks and such hard steel that it's impossible to stab the wearer to death even when he has fallen from his horse and lies helpless on the ground. At Varna the Turks could not open the armor of some of the German knights even with a sledge hammer."

"How much you know," she said caressingly. "How much you've seen! But women have their armor too. The strongest man cannot force that if the woman be unwilling. That is something the Turks will shortly discover. But there are not so very many of those women."

"Only you," I said, and my voice shook. "Only you, Anna Notaras."

Conscious of her beauty she turned and twisted with maddening deliberation, and emerged, slender as a youth, from the close plate armor.

"You make a handsome boy with that short hair," I said. "And yet you're lovelier than ever."

"I'm no boy," she returned, playing with me tenderly. "Can you tell that now?" Once more a round-shot set the wall quaking. Laying her bare arms about my neck she said, "Have no fear of the guns, beloved; I have none. My mouth is a cooling spring; drink! My body is bread for you; eat of it. Enjoy me as I enjoy you. Our life's thread is dwindling and will soon have burned to the end. Death is long, and love without the body is a lean love."

Perhaps her words were sinful, but in that hour, as death rumbled overhead, they were true.

"My only fountain," I whispered. "My only bread. Man needs water and bread to live."

But our love was bitter as salt, which stings the lips and heightens thirst, and we embraced time after time with unquenchable desire. In that stone chamber, filled with the musty smells of leather, rancid oil, wine, gunpowder and sweat-soaked clothes, we embraced; while above us, little by little, death ground the ramparts into dust. Yet our love was not altogether of the body, for every time I looked in her face I met those eyes—candid, naked, trustful—and it was as if through them I gazed through and beyond all temporal things.

"I will come back, beloved," I whispered. "I will come back one day to take up the fetters of time and space and find you again. People, names and places shift and change, but from the ruins of these walls your eyes will look at me one day like velvet-brown flowers. And you, to whatever people or age you may belong, will one day brush this dust with your hand, touch my cheek across the ages, until we find one another again."

Smiling she stroked my neck and shoulders, while tears of passion ran down her burning cheeks. "My most dear," she said. "Perhaps there is nothing more. Perhaps there is only this hour. It is enough. I am content. I am filled with you—I am you. It will be easy, sweet to die after this."

She looked about the gloomy vaulted chamber which was lit by a flickering lamp, and said, "How beautiful—how beautiful it all is. It has never been as beautiful as this."

Resting wearily with my mouth on her warm shoulder I debated with myself whether I should tell her my secret. It seemed vain and irrelevant; yet I would not, could not keep anything from her now. Therefore I said, "Beloved, when I was born into the world my mother clutched a fragment of porphyry in her hand. I was born in the purple. I will tell you about it, since it can make no difference now."

She started up on her elbow and regarded me wide-eyed.

"I was born with purple boots," I repeated. "My father was half-brother to old Emperor Manuel. Emperor John was my grandfather. You know, the man who went to Rome and Avignon, forsook his old religion and acknowledged the Pope, though without compromising either his people or his church. He did it so to induce the Pope to marry him secretly to a Venetian woman whom he loved. He was then forty. The Signoria paid his debts and restored to him the Byzantine Crown Jewels which he had pawned. The Pope and Venice also promised him the support of the west, and a crusade. But his son Andronikos betrayed him and rebelled, and the son of Andronikos too. When the western nations also failed him, he was forced to make a treaty with the Sultan and acknowledge his son Manuel as his heir, though in fact my father was the only lawful successor. And so Manuel sent out his angels to find him and blind him. After this my father no longer desired to live. He threw himself over a cliff behind the Papal

Palace in Avignon. The goldsmith to whom he entrusted his documents and money cheated me after my father's death. Not until I had taken the Cross did I journey to Avignon and set the point of my dagger to his throat. He still had the papers proving the legitimacy of my birth. So far as I know, both the Curia and the Venetian Signoria are aware of my existence, though they have lost sight of me. I am the Basileus, but I desire no power. Power is not for me; but I have the right to perish on the walls of my city. Do you understand now why I must accomplish my destiny?"

She was still gazing at me in shocked amazement, and now let the tips of her fingers glide over my face. I have not troubled of late to disguise myself by shaving, and my beard has grown.

"Do you believe now that everything has its purpose?" I asked. "I had to meet you and your father so as to withstand the final temptation. As soon as Constantine had proclaimed the Union I might have made myself known, and with your father's help headed a revolt, handed the city over to the Sultan and reigned here as vassal-Emperor. But would that have been worthy of my birth?"

She said in distress, "If what you say is true, then I recognized you only from Emperor Manuel's portrait. You resemble Constantine too. Now that you tell me, it seems strange that no one else has noticed the likeness."

"My servant Manuel saw it at once," I said. "Blood is a mysterious thing: it returns to its source. When I reverted to the Church of my fathers it was also the apostate John who in me won back his part in the holy mysteries. In me, destiny brings a manifold reconciliation."

She said, "Basileus John Angelos, of the Palaeologos line. And Anna Notaras, the daughter of Megadux Notaras. Much indeed is reconciled when our destinies are fulfilled.

"Now I don't believe in anything!" she cried. "I don't believe that you will come back—I don't believe that I shall. I don't believe in anything enduring. Only in the likeness that attracted me unawares. It was the imperial blood in you that I recognized—not the man I had met in a former life so that when I looked into his eyes for the first time he was known to me. Ah, why did you tell me this? Why have you taken from me a faith which would have been my comfort in death?"

Bewildered by her grief I said, "I thought it might gratify your woman's vanity. Our families are equal in birth. You did not degrade yourself in choosing me."

She said vehemently, "What do I care for birth and lineage? It is you I care for. But I thank you for the wedding present—I thank you for the invisible crown. I am Basilissa, then, if it will please you. I am anything that will please you."

Naked as she was she rose suddenly and lifted her lovely head in pride.

"Be angel or Basileus, then, whichever you prefer!" she cried. "Array yourself in your invisible, nonexistent glory! I'm a woman, and a woman only. And you have nothing to offer me—no home, no children, not one night in which when I am withered and old I may hear you breathing comfortably by my side. I could touch you then, kiss your mouth with my wrinkled lips. That would be happiness. You grudge it me because of your mad lust for honor and glory. Where is the sense in dying for a lost cause? Who will thank you for it? Who will even remember you when you lie in your own blood, and dust settles upon your face? Your sacrifice is so futile that it would make any woman weep."

She sobbed as she spoke, and raised her voice; then she broke into bitter weeping, threw herself over me, embraced me and kissed me wildly.

"Forgive me!" she begged. "I had promised myself not to

torment you any more, but I am weak. It's you I love! If you were a beggar or a traitor or cast out by everyone, I should still love you, that I might live with you. Perhaps I should be discontented and hurt you continually, but I should still love you. Forgive me."

Our tears mingled; I drank the salt of them from her cheeks and mouth. The futility of all things scorched my heart like a red-hot iron—like a flame that springs high before going out. In that hour I doubted myself, and wavered. And this was my last temptation, harder than the temptation on Constantine's column. Giustiniani's ships are lying in the harbor, ready to sail if the need should arise. Not all those hundreds of Turkish vessels could stop them from breaking out if the wind were in our favor tomorrow.

Before sunset Giustiniani knocked at the door and called us. I drew the bolt and he stepped in without allowing his eyes to wander indiscreetly.

"All's quiet among the Turks," he said. "Their silence is more horrible than the noise and the fires. The Sultan has divided them into companies of a thousand, and has allotted to each company its own hour for attacking. He spoke to them, not of Islam but of the mightiest pillage of all time. Of the treasures in the palaces, the sacred vessels in the churches, of pearls and precious stones. It's said that for two hours he was induced to tell of all there is to be looted and carried off—nor did he forget the beautiful Greek youths and girls whom no man has ever even looked at. For himself he claims only the city walls and all public buildings. The Turks have cut up cloth to make pennants of with their lances, so that each man may mark out his claim to a house. Those dervishes who can write have covered these standards with all the characters and ciphers of Islam, and this has given them more work than even the whetting of blades and the making of scaling-ladders."

In the course of the day Giustiniani had had his beard trimmed and dyed and braided with gold thread. His armor was specklessly bright, and the dents in it had been beaten out. He smelled of good salves and was in every way a splendid and impressive figure.

"Are you not coming to church, my children?" he asked. "The Turks are enjoying their beauty sleep before the assault. Anything their artillery can knock down before then my men can repair. Make haste now and dress yourselves decently, so that like other honest fellows you may make your last communion and take a vow of purity for tonight." He glanced at us and could not resist adding, "From your faces I see that this will be easier for you than for many others."

We rode together to the church as day was fading behind the Turkish camp and shedding a last gleam of blood on the green domes of the churches. Emperor Constantine arrived at the great building with all his courtiers, senators and archons in the prescribed ceremonial order, each arrayed according to his rank and position. In my heart I knew that for the last time a doomed Byzantium was gathering to dedicate itself to death.

The Venetian bailo, the Council of Twelve and the Venetian nobles were also in ceremonial dress. Those who came hither from the ramparts wore gleaming armor instead of silks and velvets. Giustiniani's officers grouped themselves about him. Then came all the Greeks of Constantinople to fill Justinian's holy church, despising it no longer. At this eleventh hour many hundreds of priests and monks came too, in defiance of the interdict. In the presence of death, all quarreling, suspicion and hatred disappeared. Each and everyone bowed his head before the inscrutable mystery, according to his own conscience.

The hundreds of lamps in the church burned with fragrant flame and shed a light as bright as day. Mild yet mighty, unutterably sorrowful, the mosaic figures gazed down from the golden walls. When the choirs in pure, angelic harmony sang the sacred hymns, even Giustiniani's puffy eyes filled with tears and he had to wipe them with both hands. Many valiant men wept aloud.

In the presence of us all the Emperor confessed his sins in the phrases that centuries have hallowed. The Latins joined with him in murmuring chorus. The creed was recited by the Greek Metropolitan, who omitted the offending words *"and from the Son."* Bishop Leonard repeated the Latin creed for the Latins. In the Greek intercessory prayers the Pope was not named. The Latins included him in theirs. But tonight no one was disturbed by these divergences. All proceeded as by tacit agreement, and the Greeks in their relief wept more loudly than before, because their faith was no longer contemned.

There were so many in the church that the bread would not go around. But each one willingly shared with his nearest neighbors the morsel he had received, so that all who came might have at least a crumb of the sacred Body of Christ. Whether the bread were leavened or unleavened made no difference now.

During the service, which lasted several hours, we were moved by a strong and radiant ectasy, more wonderful than any I have known in any church. We stood beside one another, Anna and I, hand in hand. Hand in hand we shared the holy bread and made our vow of purity. So light did my heart seem, and my whole body, that I felt I might have walked without touching the floor. Her eyes, her brown eyes were close beside me, yet already remote, in a hallowed radiance. But as they withdrew from human warmth and bodily presence they still shone for me with the light of eternity, candid, dearly known, even as one day I shall see them again.

After the service, Emperor Constantine spoke to his people and said in a voice that trembled, "The Turks have their guns and their vast army, but we have God and our Savior. Let us not lose hope."

He embraced each of his friends and begged their forgiveness for any injury he had done them. The nearest of the common people he kissed too, embraced them and asked their forgiveness. His example induced even the Latins to hug one another and beg one another's pardon; the Venetian bailo with tears in his eyes put his arm about Giustiniani and implored him to forgive his malicious thoughts. Venetians and Genoese embraced and promised one another to fight bravely and vie with one another in the pursuit of glory. I believe that on this day every man of them was sincere.

It was dark when we came out of church, but candles were burning in all the houses, and the main street was illuminated with torches and lanterns from St. Sophia's all the way to the Blachernae and the Kharisios Gate. Bells were ringing in church and cloister, so that we seemed to be celebrating some great and joyous festival.

But above the lights of the city the stars shone brightly in the black sky. The thoughts of the stars were with us, and our astral bodies prepared to leave their earthly husks and return to their homes. That was why I felt this marvelous lightness; that was why Anna Notaras' eyes shone with so unearthly a beauty.

On reaching the Church of the Apostles we left the Emperor's following. Once more Constantine embraced Giustiniani and entreated his forgiveness. Most of the Greeks went home to doff their holiday dress, bid farewell to wives and children and put on their armor before hastening back to the walls.

During this interval I met the German, Johann Grant, and dismounted from my horse to embrace him and thank him for his friendship. His face was peppered with gunpowder, he moved painfully and blinked his smarting eyes continually. But even on this last evening he was entirely given over to his insatiable desire for knowledge. He pointed to two aged, bald and toothless men who were staggering by, led by a youth in the costume of an imperial technician on which was a red badge of honor which I had not seen before.

"Do you know who those are?" he asked. I shook my head and he told me, "They come from the most secret underground chamber in the arsenal where the Greek fire is made. Do you see how yellow the boy's face is, and how thin his hair? The old men have lost all their teeth and their skin is peeling. I should much like to talk to them, but they're guarded, and anyone seeking to address them is cut down on the spot.

"Their stock of raw materials is exhausted," he went on. "The last remaining crocks of fluid have now been carried to the wall and to the ships. I know some of the ingredients, but not all, nor how they are blended. The most remarkable feature is the way the fluid ignites of itself as soon as it spurts out. It's not the effect of the air, but of some combustible in the vessels themselves; there must be some device in the muzzle of the mortar that sets it burning. There's a good deal of naphtha in it, since it floats on water, and water cannot put it out. Only sand and vinegar can quench it. The Venetian sailors say that in a pinch they can extinguish stray drops of it with urine. Those old fellows are the last who know the secret, which has been preserved for a thousand years. No one has ever been allowed to write it down, and in former days they cut out the tongues of all who worked in the underground chambers. If the Turks capture the city tomorrow, the last duty of the arsenal guards will be to kill these old men, so that they may carry their secret to the grave. That's why they have been allowed to come to church today for the first time for who knows how many years." He shrugged his shoulders. "Many secrets will perish with this city—much priceless knowledge—and to no purpose. John Angelos, there is nothing more detestable than war! I say this, after having destroyed nineteen Turkish mine tunnels and used all my skill and art in helping the Emperor's technicians to kill more Turks than ever before."

"Let us not lose hope," I said, though I knew that all hope had fled.

He spat and said bitterly, "My only hope is for a place in a Venetian vessel, always supposing I can reach the harbor in time. I have no other." He laughed at himself, wrinkled his singed forehead and added, "If I was a resolute sort of fellow I should rush to the library as soon as the city falls, and sword in hand seize the manuscripts I covet, to take on board with me. But that is what I cannot do, being a German and bred to loyalty. If I were Italian I might, for Italians are freer and more sensible than we northerners. But I can't, and so I despise myself."

I said, "I pity you, Johann Grant, for your besetting passion. Could not even the holy mystery this evening release you from your Self?"

"No," he answered. "Nothing but knowledge can release me from my Self. Knowledge is man's only freedom."

But when we parted he embraced me and said, "You're not self-righteous and you never force your faith on others. Therefore I have been fond of you, Jean Ange."

As we approached the Gate of St. Romanos, moving through

the cool night, the fearful stench of corruption came to meet us—a stench we hardly noticed so long as we remained constantly on the wall.

Anna Notaras trembled, but when we had dismounted, Giustiniani said, "Rest my children, and sleep for a while. We have an hour or two or perhaps even three before us. As soon as I have gone my rounds I shall come and sleep for a little too, this sinless night, with a clear conscience as my pillow. I have been betrayed, but by God's grace and through no merit of my own, I have not had to betray."

Then he added, "Later, when all are at their posts to defend what is left of the outer wall, the sally ports will be locked and the keys handed to the Emperor. So it has been agreed. Sincc everyone knows this, no one will be tempted to run away. Those on the outer wall must fight on or fall. That is why we have made our communion and shall pass the night without sin."

Anna Notaras asked, "Which will be my place?"

Giustiniani laughed kindly. "I think you must be content with the great wall. In the front line we shall be too busy to look after you. To be frank, you would be in the way there."

"Go to the Kerkoporta," I said quickly. "There you will be among compatriots, and between the Guacchardis and the Venetians, and if necessary you can withdraw into the Blachernae. If you fall it will be the will of God; but it would be no sin for you to escape on one of the Venetian ships. We will not be anxious for one another."

She had turned deathly white as I spoke; her grip on my arm startled me and I asked, "What is it? Aren't you well?"

She whispered, "Why did you mention the Kerkoporta? Did you mean anything special by that?"

"I meant only what I said," I answered, though this was not the whole truth. "What can be the matter?"

She said lamely, "Perhaps the stench has made me feel sick. I'm a poor soldier, and I don't want to get in your way. I will go to the Kerkoporta, and after that we will not be anxious for one another. But until midnight we can be together. That I beg of you."

I rejoiced that she so willingly agreed to my suggestion, for I have a plan and I had feared that I should have to try to persuade her against her will. The Kerkoporta is the safest place during an attack, and I would not have her forced to try and defend herself against the lightning blade of a janissary.

She has fallen asleep now; but how should I sleep, when for the last time I may enjoy her presence? I have been writing meanwhile, and even down here in this vault one can catch the muffled murmur of a hundred thousand Turks moving about their camp, dragging up scaling-ladders and stacking arrows for their archers.

Soon it will be midnight, and Manuel will come to fetch my papers. I have written rapidly; not for nothing was I clerk to the synod for two years. Giustiniani has already emptied his chest and burned such papers as should not fall into Turkish hands. Flames have been shooting from the great chimney of the Palace of Blachernae too, and charred fragments of paper have been scattered by the night wind. It's blowing up from the north: this may mean safety for hundreds of Latins.

This evening more than forty youths from Pera reported to Giustiniani for leave to fight with their compatriots. Their honor would not allow them to remain on neutral ground, although the podesta has let himself be intimidated by the Sultan and has threatened death to anyone who endangers Pera's neutrality. He has locked the gates of that town, but the striplings climbed the wall near the shore while the sentries looked the other way and turned a deaf ear to squealing row-locks.

Tonight no one accuses his neighbor, all sins are forgiven and each man allows others to obey the voice of conscience. Should anyone, even now, escape aboard a Venetian ship and bribe the captain, it will be his own affair. Should anyone slink from the wall at the last minute and hide in the city, he will be answerable to his own conscience alone. Deserters are no longer seized. There are not many—indeed they are incredibly few, having regard to all the cripples, old men and ten-year-old boys who in the course of today have come to the wall to die for their city.

This is the Greeks' night. I have seen their dark eyes, drenched in the melancholy of many hundred years. Outside, bells are ringing the death knell of the Last Rome.

Manuel will soon be here. He is of those who never go under.

29 May 1453

Aleo e polis!

The city is lost.

That cry will echo so long as the world endures. If in some century to come I am born again into this world, those words will bring horror to my eyes and set my hair on end. I shall remember those words and recognize them, though I should remember nothing else—though my soul be like a smoothed wax tablet. I shall recognize those words.

Aleo e polis.

Yet I still live. It was so intended, then. I am to drain the last cup, and behold the downfall of my city and my people. So I write on. But to write this fittingly, I should dip my pen in blood—and blood would not be lacking. Blood fills the gutters in a congealed and sticky sludge. Blood from the wounds of the dying collects in warm pools. In the main street, by the Hippodrome and about the great church lie so many corpses that one can barely walk there without treading upon them.

It is night once more. I am sitting in my own house, which is guarded by a pennant on a spear shaft. I have stuffed my ears with wax to escape the shrieks of outraged women and children, the howls of pillagers fighting over their spoils, the ceaseless death-cry rising from my city.

I am forcing myself into detachment. I write, although my hand shakes. I am shaking all over—not from fear, not on my own account; my life is worth less than a grain of sand in the street. But on account of the suffering and pain now welling from a thousand sources round me in this night of boundless terror.

I have seen a young girl, marked by bloody hands, hurl herself down a well. I have seen a wretch tear a babe from its mother and laughingly impale it on a comrade's spear, so as to throw down the woman. I have seen all the worst that human beings can do to one another. I have seen enough.

Soon after midnight, those who had dedicated their lives to the defense of the outer wall took up their positions. After that the sally ports in the great wall were locked, and the keys handed over to the commanders-in-chief of the various sectors. Some prayed, but most lay down to rest; many even slept.

Meanwhile the light vessels of the Turks began moving, and approached the harbor wall. The main fleet in the Port of Pillars sailed from the Bosporus and spread out along the sea wall from the Marble Tower to Neorion and the boom. In this way the Sultan threatened the entire circumference, so that no men could be released from any point to reinforce others. The enemy everywhere had been commanded to attack in earnest, without mock assaults as hitherto. Therefore their ships too were equipped with scaling-ladders and bridges while archers swarmed in the rigging.

To the first who should maintain a footing on the wall the Sultan had promised a horsetail and the governorship of a province. To any who should retreat or surrender he had promised death. His forward assault troops were flanked by *tsaushes.*

Three hours before dawn, pipes and drums sounded and a fearful din broke out as the first storming parties by means of yells egged themselves and each other on to the attack. The breach we were defending by the Gate of St. Romanos was more than a thousand feet wide. The Sultan first sent in his auxiliaries: herdsmen and nomads who had come from the countries of Asia to share in Islam's holy war. They were armed only with a spear or a sword, and carried a narrow wooden shield.

As they approached the wall the Turkish culverins and harquebuses opened up, and a cloud of arrows came singing toward and over us. Hundreds of scaling-ladders were raised simultaneously against our provisional earthwork; then with howls and wails of terror and appeals to Allah, the first groups of a thousand raced up them. But the ladders were overturned, Greek fire spurted over them and the welter of struggling men at the foot of the rampart was showered with arrows as well as seething pitch and molten lead from long-handled dippers. So deafening was the noise that soon we could hear nothing. The enemy were attacking along the whole length of the landward wall; their artillery now resounded from the harbor too, and from the sea.

Many of the assailants, badly burned and screeching, tried to run away, but the *tsaushes* posted by the ditch clove their skulls with their swords and threw their bodies into the ditch to help fill it in. Soon piles of corpses lay all the way along it, here and there reaching halfway up the sides.

After these irregulars, the Sultan sent in his Christian allies and also the renegades of every nation who had rallied, thirsting for plunder, to his standard. They were fighting for their lives, and many secured a footing on the wall before being hurled down upon the mounds of corpses. It was a terrible thing to hear them invoking Christ and the Blessed Virgin in all the tongues of Europe, alongside Turks who called upon Allah and his Prophet. Many a time I was confronted by a face distorted in horror, which the next moment vanished into the darkness below.

Many of the iron-clad Genoese were wounded or killed by leaden shot, for the Turks continued firing from beyond the ditch without regard for the lives of their own men. Wounded Genoese fought on their knees at the edge of the rampart without attempting to crawl to cover, until their assailants hauled them down with iron hooks.

After about an hour the Sultan allowed the survivors to withdraw, and fired off his heavy guns. Their appalling stone missiles smashed our breastworks, sweeping crates and barrels of earth into the alley between the walls. The din of falling timber filled the air. The dust had not settled nor the smoke dispersed before the Turks from Anatolia opened their attack.

These were swift, savage men who laughed gleefully as they clambered up on one another's shoulders in swarms to reach the top of the rampart. The *tsaushes* had no need to whip these fellows forward, for they were true Turks with war in their blood. They asked no quarter and died with the name of Allah on their lips. They knew that the ten thousand angels of Islam were hovering overhead and at the moment of death would snatch each one of them straight up to paradise.

They attacked in close waves of a thousand, yelling and reviling the Christians with menaces too frightful to record. But our men stood their ground. The gaps in our ranks were filled, and wherever the living wall of iron seemed to waver, thither dashed Giustiniani to encourage his men and cleave Turks to the midriff with his two-handed sword. Wherever he appeared, there the assault slackened and the enemy raised their ladders at some other point.

As the Anatolian attack was ebbing out, the first corpse-gray light of dawn appeared in the sky. My body was tender and bruised all over, and my arms were so weary that after each stroke I fancied that I could not for my very life raise them for another. Many of the iron-clad Genoese were panting and wheezing and gasping for water. But as the Turks started to withdraw, hope revived in many of them and a poor fool here and there could be heard shouting "victory" in a choking voice.

One could now distinguish a black thread from a white, and as night faded we could make out the tall white felt caps of the janissaries in well-dressed ranks opposite, on the other side of the ditch. The men stood in companies of a thousand, one behind the other, silently awaiting the order to attack. Sultan Mohammed himself could be glimpsed in front of them, bearing his iron hammer of command. Hastily we trained culverins and harquebuses on him and fired, but failed to hit him. Several janissaries fell round about him, but the ranks stood motionless. Fresh men stepped forward to fill the gaps, and I knew that they rejoiced in the honor of joining the front rank beneath the eye of their Sultan—a position to which neither their age nor length of service would otherwise have entitled them. Green-clad *tsaushes* quickly placed themselves between us and the Sultan, to shield him with their own bodies.

The women and old men on the great wall took advantage of this pause to lower big jars of water mixed with wine; for although even this main rampart was so badly damaged that at many points it stood no higher than the earthwork before it, it was still too steep to climb down.

What followed I can merely relate as I saw it, and perhaps another would tell the story differently, since man's powers of observation are always faulty. Nevertheless I was standing close by Giustiniani and I believe I saw what happened.

I heard the warning shouts in time and threw myself down as the Turks once more discharged their great cannon and all their other pieces in a tremendous volley. The wind had freshened and soon swept away the rolling black clouds of smoke. As the din and the cries died away I saw Giustiniani slowly sink down and sit upon the ground. At one side of his cuirass gaped a hole the size of my fist, from a leaden ball that had struck him diagonally from the rear. In an instant his face turned gray and all vitality drained from him, so that he seemed an old man despite his freshly dyed hair and beard. He spat out a mouthful of blood, and blood was also running down the fold of his groin below the armor.

"Fair and square," he said. "This is the end of me."

The men nearest him stood around him to prevent the rest seeing that he was wounded. They looked about them menacingly.

"That ball came from behind," said one.

Two came up to me, seized me by the arms and snatched the iron gauntlets from my hands to see if my fingers were stained with powder. Then they went up to a Greek technician a little distance away who was hurriedly loading his harquebus; they knocked him down, tore his beard and kicked him with their iron-shod feet. Everyone looked up at the great wall and shook his fist.

"For Christ's sake, brothers," said Giustiniani feebly, "don't quarrel now. It makes no difference where the bullet came from. I may well have turned to look at the wall and the water jars, and had my back to the Turks at the time. It's all one to me. You'd do better to call for a surgeon."

His men began shouting in chorus for a surgeon, but the Greeks on the wall replied that no one could get to Giustiniani because the postern was locked. A brave man might have slid down the face of the wall, but it was understandable that no physician was willing to do this even for Giustiniani's sake, for just then the copper drums of the janissaries began to roll and they struck up their assault-music.

It is beneath the janissaries' dignity to invoke Allah as they charge. They raced silently, savagely toward our earthwork. In many places they had no need of ladders, so high lay the heaps of corpses before the ruins of our outer wall. Their onslaught was swift and violent, and few of the defenders had time to drink, though we were all perishing with thirst. Jars were knocked over beside us and in another moment a hand-to-hand struggle was raging all along the top of the wall.

This was now no mere vulgar killing—it was war. The janissaries wore either scale armor or chain mail. Their swords struck swiftly as lightning and by sheer weight of numbers they forced the defenders back. Giustiniani's Genoese and the Greeks who had been sent to our relief were compelled to bunch up in order to resist the pressure with united strength.

Just then the Emperor, mounted on his white charger, showed himself upon the battlements. His face glowed and he shouted jubilantly, "Stand fast! Stand fast but once more, and the day is ours!"

Had he been down there among us and felt the leaden weight of our limbs he would have held his peace.

Giustiniani raised his bull's head from his hands, gritted his teeth in agony, spat out another blood clot and with a coarse oath bade the Emperor hand over the key of the sally port. The Emperor shouted in reply that Giustiniani's wound could not be as serious as all that, and that it would be unbecoming in him to forsake his men just now on account of his present pain.

Giustiniani shrieked in reply, "Blasted Greek perjurer! I'm the best judge of that. Throw down that key or I'll come up and strangle you with my own hands."

Even in the fury of battle his men burst out laughing, and after a moment's hesitation the Emperor threw down the great key at Giustiniani's very feet. He picked it up and showed it meaningly to those nearest him. The conflict was raging only a few paces away, loud with the clash and squeal of blades on armor. There a huge janissary was laying about him with a captured two-handed sword, until the iron-clad Genoese contrived to surround him and bring him to his knees. So impregnable was his armor that they had to slay him piecemeal.

As the first wave of janissaries withdrew to get their breath the next surged forward. Giustiniani called to me and said, "Give me your arm and help me away from here. A good commander fights as long as there's a chance, but no longer."

I took one arm and the man nearest him the other, and we succeeded in getting him down the rampart and through the sally port into the city. The Emperor met us in great agitation, attended by his suite. He was without armor, so as to move more freely, and wore a purple shirt and a mantle of imperial green stitched with gold. Once more he urged Giustiniani to stand fast and return to the battle; the wound, he said, was not necessarily so very serious. But Giustiniani never answered, nor even looked at him; he had enough to do to endure the hideous agony that every step entailed.

The Emperor returned to the wall to observe the course of the battle and encourage the Greeks with his counsel. We managed to remove Giustiniani's armor; blood slopped from it as it fell to the ground. Giustiniani signed to his next in command and said, "You will answer for the men's lives."

The officer nodded and returned to the wall.

The daylight grew brighter.

"Giustiniani," I said. "I thank you for your friendship. Now I must go back."

He put out his hand, grimaced with pain and said laboriously, "That be damned. The battle's lost—you know it as well as I do. How can a thousand exhausted men hold their ground against twelve thousand janissaries in full armor? There's a place for you aboard my ship; you've earned it honorably."

He groaned for a while with his head in his hands and then said, "In the name of Christ, go up on the wall here and then come back and tell me how it goes."

He wanted to get me out of the way, for now through the sally port single Genoese were beginning to stagger in, bloody from head to foot. They gathered about him. I mounted the wall and in the growing daylight I could see Sultan Mohammed by the filled-in ditch. He was brandishing his iron hammer and cheering on his janissaries as they tore past him to the assault.

The battle was raging along the whole of our part of the outer wall. The Genoese closed up continually, and here and there I saw one tap another on the shoulder and take his place; they were withdrawing one at a time to the sally port. I saw that the battle was lost. The copper drums of the janissaries thundered yet more loudly; it was the dirge of my city.

Suddenly someone beside me pointed northeastward along the wall in the direction of the Blachernae. Women and old men who had been wringing their hands and crying aloud in their distress fell silent and stared, incredulous. In the light of the rising sun the blood-red banners of the Sultan, with their silver crescent, were floating from the tops of both the undamaged towers of the Kerkoporta.

It was a sight I shall never forget. The whole city saw it at the same moment, for along the wall there spread first in a disbelieving murmur, then in a mounting shriek of horror, the cry of our defeat: *"Aleo e polis!"*

The storming Turks joined in the cry with a hoarse howl of jubilation from a hundred thousand throats. For an instant I was nonplussed; it was against all reason that the best-preserved part of the wall should have been captured first. By the Kerkoporta even the outer defenses were almost undamaged.

Yet there on the great wall floated the Turkish crescents. At that instant a fresh wave of janissaries swept Greeks and the last of the Genoese down into the lane between the walls. The foremost at once continued the assault, and lithe as cats began climbing the great wall, clinging to every ledge and crack. Terror lent strength to the women and boys above and they rolled great blocks of stone down upon them. The bronze mouth over the gate began to spew forth flames once more, now that there was no danger to ourselves in setting fire to the wooden wreckage without; one of the Emperor's technicians stamped and dragged with the strength of despair at the levers of the flame-thrower, but soon the burning stream dwindled and the last drops soaked impotently into the earth. The Greek fire was at an end.

All this happened in a shorter time than I can write it down. I shouted to the Emperor and his retinue that it was high time to open the counterattack. As they didn't hear me I dropped from the crest of the wall to hurry back to Giustiniani. The death-cry of the city was ringing in my ears: *"Aleo e polis."* The very stones seemed to join in as the wall shook to the tread of running feet.

Giustiniani's Genoese had helped him onto the back of his great charger and with drawn swords surrounded him in a threatening group. In the beginning they had consisted of four hundred men in plate armor and three hundred arbalestiers. One hundred in all remained. I could not reproach him for trying to save them. I waved to him and shouted, "Good luck! May you soon be well again and take Lemnos from the Catalonians. You have deserved it a thousand times over."

But from his leaden face and closed eyes I saw that it was a dying man the soldiers were leading to the harbor. He could no longer turn his head to answer. His men supported him in the saddle on both sides. No sooner had he disappeared round the first street-corner than the great flight from the walls began. Everywhere men were leaping from the battlements, throwing away their weapons and rushing blindly in among the houses. The Emperor could not halt them.

When Giustiniani had gone, his most trusted man held the sally port open and threatened the Emperor's guards with his drawn sword when they attempted to shut it. He received one reeling, stumbling Genoese after another, mustered them in groups of ten and sent them off to the harbor on the double. In this way he saved about forty. He was an ugly, pockmarked man. He spared the time to spit on the ground at my feet and yell, "To hell with you, damned Greek!"

Just then the first janissaries appeared in the archway with drawn scimitars, panting from their charge. With united strength we contrived to slam the gate and bolt it before enough came to prevent us.

I could see from the look on the man's pockmarked face that he would have liked to split my head in two just for being Greek. But he wiped his blade on his thigh and marched off with the last of his men. Their honor would not permit them to run, although the street was already full of fugitives.

I remain alone by the sally port, awaiting the signal for the counterattack.

I was alone, but suddenly there stood at my side the one I had met at the time of the earthquake in Hungary, and later at Varna, beside the body of Cardinal Cesarini. He was dark and grave—he was my own image. I recognized my face, my look. I said, "We meet at the Gate of St. Romanos, as you promised. I have not fled like the merchant of Samarra."

He gave a cold smile. "You keep your promises, John Angelos."

I said, "At that time I did not even know where this gate was. But destiny has brought me here."

Above us on the battlements janissaries were already running. The first rays of the morning sun tinged their white felt caps with red. Red, too, was the flash of their swords as they cut down the last of the defenders: soldiers, technicians, women, boys and old men, without discrimination. Near us, Emperor Constantine was shouting and beckoning the fugitives to rally. But from the group around him many slunk away each time he turned his back, so that his retinue dwindled steadily.

When the Emperor perceived this, he clapped his hands to his face and cried, "Is there no Christian to take pity on me and cut off my head?"

The angel of death nodded to me and said smiling, "You see, he needs me more than you do." And the dark stranger, my likeness, moved silently to the Emperor and spoke to him. The Emperor dismounted, tore the chains from his neck and cast his gold-embroidered mantle to the ground. He set a helmet upon his head, took a round shield that someone offered him and went in the forefront to meet the janissaries, who were falling, rolling and leaping from the wall. His courtiers and lifelong friends, who had dedicated themselves to death, followed him with drawn swords; his example induced some of the fugitives to turn and follow him also.

There were perhaps a hundred of us who in close formation first walking, then running, advanced to the last encounter, when the janissaries had already hoisted their flag on the great wall and were pouring into the city. Then all was a tumult of crashing shields and flashing blades, until in the mêlée I lost my footing and was flung headlong, unable to raise my sword. I received a cut in the shoulder and another on the head, and a dazzling blaze of red quenched my consciousness. Like a raging tempest the Turks poured over me and trampled me to the ground.

The sun had risen some way above the horizon and was yellow by the time I came to my senses. At first I could not make out where I was; then I managed to roll aside the warm bodies lying across me. I sat up and found that I was not badly wounded, though countless bells were chiming in my ears.

As I sat there half-dazzled by the sun I saw a couple of green-clad *tsaushes* walking along the top of the wall looking for wounded. Now and then they bent to sever a wailing head from its body. I called to them in Turkish and asked them to give me the *coup-de-grâce,* but the elder of the two recognized me and bowed deeply, touching his forehead. He had perhaps seen me in the Sultan's suite during the seven years I had been with Murad and Mohammed.

He fetched water and bathed my face, helped me to remove my helmet and coat of mail and handed me a Turkish cloak which he took from the least bloodstained of the dead janissaries that lay near. I don't know whether he thought I had taken part in the assault or had been living in the city as the Sultan's spy. In any case he told me his name and begged me to remember him. When he perceived the confused state of my wits he told me the passwords of both janissaries and *tsaushes,* took up a spear to which a strip of cloth was knotted and said smiling, "Great is Allah's reward. No one needs this now; take it as your sign and mark a house for yourself."

With the spear as my staff I staggered off along the foot of the wall toward the Kerkoporta. As I drew near the Kharisios Gate I could hear that the battle was not yet over, though the Sultan's crescent now waved above the Blachernae. I came just as the Guacchardi brothers were withdrawing their men. Their bastion had held out long after the Turks had broken through the wall on either side and stormed into the city. Now they were mounting their horses, and so great was the terror their valor had inspired that the Turks from Anatolia would molest them no further, but let them alone and set off after plunder.

The brothers were not laughing now. The eldest of them called the others and said, "We're still alive, but the city is lost. Sun, tremble! Wail, O earth! The battle is over. Let us save our lives while we may."

They ordered the last of their men to catch hold of the stirrups, girths and tails of their mounts and rode off, leaving copious trails of blood along the street. Even janissaries made way for them and averted their eyes as if they had not seen them. In this way they showed their respect for the gallantry of the Guacchardis, reflecting perhaps that certain loot was preferable to a useless death in the hour of victory.

The Guacchardi brothers reached the harbor, although the enemy now occupied the whole city, and escaped aboard a Latin ship. Their names are Paolo, Antonio and Troilo, and the eldest of them is not yet thirty. They did not hate the Greeks as other Latins did. May their name endure.

I came then to the Kerkoporta. The Venetians appeared to have made a sortie from the Blachernae, for many fallen janissaries lay about, also a young Venetian or two, rigid in death, soiled with blood and earth. The place was deserted. The janissaries had already abandoned the towers on the wall which they had captured, and left only the Sultan's banners behind. The Kerkoporta itself was locked and barred. And before it—

Before it lay the body of Anna Notaras, with blood in the cropped hair and eyes half-open. Swarms of flies were already crawling over her eyes and mouth. Her helmet lay at a little distance. Throat, armpit, groin—all the parts unprotected by her armor were full of deep stabs, so that the blood had drained from her body, which lay in a distorted, dreadful posture.

"Stranger, my likeness, where are you?" I cried. "Come to me, dark shade; this is your hour."

But he did not come. I was alone. I clutched my head and shrieked, "Manuel, Manuel, the fault was yours! I shall seek you out, though you hide in hell! Why did you not obey me?"

I tried to lift her body, but I was too weak. I sat down beside her and surveyed her dead face so as to harden my heart, since she was gone. As I beheld her lying there, while dying shrieks rose all around me from house and street, I no longer believed in God or in rebirth.

"Stone is stone," I said to myself. "A body is a body. What

breathes not, is not. The astral body is fantasy, like other fantasies."

I stood up, thrust at the body with my foot so that the flies buzzed up, and went on my way. A corpse is only a corpse, and with corpses I have no concern.

Leaning on the spear I walked along the main street into the center of the city, hoping to meet someone who would exercise compassion on me with his sword.

But no one raised a hand to me.

In the street leading to the Khora convent lay smashed icons and the trampled corpses of many women. Some still clutched tapers in their convulsively clenched fingers, and their faces were distorted in a mute scream of unutterable horror.

Here and there fighting still raged about the largest houses, whose inmates had barred the doors and were defending themselves against the besieging janissaries with crossbows, stones and kitchen implements, boiling water and burning brands. But from most of the houses fluttered the pennants of the victors, and from within could be heard the weeping and screaming of many women.

All the way to Emperor Valentine's aqueduct the main street was strewn with Greek dead. There the blind massacre seemed to have stopped. I began to meet long strings of Greeks bound together, guarded only by a barefooted herdsman or so with a spear in his hand. The women had been robbed of their jewels, their clothes were torn from being searched for hidden money, and their hands were tied behind them with their own girdles. High and low, old people and children, artisans and archons walked side by side, to be separated later in the Turkish camp, that the poor might be sold as slaves and the wealthy pay their ransoms.

I started to walk down toward the harbor. Some quarters still seemed deserted and no Turks were to be seen. The harbor wall opposite Pera, which was guarded by the fleet, was still in Latin hands. A vast, seething mob was densely massed before the harbor gates; the people stretched out their arms in entreaty. All were begging for mercy and a place on board one of the ships. But the guards had locked the gates and thrown the keys into the water, except for the seamen's gate, which was sternly held by marine-soldiers armed with spears and swords. Up on the wall the sentries waved their smoldering matches and in hoarse, cracked voices threatened to discharge their swivel guns and harquebuses into the thick of the people unless they withdrew and made room for the Latin men-at-arms, who from time to time ploughed their way through, covered from head to foot in blood and reeling from exhaustion, toward the safety of the harbor.

Many women had cut their hands severely in snatching at the swords of the marines. A number of the richer and nobler people held out heavy purses, in the vain hope of buying a place on some ship.

I went farther up the hill so as to see over the wall. Here and there ladders were placed against it and the more enterprising among the people were letting themselves down into the water and swimming out to the ships. Heads bobbed like black dots on the surface. At the top of the rope ladders armed seamen kept guard, resisting the swimmers or directing them to other vessels. Many were thus forced to swim from ship to ship until their strength gave out and they sank. Some ships, however, being short of their full complement, accepted the most powerful of the fugitives.

Packed boats were continually pulling out to the ships and returning for fresh loads. They carried not only Latins who had escaped from the walls but also chests and bales. In the confusion that prevailed all day, the fleet alone seemed to have preserved some sort of order. A certain number of Greeks were taken aboard too, if there was room and if they had connections among Genoese or Venetians.

Standing there on the hillside I saw the largest Genoese vessel set sail and with the aid of wind and oarsweeps bear straight down on the boom in an attempt to snap it. She was a mighty ship with at least two thousand men on board. The chain yielded but did not break, and the ship was brought up with a jerk that shook her from stem to stern. Yet her masts did not snap, for the Genoese are skilled mariners and know what they're about.

The northerly wind pressed the vessel against the boom until this curved outward like a bent bow. Two big sailors leaped out onto it, each with a broad-bladed axe. With the energy of despair they hacked steadily at the chain until suddenly it parted; the proud ship headed out of the harbor under bellying canvas and the two men were only just able to scramble aboard again. After the great ship there followed three lesser ones, but the Venetian vessels still lay peacefully at anchor.

Not a single Turkish galley pulled out to attack the fleeing ships, for the Turkish sailors had left them all along the Marmora shore. Soldiers and sailors were all busily engaged in carrying plunder down to them, and in driving their flocks of slaves. Many of these were Jews, for the seamen had come first to Giudeca, the Jewish quarter, and lingered there to search for the much talked-of gold and jewels of the inhabitants. This was why so many townspeople had been able to reach the harbor, although the greater part of the city was now in Turkish hands.

While the first ships were making their escape, the imperial standard still floated above the tower on Acropolis Point. There the Cretan seamen had made their stand, and the Turks seemed unwilling to launch a full-scale attack upon it when they saw that the defenders did not mean to capitulate even after the city itself was taken.

I had nothing to do in the harbor, and I went on up the hill to my house. It seemed deserted. No Turks were to be seen, though the tavern opposite had been sacked and before the steps lay a pool of wine.

I thrust the spear with its strip of cloth into the ground beside the stone lion, and so took possession of my own house. I went in and shouted for Manuel. After a time a quavering voice came from the cellar: "Is that you, master?"

He crawled up on all fours and tried to embrace my knees. I kicked him hard in the chest, heedless of his frailty and his gray beard.

"Why did you not obey me? Why did you not do as I ordered?" I shouted in fury, and with my powerless hands tried to draw the sword that had stuck fast in the scabbard. Only now did I realize that my sword was a Turkish scimitar and that the cloak the *tsaush* had given me and the turban he had used to bind up my wounded head made me look like a Turk.

"God be thanked that you do serve the Sultan after all!" said Manuel sincerely. "You were clever indeed to keep your secret so well up to the last minute, so that even I was almost deceived. Surely you will take me under your protection? I've already marked down a number of houses which I can help you to plunder."

Glancing at me he added hastily, "I mean—to pass the time I've been thinking what I should do if I were a Turk. Tell me, is it true that the Emperor has fallen?"

When I nodded, he crossed himself heartily and said, "God be praised! In that case there's no longer any doubt: we are all lawful subjects of the Sultan. Master, take me as your slave, so that I may appeal to you if anyone tries to carry me off."

I could endure him no longer. Seizing him by the beard I jerked up his chin so that he was forced to meet my eye.

"Where is my wife Anna Notaras, whom I entrusted to you and whom you swore to save?"

"She is dead," said Manuel simply. He blew his nose in his fingers and burst into bitter weeping. "You said that when all was lost I was to hit her over the head if she would not come with me willingly, and row her out to Giustiniani's ship. I had already hidden away a donkey for this purpose, though I should have lost this by now if I hadn't been so lucky as to sell it to a Venetian who wanted to carry an inlaid cabinet from the Blachernae to the harbor. It was an exquisite cabinet."

"Anna!" I bawled, jerking his beard.

"Don't tear my beard, master; it hurts," said Manuel reproachfully, defending himself with both hands. "I did what I could and risked my life for that mad woman out of sheer loyalty to you, asking nothing in return. But she would not obey me. And when I heard her reasons I could only stay with her and wait for morning."

Again Manuel looked at me with reproach, then rubbing his knees furiously he went on, half-sobbing, "And this is my thanks for it—you pull and tear at me though my knees have begun aching again and I have a sore throat as well. You see, your wife could not bring herself to tell you of her father's shame, because you take everything so seriously. But while in her father's house she had come to know of his plan to let the Kerkoporta stand open and unguarded during the assault. As a testimony to the good will of the Greeks, of course; not even the Megadux can have believed it would be of any service to the Sultan. The Turks could not have reached that point between the inner and outer walls until after the outer wall by the Kharisios Gate had been taken—and then only with a very small force. But he considered that to leave that gate open would have great political significance, as proof of the willing co-operation of the Greeks."

"No doubt," I said. "The borderline between political opposition and treachery is as fine as a hair. But to leave a sally port open and unguarded is treachery. No one can deny it. Many have been hanged for less."

"Treachery of course," Manuel agreed readily. "That is what your lady thought, and so she ran away to you. And of course because she loved you, though she had no very high opinion of your sense. But for her father's sake she wanted to prevent this betrayal and see to it that the door was not left open. I went with her to the Kerkoporta, as you ordered, thinking it was a safe place—defend us from such safety! And there we stayed, though the Greek guards repeatedly tried to drive us away, saying that no one wanted us there. Who they were I don't know, as they were careful to keep their faces hidden in the darkness. Most likely they were the Megadux's people, who had come on guard at his order and dismissed the other sentries.

"And then when it started," Manuel continued, "they simply lifted away the bar and unlocked the door—for they had a key. Your lady went up to them sword in hand and demanded the key from them. At first they tried to frighten her away, but when they found she wouldn't give in they all seized her at once—there were five of them—and stabbed her to death before she could cry out."

"And you—what did you do?" I asked.

"I ran," said Manuel artlessly. "I ran as fast as I could, and in the dark they couldn't catch me although my knees were hurting. And since I could do nothing else I sold my donkey to a Venetian, as I said."

"Dear God!" I cried, "Why didn't you give the alarm to the Venetians?"

"I tried to," said Manuel, "but they wouldn't believe me. They had enough on their hands with the defense of the Blachernae wall. And their commander showed me a plan whereon the Kerkoporta was marked as being in the Greek sector, not theirs."

Manuel began tittering behind his hand.

"He must have thought I was mad, or else that it was a ruse of the Greeks to dismay the Venetians. The wall near the Blachernae is scribbled all over with 'Go home, Latins,' and so on. At last he threatened to hang me if I troubled him any further. So then I went to seek help from the Guacchardis, but by then it was late and they had enough to do to keep the Turks out of the breach in the great wall. After that—well—"

Manuel gave me a timid glance and said despondingly, "I don't suppose you will believe me, but it occurred to me that I was Greek, too, and that my father was wood-carrier to Emperor Manuel. Of course I also thought sadly of my hidden money, and my life—still, I took a dead man's sword and ran back to the Kerkoporta."

Amazed now, it seemed, at his own rashness, he threw out his hands and cried, "As sure as I'm standing here, master, I ran back to the Kerkoporta thinking I might somehow get it shut again. But luckily my courage came too late. I was met by the Sultan's janissaries, and so I quickly threw away my sword, raised my hands and prayed to the Blessed Virgin of the Blachernae to protect me. And my prayer helped me strangely, for the Turks gripped my arms and held me as if in a vise, and ordered me in bad Greek to take them to the Khora convent, though there were only about twenty of them. And we ran there as fast as our legs would carry us. They were brave men—I'll say that for them."

"That was just when the Turks broke through by the Gate of St. Romanos," I said. "No, the treachery at the Kerkoporta can have made no difference. And the gate was locked when I saw it this morning."

"Yes, as soon as the Venetians saw the Sultan's banners they made a valiant sortie," said Manuel. "When I looked round they were just dashing out of a door in the palace wall with flashing swords, and armor, and the Lion banner. They slew the janissaries who had stayed by the gate, and locked the Kerkoporta before they went back into the Blachernae."

"And you?" I asked.

"I showed the Turks the way to the Khora convent, hoping that the miracle-working Virgin would calm their wild spirits," said Manuel, troubled. "But so vile is human nature that their greed for spoils conquered all else in them. The whole church was bedecked with roses and packed with praying women, who held tapers in their hands. But the janissaries defiled the temple: they began cutting their way through the helpless women straight to the iconostasis. They smashed the door there and hacked the miraculous icon into four pieces. At this I was really shocked—I would not remain in such godless company and I ran away with the women.

"I was in time to go with the Venetians when they left the Blachernae," Manuel said. "Luckily there were some who recognized me, or they would have killed me just for being Greek. As they cut their way through the city they slew Turks and Greeks impartially and looted several houses on the way, since they had plenty of time. They were enraged because so many of their men had died on the walls in vain—and by the way their bailo has been taken prisoner by the Turks. I went with them to the harbor and then hid here in the cellar, commending my life to God. I did not mean to creep out until tomorrow when the Turks should be a little quieter. Today they look as if they would slay everyone they meet for the sheer joy of it—except the women, of course, from whom they derive a different pleasure."

"You're safe here as long as that spear stands before the door," I told him. "That is my mark now, and no one else will break in. It's a small house and there are no women in it. But if they do find their way here, just say that the house is taken—tell them my name in Turkish and say that you're my slave. Then you'll come to no harm. God be with you."

Manuel clung fast to me in an agony of fear and cried, "Where are you going, master? Don't forsake me!"

"I am going in search of the conqueror," I said. "And conqueror is his proper name. Among all Sultans may he be called hereafter Mohammed the Conqueror, for he will be the greatest of them and will rule over east and west."

I went right down to the shore where the crews of the Turkish ships were busy with their pillage, and I saw that the Sultan had indeed placed Megadux Notaras' house under the protection of *tsaushes*. I spoke to them and they told me that Megadux Notaras and his two sons and his sick wife were all in safety within those walls.

At noon I returned to the great church and from there beheld the last of the Christian ships, deeply laden, leaving port. But not even now did a single Turkish ship attack them. Their sails swelled before the fresh northerly wind, and from their mastheads the emblems of many Christian nations waved an unconquered farewell to dying Constantinople.

"You bear tidings of death to Christendom!" I shouted. "Tremble, ye western nations! It will be your turn next. Do you not see that you carry night with you over Europe?"

Now Turkish soldiers began gathering from all parts, and along the main street the Sultan's brilliant retinue advanced, escorted by green-clad *tsaushes,* the bodyguard with their gilded bows bent, and runners swinging censers. The horses trod on Greek bodies still lying in the street, and curly-haired boys of the harem sprinkled rose water in front of the Sultan's charger.

Before the bronze gates, which had been forced, the Sultan dismounted from his snow-white horse. His fiery young face was twitching with weariness, but in the gold-glistening eyes shone a cold triumphant joy which I had never yet seen in any man. I saw his lean face, his narrow, aquiline nose and pointed chin, and I was spellbound by the same horror and attraction as held me in the days when I lived at his court.

Having dismounted, he took his iron hammer in his left hand, bowed low, and grasping a handful of earth from the ground, strewed it over his head. The janissaries thought that he was humbling himself before the one God, and were reverently silent. But in fact I believe he was dedicating himself as a son of the dust, and desired in this way to show his respect for death.

He entered the church with his suite and I was among the foremost with him. On the floor lay a few bloodstained corpses and a crowd of janissaries were busy looting the place, smashing icons, tearing away their frames of gold and silver and collecting all valuables in altar cloths and pearl-embroidered copes. In the middle of the floor a janissary was hacking one of the marble flagstones to pieces with an axe, in search of hidden treasure.

Sultan Mohammed strode up to him, struck him pitilessly down with his hammer and cried with a lowering visage, "Do not touch my property! All that is movable I have promised you, but the buildings are mine."

Comrades of the janissary quickly dragged him out by the heels before the Sultan could kill him. One might have supposed that the Sultan's boundless fury arose from envy because his subordinates were amassing such huge wealth. But such is not Mohammed's nature. It is not treasure he desires, but power.

He stood there looking around the church as if incredulous of its vast size and splendor. The young officers of his suite could no longer contain themselves; one of them wetted his hand in a pool of blood, crouched by the wall and sprang up, slapping his hand as high on the wall as he could reach. "There's my mark!" he yelled. The red print of his hand was so high that three men would have had to mount on one another's shoulders to reach it.

Sultan Mohammed took a gilded bow from one of the bodyguards, aimed upwards and shot a quivering arrow straight into the mighty dome. "There is mine!" he cried; then looking around he ordered the janissaries to break down the iconostasis so as to disclose the altar.

As the wall crashed down he commanded, "Shout this together, all of you: 'Mohammed, Emir of the Turks and son of Murad, is come to dedicate the greatest church of Christendom to the one God!' "

The soldiers who, momentarily forgetful of pillage, had crowded into the church after the Sultan, joined in the shout, which echoed long under that most marvelous dome. Then a wonder took place: from behind the altar arose, one after another, twenty Greek bishops, priests and monks arrayed in ceremonial vestments and all the emblems of the Church. They approached the Sultan, knelt before him and committed themselves to his hands. Among them was Gennadios. They had been hiding throughout the siege in one of the many secret chambers of the church.

This all seemed to be taking place in accordance with some secret agreement, and may explain the Sultan's wrath when he saw one of his men trying to tear up the floor.

Now he said to the janissaries, "These are my prisoners;

they have surrendered to me. No one is to touch them, but I will pay you a hundred aspers in compensation for each of these exalted Christian priests. Lead them to some monastery of their own choice and place them under the protection of the *tsaushes*."

With one accord the bishops and priests declared, "We choose the Pantokrator!"

At that moment the dervishes and learned men in attendance on the Sultan cried out that it was the hour of the noon prayer. The Sultan commanded water to be brought, and washed rapidly while the janissaries led away the Christians. Then he stepped barefooted onto the altar, trampled the cross underfoot, turned his face to the east and led the devotions. His suite and all his soldiers prostrated themselves, pressed their foreheads to the ground, and with their Mohammedan prayers dedicated Christendom's most glorious church to Allah.

After the prayers the Sultan ordered the dervishes to see that the building was cleansed with rose water from all Christian impurities.

As he crossed the vast floor on his way out I stepped before him, and no one hindered me. I stood in front of him without a word and he recognized me. His face turned the color of clay and looking about him he whispered, "Angel, have you come for me already?"

When he had recovered himself, he raised his hand and said to his attendants, "Don't touch him."

Then he stepped close up to me, touched my face, laughed and exclaimed, "You're still alive, then, Incorruptible! Now do you believe that I shall stable my horses in the churches of your Pope?"

I said, "You knew better than I. It was not intended that I should die upon the walls of my city. Have me beheaded now, that your victory may be complete."

He smiled with the yellow glint in his eyes and said, "Patience, Angel! There is a time for everything."

Without concerning himself further with me he left the church. I joined his suite to be near him, for my longing to die was stronger than any longing I had known. Among the retinue were many who knew me, but no one would speak to me.

Meanwhile Megadux Notaras and a group of noble Greek prisoners had been brought to the church. They knelt before Sultan Mohammed. He spoke to them sternly and asked why they had offered so obstinate a resistance, thereby causing unnecessary damage to the city and losses to the Sultan's troops.

Notaras looked silently at Grand Vizier Khalil who, a long-bearded, broken man, stood at the Sultan's right hand; for the Sultan deliberately took him everywhere to show him the completeness of his victory.

"Speak freely," said the Sultan.

"Could we do otherwise, when in your own camp—even among your closest advisers—there were those who urged us to resist?" said Megadux Notaras resentfully, still looking accusingly at Khalil.

Mohammed turned to Khalil, seized him roughly by the beard and shook the trembling old head.

"I know you, you pro-Greek!" he cried aloud, that the janissaries might hear him. "But you served my father faithfully, as your father and grandfather served, standing at the Sultan's right hand as Grand Vizier. Therefore I will have mercy on you and not behead you, though you have deserved it. But never let my eyes fall upon you again. Hide like a beggar in the remotest corners of my Empire, as like a beggar your grandfather once stepped into the presence of his Sultan."

The sudden pronouncement of this sentence was bold. But it was the moment which Mohammed had been longing for from his youth up, as hotly as he had longed to conquer Constantinople. The young officers of his suite began reviling Khalil, and after some hesitation the janissaries joined in the outcry. Sharply scrutinizing those about him the Sultan pointed out a few old men who would not condescend to applaud his just doom.

"Go with Khalil!" he commanded. The *tsaushes* sprang forward and stripped the kaftans of honor from these old men who, half-naked and abusing one another, walked away with Khalil on their path of humiliation. The janissaries vied in abuse, and flung blood-soaked clods of earth after them.

When they had gone, the Sultan turned once more to the Greek prisoners and asked, "Where is your Emperor? What do you know of him?"

The Greeks looked at one another and shook their heads.

The Sultan, feigning wonder, sneered, "What, is it possible? Did you not fight at his side?"

Some of the senators hung their heads in shame, but Lukas Notaras answered defiantly, "Emperor Constantine betrayed our faith and sold us to the Pope and the Latins. We do not acknowledge him as our Emperor, and prefer to serve you."

The Sultan ordered proclamation to be made everywhere that the Emperor's body must be found, if he had fallen in battle. He promised a reward to the finder, and also to the man who could prove that he had slain him. The runner had no need to depart upon this errand, for at once two janissaries pressed forward to the Sultan. Each swore by Allah and his own beard that he alone had given the Emperor the *coup-de-grâce,* and began a violent dispute in Mohammed's presence. They were sent to find the body and hurried away, vehemently pointing and shouting one another down as they described how their fatal blows had fallen.

The Sultan continued talking cordially to the Greeks, promising them gold and lands, and he said that he would leave the government of the city in their hands, since they were qualified for the task and were trustworthy men. He therefore asked them to name others who might be useful to him and whom he might buy back from their captors.

Lukas Notaras mentioned about thirty names, and when the other Greeks had conferred together they added those of their own friends. At this I could no longer contain myself, but stepping up to Notaras I cried, "Mad traitor! Would you drag down others with you to destruction?"

Notaras was wroth to see me in the Sultan's suite and said hotly, "A flexible policy is no betrayal. It is the only resource of a people in extremity, and if I have soiled my hands it was for the sake of my people. Someone had to do it. Perhaps more courage is needed for that than for throwing one's life away. You don't know me well enough to judge me."

I said, "Your daughter knew you and judged you! Your people murdered her at the Kerkoporta as she was striving to cleanse your name and fame from the stain of treachery!"

Notaras paled in horror, and his face was rigid. He exclaimed bitterly, "I have no daughter—I have never had a daughter! I have only my two sons. What is this nonsense about the Kerkoporta?"

He looked beseechingly now at the Sultan, now at his countrymen, who drew aside, leaving a space around him. With a powerful effort he overcame his agitation, smiled—though the corners of his mouth were twitching—and appealed to the Sultan: "This man, your envoy, has deceived you. He can bear witness that I have often begged him in vain to collaborate to your advantage. But from sheer greed and ambition he rejected my support, preferring to play a lone hand and gain your favor at my expense. I do not know what he may have done for you, but it cannot have amounted to much. He was the friend of Giustiniani and the Latins. God be my witness that I have been of better service to you than he has."

Mohammed smiled coldly, signed to me and said again, "Incorruptible, have patience!"

He gave an order to his treasurer, then turned to the Greeks and said, "Go with my treasurer and search among the prisoners in the camp and aboard the ships for the men you have named. Many may have disguised themselves to conceal their rank, and would not dare to step forward if my treasurer alone were to inquire for them. But you they will recognize and trust. Buy them back from the slave dealers and soldiers. I permit you to pay one thousand aspers for each of them, so important do I consider them for my plans."

The Greeks were delighted at this mark of favor and willingly accompanied the treasurer, conversing eagerly the while and already distributing among themselves the most profitable appointments in the city. But Mohammed regarded me with a smile, knowing that I read his heart. Notaras was escorted back to his palace, with the Sultan's kind wishes for his lady's rapid recovery.

Upon me he bestowed not another glance, but rode back with his followers to his camp for the victory celebrations. I went with him as far as the Palace of Blachernae. There he halted to glance at the halls that the Venetians had ravaged and plundered, and quoted aloud to his suite:

"Owls screech in the pillared halls of Efrasiab,
Spiders are sentinels at the Emperor's door."

I now returned to the Kerkoporta and buried Anna Notaras' body in a great hollow that a cannon ball had blown in the wall. I could think of no better or more honorable tomb. And I thought that, truly, one day her brown eyes might open again there as dark flowers and survey their city from its ruins.

In this city, now intoxicated with blood and pillage, human life was cheaper and of less significance than I could ever have imagined. As soon as the Sultan had departed, the Turks began slaying one another recklessly in the struggle for slave-women. Ignorant dervishes worked themselves up into religious frenzies and mutilated with their knives many Greek slaves who refused to acknowledge the Prophet.

Through this appalling chaos I wandered, stony with sorrow, but no one came near me. I did not direct my steps but let chance lead me, since it was my destiny to see all that was coming to pass. But there are bounds set to what a man can endure, beyond which all the senses are mercifully dulled; eyes see and perceive not. Nothing wounded my heart now.

I wandered farther. From the sheds where wounded Greeks and Latins had lain on blood-soaked straw, all Christians had been dragged out and beheaded, and their bodies stacked up by the doors. Wounded Turks had taken their places. Their cries, their stench, their helplessness were like those of the Christians. They wailed in many languages for water, or besought their comrades to put an end to their torment.

The wounded were tended by a few Turkish surgeons, old dervishes and Greek nuns who had been taken as slaves and forced into this filthy, stinking work, since by reason of their age and appearance they had no charms for the conquerors. A number of *tsaushes* kept order and prevented the Turks from robbing their own wounded.

Among the nuns I recognized Khariklea. Her cloak was torn to shreds, she was bruised and her ugly face was swollen with weeping. She was kneeling on the straw holding the hand of a very handsome Anatolian youth. On his lips and chin the first silky black down was appearing, but his face was already pale with a yellow pallor and he was bleeding profusely through the bandage around the upper part of his body.

"Khariklea!" I said. "You're alive! What are you doing here?"

She glanced at me as if it were the most natural thing in the world to find me beside her, and replied, "This wicked Turk has caught hold of me and won't let me go. I don't understand what he's saying." She added with a sob, "Truly he's so young and handsome that I haven't the heart to take away my hand. He will soon be dead."

With her free hand she wiped the death sweat from the boy's brow and stroked his childishly round cheek, so that his face which had been distorted in agony grew peaceful.

Khariklea burst into tears and sobbed compassionately. "And the poor boy can't even join in the looting, though he well deserves it. He fought so bravely. He is wounded everywhere and the bleeding won't stop. He might have found treasure and money and lovely girls, but now his only reward is my gnarled old hand."

The youth opened his eyes, looked through us and murmured something faintly in Turkish.

"What is he saying?" asked Khariklea, impelled by her inveterate curiosity.

"He says that God is the one God," I translated. "He is asking whether he has deserved paradise."

"Why, surely, surely!" said Khariklea. "Turks must have their paradise just as we Christians have our heaven. Of course he shall go there, poor boy."

A passing dervish pressed his stinking goatskin to his chest, bent over the dying lad and recited to him those verses in the Koran which tell of the cool waters of paradise, its fruit trees and ever-virgin maidens. The boy smiled faintly. When the dervish had gone he said twice, in a broken voice, "Mother, mother!"

"What is he saying?" asked Khariklea.

"He thinks you're his mother," I said.

Khariklea wept again and cried, "I never had a son, for no man ever cared about me. But if he believes that, I cannot disappoint him, and surely it's no sin."

She kissed the youth's hand, pressed her cheeks to his and in a surprisingly gentle voice began whispering caressing words in his ear, as if in the midst of all the devastation and useless death she had wanted to express to the full the tenderness that lay buried in her heart. The boy clutched her hard hand, closed his eyes and breathed heavily and painfully.

Then I remembered something. Looking neither to left nor right I walked straight through the city to the Pantokrator monastery. I must be sure—I must see for myself.

Turks had made a fire in the cloister garth of all the smashed icons, and were cooking their food. I went past them to the fishpool, found a fish spear and soon brought out one of the sluggish, muddy-gray fish. As I lifted it from the water I saw it turn red as rust. The scales gleamed red in the rays of the setting sun, as the monk Gennadios had foretold.

Then dusk fell. The night of wild beasts set in. With drooping head I returned to my room and sat down to write.

30 May 1453

This morning a *tsaush* arrived to guard my house, and by this I knew that Sultan Mohammed has not forgotten me. Manuel prepared food for him. Neither of them disturbed me.

Nor did the Sultan's man stop me when I went out. He simply followed me at a distance of twenty paces.

In streets and squares the corpses are beginning to swell. Both from Europe and Asia the ravens have gathered in their flocks. Dogs howl in the courtyards; some have already run wild. They lick blood and gnaw at the bodies.

During the night the Sultan's army had strangely altered its appearance. *Tsaushes* can be recognized by their green kaftans and the janissaries by their white felt caps; but the other men walking the streets have garbed themselves as if for some wild and horrid feast. A herdsman who yesterday went barefoot now wears soft shoes and a mantle of silk or velvet. From the shoulders of a pockmarked Negro hangs a heavy, gold-embroidered cloak. All have washed and purified themselves as Islam enjoins, yet the stench of corpses hangs over the city and finds its way everywhere.

The plundering is now going forward in a more orderly fashion. House after house is emptied of furniture and kitchen implements. Countless carts and ox-sledges are loaded high and driven out through the city gates. In every market place there is buying and selling, and packs are laid upon the backs of donkeys and camels. The more cunning of the Turks have begun to search the cellars of wealthy houses, tapping the walls and breaking them down with pick and sledge hammer. Now and then shrill cries announce the discovery of fresh hoards. People in hiding are dragged by the hair from bricked-up vaults and empty water cisterns.

Emperor Constantine's head lies between the forehoofs of the imperial equestrian statue in the center of the city, upon which it gazes down with rotting eyes. Sultan Mohammed had it set up there on the pedestal to remind the Greeks that their Emperor is dead and that the power now lies in the Sultan's hands.

Mohammed rides restlessly here and there inspecting palaces and churches. On Acropolis Point he said, "This is where my seraglio shall stand." His place of execution is by the Arkadios pillar. Here among other bodies I found that of Minotto, the Venetian bailo, headless and distended.

This is my proper place, I thought, and sat down to wait for the Sultan to come and establish his Greek government.

I had to wait until afternoon. In the course of the day the Sultan's bodyguard and *tsaushes* brought hither nearly fifty Greeks whose freedom had been purchased with the Sultan's money. They were given water and stew and clothes befitting their rank. But they did not rouse themselves from their despondency. Only a few ventured to whisper nervously among themselves. From time to time *tsaushes* would arrive carrying the heads of other distinguished persons, and laid them in a row along the marble balustrade of the square. The captives pointed to them and whispered well-known names. Many had perished on the ramparts, where their bodies were sought for and found. Others had been slain while defending their own homes.

At last the Sultan appeared, attended by his young viziers, and dismounted unsteadily from his horse. His face was swollen from wine and lack of sleep. The sun dazzled his eyes and he had to shade them with his hand.

The prisoners prostrated themselves before him and pressed their foreheads to the ground. He spoke to them with affected cordiality and bade them stand up. While his treasurer called the roll, Mohammed intently scrutinized each man and demanded that all should testify to one another's identity. Most of them belonged to families dating back many centuries, and their names were familiar whether for good or evil in the city's history. Only a few of the names on the list were unaccounted for.

Mohammed sat cross-legged on a block of marble, rubbed his aching forehead and said, "Weary though I am, and oppressed with cares, yet my sense of duty forbids me to let these noblemen continue in uncertainty. I have come as I promised to establish a Greek government on a new basis, so that the Greek people and my own may dwell together in amity and peace. I have been told that you are all right-thinking men who unwillingly took up arms against me. Now that you have lost the city you are willing to recognize me as your Emperor and to place at my disposal all your knowledge and experience in matters of state, so that the Greek people may submit to my rule without misgivings. Is this true?"

The prisoners shouted eagerly that they would serve him to the best of their ability. Mohammed wrinkled his brow, looked about and demanded with affected astonishment, "Where are the Greek people?"

The soldiers assembled in the square and the Sultan's followers also looked about, and with laughter and shouting repeated the question: "Where are the Greek people?" Soon they thrust forward with kicks and cuffs a handful of half-naked, terrified women and old men, pointed to them and cried. "Emir, father—see! Here are the Greek people."

Mohammed nodded haughtily and said, "Let your own people then be your witnesses. Do you promise and swear by your God and all your saints, and are you ready to kiss your cross in token of your submission and in confirmation of your oath, that you are willing to serve me faithfully unto death, however high the position to which you may be raised?"

The prisoners shouted and made the sign of the cross, plainly showing their willingness to confirm their oath. Only a few stood silent, regarding the Sultan attentively.

"So be it," said Mohammed. "You have chosen. Kneel in turn, then, and stretch forth your necks, so that my executioner may behead you all. In that way you will serve me best and most faithfully, and your heads I will raise up on a pillar beside those of your brave compatriots. And in this I am not dealing unfairly with you, since you have just sworn to obey my commands, whatever they may be."

The Greeks stared at him thunderstruck. Then they began crying out and shaking their fists, and some wounded themselves on the spears of the guards in trying to attack the Sultan. But others said, "Brothers, let us die like men, since we have dug this pit for ourselves."

The Sultan raised his hand and said in simulated gentleness, "There is nothing to prevent you from establishing a Greek government in your Christian heaven, since the Greeks there far outnumber those in Constantinople. Hasten, then, to agree upon your appointments."

His words were a cue for the executioners, who now stepped forward. Soldiers seized the captives by the arms and forced them to their knees. As blood spurted in fountains from the severed arteries their heads rolled toward the Sultan, who had them set up in a row on the balustrade, until tearstained, bloodstained, grinning heads encircled the whole square of Arkadios.

The Sultan now turned to the petrified old men and the women and said in his broken Greek, "With your own eyes you have seen that I come not as conqueror but as liberator, since I am freeing the Greeks of Constantinople from their thousand years of slavery under emperors and nobles. You alone are to blame for the sufferings that have overtaken you now, because you did not cast off your yoke in time and appeal to me. But these distresses will soon be over. Therefore I ensure to every survivor his house, property and livelihood, and any fugitives who return shall enjoy the same rights. Allah is merciful and compassionate, as you shall see, you poor folk. You have been fleeced, deceived and despoiled for so long that you do not yet know what real freedom is. But I will bring your city to such a flowering as no one has ever dreamed of before. It shall be the most glorious jewel in my turban, and reign supreme in the east and in the west."

He bade his treasurer give ten aspers to each of the Greeks whom he had summoned as witnesses, so that they might purchase their freedom. This was a good price, for slaves that are in any way injured or infirm are going for a single silver coin in the market. But the women and the old men who had endured a day and a night of terror, slaughter and rape stood there dazed and apathetic, without understanding what had happened to them.

I looked about the blood-drenched square in surprise, and going up to the Sultan, I said, "But the Megadux, Lukas Notaras? I don't see him here. What is to be his place in your just plan?"

Mohammed regarded me benevolently, nodded and replied, "Be patient yet a little while, Angel. I have sent for him and his sons, but they linger." He gave me a searching, inquisitive look and explained, "Notaras has hidden his daughter from me and denies all knowledge of her. Therefore I sent my white eunuch to his house with orders to fetch Notaras' younger son for my pleasure. He's a handsome boy and I want his father to bring him to me himself, for me to do as I like with."

"You've been drinking," I said. "You offend against your Koran."

Mohammed bared his gleaming wild beast's teeth in a smile and said, "I am my own law. I need no angel to whisper in my ear that I am mortal, for I know that I am more than any mortal. Not God himself can compete with me in earthly power. At a sign from my hand, heads fall to the ground. Before my cannon the mightiest walls collapse. Do you still deny that I am more than a man?"

I looked into his eyes and knew that in his fashion he was right, since he had chosen truth as man sees it, and material death, rather than the reality of God.

I said, "In believing that you can shake off the past like an old prejudice and set yourself up as the standard by which all things are to be measured, you are forging worse fetters for yourself than anyone has ever borne before you. The fetters of time and space are eating into your flesh and choking your spirit. When you die there will be nothing of you left."

He cried, "My memory shall endure so long as there are men living on the earth. I have told you, I need no angel to whisper in my ear."

"Then kill me," I begged him. "I forsook you in the autumn when I saw what you are, what you want and what is to come. Take pity on me and give me death, so that my blood may mingle with that of my Greek brothers."

But he smiled his mocking, wild beast's smile and repeated, "Have patience yet a little while, Angel. Let us first see how low even the noblest Greek can stoop."

I had to step aside, for just then came the eunuchs with Lukas Notaras and his two sons. When Notaras received the Sultan's message he doubtless guessed what his fate was to be.

He walked with a straight back and did not kneel to Mohammed now.

The white eunuch said to the Sultan, "Lord, he would not obey your commands or deliver his son to your harem. Therefore I have brought them all, as you ordered me."

Mohammed indicated the heads lining the square and said, "Why do you not obey me, now that I have established a Greek government and minutely followed the advice you gave me?"

Notaras looked around with a rigid face, slowly crossed himself, gazed heavenward and cried, "My Lord and my God, I acknowledge Thy justice. Thou art indeed a righteous God."

He walked slowly round the little square, pausing at each of the heads and saying, "My brother, forgive me. I knew not what I did."

When he came back to his place he laid his hands on his sons' shoulders and said to them, "Let us now show that we can die like men. Let us also thank God that we may die like Greeks, true to our faith."

The Sultan threw out his arms and cried in mocking wonder, "You need not die! I have promised to exalt you above all these Greeks. You have only to obey me and tell your handsome son to obey me, whatever I may order him to do."

Megadux Notaras answered, "You need not condescend to find an excuse for my execution. I have humbled myself before God; why should I any longer humble myself before you? It would save neither me nor my sons. But I would beg you to satisfy my human curiosity. Why must I die, in defiance of all the rules of sound politics?"

Sultan Mohammed bent his young, fiery face toward him and whispered, "You betrayed your Emperor. You would betray me too."

Megadux Notaras bowed his head and said again, "Truly Thou art a righteous God."

He then begged as a favor that he might see his sons beheaded first, so that he might be sure they would not abjure the Greek religion to save their lives. The Sultan permitted this. Notaras himself pressed his sons to their knees, first the elder and then the younger, talking calmly to them as the executioner struck off their heads. Not a single tear came into his dark eyes, though Sultan Mohammed bent forward inquisitively to observe his face.

When both the young men were dead, Notaras said, "My Lord and my God, I stand before Thy judgment seat. Thine is the right to judge me, but no man has that right." Then he humbled himself, bowed his head, and shedding burning tears he prayed as simple people pray: "Jesus Christ, Son of God, be merciful to me a sinner."

For a while he prayed apart, then rose; and having walked with the *tsaushes* to the Arkadios column he knelt in his sons' blood and waited tranquilly for death. The Sultan had his head set up on the column, above the heads of all the other Greeks. Then he turned away, weary of the blood and the stench of carrion, and rode back to his silken tent. Me he dismissed, though I had expected everything to be accomplished now.

But when I turned to go home a green-clad *tsaush* followed me at a distance of twenty paces. So he has not forgotten me.

EPILOGUE

Manuel the son of Demetrios writes this. That Demetrios who was wood-carrier in the service of the old Emperor Manuel. But Manuel who writes this has served Master John Angelos, whom the Latins called Jean Ange and whom the Turks called the Angel, and feared.

When my master had written what he had to write I showed him the money I had hidden in the cellar and a communion chalice of gold which I had rescued from the Khora convent. I said, "Many Latins have bought their freedom from the Sultan's viziers. Buy your own freedom and let us flee from this city of death."

He said, "No, no. Death is the greatest boon that can be granted me. But you must live on and trust to Turkish favor; you are of those who always survive because they are what they are and can do nothing to alter it."

My master had kept vigil many nights, and of recent days he neither ate nor drank, but fasted entirely. Therefore his head was so confused that he no longer knew what was best for him.

On the third morning after the capture of the city Sultan Mohammed sent for my master. I followed him at a little distance, and no one hindered me. Other Greeks were gathered around Constantine's column to see what was to happen.

Sultan Mohammed pointed at Emperor Constantine's head;

the eyes had run out and it was beginning to stink. He cried, "I have captured Constantinople with the sword, and with the sword I have struck down the Emperor of the Greeks, from whom I won this city. Are there any to dispute my inheritance?"

My master stepped forward and said, "I dispute the inheritance, Turkish Emir Mohammed! I was born with purple boots and I keep them until my death. I am of imperial blood; I am the only rightful Basileus of Constantinople, though this you did not know."

But Sultan Mohammed was not at all astonished at his words; he shook his head and said, "I know all I need to know. My father knew your origins, though you fancied you had kept them a secret from everyone. This is no news to me, for I have eyes and ears in all Christian countries—even in Avignon. Why do you suppose I allowed you to go your way last autumn, and gave you a handful of jewels as a farewell present?"

My master said, "I know that you collect people as Aristotle collected nature's freaks. You once said that nothing human could astonish you, because you could see through everyone. Have I not astonished you?"

Sultan Mohammed answered, "Yes, Angel, you have astonished me. I let you go to Constantinople when war broke out because I hoped that your own good sense would prompt you to stir up a revolt here and compete with the Emperor for power. So you were given means to sow dissension among the defenders. But you astonished me. Am I to believe that in you I have met the only man on earth who does not strive after power?"

My master said, "Only now is my hour come. In the presence of your army and of the Greek people I dispute your right of inheritance and claim my Empire from you."

Sultan Mohammed shook his head pityingly and said, "Don't be a fool. Kneel and adore me as conqueror and I will spare your life. Otherwise I shall grow weary of this and toss you onto the midden, as Aristotle grew weary of carrying the whale's vertebra."

My master replied, "It is not you who are the conqueror, but I!"

His obstinacy irritated Sultan Mohammed, who clapped his hands as a signal and cried, "Be it as you wish. Give him his purple boots, that he may die with them on, as he was born. I do not dispute his birth."

At once his executioners seized my master and stripped him of all but his shirt. They held him by the arms and severed the arteries of his legs so that his blood ran down and colored his knees and calves and feet quite red.

While my master's blood ran down he supported himself on the shoulders of the executioners, raised his eyes and prayed his prayer, saying, "Inscrutable God, I have thirsted after Thy reality all my days. But in the hour of my death I beseech Thee, let me return! Give me once again the fetters of time and space, Thy wonderful, terrible bonds. Grant me this, for Thou knowest why I ask it."

The Sultan lifted his quivering chin and with head erect he said, "Behold your city, Basileus John Angelos!"

With the last of his strength my master said, "I see the beauty of my city! To this place my astral body will one day return—return to the ruins of the ramparts. As a wayfarer shackled by time and space I shall one day pluck a dark flower from the wall, in memory of one I have loved. But you, Mohammed—you will never return."

Thus passed my master John Angelos, wearing the purple boots. When his life had fled, the Turks struck off his head and flung his body into the harbor, where other bodies poison the water.

But when the Sultan had proclaimed himself the Emperor's heir he sent away his army and his ships and allowed the Greeks who remained to choose themselves a patriarch. We chose Gennadios, who is the holiest of the monks in the city and whom the Turks have spared because of his great reputation. The Sultan received him in his quarters and appointed him Patriarch of Constantinople, as Emperors have appointed men before, and he gave him a costly crosier and a golden chalice in token of his favor. Thus the Sultan kept his promise and allowed the Greeks free exercise of their religion and the administration of their own justice. The Sultan also gave us certain churches where we might hold our services, but the rest he has purified and they are now mosques to the glory of the God of Islam.

To the town of Pera beyond the harbor the Sultan has restored former trading concessions, as a reward for its neutrality. But the walls of Pera on the landward side he has pulled down, and the houses of those who fled from the town have been sealed and their property listed, so that everything of theirs passes into the Sultan's hands unless the owners return within three months to claim it.

Many fugitives returned to Constantinople too, and the Sultan promised his especial favor to all returning Greeks who could prove that they were of noble birth. These he beheaded without delay. He spared only the poor, and allowed them to work for the good of the realm, each in his own calling. He showed mercy also to learned geographers, historians and to the Emperor's technicians, and took them into his service. But philosophers he did not spare.